PENGUIN CANADA

BIG MAN COMING DOWN THE ROAD

BRAD SMITH is the author of *Busted Flush, All Hat,* and *One-Eyed Jacks,* which was nominated for the Dashiell Hammett Prize and the Arthur Ellis Award. He lives in a farmhouse near Dunnville, Ontario.

Also by Brad Smith

BIG
MAN
COMING
DOWN THE
ROAD

a novel

BRAD SMITH

PENGUIN
CANADA

PENGUIN CANADA

Published by the Penguin Group

Penguin Group (Canada), 90 Eglinton Avenue East, Suite 700, Toronto, Ontario, Canada M4P 2Y3
(a division of Pearson Canada Inc.)

Penguin Group (USA) Inc., 375 Hudson Street, New York, New York 10014, U.S.A.
Penguin Books Ltd, 80 Strand, London WC2R 0RL, England
Penguin Ireland, 25 St Stephen's Green, Dublin 2, Ireland (a division of Penguin Books Ltd)
Penguin Group (Australia), 250 Camberwell Road, Camberwell, Victoria 3124, Australia
(a division of Pearson Australia Group Pty Ltd)
Penguin Books India Pvt Ltd, 11 Community Centre, Panchsheel Park, New Delhi – 110 017, India
Penguin Group (NZ), cnr Airborne and Rosedale Roads, Albany, Auckland 1310, New Zealand
(a division of Pearson New Zealand Ltd)
Penguin Books (South Africa) (Pty) Ltd, 24 Sturdee Avenue, Rosebank, Johannesburg 2196,
South Africa

Penguin Books Ltd, Registered Offices: 80 Strand, London WC2R 0RL, England

First published 2007

1 2 3 4 5 6 7 8 9 10   (WEB)

Copyright © Brad Smith, 2007

Pages 359 and 360 constitute an extension of this copyright page.

*Publisher's note: This book is a work of fiction. Names, characters, places and incidents
either are the product of the author's imagination or are used fictitiously, and any
resemblance to actual persons living or dead, events, or locales is entirely coincidental.*

Manufactured in Canada.

ISBN-10: 0-14-305177-6
ISBN-13: 978-0-14-305177-0

Library and Archives Canada Cataloguing in Publication data available upon request

Visit the Penguin Group (Canada) website at **www.penguin.ca**

Special and corporate bulk purchase rates available; please see
www.penguin.ca/corporatesales or call 1-800-810-3104, ext. 477 or 474

For Gilly
who has gone on ahead

ONE

There were snapping turtles in the creek. Of the species *Chelydra serpentina,* they were hulking, ominous creatures, sometimes measuring two feet across, with rough dragon's claws and prehistoric beaks that could break bone like it was penny candy. They swam suspended beneath the surface of the muddy stream and they fed on virtually anything and everything—invertebrates, carrion, aquatic life, mammals, birds, fish. As predators they were indiscriminate, unbiased in a manner rarely encountered.

The creek merged with the river at roughly a forty-five-degree angle; it descended from the northeast, draining a marshy area a quarter mile inland and serving double duty as the northern boundary of the Eastman farm. Here the Grand River was rather wide and quite shallow, although not as shallow as it was a few miles to the north, where it came tumbling out of the Elora Gorge, gurgling around rocks and scraping across the pebbly bottom like a rasp over a woodcut before easing into the steady flow that drifted in front of the farm known as Crooked Pear. The riverbank was neither rock strewn, as it was to the north, nor reedy, as it sometimes was in the low-lying areas farther south. Here the bank was of solid earth, plush with grass and dotted with cottonwoods and maples. The farmhouse itself was on a rise south of the creek and east of the river, and it sat back a perfect five hundred yards from each, a geometric quirk left from the farm's first owner who'd built the original dwelling some hundred and sixty years earlier.

In the spring several families of mallards nested in the marshy upper reaches of the creek, and by May the stream was scattershot with the hens and their ducklings swimming out from the swamp and toward the river, gliding along in single files, quacking and squawking as they dove for food beneath the budding lily pads.

The snapping turtles came up the creek from the river, hungry after a winter's hibernation, voracious by abstinence as well as by nature. A downy duckling, its head beneath the surface of the creek as it foraged, was an easy prey. A snapper, lying still and dark in the murky water, would attack in a flash, clamp its iron jaws over the baby's bill and drag it down to the bottom, hold it there until the duckling drowned and then devour it at its leisure. On the surface the mother duck would be in full panic, screeching loudly and flapping her wings as she gathered her remaining brood close to her side.

Everett Eastman had decided, over the past couple of years, that he hated the turtles and that he would devote his flagging energies to their extermination, if not from the earth, then at least from Everett's little corner of it. The passion he had for this pursuit was a little surprising, considering that he'd passed his first seventy-six years on the planet without giving *Chelydra serpentina* a second thought.

They had come to his attention two springs ago, during a period of limbo between the third coronary and the first bypass. Bored by inaction and desperate for something to do, Everett had decided to repair the dock he'd had built thirty years earlier, the dock off which the kids had fished when they were small and to which Everett used to tie his cedarstrip runabout. The boat was now in the barn, upside down across sawhorses, its planking shrunken, the spar varnish on the deck flaking away like sunburned skin.

It was odd that Everett was even staying at the farm, and odder still that he would attempt to rehabilitate the dock himself, having spent a lifetime hiring such chores out. But boredom was a powerful catalyst. He'd been ordered by the medical profession to stay away from the distillery in Waterloo, and the auto parts plant in Mississauga, and the entire city of Toronto—so he'd been cooling his heels on the farm, waiting for a date to be scheduled for the surgery and looking for something to do.

He'd been advised to relax and one day, while pretending to do so, the rotted dock boards caught his eye. After lunch, and some half-ass planning, he drove next door in the Dodge pickup and got some white oak planking from Will Montgomery, who periodically cut trees from the bush lot at the back of both farms and had it sawn into planks that he stored in the rafters above his granary for curing. The tops he cut up for cordwood. There was an unspoken agreement between the two men that Will could harvest whatever he deemed usable from Everett's bush, to keep the lot thinned out. In return, Everett would receive firewood and whatever lumber he might require. In the twenty years they'd known each other this was the first Everett had asked for planking of any kind, although he did burn cordwood in the farmhouse on the rare winter days he or the extended family might be there.

On the day of the dock repair Everett was attempting to nail the planks onto the framework of the old pier and not having any success, as the white oak was too hard to take a nail. Will Montgomery might have mentioned this when he'd helped load the boards into the pickup, but Will wasn't one to offer unsolicited advice, a trait that Everett usually appreciated. Still, Will would have surely suspected that Everett—in a lifetime of buying and selling companies and commodities—had never stumbled upon the knowledge that a white oak board required drilling before nailing. If so, he kept any such suspicions to himself.

In any event, Everett, having twisted a couple dozen three-inch Ardox spikes into pretzels, was about to give up when he heard a frenzied squawking from the creek behind him and turned to see a pair of webbed feet sticking straight up out of the water and thrashing about in the most urgent way. Several mallard hens and their offspring—maybe thirty or forty birds in all—were scurrying back and forth and raising a cacophony of noise in protest against their friend's dilemma. Everett walked to the creek bank, regarding the strange sight and not quite fathoming what it was he was seeing, then decided to wade into the stream to find out. The reason for the duck's balletic display was evident as soon as he grabbed the bird by the feet and lifted. The duck came out of the water and with it came the enormous turtle whose jaws were clamped like a steel vise on the bird's bill. The snapper weighed thirty-three pounds, he would determine later, and was thoroughly dedicated to its grip on the duck, never giving an inch while Everett dragged both bird and turtle ashore. He finally separated the two by clubbing the snapper several times over the head with the same length of white oak that had refused to take a nail.

The turtle ended up expiring on the bank. Everett carried it to the house and weighed it on the bathroom scale and then handed it to Johanna, telling her to make soup of it, although Everett had never tasted turtle soup and as such had no idea if he cared for it. Johanna had agreed, then waited until he'd headed back to the river and taken the huge turtle out and tossed it behind the old manure pile, where the barn cats soon cleaned it up, leaving nothing but the hollow shell.

Yes, there were snapping turtles in the creek, and from that day on, Everett would wage war upon them. Quite typically, he chose to disregard an animal's biological needs, choosing instead to take the attacks on the ducklings personally. Everett liked to pick sides. The baby birds became his baby birds and the snappers became an enemy to a man who had passed nearly eight decades delighting in confrontation and the vanquishing of foes. His health now almost completely failing him, he was not one to reflect upon the seemingly inconsequential nature of this latest feud. Fights, by nature, were worth fighting.

Now, two years past the rescue of the mallard duckling, he walked nearly every day to the creek bank, his canvas bag in his hand, his veins heavy and sluggish under doses of Lipitor and beta blockers, his glycerin tucked inside his jacket pocket along with the flask of Dalmore. He had put up a crude one-sided blind twenty yards or so from the shore, with pine boughs protecting him from the west winds, which he found chilling, even though the mid-May temperatures were often well into the sixties. He'd hauled a faded green Adirondack chair down from the porch and positioned it on the grass a few feet from the windbreak, facing the creek where his enemy skulked. Some days the hens and ducklings would be already skimming the surface, clucking and chortling. Other days they would be holed up in the marsh to the east, where he could hear them as they fed.

Regardless of the birds' whereabouts, Everett would settle in the chair and then open the bag and bring out the old cap-and-ball Colt. He would take his time loading it, enjoying the ritual, donning his reading glasses to measure the powder by eye, doling out enough to bring the ball flush with the front of the cylinder. He didn't bother to grease the loaded chambers, reasoning that it was a little late in the game to be growing cautious. After loading all six cylinders he would place the number eleven caps on the nipples, put the heavy revolver on the arm of the chair, and only then take the first sip of scotch as he waited and watched the area beyond the sunken logs on the far side of the creek. Some days the sun would come out and he would hear the ducks approaching and he would smile and take a long drink, the Colt in his lap, turtle vengeance in his heart. This, the last of his pleasures, it seemed.

WILL MONTGOMERY saddled the buckskin mare in the box stall and led her outside by the reins, opened the lane gate and then grabbed a handful of mane and pulled himself into the saddle. The buckskin balked before sidestepping through the gate, which Will leaned over and pulled shut behind them. Then he reined the fidgety horse onto the grass on the high side of the lane and kicked her into a lope.

The lane itself was a quagmire. The rain, which had amounted to very little ("four-fifths of fuck-all" was the assessment of his hired hand Dalton Myers) in April, had barely stopped to catch its breath here in the second week of May, rendering the lane impassable by truck. Will could've driven the tractor to the back acreage but that would only have cut deep ruts he'd end up cursing all summer long. Besides, the buckskin had been lazing in the front pasture field with the cattle since he'd turned the herd out and she needed the exercise.

He ran her out until she started to behave and then slowed her to a walk as he approached the creek where it cut the lane in front of the bush lot. They went through the gurgling stream, rider and horse, then swung around the bush and into the field of winter wheat behind.

Will climbed down from the horse and gave the reins a turn around what remained of a rail fence. He walked into the field. The sixty acres that had looked so good after he'd planted it in the fall was barely holding its own now. It had been a cold winter with little snow, and then the reluctant spring. The downpours of recent days had washed the crop completely away in the low areas. What was left was yellow and sickly. Still, a jump in the temperature and some sunny days would bring it back, he reasoned. There was no sun, however, in the forecast.

Walking around a point of cedar trees that extended from the bush lot into the field, he surprised a flock of wild turkeys, sixty or seventy strong, fanned out across the field and snacking on his already suspect wheat crop. The birds scattered at a dead run when they saw him, running pell-mell into the woods, clucking urgently one to another as they fled. He watched them disappear into the brush and then walked back to the mare and climbed into the saddle again.

He pushed her back to the spot where he'd seen the turkeys and continued on, circumventing the bush lot and heading to the back of the Eastman farm. The buckskin was, uncharacteristically, acting just fine. Will had never been overly fond of the animal; she'd been Denise's horse and when Denise had still been there she'd been a problem, having a tendency to attempt to rub riders off on nearby trees or to roll on the ground with someone in the saddle. Will had one day broken a shovel across her back after she'd kicked him in the thigh while he was cleaning her stall. Now, however, with Denise packed and gone, the mare seemed a little less tense. Her and Will both.

When he'd flanked the Eastman woods he came upon the creek again and followed it toward Crooked Pear, keeping to the high side and out of the marsh that had, with the rain, spread across the big field in front of the bush, completely flooding the swale that extended all the way to the southern boundary of the farm.

As he approached the Eastman farmhouse he saw Everett in position, hunkered down in the old wooden chair, sheltered by the makeshift wind-block on his left. Although he was still too far off to see, Will knew the old man would be further fortified with a single malt and a six-shooter.

He rode the mare through the twisted wild pear trees that ran along the creek bank from the barn to the road and that—at Everett's daughter Kathleen's suggestion—had given the farm its name, and when he was a hundred yards or so from the old man he saw Everett raise the revolver in both hands and sight it toward the far shore. Will reined the mare to a halt. There were a couple dozen ducks and ducklings swimming aimlessly out in front of the old man, and when he pulled the trigger the explosion that rocketed through the air scared the birds completely senseless. Putting up a squawk that rivaled the gunshot in pure decibel level, they half-swam and half-flew back up the creek, past Will where he sat the mare, which was little more impressed with the revolver blast than was the waterfowl. Will kept a tight rein on her or she would have followed the ducks upstream.

"You ought to get a silencer for that thing," Will said as he walked the reluctant buckskin out of the trees a few minutes later. "If you're gonna scare those birds to death, you might as well let the turtles have them."

"I think they're getting used to it."

"Yeah, they seemed real relaxed when they went squawking by me like their asses were on fire." Will looked at the sunken logs across the stream. "What'd you hit?"

The old man pointed with the heavy revolver. "Missed a big snapper by, oh ... maybe a quarter inch." He placed the gun on the arm of the chair. "You're riding a horse."

Will nodded. As his health continued to founder, Everett had fallen into the habit of pointing out the obvious. Getting dark, he would say. Raining out.

When Everett took a drink from the flask and then offered it up, Will got down from the saddle and took it from him. The old man's hand shook as he handed it over. He looked thinner than ever. He'd stopped cutting his hair about six months earlier and the gray locks hung down from beneath the straw hat he'd taken to wearing. He was beginning to resemble a sage old Indian in a movie.

"Out looking at the ground?"

Will took a drink. "Yeah."

"Won't be seeding anything for a while. Damn wet."

"Damn wet is right. I was hoping to plant oats in that big field of yours in front of the bush. Too late in the season now. Might have to do the whole farm in soybeans."

"You'll make money off soy."

"And use it to buy oats." Will looked across the swollen river.

The old man got up stiffly from the chair, took a couple of steps toward the creek and unzipped. When the meager stream eventually came forth, he looked back and said, "I gotta take a piss."

Will nodded and looked at the gun on the chair arm and at the pill bottles visible inside the canvas rucksack. "How you feeling, Everett?"

"Like a teenager," Everett said, zipping up. "Had half a mind to throw it into Johanna last night."

"That's all you need, a sexual harassment claim from your house-keeper," Will said.

"How do you know she's not aching for it? Maybe she's been wanting it all these years, watching all my wives come and go. She might be a little curious. You know how women are."

Will took another drink of the scotch and handed the flask back over before mounting the buckskin again. "I know a lot of things, Everett," he said, reining the horse around. "But I wouldn't go so far as to say that I know a goddamned thing about how women are."

He pushed the mare toward the barn and then down the drive to the road. As soon as the horse knew she was headed for home she wanted to run, and he let her, galloping flat out alongside the paved river road, the mare's hooves throwing clods in the air behind them. It was a half mile from Crooked Pear to Will's place, and by the time they got there the out-of-shape buckskin was blowing hard. He reined her in at the end of the lane and reached down to collect the mail from the box. He tucked the letters and flyers inside his jacket and rode to the barn. Getting down from the horse, he walked her around the yard for five minutes then gave her a rubdown with a burlap bag and brushed her out. He put her in the box stall; he would turn her out with the cattle later in the day.

It was lunchtime when he went inside. He scrambled some eggs, and while he was waiting for them to cook he opened the mail, or at least he opened the letter from Denise's lawyer. In it were listed the specific items she wanted from the marriage, aside from the money, which had already been decided. Included were items of jewelry, furniture, paintings and some glassware. Last on the list was the 1968 Mustang fastback that was sitting in the back corner of the machine shed. Will had owned the car for ten years before he'd ever met Denise. He knew she would now claim that he'd said he would fix it up for her, and she'd be right in saying it. But then, they'd both said a lot of things, early on. As Will had mentioned to Everett Eastman earlier, he didn't know a hell of a lot about women but there was one thing he did know—he would pull the Mustang out of the shed, douse it with gasoline and burn it to a cinder before he would sign the ownership over to his ex-wife.

Looking at the paper again as he ate his eggs, he realized that the buckskin mare was not listed. He smiled, recalling the times that she'd told him she loved that horse with all her heart.

BY THE TIME the flask was empty the ducks and ducklings had still not returned. Everett huddled in his canvas jacket and felt the day grow cold and then colder, even though the sun shone and the weather channel had that morning called for warm temperatures. He began to drift into an uneasy sleep. While floating, he dreamed himself on the opposite bank of the creek, watching himself in the chair. It was a curious sight and it lasted a few seconds only. When he awoke again he thought he saw Kick, as a young girl, chasing frogs in the shallow water by the dock.

He lurched back to full consciousness late in the afternoon; he was freezing and nauseous now as well. He thought of a long bath and of lighting a fire in the front room. When he tried to reach for the revolver he found that his left arm would not move at all and then he knew at last that he was in some trouble. He concentrated on taking a single breath, wondering if he was already gone. He managed to get his right hand on the gun. He fired a shot in the air.

WILL AND DALTON MYERS were in the drive shed, replacing broken tines on the cultivator and greasing the bearings in readiness for working the ground whenever the rain decided to stop. Dalton had gone into town for the new tines and he'd picked up coffee and fritters from Tim's. They ate the fritters while their hands were yet clean, and then drank the coffee while they worked.

They heard the gunshot from the farm to the north, the roar echoing across the quiet afternoon like a sudden crack of thunder. Will straightened from the grease gun and looked off in that direction.

"Everett's after them turtles again," Dalton said. "That old horse pistol gonna blow up in his face, one of these days. Somebody ought to take it away from him."

"Let me know when you find somebody wants to try," Will said and he went back to work.

TWO

A rancher named Dawe went crazy over the weekend and shot up a drilling rig near Spotted Horse, north of Gillette, and on Monday morning Kick decided that they should drive up and have a look around. By then they had moved down from Belle Fourche and were staying at the Ramada in Casper, so in effect they'd be backtracking, but then how were they to know that a rancher would go nuts?

Kick got up at dawn and went for a run along a stretch of abandoned train line, then ate some fruit in her room while she read the newspaper and flipped through the morning shows. They were talking plastic surgery on *Good Morning America* and spring salads on *The Today Show,* so Kick had to assume that war and pestilence and famine had pretty much been eradicated throughout the world. Buoyed by that consideration, she put on jeans and a sweater and her hiking boots and then went down to meet Tom in the parking lot, stopping at the motel restaurant for takeout coffee for them both.

Tom Thomas, whom Kick referred to as the cameraman so nice they named him twice, was leaning against the Land Rover, wearing his shades and his archaic Expos cap. He took a critical sip from the coffee and they set out.

Tom drove and Kick assumed control of the map and the CD player. She duct-taped the printout of northern Wyoming to the dash and then went through the jumble of CDs on the back seat for a suitable disc.

"You feel like a little Joni Mitchell?" she said.

"Can we turn on the news?" Tom asked. "Kinda like to know what's going on with the world."

"Botox is cool and avocados are fun. Got it straight from the networks." Kick turned up the volume.

They headed north out of Casper on Highway 25. The day was clear and they traveled under a Wyoming sky every bit as big as its better advertised neighbor to the north. It took them a couple of hours to reach Buffalo, crossing over the south fork of the Powder River while Canada geese flew overhead and Mitchell sang "Chelsea Morning." By the time they reached Johnson County the north-bound geese had outdistanced them and Kick had moved on to Gordon Lightfoot, whom she accompanied.

"*The legend lives on from the Chippewa on down, from the great lake they call Gitchee-goomee.*" She looked over at Tom. "I love that name. Gitchee-goomee. Why don't you ever tell me how much you love my singing?"

"Because my mother used to hit me with the flyswatter when I lied," Tom told her.

"That doesn't sound very hygienic."

"Stopped me from lying."

They pulled in to a truck stop for gas in Buffalo. Tom pumped while Kick checked the oil and washed the windows. The rest of the truck was filthy. When Kick went in to pay for the gas she had the cashier try three credit cards before one cleared.

From Buffalo they angled northeast, following the Clear River as it jumped and twisted through rocks and switchbacks, readying itself to join up with the Powder farther north. Kick went into her knap-sack and found the CD she'd received in the mail the previous day, forwarded to her hotel from her Toronto address. She slid it into the player. The singer's voice crept in under the dirge of a harmonica, the tone thin and reedy, the melody practically nonexistent.

"What the hell is that?" Tom asked.

"That," Kick told him, "is my brother Ethan's demo tape. So watch what you say."

Tom, under Kick's challenging glare, opted for silence. After a moment's more listening Kick acquiesced and began to punch through the other songs, giving each a half minute or so before moving on, like an index-finger gong show. When the last song began she was ready to pop the CD from the player, but then she stopped. There was an acoustic guitar, a couple of simple chords and then Ethan's voice, but this time it came from another place. His tone was assured and his pitch as clear as the tumbling stream outside:

I see his suitcase on the front porch,
I hear his footsteps in the hall,
I knew a man all my life
I never knew at all

"I'll be goddamned," Kick said when the song was finished.

It was early afternoon when they drove into the town of Spotted Horse. Kick pointed out a diner on the main street and they parked and went inside.

A waitress wearing a tracksuit brought single-page menus laminated in plastic. When Kick asked if there was a special she offered a strange look in reply and went back to the counter, where a half dozen cowboys sitting on stools were talking softly, nursing coffees and taking turns sneaking glances their way. Kick smiled over at them, and when none returned the effort she glanced at Tom, who shrugged and went back to the menu. Kick regarded the reticent bunch a moment longer.

"Well, I'd rather be hung for a rabble-rouser than mocked for a coward," she said and then raised her voice to address the counter. "Hey boys, how you doing today?"

A couple of the cowboys turned away as soon as she spoke. Kick half expected them to cup their hands over their ears. The waitress came back.

"Ready to order?"

"Turkey club on rye," Kick told her. "My compatriot will have a cheeseburger and fries, gravy on the fries. Coffee for us both."

"I can order my own lunch," Tom said. He looked at the menu again and then asked for a cheeseburger and fries with gravy.

"Don't take anything too personal," the waitress said then. "Just that people around here are kind of distrustful of reporters. With the trouble and all."

"What makes you think we're the press?" Kick asked.

"Come on. Truck outside full of equipment. Pretty girl, looks like she could be on the television news."

"Good-looking camera guy," Tom added.

"I'm a filmmaker," Kick told her. "Documentaries."

"What's the difference?" The waitress moved off.

While they were eating, a fleshy-faced man in a brand-new Stetson hat slid down from his stool and made his way over. Drew the short straw, Kick thought as she watched him approach their table, a large man with the walk and the earnest look of a child who'd just accepted a dare from his playground buddies. He sat at the next table and turned his chair sideways so he could face them. He didn't, however, say a damn thing. Kick took a bite of the club, looked at him thoughtfully as she chewed and swallowed, and then got to it.

"Do you know Stanley Dawe?"

"I do," the man said. He was talking to Kick but looking at Tom, who was attempting to fit his mouth around the large burger.

"Would you know why he took a Winchester 30-30 and shot up one of GreenPower's rigs on Saturday night?" Kick asked.

"I expect he was aggravated."

"I'm guessing that's a fairly common emotion in those prone to shooting things up," Kick suggested.

"Well, some will do it for fun."

"But not Stanley Dawe."

"I expect not."

Kick tipped the creamer over her coffee. "Any notion as to the source of his aggravation?"

"I got more than a notion," the man said and he took off his hat to reveal curly red hair, thinning on top. The skin above his hat line was startlingly white. "Fact is, they can expect more of it. They keep that drilling up, sure we'll have all kinds of natural gas. Methane too. But no damn water. We're ranchers, most of us. You need water to run a ranch."

"I know," Kick said. "We've been talking to some ranch families over near Belle Fourche and they—"

"I've got kin in Belle Fourche."

"Would you be willing to talk about this on camera? I'd like to film you at your ranch. You can talk about whatever you want, what makes you happy, makes you sad, gets your dander up. Would you do that?"

"I'd have to clear it with the missus first."

Tom looked up at him from his fries, then glanced at Kick.

"I'll give you my cell number," Kick told the man.

The red-haired man didn't require permission from the missus to give them directions to the GreenPower drilling site in question. In fact, he drew them a rather comprehensive map on a paper napkin. He took Kick's phone number and then ambled back to the counter.

The site was just ten miles out of Spotted Horse. On the way there were smaller ranches scattered in the valley, fencing stretching up into the hills, pasture fields dotted with rocks and the occasional rusted-out shell of a vehicle.

At the drilling site a brand-new gravel road ran north off the highway, and near the entrance to the road a huge sign constructed of white laminate read:

GreenPower Gas & Oil
Fiscally Sound
Environmentally Safe

"Who do they think they're fooling, putting green in the name?" Kick asked as they turned onto the rough roadway.

The road ran through rock cuts and scrub evergreens. There were generators on wheels parked here and there off the narrow path, and the odd bulldozer or skidder on rubber-tired floats. All the tires, and most of the equipment itself, were fairly well perforated with bullet holes and perimetered off with yellow police tape.

They'd gone maybe a mile when they spotted the rig through the pines, the derrick reaching well above the tree tops. Rounding a small curve, they came upon a parking area. There were three police cruisers in the lot and a number of GreenPower pickups, most featuring the same ventilated look as the equipment they'd seen earlier. The rig itself, being primarily of steel, appeared largely unscathed other than being pockmarked from gunshots, but the enormous diesel engine that powered it must have taken a hit. There were several men in coveralls at work disassembling it. There was another group, including several cops, gathered in a circle near the base of the rig. As soon as the Land Rover pulled up a man in jeans and a sheepskin coat broke away from this bunch and approached, his right hand in the air like he was being sworn in for something. Tom stopped the truck and Kick got out immediately and walked to meet the man.

"You can't be here," he said flatly.

"So much for the meet and greet," Kick said and she took a card from her pocket. "I'm Kathleen Eastman and I'm a documentary filmmaker. Is there any chance—"

"You can *not* be here."

"What do I need—a hard hat?"

Tom shut the engine off now and got out.

"Get back in the truck, sir." As the man spoke he turned and looked pointedly toward the rig, where one of the cops was waiting his cue.

"I just have a couple quick questions," Kick said. "We've got ranchers telling us that GreenPower is sucking all the groundwater from beneath the surface and letting it run off in the streams. They claim they have Artesian wells running dry and they also say that some of the water being pumped from the deeper aquifers is so contaminated with salt it's poisoning the creeks and killing the aquatic life. Can you respond to any of this?"

The man in the coat just looked at her and waited for the approaching cop. "They have no clearance to be here," he said when the man arrived.

The cop wore a trooper's hat low over his eyes, the brim actually resting on the top of his sunglasses. His mustache was so thin and wispy that it hardly qualified as such, but he had a jaw that would make Dudley Do-Right blush.

"What is your business here, ma'am?" the cop asked.

"We heard about the incident on the news," Kick said.

"She claims to be a reporter," the man in the coat said.

"The hell I did," Kick said, looking at him.

The cop then extended his left arm straight out from his body and made a sweeping gesture with his right toward the Land Rover, like he was directing traffic in a parade.

"You asking me to dance?" Kick inquired. "We've just met."

"This is a crime scene, ma'am."

"That's exactly what we've been hearing," she said. "Oh—you're probably talking about the guy with the rifle?"

The cop was holding to his let's-waltz pose. "This site is closed to any persons not involved with the investigation. You're required to turn this vehicle around and evacuate the premises."

Kick looked at Tom. "I love the way these guys talk." She turned to the cop. "Where's Stanley Dawe?"

Perhaps in surrender to muscle fatigue, the cop finally dropped his left arm. "I am not at liberty to discuss any persons of interest with regard to this case. I'm going to tell you one last time, ma'am. You are to leave this property. Until our investigation is complete, this site is off-limits to any unauthorized personnel who might contaminate the crime scene."

Kick turned and made a point of looking over the site—the huge rig, the machinery and trucks, the generators running at full speed. "I guess we're out of here," she said to Tom. "The last thing we want to do is *contaminate* the area. Oh, the irony."

Tom got back behind the wheel of the Land Rover. Kick climbed into the back seat.

"Take your time turning around," she told him as she reached into the back and grabbed a Betacam. She did a battery check, then rolled down the side window and began to shoot as Tom started the engine. The man in the coat saw and began walking toward them, his expression dark. Kick leaned out the window as they turned around, got the rig and the shot-up pickup trucks. As Tom started the truck on the way out, she swept across the site with the camera and then took a long last shot of the man in the coat as he paced quickly after them. The perception was the reality—he was running them off.

They drove back toward Spotted Horse in silence. Kick crawled over the seat as they left the gravel road, and after a moment she put Lucinda Williams in the CD player but neglected to turn the volume up. She sat with the camera on her lap, watched the playback on the little screen and then tossed it into the back seat.

"What?" Tom asked.

"We have to stick around for this."

"For what?"

"Everything. First we're going to have to talk to this Dawe guy—"

"The news said he was locked up."

"He'll make bail. It's not much of a crime, shooting up a bloody drilling rig. But we need this guy, Tom. And we have to be here for the trial too. This is our chance to put a face on this thing. This guy could be a cowboy Che Guevara. Or Tom Paine, at least."

"What if he's just a nut?"

"Then he's a nut with a point. You saw what they're doing out there."

Kick turned up Lucinda then, watched out the window for a time.

"If he's our guy," Tom asked, "how come you're looking so unhappy?"

"Because we don't have any money left. I've been maxing out credit cards like a Hilton sister."

"What about the editing budget?" Tom asked. "Didn't the grant cover that? Can you rob Peter to pay Paul?"

"I robbed Peter blind a long time ago," Kick said. She looked over, turned down the volume. "What about you, Tom-Tom? You've got credit cards. You can't spend any more than about twelve bucks a year on clothes. You wanna pitch in a little? Get you a producer's credit."

Tom looked down at his attire, shrugged. "I'd have to clear it with the missus first."

"That damn rancher."

"I told you before, Kick. Ella handles all the money. She puts a high priority on certain things like mortgage payments, food for the kids, utilities—"

"What a lunatic. I can't believe you married that woman."

"I don't expect you to understand it," Tom said. "It's called a personal life. You should try it sometime."

"Don't start with that shit."

They were on the main street of Spotted Horse again, driving past the diner where they'd had lunch. Kick wondered if she'd hear from the red-haired rancher.

"See if this town's got a police station," she suggested. "They've got to be holding Dawe someplace."

AT TEN O'CLOCK that evening she was sitting in the lounge at the Ramada back in Casper, drinking rye and water and watching the Mariners play the Angels on the screen above the bar. Monday night was not a happening time in the lounge. There was a middle-aged couple at a table in the center of the room. When Kick came in a waitress had just cleared their dinner plates, and while waiting for their coffee they'd danced to Tony Bennett on the jukebox. Three guys in suits, their ties and tongues loosened, were at a table near the end of the bar and they'd eyed Kick lasciviously when she walked in.

She was on her third rye when she felt a presence at her elbow and turned to see one of the loose ties standing there.

"We were wondering," the man began, then he smirked, glanced back to the others. "We were wondering if you wanted to join us for a drink."

"Is that what you were wondering?"

"Yeah."

"I think I'm good right here."

"Come on, just a drink. You're all alone up here."

Kick looked over at the table where the other two men were watching like expectant teenagers. They had to be in their forties, the three of them. Paunchy, cocky in their drunken camaraderie, away from the family for a night or two.

"You know," the loose tie beside her said then. "My buddy says you got maybe the nicest ass in alla Casper."

"Gosh, what a charmer," Kick said and she looked over again. "Which one came up with that—the dumb-looking fucker with the earring or the moron with the glob of ketchup on his shirt?"

When the loose tie got back to the table she heard him tell the others that she was a dyke. A moment later they were flirting with the waitress whose ass, Kick suspected, might just have supplanted hers as the finest in the city.

While she was drinking the third rye and considering various cable markets that might be convinced to pony up the cash she needed to finish her film, a cowboy came in and sat down a couple of stools over. He was maybe ten years younger than Kick, twenty-five or twenty-six, she guessed, and he wore a sweat-stained Stetson and a denim jacket. Boots and jeans. He was a bit of a looker. There were worse reasons than that to say hello to a stranger, she reasoned. She said hello.

"Ma'am."

Kick sighed. In these parts, it seemed if she wasn't a lesbian, she was a ma'am. The cowboy ordered a beer and asked the bartender if he had any peanuts. He was a polite kid.

"You a rancher?" Kick asked when he had his beer.

"Not really. I buy and sell cattle." He had brown eyes and long lashes. Kick wished he would take the hat off.

"From here?"

"Calgary."

"Hey, I'm from Ontario."

He nodded as he took another drink of beer.

"You wouldn't know anything about the oil and gas drilling that's happening around here?" she asked.

"I'm from Calgary."

"Yeah. You said."

He drank his beer and ate a few peanuts. Kick wasn't at all sure if he'd actually looked at her yet. The loose ties were telling jokes now, piling one on top of the other, each man in turn laughing loudly and briefly before exclaiming, "Wait, I've got one!"

"I'm just heading home from Wichita," she heard the young cowboy say. "I don't know much about this area. I tend to mind my business."

"It's never been my strong suit," Kick told him. "Although it has been suggested to me a good many times. As recently as this afternoon, in fact."

The cowboy continued to focus on his beer. Kick watched him for a moment, then drank off her rye. She hadn't eaten since lunch in Spotted Horse and she was feeling the effects of the whiskey. She toyed with the notion of another, considered getting herself drunk. Maybe the young cowboy would follow suit and they could end up in her room. He was a slow talker and, quite possibly, a slow thinker. Maybe she'd get lucky and he'd fuck the same way.

She entertained the thought for a moment or two, then pushed her glass away and stood up. "I just don't know what we'd talk about in the morning," she said.

"What?" he asked, finally looking at her.

"Nothing, young cowboy," she said and she left. Standing alone in the elevator, she began to sing:

"As I was out walking the streets of Laredo,
As I walked out in Laredo one day,
I spied a young cowboy all wrapped in white linen—"

Her cell phone began to ring and she fished it from her vest pocket. She answered it by singing:

"Wrapped in white linen as cold as the clay—"

Then a voice she didn't recognize told her that her father was dead.

THREE

Ben got the call as he and Teddy Brock were walking into the strip bar in the industrial mall in Mississauga. When the cell phone rang, he waved Teddy on. Two minutes later, he joined him inside. They sat at the bar along the stage and ordered scotch on the rocks.

"Everything okay?" Teddy asked.

"Yeah," Ben said. "My old man died this afternoon."

Teddy watched as Ben stuffed some bar pretzels into his mouth. "Really?" he asked after a moment.

Ben took a drink. "He was old, don't worry about it."

"How old?"

"I don't know. Seventy-five or eighty. You make a tee time for the morning?"

"Yeah, but if you have to take care of things—"

"What am I gonna do—embalm him?" Ben asked. "What's the tee time?"

"Eight-fifteen."

Ben slept until a quarter to eight the next morning. Ben Junior had already left for school by the time he went downstairs. Meredith was washing breakfast dishes. She was dressed to go out, he saw, wearing cotton pants and a blouse. She had her makeup on. Ben poured a cup of coffee from the carafe on the island.

"Why are you washing dishes?"

"Eleanor has a doctor's appointment."

"Woman has a lot of doctor's appointments, doesn't she?"

"It's her health, Ben. I don't think she does it to aggravate you. You want breakfast?" she asked. She moved behind him, ran her hand across his back.

"No, I'm late."

"You were late last night. I wondered where you got to."

When he didn't comment, she went back to the dishes. He drank his coffee standing up, took a banana from a basket on the counter and put it in the pocket of his khaki shorts.

"I assume by the golfing attire you're not going in to the office," she said then.

"No. Got a grudge match with Teddy Brock."

"You used to golf on weekends."

He looked at her, then had another drink of the coffee and set the cup down. "I still do," he said and walked out.

Wilson was trimming the shrubs along the drive with hedge clippers. "Looks good, Wilson Pickett," Ben said as he got into the Corvette.

It was only a ten-minute drive to the course. On the way he ate the banana and tossed the peel out the car window. Then he called Louise.

"Hey, it's me."

"Hi," she said. He could tell she was on the headset.

"Anything you need me for this morning?"

"Not a thing."

He could never tell if she was being sarcastic or not. He was quite sure she was aware that the plant ran just as smoothly when he was away as when he was there, but the woman was such a blank slate he had no idea what her opinion was of him. Fortunately, he didn't give the matter a lot of thought.

"Okay, my cell's gonna be off for a few hours," he told her.

"Hit 'em straight."

Brock and Leo and Leo's brother-in-law—Dan or Don or Doug, Ben couldn't remember which—were waiting on the first tee. It was a cool morning. Ben pulled on a wind-shell before he got his clubs from the trunk and walked over.

"Gentlemen," he said.

"You remember Doug," Leo said.

Ben shook Doug's hand. "Slash away, whoever's ready," he said then.

The first hole ran parallel to the highway. There was a creek with an iron bridge crossing about one seventy-five out and to the right was a stand of willow trees. Ben teed off last and hit a towering slice over the willows and then, apparently, well across the road.

"I don't know," he said as he watched the ball disappear behind the willows. "I better hit a provisional."

He rode in the cart with Teddy Brock, who'd hit a draw into the light rough on the left-hand side of the fairway.

"I'm going to divorce Meredith," Ben said as they crossed the iron bridge. "I want you to handle it."

Teddy took a moment. "First of all, I'm not a family lawyer. Secondly, when did you decide this?"

"This morning, when I was drinking my coffee."

They arrived at Teddy's ball. Ben got out of the cart and grabbed an iron from his bag. "I'm gonna have a look for my first ball."

He walked toward the willows, and when he got there he turned and waited until Teddy was in his backswing then dropped a ball from his pocket in the long grass beneath the trees. He waited until Teddy arrived with the cart before "finding" the ball he'd just dropped. He hacked the ball out of the heavy rough with a five iron and left it ten yards short of the green.

"What does Meredith say?" Teddy asked when they were back in the cart.

"She doesn't know yet."

As they drove Teddy glanced across the highway to the right. There was a ball on the far side, resting on the gravel shoulder.

"What'd she say about your father dying?" Teddy decided to ask.
"Sonofabitch. I forgot to mention it."

ETHAN AND JANEY arrived at Crooked Pear early that evening, having flown in from Victoria where Janey's parents had a condo and where they had been living since they'd finished tree planting the previous fall. The call came at an opportune time—Janey's parents had spent the winter in Mexico and were due home in another week. Janey and Ethan had intended to go back to the north of the island to plant but the crew had been downsized. The timing of the call couldn't have been better because she was aware that her father was less than enthusiastic about their relationship. He was prone to asking what Ethan intended to do if his musical aspirations didn't pan out. That is, he was prone to asking Janey those types of questions. He rarely said anything at all to Ethan.

They landed at Pearson in the late afternoon and rented a Ford Taurus on Janey's Visa card. They took the 401 west, Ethan driving, then headed north on Highway 6 and arrived at Crooked Pear as the sun was setting over the Grand River. Cresting the hill as they approached the farm from the south, Ethan pulled over to the side of the road and shut the motor off, then produced a joint from his shirt pocket and lit it. Janey took a hit and then handed it back as she looked out the windshield at the farmhouse.

She saw a three-story red brick jumble of els and additions, porches and terraces, dormers and walkways, French doors and bay windows. There was a glassed-in sunroom all along the southern exposure of the house and even from this distance she could see blooms and greenery inside. Behind the absurd structure was a large barn of red steel, and behind that a stable with a corral alongside. A stout workhorse was standing in the corral, its head over the top rail as it looked off toward the horizon. A black goat stood nearby, pulling at a tuft of grass.

The front yard of the house sloped down to the road, which ran along the river to their left and was dotted with ancient hardwoods. There were other, twisted trees beyond the house, along the bank of a creek, and a stand of cedars on the stream's far side. Janey had another toke and then turned her attention back to the house.

"Looks like Frank Lloyd Wright got into some bad acid."

Ethan leaned back and exhaled into the roof of the rental. "Throw my troubles out the door, I don't need them anymore, 'cuz tonight I'll be staying here with you."

A blonde woman let them in. She was in her late forties, Janey guessed, very fit, wearing tan khaki pants and a V-neck sweater. She wore no makeup. Her hair was pulled back, revealing freckles on her shoulders and neck. Her hands and forearms were strong, the fingernails clipped short.

"Hello, Ethan," she said when she saw them. Her voice contained the faintest remains of an accent—Dutch or possibly German, Janey guessed—and her tone held little emotion, but her eyes showed a certain cautious warmth that suggested she was happy to see him.

"I'm glad to see you're still alive, you're looking like a saint," Ethan told her.

"Okay then," the blonde woman said, her eyebrows raised.

"I'm Janey," Janey cut in. "Ethan's … girlfriend. I'm really sorry to hear about Mr. Eastman."

Ethan looked past Janey to the sunroom, where brilliant daffodils and tulips were closing down their blossoms for the day. He walked toward the flowers, following his stone. Watching him, Janey was aware of her own enlightened state; face to face with the blonde woman, she felt suddenly like a kitten that had scaled a set of drapes and was coming to the gradual realization that it had no exit strategy.

"I'm Johanna," the woman said and then she smiled. Janey got the sense that she'd seen kittens in this predicament before.

"Ethan's told me about you," Janey said. "This is a ... um, a lovely house."

"Actually, it's not such a lovely house," Johanna said. "But it is an interesting house."

"Do you look after it all by yourself?"

"Yah. But it is not as big a job as maybe you think."

"Oh. Well, Ethan said that you ... well, he said that you kinda raised him."

The woman Johanna took a moment—of judgment more than decision, it seemed to Janey. "I supposed I helped. What do they say—it takes a village? We had quite the village here. With the children, and the odd wife. Notice I said odd. And Everett himself from time to time. And all of the time these past two years. But I guess you know all that."

Janey felt herself inching down the curtains. "I don't, actually. Ethan told me about you, but he doesn't talk much about his family."

"But he has shown up now. And damn quick."

"Well, it was his father."

"Yah, he was. He was his father when he was alive, too."

"I don't know what to say," Janey said. She felt cornered and regretted toking in the car. "I never knew him."

"Oh, he was quite an impossible man," Johanna said, relenting a little.

"I guessed we missed the funeral. We just heard—"

"There was no funeral," Johanna told her. "So where are you two staying?"

Janey glanced toward the sunroom, where Ethan was now seated in a wicker settee, his feet up. His expression seemed to pass from serene to anxious in a blink of an eye.

Johanna nodded. "You can take Ethan's old room. I'll see to the linens."

KICK STAYED AN EXTRA DAY in Wyoming, thinking that the wrathful rancher Stanley Dawe would make bail and she might get him on film while he was still, presumably, in an incendiary frame of mind. As it was, the bail hearing was postponed at the request of the state police, who claimed they needed more time to assess the damage at the drilling site. Kick flew home the next morning.

She stopped at her apartment in Toronto to dump off her film equipment and pick up her Jetta from the underground parking. She did a couple of quick loads of laundry while sifting through a depressing stack of mail—credit card bills in the main, with nary a successful grant request in the bunch. Then she filled the Jetta with fuel and headed to Crooked Pear.

There was a Taurus with rental plates in the drive, and Johanna's Volvo wagon alongside. Kick parked and sat for a time behind the wheel. Whatever her emotions for the conventional concept of coming home, they were tied to Crooked Pear. This in spite of the fact it had been a temporal home at best—summers growing up for the most part—and that she'd spent a good deal of her childhood in various places in Toronto, the specific location determined by her father's marital status at the time. The fact of the matter was that she considered herself a nomad. Still, if she was obliged to label a place home, this farm called Crooked Pear would be that place.

Maybe it was her olfactory sense, and not her heart, that made it so. Walking through the front door, she was immediately assailed by an assortment of aromas from the kitchen. The pungent, yeasty smell of baking bread, permeated by another odor—a mix of basil and tomato and oregano. There was something else in the air—quite possibly apple pie. Kick followed her nose to the kitchen and found it, albeit cloaked in the delectable odors, quite empty otherwise. She decided against looking inside the oven, fearful of causing a culinary collapse.

She walked to the French doors and stepped outside. The backyard was large, sloping away from the house to the outbuildings. The grass was just beginning to green up. The barn had been recently painted, red with white trim. The line of blue spruce trees she and Johanna had planted when Kick was in high school were now ten feet tall or higher. Kick went back inside and carried her knapsack upstairs to her old room. She found Johanna there, changing the sheets on the bed.

"Somebody been sleeping in my bed?" Kick asked.

Johanna glanced at her. "No."

"That means you're changing clean sheets."

Johanna pulled the duvet over the bed and straightened. "Are you going to be a smart-ass or are you going to give me a hug?"

"Can't I do both?" Kick asked. They hugged for a long time, and it seemed to Kick that Johanna's eyes were damp when they quit.

"You could always do both," Johanna said.

"Is that lasagna I smell?"

"It is lasagna you smell," Johanna said and they went downstairs.

THEY ATE IN THE LARGE DINING ROOM turned family room. Ethan and Janey had gone for a walk down by the river and they returned as Kick was opening a bottle of wine and Johanna was lifting the lasagna from the oven. Kick looked at Ethan for a moment—the lank hair hanging in his eyes, the baggy pants, the stoner's gaze—and then she gave him a hug.

"What's going on, bro?" she asked.

"Oh sister, when I come to knock on your door, do not treat me as a stranger" was his reply.

"Okay," Kick said and she turned to Janey. "I'm Kathleen."

"I'm Janey."

Kick poured the wine and they sat around the big oak table and ate. Ethan was ravenous—predictably so, Kick thought—and he had little to say as he scarfed down the pasta and fresh bread. Janey picked at her plate. Kick could sense her nervousness at being the newcomer. From Johanna she could feel a certain joy at having part of her brood back at her table, but she too was uncharacteristically quiet. In the end, the formality was too much for Kick.

"So when do we start reminiscing about the hale and hearty times we had here with dear old Dad?" she asked finally.

Ethan, his mouth full, looked at her and shrugged.

"Ah yes, there's a slight problem with that plan, isn't there, Ethan?"

"Yeah, we never had any."

"That's right," Kick said. "Guess we'll have to make 'em up."

Janey smiled at her then, and Kick could actually feel her relax.

"Everett wasn't cut from the Norman Rockwell mode," Kick told her. "As a father, he was more of a … well, a sperm donor. Which made it hard to find a suitable card for Father's Day."

"Now, now," Johanna said. "He took care of this family. Maybe he wasn't always … accessible. But he took care."

Kick pushed her plate away and had a drink of wine. "Well, he's managed to bring us together here tonight. That's something. Where did you kids come in from?"

"Victoria," Janey said.

"What do you do there?" Kick asked.

Janey glanced at Ethan. "Different things," she said when he made no effort to reply. "We plant trees on the island during the season. And Ethan has his music."

"How's that going?" Johanna asked.

Ethan shrugged. It appeared that Janey would be the spokesperson. "Well, he did a CD. A demo."

"I got the copy you sent," Kick said. "Show it to any distributors?"

Janey glanced over at Ethan again. "Yeah," she said slowly. "We, um, never got a deal."

"Who turned you down?" Kick asked.

"Everybody," Ethan said and he finished the last forkful.

"What do you do?" Janey asked.

"Documentaries," Kick said. "So I know all about rejection."

"What do you mean?"

"That was a joke," Kick said. "I make docs."

"Are you working on something now?" Janey asked.

Kick looked at Ethan, who was staring glassy-eyed at the wall, having had his fill of the pasta and possibly the conversation too. She was surprised that he hadn't asked what she thought of the CD. It wasn't something she wanted to get into for the moment. "I'm in Wyoming," she said, turning to Janey. "Do you know AmCom?"

"Yeah," Janey said. "They make pharmaceuticals, don't they?"

"They make everything," Kick said. "They probably made this lasagna sauce."

"*I* made the sauce," Johanna said.

"Oops," Kick said. "They make everything else. They have a gas and oil division. GreenPower. A few years ago the Bush administration signed off on an agreement allowing them to drill tens of thousands of gas wells in Wyoming. However—in order to pump natural gas out of the ground, you have to pump the aquifers dry first, both fresh and saltwater. It's an environmental disaster in the making. I've been shooting footage of ranchers and farmers in the area. You know—people who have the crazy notion that their government might actually want to protect the water supply."

"AmCom?" Janey asked. "Weren't they involved in some controversy over the Katrina cleanup?"

"Yeah," Kick said. "They hired a couple thousand immigrant workers and then forgot to pay them. Just like the five hundred thousand meals for the soldiers in Iraq that they were paid for and never delivered. That's AmCom. A big, fat, insensitive blight on the landscape."

And with that Ben arrived.

He came through the French doors without knocking, slouching into the room like a surly teen. Any notion of familial handshakes or hugs was dispensed with at once as he went to the far end of the table and flopped into a chair. He was wearing shorts and a windbreaker bearing the logo of some Scottish golf course.

"Guess I wasn't invited to dinner," he said.

"I called your office at three o'clock but you weren't there," Johanna said. "I'll get you a plate."

"Don't bother," he said. "I had a steak at the club. Prime beef."

"So you're just whining for the pure joy of whining?" Kick asked. "How are you, Ben?"

"I'm okay." Ben looked down the table, where Ethan was looking at the cove molding above his head. "Ethan."

"This is Janey," Kick said. "Ethan's friend."

"Hi," Janey said, but Ben ignored her.

"So what do we have here?" he asked. "A little strategy meeting behind my back?"

Johanna got up and began to clear the table. She gave Kick a short look of reprimand as she left the room, the same look she used to offer when Kick was about to slap the hell out of Ben when they were kids and Ben was acting the fool. The look had rarely been effective.

"Why would we be having a strategy meeting, Ben?" Kick asked. "With or without you?"

"Duh," Ben said. "The reading of the will is tomorrow."

Kick looked at Ethan, who was now staring off into the kitchen, perhaps with visions of dessert dancing in his mind. Janey was watching Ben openly.

"I don't claim to be any kind of an expert in the field of last wills and testaments," Kick said. "But I'm thinking if you want to influence such a document, you probably need to do it while the person is still *alive*. That make sense to you?"

"You've always got an answer for everything, Kick."

"Wouldn't that be nice?" Kick said. "How's Meredith and little Ben?"

"They're fine. Why would you ask that?"

Kick shook her head and got up. "We're gonna need another bottle of wine."

It was indeed apple pie Kick had smelled earlier and Johanna brought it out while Kick opened another bottle of red. Ben refused both the pie and the wine and suggested that Johanna fetch him a vodka and tonic instead.

"So what're you doing these days, Ethan?" Ben said when he had his drink.

Ethan, fully engaged in the pie, looked up. Kick was certain he didn't want to attempt to explain to his older brother that he was a struggling musician. "Planting trees," Ethan said after he swallowed. "Vancouver Island."

"Tree planter," Ben said. "Isn't that another word for pothead?"

"And what've you been doing, Ben?" Kick asked. "Other than perfecting the art of obnoxiousness?"

"Oh, I missed you too, Kick," Ben said. "You know what I've been doing. Running Eastman Technologies, that's what I've been doing. I happen to live in the real world."

"I'm sure the real world is thrilled to have you aboard," Kick said, and with that Johanna got up from the table and left the room.

When she was gone, Ben took a drink of vodka and then reached across the table and cut off a large slice of pie and slid it onto a plate. He offered Kick a smile as he began to eat.

"I'm thinking your tree planting days are over now, Ethan," he said around the pie. "What do you figure to do with your share?"

"Oh, they'll stone you when you try to be so good," Ethan replied.

"What the fuck's he talking about?" Ben asked.

"It's a song," Kick said.

"I ask what he's gonna do with his money and he sings me a song?"

"What money?" Kick asked.

"The will, Kick. Try to keep up."

"We don't know anything about the will," Kick said. "Don't you think we could talk about something else tonight?"

Ben looked at her a long moment and shrugged. "Whatever," he said and then took another bite of the pie he hadn't wanted.

Kick glanced at Janey, then turned back to Ben. "So what grade is little Ben in now?"

"What *grade* is he in?" Ben asked. "Shit, I don't know. Four or five, I guess."

That was enough for Kick. She drank off her glass of wine and got to her feet. As she was walking out of the room, though, Johanna came back in carrying a photo album.

"I thought you might like to see some old shots of the farm, Janey," Johanna said.

Janey hesitated. "Sure."

Kick lingered in the doorway a moment and watched while Johanna opened the book on the table in front of Ethan and Janey. "This is how the place looked when I first arrived, twenty-nine years ago. See, there's the old garage. Everett burned it down by accident."

"How did he do that?" Janey asked.

"He thought he knew how to weld," Johanna said. "There's the kids on their raft." She turned the page quickly.

"That was Ethan?" Janey asked. "Go back."

Johanna glanced over at Kick as she turned back the page to reveal Ethan at maybe five or six, sitting on a rickety raft a few feet from the shore of the creek. Kick, ever the leader, was standing at the front of the vessel, manning a pole, and Ben was staring into the camera, his chubby cheeks as red as the baseball cap on his head.

Four or five album pages later, both Ben and Kick had, predictably, been drawn in. The five of them huddled around the book for the next hour, looking at themselves and times past, at pets and projects and hay rides, and snow forts and cookouts on the riverbank. The memories within the album had been perfectly filtered—there was no pettiness between the pages, no silly arguments or crying jags over who got the biggest slice of watermelon. The only hardships to be found in the cracked Kodak prints were sunburns, and skinned knees, and the cast on Kick's arm from when she broke it falling out of the tree house on the front lawn. She'd been eleven years old at the time and forlornly in love with Will Montgomery, who'd just gotten his driver's license.

When Johanna closed the book the memories remained, as if floating on the air, as tangible and tantalizing as the earlier aromas of baked bread and apple pie. Kick and Ethan and Ben were caught, at least temporarily, in the unfettered yet false world of remembrance, a conspiracy of the times they'd shared, back when Crooked Pear was all the world they knew or needed.

When Kick was a little girl she'd been convinced that Johanna was not only the smartest person she knew but in all likelihood the wisest woman on the planet. Going to bed later that night, she decided she had been right way back then.

THE READING WAS SET for eleven the next morning. Kick went for a walk along the creek beforehand and when she returned she found Ben sitting in his new Corvette in the driveway. Sitting there, the engine off, looking at the house. There were several vehicles in the drive, including the rented Taurus, a Lincoln Town car and a black pickup truck. As Kick walked up Ben got out of the car and stood looking critically at the pickup. If nostalgia had proved to be a wonder drug against animosity the night before, the cure was short-lived.

"What the fuck is he doing here?"

"You'll have to tell me who *he* is."

"Will Montgomery," Ben said. "I suspected he was sniffing around the old man. He better not be in the will."

"Doesn't he rent the farm?"

"Yeah."

"That what you call sniffing around?" Kick asked.

"He better not be in the will. There'll be challenges if he is. You can bet your life there'll be challenges."

"Life is full of challenges, Ben," Kick said. "You ought to know that."

"What's that supposed to mean?" They walked together to the front door.

"Would you relax? You look like a man in a laxative commercial. Where's Meredith?"

"Home. This has got nothing to do with her."

The reading was to be in the living room. When they walked in Raney Kilbride was seated in the leather easy chair by the fieldstone fireplace, a sheaf of papers on his lap and a tumbler of water on the table beside him. His hands shook slightly as he leafed through the pages. Kick guessed he was at least as old as her father, and one of the few men her father had come up with that he never managed to alienate. This was largely due to the fact that Raney had developed a propensity, early on, of telling Everett to go to hell when he needed to be told.

Ethan was sitting on the couch beside Janey. He had a video game on his lap and was thoroughly engaged in the little screen.

Will Montgomery, drinking from a cup of takeout coffee, leaned against the fireplace that occupied the entire west wall. He was wearing a canvas coat and work boots. His body language suggested that he hoped to be there for as short a time as possible.

"Hello, Kathleen," he said to Kick, who smiled at him.

"Will," Ben said, extending his hand. "Didn't expect to see you here."

"You never know what to expect these days, Ben."

Johanna came in then, carrying a tray with coffee and a pot of tea. She put the tray on an oak sideboard and then hesitated until Raney gave her a nod of dismissal. She shot Kick the same look of warning as the night before. Kick gave her a wink as she left.

"All right then," Raney said when she was gone. "It looks as if we've got all the chickens in the coop. First of all, we're doing this reading here because I closed my law office last year and frankly, I didn't want the whole lot of you over to my house."

Will, sipping his coffee, laughed and had to wipe his mouth.

"Now I'm here to read the last will and testament of Everett Edward Eastman," Raney went on. "This thing's got more twists and turns than a mountain road so I'm just going to give you the highlights and then you'll each get a copy of the document and you can retire to your respective corners and come out swinging, if you like. The first thing you might want to know is what will happen to this house. Well, Johanna will remain here for as ever long as she pleases, and there's been a salary and living expenses designated for the duration of her stay. She's been informed of this. The numbers are in the document. The farm itself will continue to be leased to Will Montgomery, for as long as *he* desires. If you're thinking that's why he's here today, well, you're wrong. I could've given him that little piece of information over the telephone. Will is here because he's the executor of this estate."

Raney paused, ostensibly to take a drink of water, but really to let this announcement take hold. Kick looked at Ben, who was leaning forward in his chair, his red face growing even redder. Raney continued.

"Will is the executor and by his expression I have a feeling he'd rather be home, castrating bull calves. But there it is."

"Who made that decision?" Ben asked.

"Your father," Raney said. "Who the hell do you think made it?"

"I just asked a question," Ben said. "Am I not allowed to ask a question?"

"Not dumb ones, you're not." Raney coughed and took another drink.

Ben was evidently stung by this. He turned on Will. "Oh, I get it. Everett left a *will* … so you get to take care of it because you're a Will."

"So if he left a jackass, you'd be in charge?" Will suggested.

Kick laughed and said, "Moving on."

"Yes," Raney said. "We can get back to the house and property later. Everett spent the last year or so basically getting rid of most of his financial interests. He was de-diversifying, as he called it. At the time of his death, he owned just three companies—Eastman Technologies, the McDougall Distillery and Great North AudioBooks."

"Three?" Kick asked. "Gee, what a coincidence."

Raney smiled at her. "That's right. Everett's set this up to leave you all a separate piece. Ben, you get the auto parts, Ethan inherits the whiskey factory and Kathleen—you're in the books-on-tape business, girl."

"I wouldn't bet on it," she said.

"I might," Raney said. "Because we're just starting here. Everett insisted on a couple of little twists. First of all, these three properties will be held in trust for the first year, during which time certain conditions must be met before ownership is granted. Challenges, if you will. Also, if any one of you wants to sell your business, after meeting the conditions, you can do so, but only after you've run it for ten years. If you want to sell it before then—you can do that too, but then—you'll like this one—but then you have to split the profits with the other two. And I can tell you this—these three concerns have a certain amount of debt. You want to sell one off, and then split it three ways, you'll end up eating beans and wieners, not Chateaubriand."

"What the hell is this?" Ben asked.

"Looks to me as if your father is having a little fun with you guys from the great beyond," Janey said.

"Why are you here again?" Ben asked.

"Ain't it just like the night, to play tricks when you're trying to be so quiet?" Ethan asked.

"Come on, Ben," Kick said. "Everett's trying to will us responsibility. He sure as hell never passed it along genetically. It's not gonna work, of course, because while you might pretend to run the plant, you don't know anything about auto parts and haven't the ambition to learn. I'm not interested in putting out audio books, and Ethan, as much as I love him, seems to be having trouble putting together a coherent sentence these days."

"Uh, there is a reason for that," Janey said.

"I was hoping," Kick said.

"It's just not a very good one," Janey added. "He speaks mainly in Bob Dylan lyrics."

"He what?" Ben asked.

"Could be worse," Kick said dismissively. "Could be Barry Manilow. Listen, I don't want to appear selfish but I came here hoping to scrape together fifty grand or so to finish a doc I'm shooting in Wyoming on a great imperialistic land rape. I've just been informed I'm the new owner of Great North AudioBooks. Well, not for long. Could be I'll be happy with wieners and beans, Raney."

"Slow down now," Raney said. "You don't own it yet, Kathleen. I told you there are challenges to be met. I'm not gonna go through them all right now because I'm old and tired, and making this damn document has made me older and even more tired." He paused. "Besides, maybe Great North makes enough to support your little projects."

"My little projects?" she said. "You wouldn't be trying to piss me off, would you?"

Raney smiled and had more water.

"What about the capital?" Ben demanded. He looked darkly at Will. "The old man was worth a lot of money. Where is it?"

"You think he gave it to me?" Will asked before Raney could speak.

"The money is all gone," Raney said.

"Bullshit," Ben said. "He was worth a hundred million dollars. At least."

"It was more like half that," Raney said. "I have a feeling you never knew the scope of his tax problems in the States. But what does it matter how much he had, if it's all gone? You do understand the concept of nothing, Ben."

"What do you mean it's all gone?" Ben demanded.

"I mean he gave it away. Spent the last couple of years doing it. Quite enthusiastically, I might add. And I mean all of it, Ben. It was a fascinating thing to watch. He gave away a little at first and then he couldn't stop. Hospitals, schools, lost causes. He wrote a check for a million dollars for a kids' cancer camp in British Columbia. He gave ten million to Sick Kids Hospital in Toronto. And every penny anonymous. It's not an easy thing, giving away that much money. He was getting a kick out of it."

"Trying to buy his way into heaven, that's what he was doing," Ben said.

"Knock, knock, knockin' on heaven's door," Ethan said.

Ben looked at Ethan a moment, his mind obviously racing. He turned back to Raney. "Well, this sucks," he said, nearly pouting. "What about this place?"

"Like I said, Johanna stays as long as she likes, Will leases the land as long as he wants," Raney said. "Then the property reverts to the three of you. Except for the fifty acres north of the creek. That becomes a conservation area. Everett became a big fan of waterfowl in his later years."

"But not snapping turtles," Will said.

"That reminds me," Raney said and he reached behind the chair and brought out an ancient canvas carry bag. "There was one other bequeathment. He left you this, Kick."

Kick took the bag and opened it on the stone mantel. She pulled the heavy Colt revolver from the cracked leather holster inside, then laid it carefully on the mantel. Eyebrows raised in puzzlement, she glanced at Raney Kilbride.

"Congratulations," Ben said. "He left you a paperweight."

Kick reached into the bag again and retrieved a single sheet of paper, folded four ways. Ben stepped closer as she unfolded it.

"What's it say?" he asked.

"None of your business," Kick told him, then she read it out loud anyway. "It says—'Use this on them when they all start screwing up.'"

Raney chuckled as he began to gather his papers together.

"Does anyone else get the impression that our father never had a lot of faith in us?" Kick asked.

"He could have left you fifteen or twenty million a piece," Raney said. "But really, Kathleen—do you think you would have been a better person for it?"

"I'd have been willing to give it a try," she said.

Raney smiled again and got stiffly to his feet. "Well, that's the bare bones of it. You each have a copy on the table there. There's a few more specifics inside. Fact is—I'm supposed to read the whole thing but I've recently decided to quit doing whatever the hell it is I'm supposed to do. What happens when you turn eighty. Besides, I know you'll all have your own lawyers look it over anyway."

"How long will it take to clear everything up?" Kick asked.

Raney smiled. "You sound like a woman in a hurry, Kathleen."

"I damn near left my car running," she told him.

"You'd better count on parking it for a few days." Raney patted her affectionately on the shoulder and started for the door.

"Wait a minute," Ben said. He pointed his jaw at Will. "What exactly is his role in this?"

"You keep sniffing at me like I've been sprayed by a skunk, Ben," Will said.

"As executor, it's his job to see that you all abide by the conditions of the will," Raney said. "He'll be paid to do that. From where I'm standing, he won't be paid enough to oversee this squirrel hunt, but he will be paid. Your father left an account, from which Johanna's salary, property taxes, Will's fees and whatever will be paid. I might add that this account is off-limits to the three of you."

"Why would my father choose him?" Ben asked.

"I was wondering that myself," Will said. "I always thought he was my friend."

FOUR

Kick slept in her old room, at first in a chair and then in bed. Her sleep was fitful and expectedly so; at four o'clock she awoke for good and lay in bed for two hours, thinking about Everett and how little she'd known him, and wondering how she'd reached the age of thirty-six with absolutely no sense of family. Even as a little girl she had never felt familiar with her father. She used to call him *Mister Eastman* and, although the nomenclature seemed to amuse whatever adults happened to be around when she did, she hadn't been joking. She could remember being fascinated by him when she was very small, by the unknown quantity of the man. She'd loved how he smelled, of tobacco and scotch whiskey and hair tonic. The fascination had eventually given way to bewilderment as she began to wonder at his oscillating interests in his family. In her teens, she remembered being angry with him most of the time, although it had been a hard point to make when he was virtually never around. By the time she finished university she found it easier on herself if she merely ignored his existence, reasoning that the time for any genuine paternal influence had passed anyway.

At six she got up and went for a run, taking her old route, north on the river road, across the bridge that spanned the creek and up the rise toward the apiary on the corner of the town line. She took the side road east and then basically circled the concession, making note of the changes as she ran. She hadn't spent much time in the area since her late teens. She'd been four when her mother had divorced Everett but she'd continued to spend her summers at the farm, where often all three of Everett's ex-wives, and their kids, would be on the premises at the same time. Everett, of course, would be gone. Still, it was a confusing time for Kick, never really knowing where anybody stood. Each Eastman wife had remarried at least once—in the case of Ben's mother, Margie, who was flakier than a blue ribbon pie crust, three times—and so there were quite often other kids roaming around as well. When she was very young the only way Kick could keep things marginally clear was to remember that just the three of them—Ben, Ethan and herself—went by the name Eastman.

Aside from those familial confusions, she'd loved the farm. There were horses there at that time, and ducks and goats and a small herd of Charolais cattle—beige cows, she'd called them as a girl. Paula, Kick's mother, was a little too wired in general to embrace the concept of country living, artificial as it may have been, and she developed a habit of dropping Kick off for days and sometimes weeks at a time while she pursued her other interests, one of which was, ironically, the publishing endeavor Kick had so recently and reluctantly come to own. These drop-offs were hardly trauma inducing; Johanna's maternal instincts could run circles around Paula's and Kick loved the woman from the moment she met her. To an eight-year-old, a housekeeper who made fluffy Belgian waffles served with real maple syrup stacked up pretty well against a mother who had trouble figuring out the toaster.

That was then. Everything had changed, of course, over the past two or three decades, including, Kick saw as she ran into the rising sun, the countryside itself. There were a number of new houses along the town line, from brick bungalows to decidedly more garish abodes, set back in the trees and surrounded by unsightly wrought-iron fencing. The farms were what really caught her eye, though. It took her a while before realizing what was different about them, and then, cutting back on the mud road that ran down to the river, she did.

They didn't look like farms anymore. The fencing was virtually gone and the properties that had once been cut up into neat little ten- and twelve-acre squares were now vast plots of land. The farmers' lanes were also gone, along with the maples and oaks and elms that had lined them. It was still farm country but it was industrialized farm country; everything was bigger, cleaner, blander. Except for the Montgomery farm, where a herd of beef cattle grazed in a pasture field, there were few animals in evidence. Certainly no chickens scratching in the barnyard, no ponies grazing along streams, a paucity of workhorses in harness.

"I read too much Steinbeck when I was a kid," Kick said to herself, stopping to catch her breath as she reached Crooked Pear. She retrieved the morning paper from the roadside ditch and then ran up the drive to the house.

Johanna, wearing faded jeans and an Emmylou Harris T-shirt, was mixing waffle batter when Kick walked into the kitchen. Kick, sweating from her run, kissed her on the cheek and then poured a cup of coffee from the pot.

"You're a mind reader, Johanna."

"You think I need a crystal ball to tell me what you want for breakfast?"

Kick sat down at the counter and opened the paper. She looked absently at the headlines, feeling Johanna's presence. After a moment, she realized she was also feeling her father's absence, and the realization surprised her. After all, not being there had been his stock in trade.

"Nobody told me what happened," she said, setting the paper aside. "Some stranger tells me my father is dead and when I ask for details, I'm treated like an intruder."

"He died down by the creek, sitting in a chair," Johanna said as she poured the batter. "Every day he would go down, to kill the snapping turtles." She looked over. "I guess they turned the tables on him."

"I guess," Kick said. "And he didn't want a service."

"No. He was cremated the next day. Raney Kilbride scattered his ashes somewhere, but he won't say where. Everett had it all planned out; it was the way he wanted it to be." She lifted the lid of the waffle maker, had a peek. "I assume you have talked to your mother?"

"Yeah."

"Where is she?"

"England. Got a new man. Some twit ten years younger than her, his family owns newspapers. You know Paula—she's always been impressed by the printed word. Although I don't recall her ever reading a fucking book."

"Watch that mouth."

"Oops."

When the waffles were ready Kick carried the syrup and butter to the counter. Johanna had already eaten something, she said. She sat down opposite and drank coffee while Kick ate. The sun that came through the French doors crossed Johanna's face. To Kick she hadn't aged at all in the nearly thirty years she'd known her. She'd been barely twenty-one, freshly arrived from Holland, when she first came to Crooked Pear. Kick had asked her more than once why she had signed on as nursemaid to the Eastman bunch and, more significantly, why she had stayed. She'd never received anything resembling a reply. Quite likely Johanna didn't fully know the answer herself.

"When was the last time you saw him?" Johanna asked now.

Kick poured syrup over her waffles, meticulously filling each square as she'd always done. "It was ... Christmas."

"He was here Christmas. You weren't."

"Shit," Kick said. "Then it was the Christmas before that. I guess I should feel guilty about that. Do you think he cared?"

"I don't know what he cared about. I really don't."

"Was he different at the end?"

"Different?" Johanna asked. "No. People don't change. At least people like Everett Eastman don't change. He quit eating. He might have one meal a day. But I don't think there was anything to it. He just didn't feel like eating." She took a drink of coffee. "He was focused on the turtles."

"He was focused on the turtles," Kick said. "Yeah, I could see that."

Janey came down the stairs as Kick was starting in on her second helping of waffles. She had her blonde hair pulled back in a ponytail and she wore a tank top and madras pajama bottoms. Her eyes were a little red around the edges.

"Good morning," she said.

Kick, her mouth full, nodded to her.

"Are you having breakfast?" Johanna asked, getting to her feet.

Kick nodded to her again, this time emphatically.

"Sure," Janey said and she sat down.

Kick swallowed and then lifted another forkful. "Ethan up?"

"No. He said he's gonna sleep in."

"In those words?"

Janey smiled. "Go away from my window, leave at your own chosen speed."

"That's pretty good," Kick said. "How long has this been going on?"

"I don't know," Janey said. "Three weeks."

"I'd have slapped him about twenty days ago."

Janey looked out the French doors to the barn. The big Belgian mare was in the corral; the little goat was dozing on the ground nearby. The sky was overcast, the clouds racing on the wind.

"How did you guys meet?" Kick asked.

"I was working in television in Vancouver," Janey said. "Doing PR for a local show on the arts. I met Ethan at a talent night at a club, a couple of years ago. The show got canceled and we decided to go tree planting, get out of the city for a while." She glanced over at

Kick. "He's okay most of the time. When he's uncomfortable or … I don't know … feeling challenged, he reverts to Dylan. He's been going through some changes." She looked away again. "He had high hopes for the CD."

"What's he taking?" Kick asked.

"What do you mean?" Janey asked.

"Don't do that," Kick said. "He's my brother. He's been suffering from depression since he was fourteen. He's ingested more drugs than the Grateful Dead. So what are they giving him now?"

"That's the thing," Janey said. She looked over at Johanna, who made no attempt to hide her interest. "He hasn't taken anything for months. The drugs really … mess with his creative process. He can't write music. But he's down now because of the CD not going anywhere. So he can't write with the drugs, and he's not doing anything without them."

"Which explains the sleeping till noon," Kick said.

"He's been sleeping a lot, yeah," Janey said. "I was hoping seeing all of you might help." She looked at Kick. "He thinks you're invincible."

"Good God, he is deranged."

Johanna set a plate of waffles in front of Janey and then poured more coffee for herself, and for Kick, who was mopping syrup with a last piece of waffle.

"How would I find the distillery?" Janey asked.

Kick glanced at Johanna. "Follow the river south. It's right on the north edge of Waterloo. Ethan knows where it is. Or he did anyway."

"I thought I'd drive over on my own and have a look. Want to go with me?"

"No thanks," Kick said. "I've got my own row to hoe."

RANEY WAS SITTING on the front porch of his fieldstone home on Brant Street in Waterloo, waiting for her. He had an unlit and unloaded pipe in his mouth and he wore a heavy cable-knit sweater against the spring chill. He looked like a retired Maritime fisherman. When Kick parked on the street and started up the walkway, he came down off the porch and met her halfway.

"You're late," he said, putting the pipe in his pocket.

"I was eating waffles."

"As excuses go, that's first rate," he said as he got into the car and fastened his seatbelt. "My Alma feeds me All-Bran, every damn morning. She says it'll make me live longer. I told her I don't know if it'll make me live longer but I do know it's going to seem longer."

Great North AudioBooks had its head, and only, office in downtown Waterloo, on Colborne Street. Kick had worked there for a summer as a high school student but had been shown such deferential treatment as the boss's daughter she'd refused to return the following year. As they drove she admitted to Raney that she was a little surprised the family still owned the business.

"I mean, this was basically my mother's thing, wasn't it?"

"Initially."

"In my more cynical moments, I assume that Everett financed this little endeavor, tucked conveniently away in the backwoods, to keep her busy and to allow him to do whatever, and whomever, he wanted elsewhere."

"You're awful hard on the dear departed, Kathleen."

"But I'm right, aren't I?"

"Might be a kernel there."

"More like a whole cob, you ask me," she said. "What I can't figure is why he held on to it."

"It was offered as part of the divorce settlement. But your mother was bored with the whole thing by then. The novelty of it ... you know your mother. Besides, she wanted cash."

"So why didn't Everett sell it?"

"That's a good question. I'm sure he always intended to. The company won a couple of awards back in the nineties—environmental tapes or something like that. Your father reached a point in his life where I think he delighted in countering his image as a ruthless bastard." Raney looked over at her. "Maybe he held on to it so he could give it to you."

"Ruthless bastard."

They parked in a lot across from the building. Kick had an anxious moment crossing the street when Raney, whose pace was that of an eighty-year-old, barely made it through the crosswalk before the light turned red.

The meeting with Blaine Steward was set for eleven; in spite of Raney's admonishment they were barely five minutes late. A receptionist in the outer office looked at them blankly and picked up a phone, spoke briefly into it. A moment later Steward strolled down the hall; his clumsy stride suggested that of a busy man called away on some trivial matter. He actually looked at his watch as he approached.

Everyone exchanged feigned hearty hellos and then Steward led them into a room off the foyer. There was a cherrywood table and a half dozen chairs. Steward offered coffee and they both declined.

"So you're now representing the next generation, Raney. I thought you'd retired with all your millions."

Kick looked quickly at the old lawyer, who just smiled and refused the bait as he sat down. Steward extended a beefy palm toward a chair opposite and she walked over and sat. Talking to Steward on the phone earlier, she had tried to remember what he looked like and couldn't come up with an image, even though he'd been the managing editor back when she'd worked there. She remembered him now. He had changed little over the years; he was a big, soft man, with a red face and pink hands. If anything, he was now bigger and softer, more florid. He wore a polo shirt, untucked to hide his expansive stomach, and Dockers. He had a lawn-bowling pin fastened to the collar of his shirt.

He sat down at the head of the table and put one hand on a file there. "I've put together a little package for you, Kathleen, like you asked." His tone matched his put-upon pose. "I'm not really sure what you want to see. I'm not at all sure what you already know, for that matter."

"The last time I was here you were still using typewriters," Kick said. "I need an update. Tell me what you're doing."

"Well," Steward said slowly. "We still publish a few textbooks, but our business is largely audio books these days. Technical manuals, school texts, novels. We do a few kids' CDs—Humpty-Dumpty, that sort of thing. We're pretty much self-sustaining, a turnkey operation. I don't know what else to say. We, um … we're just chugging along."

Kick watched as Raney removed his glasses and held them to the light. "All these technical terms," she said to Steward. "Any chance you could elaborate on chugging along?"

He pushed the file folder toward her. "Here's our numbers for the past year. I put this together real fast for you this morning. I assumed you'd just want a quick overview."

"That's an odd thing to assume," Kick said as she opened the file and began to leaf through it. After a few seconds Steward began to drum his fingertips on the tabletop. When she looked up at him, he stopped.

"Are you making money?" she asked.

"A little," Steward said after a moment.

Kick watched his eyes until he turned away. It was her experience that anyone who said they were making a little money was probably making a lot. And the man who bragged he was making a killing was in all likelihood not.

"This is just a small business, Kathleen," Steward decided to add. "It's not an investment opportunity per se. We have administration and some production staff, but the recording itself is freelanced out, along with the design. At the end of the day, we put out a good product, and make enough money to pay everyone's wages. And we've been doing it for thirty years without any—"

Kick smiled as he caught himself. "Outside interference?" she suggested.

"I didn't mean that. I figured you wanted to stop by and check things out before you head off to—well, I don't even know where you're based these days."

"I'm usually based in my vehicle." Glancing up from the file, she saw Steward make eye contact with the receptionist through the plate glass.

"I just wanted you to know that the operation here pretty much hums along on its own. It's not something you have to worry about."

Kick nodded absently, leafing through the papers. "So this is what you call an overview, right? But you must have figures for the individual interests. I'm assuming that they all perform at different levels. Trade manuals versus novels, stuff like that. Keep in mind that I know nothing about the business."

Steward's cell phone rang and he snatched it from his belt.

"Steward," he said and he listened a moment. "Right. I'll be there … as soon as I can."

When Kick turned, she thought she saw the receptionist in the act of returning the phone to its cradle.

"I wasn't aware that you wanted to get that specific," Steward said.

"Didn't think my pretty little head could handle all those numbers?"

"Now you're being silly."

"Well, I'm the new owner. Humor me." She smiled to deflect any sense of tone. She could see that he was fuming behind his own benign expression. "Does everything make money?"

"That's a complicated question. It's a cyclical business. I like to compare it to a horse race. At any given time, any one of the publications could be in the lead. The next quarter might be a different story. For example, audio textbooks show the strongest in the fall. Back to school, right? So there's your lead horse."

Kick got to her feet. "I'll tell you what I'd like. I'd like the specific numbers on all these … horses. Round 'em up, to beat that metaphor completely senseless, and have them sent out to Crooked Pear. Could you do that, please?"

"I guess so," Steward said. He stopped just short of sighing heavily. "It'll mean taking someone off something else."

"Let's do that," Kick said. "Everyone likes a little variety in their workday." She looked at Raney, who wore the expression of a man who'd just come from an enjoyable night at the theater.

Steward walked them to the foyer. While they waited for the elevator Kick made an inspection of the various plaques and awards on the walls. She had a thought as the doors opened and she turned to Steward.

"When was the last time my father was up here?"

"I … it's been some time," Steward said.

"As in, more than ten years?"

"I would say so. Yes."

SHE OFFERED TO BUY Raney lunch but he declined, explaining that he and his wife had plans to meet her brother and his wife at the country club.

"Quite possibly the two most boring people on the face of the earth," he said. "However, it is Friday. And that means fresh Lake Erie perch at the club."

"Speaking of boring," Kick said as they idled at a light. "I sat down with my copy of the will last night. Or, as I've decided to call it, Raney Kilbride's War and Peace."

Raney chuckled.

"You ought to laugh. You're lucky I know you, otherwise I'd suspect you were charging Everett by the word."

"It's an interesting document."

"I wouldn't know," Kick said. "I got to the third page and fell asleep in the chair. Woke up at four in the morning with a stiff back, probably strained it lifting the goddamn will."

"You'd do well to read it through," he told her.

"Can't I hire you to do it?"

"No."

They were on his street now. She pulled up to the curb. When he made no move to get out, she put the car in park and waited.

"What are you going to do with Great North?" he asked.

"I was hoping to use it to my advantage," Kick said, looking out the windshield. "But somehow I doubt that's gonna happen. I'm up to my ass in debt on this movie. I've got feelers out to PBS, HBO, the Discovery Channel. Nobody's biting. There's a great right-wing conspiracy against me."

"You don't believe that."

"Naw," she said. "But I gotta blame my woes on something. If I can put together a rough cut, I should be able to sell it. I've got some great footage, real American Gothic versus the soulless industrialists type of thing. There's a trial I need to cover out in Wyoming, a rancher who I hope turns out to be James Stewart and not Charlie Manson. But I don't have two nickels to rub together at this point." She glanced over at the old man. "Whatever I can squeeze out of Great North, I'll squeeze."

"Just take it slow," Raney said. "You don't want to trade in all your tomorrows for today."

Kick laughed. "Sure I do."

He gave her a stern look and then opened the door.

"Hey," she said to stop him. "Was I being a bitch back there, Raney? Tell me I wasn't."

"You weren't."

"Then what was the problem?"

"You weren't telling him what he wanted to hear. He wanted to hear that it was going to be business as usual. In other words, an absentee ownership. You heard him—your father didn't show up once in a decade. People don't like change, especially self-important dullards like Blaine Steward."

"So that's all it was?" Kick asked. "You don't think he's hiding anything?"

"That dummy couldn't hide a penny in a snowbank."

AS KICK HAD SAID, Janey had only to follow the river south to find the McDougall Distillery. It was a red brick building of indeterminate years, three stories high, with a copper roof turned to green patina with age and exposure to the elements. The property was perched above a rock gorge through which the river ran noisily. There was a waterwheel turbine that protruded out into the stream. It had once provided power for a grist mill, which the distillery had originally been, and was now the source of hydroelectricity for the plant.

Janey parked in the lot, in a spot designated for visitors. On the drive there she'd been rehearsing what she would say in an attempt to gain entrance to the plant and her story had seemed increasingly lame as the distillery grew closer. Still, she went bravely through the front door and approached the reception area. A middle-aged woman with a bad hair-color job—auburn verging on purple—was at the counter.

"Whoa," the woman said when Janey had just begun. "Did you just say that you own this place?"

"Actually, my boyfriend is the son of Everett Eastman—"

"Whoa," the woman said again. Janey felt like a draft horse. "I'll be right back," the woman said and she disappeared through a steel door.

The walls of the reception area were covered with product displays, advertising posters and various awards for the McDougall line of liquors. Janey recognized Royal Highland Rye at once; it had been her father's choice of whiskey for years, and she'd seen Ethan help himself to her father's supply in recent months. He'd never mentioned that his family owned the company, even back when he was still in the habit of mentioning things not plagiarized from Minnesota's favorite son.

The plant's history was detailed in picture and print along one wall. The distillery had been started in 1859 by John McDougall, who had, somewhat reluctantly as the text revealed, turned to the making of rye when it became apparent that there was insufficient peat in rural Ontario to support the distilling of scotch whiskey. There was a photograph of John McDougall in his dotage, wearing huge side whiskers and pince-nez spectacles, and several more of his various descendants, the most recent being of Larry McDougall, a pasty-faced young man wearing a golf shirt and an insolent look that suggested the photographer was keeping him from the links. Janey assumed that it was young Larry who had sold the business thirty years earlier to Ethan's father, of whom there were no pictures on display.

When the receptionist returned she veered off to her post behind the counter, offering Janey a thin smile that promised she would be attended to soon. Which was true, as thirty seconds later a tall, thin man wearing a gray brush-cut came through the same door. He approached with his hand out.

"I'm Jack Dutton," he said as they shook. "What can I help you with?"

By the time Janey explained that she was Ethan Eastman's girl-friend and that she was there as his representative due to the fact that Ethan was ill (it was the best she could come up with) and that she merely wanted to have a look around on behalf of the new owner, Jack Dutton had his hand on her elbow and was steering her gently toward the front doors. To his credit, he did not tell her that he thought she was full of shit.

"We are aware that Mr. Eastman has passed on," he told her when they were standing outside on the steps. "And we've been advised through Raney Kilbride that there will be ownership changes. Unfortunately, nobody's told us anything about your involvement in this, Miss—?"

"Sims. Janey Sims."

"Mr. Kilbride hasn't informed anyone of your involvement in this, Miss Sims. You should know that this is a ship which sails along on its own. For instance, we haven't seen Everett Eastman in at least five years."

"I just thought, with the will—"

"Maybe when young Mr. Eastman is feeling better, he can stop by and we can chat."

And then she was standing on the lawn, alone, looking at the beautiful flower gardens she had somehow missed on her way in.

Driving away, she told herself that she really had no right to expect a better reception, even though she had been telling the truth when she'd said she was there with Ethan's blessing (in the form of "Don't think twice, it's all right"). But the sad truth was that in today's world you were considered a liar until you proved otherwise. What the hell did they think—that she was looking for free whiskey? All she wanted was a tour of the plant.

But there was more than one way to take a tour. She drove into Waterloo and found an internet café near the university. She was betting that McDougall would have a website and she was right. She got a coffee and a blueberry muffin from the counter at the front of the café and moments later she was looking at Jack Dutton's smiling (now) face. Jack was the master distiller, she learned, and he had been born on a farm not three miles from the distillery. The bio made no mention of his distrustful nature.

She went through everything the site had to offer, saw pictures of the vats, and of the bottling plant, and of virtually all the employees, including the receptionist who had whoa'd her, although on the screen her hair was unnaturally blonde. There was detailed information on the various libations produced by the distillery, and more on the awards she'd seen plastered on the walls. On the whole, aside from a mention of a new product, Highland Gold Liqueur, the business appeared to be an old-fashioned concern. There were no Rip-Snorting McDougall Shooters or Wild Highland Party Shots to be had.

On the way home Janey decided that she could indeed nurture an interest in the distillery business. Of course, it didn't matter what enthusiasm she might muster. It was all up to Ethan, and Ethan was apparently headed down a slippery slope.

Like a rolling stone.

FIVE

Ben found Teddy Brock at the courthouse, where he was representing a provincial police officer who was up on misconduct charges after exposing himself to a female officer in the station parking lot and then holding his Glock to the temple of the staff sergeant who confronted him about it. Pending the disciplinary hearing, the cop had been suspended with pay for twenty-two months. Today was to be the day of reckoning but Teddy, after talking to his client outside the courthouse, had concluded that the officer's doctor was still in the process of fine-tuning his patient's meds. Teddy decided that the prudent move would be to ask for yet another remand.

"I'll buy you lunch," Ben said when the stay had been granted. They went to the Stone Mill.

"Double vodka tonic," Ben said to the waitress. "And the special, whatever it is."

"There are, like, three specials," she told him.

"Pick one, baby."

Teddy ordered a beer and a steak. "You're a little wound up today, Ben."

"Yeah, well," Ben said and he didn't say anything else until his drink arrived.

Teddy watched him and wondered what to do about his problem back at the courthouse. The cop in question was a certifiable nut who had no business driving a car, let alone carrying a gun. However, the union had hired Teddy Brock and it would behoove him in a number of ways, not the least of which would be a lucrative future defending incompetent cops, to get the lunatic off.

"You don't pick up your messages?" Ben demanded when he had his drink.

"If you leave one as a client, I do," Teddy told him. "You leave four in two hours, you're not a client, you're a nuisance. You'll find that the return time is directly proportional to the nuisance factor."

"Ha fucking ha. What if it was life or death? What if I was locked up?"

"Then I assume you would mention that in your message." Teddy had a drink of beer. "So I take it your father's last will and testament was not all you've been dreaming about these past years?"

Ben took another drink and then set the glass down. "He gave all his money away, Teddy. That crazy bastard spent the past two years throwing it by the handful out the fucking window."

"Everything?"

Ben told him about the contents of the will. He'd brought his copy with him and at one point he took it out of his briefcase and offered it over, but Teddy took one look at its sheer volume and, laughing, declined.

"So you've got the auto parts," Teddy said and he shrugged. "It's a going concern. What's wrong with that?"

"Technically, I don't even have it yet. It's in trust for a year. Before I get the keys, I have to fulfill these stupid conditions."

"What kind of conditions?"

"Oh, we have to meet this Toyota contract for ignition modules, for instance. We have to develop this fuel injection gizmo that the old man was hot on. Little shit like that. Nothing difficult, mind you."

"Your father really knew what was going on over there?" Teddy asked. "I thought he never went near the place."

"He knew," Ben said. "I don't know how, but he knew. You gotta know where he came from. He was a fucking laborer, right? He worked at a place that made concrete sewer pipes—pouring cement in these huge molds all day long, with these big pneumatic vibrators screaming in your ear. But on the side he had like a fix-it shop. Lawnmowers and chainsaws and shit like that. When he was twenty-four years old he invented this simple little accelerator pump—little diaphragm the size of a silver dollar—and he patented it and sold it to Briggs and Stratton. Next thing you know they offer him a job. And away he went, into the wild blue yonder. He built Eastman Technologies from that little pump the size of a silver dollar. He ended up with about a hundred million silver dollars before he lost his fucking marbles and gave it all away."

"Not that you care," Teddy said. He waited for Ben to scowl. "What kind of conditions are there for Ethan and your sister?"

"Don't know, don't care," Ben said. "I got this factory hanging around my neck like a fifty fucking pound weight. I can't sell it, I can't close it. It doesn't make enough money to put me where I want to be. What the fuck am I supposed to do with it?"

"You could try running it."

"I *am* running it."

"In a manner of speaking," Teddy said. "You own it now. I'm guessing you've got no idea how much it actually makes. Looks to me like your old man is forcing you to do something radical—go to work every day."

"Hey, I'm buying you lunch, you know."

"You're seeking free legal advice. Lunch is a ruse."

"I'm not asking for something for nothing. I have a job for you."

Teddy indicated the will. "What—reading the *Encyclopedia Britannica* there? That's not going to be cheap."

"More than just read it," Ben said as he took another drink. "I want you to challenge it."

"Why? You said all the money is gone."

"Yeah, but there's the distillery, and the house and property at Crooked Pear, the publishing company. I think I'm getting screwed here."

"Challenge it on what grounds?"

"That the old man was mentally incompetent. And maybe that fucking Raney Kilbride too." He swatted at the will like it was a fly. "Look at that fucking thing. You're a lawyer—you ever see anything like that?"

"Mental incompetence is a lot easier to prove when the subject is actually alive, Ben," Teddy told him. "You want me to challenge the will on the grounds that it's too damn big?"

"All I'm saying is just look into it," Ben said. "The old man was off his rocker. Who gives away fifty million dollars to strangers? And I'll tell you something else—that fucking Ethan is out of his gourd too. He's been diagnosed."

"As what?"

"I don't know. Bipolar, or manic-depressive or whatever. Been going on for years. They keep changing the lingo so they can change whatever drugs they're giving him. If nothing else, Kathleen and I should be able to get control of the distillery." Ben was fired up now. "And what about this shit with Johanna? She gets the house *and* a salary for the rest of her life? You telling me she didn't influence the old man on that? Woman lives on yogurt and bean sprouts—shit, she'll outlive us all."

Teddy picked up the will and then slid it into his briefcase. "All right, let me have a look. Might be something there. Did you call Sally Thompson about your divorce proceedings?"

"The wolverine? No." Ben hesitated. "I've decided to put that on a back burner for the time being."

The waitress brought their meals. Ben looked at the plate when she set it down.

"What the hell is this?"

"It's a tofu-based quiche with sundried tomatoes." She put Teddy's steak in front of him.

"I don't want this," Ben said.

She scooped the plate up. "Gee, maybe you should order your own food next time," she said and walked off.

Ben looked at Teddy. "What the hell is wrong with people these days?"

BEN DROPPED TEDDY OFF at his car at the courthouse and then drove to Lynn's apartment along the lakeshore in Burlington. He had his own key and he let himself in warily. He lived in fear that someday he would show up and find another guy there. He'd actually expressed that concern to one of Lynn's girlfriends one night when he'd had too much to drink, and she'd told him not to worry, that Lynn was too smart for that. The confession did little to abate Ben's anxiety.

She was still in her robe, sprawled on the couch, smoking a cigarette and drinking a takeout Starbucks and watching Court TV. Her long blonde hair was tangled and hanging loosely. She appeared to be naked beneath the robe; he could see her breasts, firm and rounded, when he walked up behind her. The very sight of them excited him, as always. He considered them to be his property, and in more ways than one. He worshiped them, he slavered over them. And he'd paid for them.

"Hey," she said when he came in, her eyes on the set.

He ran his hand down her neck toward her cleavage, then walked around and plopped down beside her. She lifted her legs and put them in his lap. She was wearing dirty tennis socks. Ben looked at the show where a heavy blonde woman was complaining that the defendant had promised her a trip to Rio de Janeiro and then ran off to Brazil with her sister instead. She was suing for breach of contract.

"You watch too much TV," he told her.

"Oh, but this is wild," she said. "The trailer trash, I'm telling you."

"Doesn't mean you have to watch," Ben said, but now he was watching too, hoping that the sister would be there as well, all tanned and well-fucked from her Rio trip.

Lynn leaned forward and stubbed her cigarette in the ashtray. When the show went to commercial, she hit the mute button on the remote.

"You went to Starbucks in your robe?"

"Carrie was here," Lynn said and she yawned hugely. "Wanted me to go to the mall but I'm not in shopping mode. Besides, she has to go in, like, every fucking store, then she bitches about the prices and never buys a fucking thing."

"Why go with her?"

"I didn't. Duh."

Ben ran his hand up her leg, over her knee and onto her thigh. Her legs were stubbly, the stubble dark in contrast to her hair.

"Don't start anything," she said. "I need a shower. I need to brush my teeth."

"You look pretty sexy the way you are."

"You're a dog. You're a humping fool, Benjy."

"Don't call me that. It's something you call a pet."

"I just said you were a dog," she said, kicking him. "You listening? What're you up to anyway? You talk to that guy, Tommy Brock?"

"Teddy Brock. Yeah, I had lunch with him. I bought him lunch in fact. He's looking over the will."

"Somebody better," she said. "Because this isn't exactly like you said it would be, Ben. Not even close. Two years I been hearing about Everett Eastman and his millions."

"I'll take care of things, don't you worry about that."

"What's your buddy Brock say?"

"He says ... he says it looks good. The old man was incompetent, that's as plain as the nose on your face. But we have to go through, you know ... channels."

The word made him look at the set. "Hey," he said, "turn the sound up. It's the sister."

BLAINE STEWARD, in spite of his petulant attitude, was smart enough to follow through. A courier dropped off a package at Crooked Pear at eleven the next morning, addressed to Kick. She signed for it and took it into the sunroom to read.

She'd déjà vued the early part of the morning—gone for a run around the concession, waffles again for breakfast, rationalizing that the run would balance out the carbs, all the while knowing it wasn't true. She'd spent an hour or so wandering around the farm, the big barn and the stables, the chicken house now empty. The Belgian mare, Cookie, was in the corral, with the little black goat. Kick hadn't known that Buck, the gelding match to the mare, had died the previous summer. Johanna had bought the team as yearlings and had trained them to the plow and the cutter, entering them in competitions at fall fairs and using them to pull the kids around the farm over the Christmas holidays. Johanna told her over breakfast that the mare had stopped eating when Buck died, and only came around when Johanna bought the goat to keep her company. The mare had to be pushing thirty, Kick thought.

Walking the farm, she found herself thinking of the photographs in Johanna's album. The days of wine and roses. Or Kool-Aid and cookies, at least. It was too bad you couldn't flatten your memories out, like the pictures in the book, define the borders to suit your needs. But memories were like creeping ivy. One flowed into another, and not all were pleasurable to revisit. After a while she realized that, as much as she loved the place, she rarely thought of the farm when she was away from it. It was obviously a subconscious decision to which she could affix no reason. It occurred to Kick that her life was full of such half-hidden denials.

But the times she'd spent there with her ever-evolving family had not all been bad. She'd always been a big sister to Ethan, somewhat of a pushy big sister she realized now, constantly steering him this way or that, telling him what was and wasn't good for him. It was a dynamic that had always worked, she thought; she was wondering now, given his problems later on, if she should have cut him a little more slack. What surprised her was the realization that she'd passed some good days here with Ben as well. He'd been a fat little kid, four years her elder, but he'd been a hoot. Not in the least athletic, he'd compensated with an acerbic tongue and a propensity for getting everyone around him in trouble. It was only in his teens that he grew increasingly neurotic, probably in large part due to the realization that he had a crazy mother and a father who had no idea who he was. In high school he was part of a group that was stranded somewhere between the jocks and the academics. They spent the four years mocking everyone else, getting poor grades and never getting kissed, let alone laid.

As for Everett, it was not as if he was never around. He would usually show up for the major holidays—Christmas or Thanksgiving. Kick suspected that he suffered from infrequent attacks of guilt with regard to fatherhood. To his credit, he never reverted to the stereotypical rich man's practice of throwing money and toys at his children. Instead, he would show up with a project, or an activity, that he would be genuinely excited about, at least in the short term. Waterskiing one year, wood-carving the next. One year Easter was early and he arrived from a business trip to Quebec with spiles and buckets and a cauldron, eager to tap the sugar maples in the bush lot. That was the year he bought the Ford tractor and the wagon to haul everything to and from the bush. Of course, when the time came to boil the sap Everett's enthusiasm for the endeavor had predictably waned, and he was long gone in any event. Kick remembered burning most of the sap to a black goo. The whole project netted maybe two quarts of usable maple syrup at—as Johanna later determined—roughly two thousand dollars a quart.

The package from Great North was comprehensive and confusing at the same time. Kick suspected that Blaine Steward intended that it be both. She sat and drank coffee and went over various spreadsheets, perspectives, market estimates and demographics. She'd never had an aptitude for such things, perhaps in rebellion against her father, who—maple syrup ventures aside—had a business mind like no one she'd ever met and the people skills of a cactus. Kick had always maintained an inverse pride that the commerce gene had apparently skipped a generation. At the same time, however, she was forced to admit that her inability to focus on the bottom line was largely responsible for her chronic state of bankruptcy. Like a lot of things in life, she couldn't have it both ways.

The contents of the envelope from Great North resembled a stew concocted by a blind man. One ingredient had nothing to do with another. Kick soon found herself jumping from one file to the next like a bee in a room full of fake flowers, looking for something— anything—of substance to suckle.

After a while Johanna came into the room, pushing the aged Hoover vacuum cleaner that had been at the house forever. Given Johanna's cleaning obsession, the machine seemed like a member of the family. One summer Kick had draped one of her mother's dresses on the thing and dubbed it J. Edgar. Johanna pushed the machine into the center of the room, plugged it in, and then turned to Kick.

"You look bewildered."

"I'm afraid my pretty little head can't handle all these numbers," Kick told her.

Johanna replied by turning the vacuum on. Kick retreated to the kitchen; she needed more coffee anyway. While she was waiting for it to brew, Ethan came down. He sat at the counter where Kick had tossed the documents from Great North. He picked up a spreadsheet, looked at it for several seconds, his head cocked. His hair was sticking out in every direction and he wore the wide-eyed expression of a young Stan Laurel. He had on baggy shorts and an unbuttoned short-sleeved shirt.

"Let me know if you can make heads or tails out of any of it," Kick said.

He took another long look at the paper in his hand then tossed it aside in dismissal. "The man in the coonskin cap in the pigpen wants eleven dollar bills, you only got ten."

Kick grabbed Johanna's jean jacket from a hook by the back door, gathered her papers and her coffee and went outside. The temperature had fallen sharply overnight and the morning continued cold and gray. Standing on the back porch she looked out over the property, seeking refuge from the madding crowds of vacuum cleaners and troubled troubadours inside. As she walked toward the corral her eyes fell on the old ice skating shack on the edge of the creek where it curled out of the marsh to the northeast. She started for it.

Kick had probably been six or seven when Everett had hired Will Montgomery's father to knock together a shack where the kids could change into their skates and take shelter from the elements. Of course, Everett being Everett, the result was a shack in name only. It was twenty-five feet by twenty, with a shingled roof, windows on three sides, a wood stove and benches along the walls. There were two rooms, the reason for the division unknown to Kick even now. Presumably Everett, a staunch and unapologetic sexist, intended to separate the girls from the boys. There was a table in the front room with an assortment of mismatched chairs around it; there the kids could play cards or drink their cocoa or plan snowball attacks on the Van Oosten clan from across the river when they came to skate.

As Kick crossed the pasture field, heading for the shack with the bulky envelope tucked under her arm, she heard two shotgun blasts, in fairly quick succession, from the bush lot at the back of the farm. She kept a watch in that direction as she walked. It was unusual to hear shooting in the spring.

She opened the door cautiously when she reached the shack. It was hard to say when the building had last been used, or what stray critters might be lurking within. The interior was varmint free, though, and surprisingly clean. After a moment Kick realized that Johanna, ever efficient, would still show up here every month or so, broom in hand, and give the place what she used to call "a cat's lick and a promise." She would drag the Hoover down here, Kick suspected, if Everett had seen fit to run hydro to the shack. Kick was a little surprised that he hadn't.

It was colder inside the building than out. Kick flipped the collar of the jacket up and set the coffee, half of which she'd spilled crossing the field, on the table and began reading again. What had been Greek in the big house was Greek in the skating shack as well. When she found herself blowing into her hands to stay warm, she decided to light a fire. There was firewood and kindling in the box; presumably both had been kept replenished by Johanna. There was, however, none of the usual supply of old newspaper to start the fire. She eyed the spreadsheets from Great North for a moment, thinking that torching them would show Blaine Steward what she thought of his trickery. The accounting was saved when she remembered Ben's stash of comic books beneath the loose floorboard in the corner. Superman and The Hulk both proved to be incredibly flammable. Once she had the kindling going she tossed on a couple of logs that immediately threatened to smother the meager blaze beneath. She was obliged to sacrifice Batman to the fire as well. While extracting The Caped Crusader from beneath the floorboard she also came up with an issue of *Playboy,* circa 1980.

Within half an hour she had a cozy shack. Shortly thereafter she found, buried deep in the mass of paperwork, a separate file that showed what each of the company's concerns, and the record label, had done over the past five years, as well as a proposed budget for the next four quarters. Which was exactly what she'd been looking for all along. Buoyed by this minor eureka moment, she began to leaf absently through the issue of *Playboy*.

A while later she heard a shout from outside. She went to the door and opened it. Will Montgomery was walking along the creek, wearing work boots and jeans and a mackinaw. He had a shotgun, the breech broke, over his shoulder, and he was carrying two very large, very dead, wild turkeys.

Kick stepped out onto the small porch. Only her father would design a skating shack with a porch.

"You yelled something?"

"I yelled hey," he said. "Saw your smoke. I've chased a few kids out of here. Didn't know it was you."

"It's me," Kick said. "Coming in?"

Will looked at his watch. "For a minute."

"You can leave those birds outside."

He left the ten gauge out there too, leaning it against the windowsill. He looked at the papers on the table when he came in.

"Going over the books of my new company," she said. She saw his eyes go to the open *Playboy* on the table. "Oh, that's Brandi. Her turnoffs are phony people and negativity. She works with children and one day hopes to be the first woman president of the United States."

"There's been bigger boobs in the White House."

"Amen to that. What're you up to, Will—other than killing God's creatures?"

"Tell God's turkeys to stop eating Will's wheat, and maybe we can come to some kind of agreement," he told her.

"Are you even allowed to do that? I assume these things are protected."

"You'd be wrong. Turkey season is open."

"You got a license?"

"I didn't say I was doing it legally."

Kick sat down. "Well, I could share my views on hunting in general but I've got the feeling you're one of those guys who would point out that the chicken breast I had for dinner last night wasn't made of tofu." She indicated the chair opposite. "You gonna sit down?"

Will looked at his boots; he'd been walking in the matted grass along the creek and most of the mud he'd gathered crossing the plowed field was gone. He gave them a wipe on the mat inside the door and then sat in the chair. He took off his John Deere cap and pushed his hair back.

"Twenty years ago there wasn't a wild turkey anywhere in the province," he said. "Government decided it would introduce a few breeding pairs. Now they're a damn nuisance."

"The birds or the government?"

"Both, come to think of it."

"But it's the birds you've decided to shoot."

"So far."

Kick began to reassemble the pages from Great North. When she looked over at him, he was working a thorn spike from the ball of his thumb. His hands were covered in thick calluses. She hadn't really paid much attention to him at the reading; her focus had been Raney Kilbride and the will. She saw now that he had some gray in his temples and crow's feet around his eyes. He looked a little stressed, she thought, but just a little. Probably weather-related. Farmers.

She tried to remember how old he was. He had four or five years on her, she guessed. Ben used to make fun of him when they were kids, called him a hick and a dumb farmboy. She was never sure why Will refrained from giving Ben a shit kicking. She wouldn't have.

"So you're back farming full time?" she asked.

"Yeah."

"Finished with the hockey?"

"Hockey's finished with me," Will said. "I was persona non grata after the strike."

"I was wondering about that," Kick said. "I saw your comments about the union. And I don't even read the sports pages. So if I saw it—"

"They were giving us bad advice. I can make dumb decisions on my own. I don't need a union rep doing it for me. But I kind of burned my bridges. I was a fourth line winger. You have to be a superstar, you want to speak your mind and get away with it."

"I hope you walked away with some equity." She laughed, at herself though. "Shit, listen to me."

"I never had enough games for the pension. Spent too much time in the minors. My father left some debt when he died. I paid that off. And I recently had another financial setback. But I'm about even now. Which is pretty good for a farmer."

"Pretty good for anybody," Kick said. "So how is—" she started, then stalled. "I know you married one of the Martell girls but I can't remember which. Darlene?"

"It was Denise, if memory serves."

Kick smiled. "Well, how is she?"

"Pretty good. She came into a little money recently."

"Yeah? How so?"

"That other setback I mentioned."

"Oh." Kick decided to have another look at her files. "I wasn't trying to pry. I didn't know."

"People get divorced all the time," he said. "So you're going to take over—what is it—Great North?"

"Not if I can help it. I have to come up with a plan here. According to the will, I won't actually own the company for a year but I'm hoping I can streamline it. I'm in desperate need of a little capital myself these days."

"Got anybody you can divorce?"

"Did that a few years ago, if memory serves."

"I heard. I always thought he was a nice guy."

"He's probably the nicest guy I've ever known," Kick said. "Talk about aggravating."

"So why do you need the money? Other than the usual reasons."

"I have a documentary that's about three-quarters shot. I need money to finish it."

"About the drilling for gas in Wyoming."

"Yeah." She was surprised. "Everett told you?"

"He talked about you … from time to time."

"Really?" She placed the papers back on the table. "I didn't think he ever gave the three of us a second thought."

"I didn't say the three of you. I said you."

She looked up at him when he said it, but he was watching out the window to the creek now. She could hear the clucking of waterfowl. "I didn't think my father cared about what I do for a living."

"I didn't say that either," he said. "I believe the context was something along the line of, She's out in Wyoming shooting some damn fool documentary about the gas and oil business. He may have added that you were gonna get yourself shot."

"That's my pop," she said, still looking at his profile. "I bet you and Everett had a few chuckles, making out the will. I'm assuming some fine scotch was sacrificed in the creation of that little masterpiece."

"I had nothing to do with it. I never knew any of the specifics until the other day, at the reading. He asked me to be executor and I didn't figure I could turn him down."

"Why not?"

He looked at her now. "He was my friend."

She nodded, ceding the point. "Well, I really don't know what he was trying to accomplish. Ben will be all right, with the plant. He can continue to not run it—underachieving is his forte. But I don't think Ethan is going to take charge of the distillery anytime soon. And as for myself—put it this way, I wish he'd gone the whole hog and given it all away."

"I just saw Ethan," Will said.

"You did? Where?"

"Back by the bush. He was planting something."

She considered this. "I think we can assume it wasn't corn."

Will shrugged, the extent of his disinterest plain. "So why not just wait and sell Great North, if that's how you feel?" he asked.

"You think that's what Everett wanted?"

"Nope." He put his cap back on and got to his feet. "Well, I got birds to pluck. Not my favorite job."

"You did shoot them though."

"I did. You'll be sure to close down that damper on the stove when you leave."

"What would I do without you?" she asked. "You know, it's coming back to me now … you were always a bit of a control freak."

"Sorry about that," he said and turned to the doorway. "Go ahead and burn the place down. Don't know what got into me."

"All right, all right. I'll close the damn damper. Before you go, let me ask you a question. As executor. If I decide to pull the plug on a couple of these imprints, and I'm thinking this lame record label to boot, am I running afoul of the will? I'm not going to bullshit you … I'm going to try to dip into Great North's cash flow to try and scare up enough money to finish my film."

He was standing in the doorway as he listened, looking out over the creek where something had caught his eye. Kick had had a boyfriend a few years back, a wannabe film director, who was a John Ford fanatic. He was constantly running Ford's movies, over and over, on a projector he'd set up in their cramped studio apartment in Toronto. Now, looking at Will Montgomery in the doorway, Kick was reminded of John Wayne in the final scene of one of Ford's movies.

"First of all," he said, turning around, "I know about as much about being an executor as you do about wild turkeys. Secondly, I think you'd better read the will before you make any sudden moves."

"I've read the will."

"You just said ten seconds ago that you weren't gonna bullshit me. You haven't read it, or you wouldn't have suggested what you just did." He turned and left. "Stop by the house sometime," he called back. "I'll make you a turkey sandwich."

AT ELEVEN the next morning Kick was back at Great North. She went alone this time, not wanting to bother Raney Kilbride. Presumably a man of eighty or so would have earned his leisure, and she doubted that babysitting her was very high on anyone's list of recreational pursuits. As such, she was a little surprised when she walked into the boardroom to see him sitting there. He was wearing the same sweater, the empty pipe protruding from the pocket.

She'd called Blaine Steward at eight that morning, when he wasn't in, and then again at nine, when he was. It was obvious now that Steward had then called Raney. There was another man there, a middle-aged accountant named Dobson, or possibly Dowson. Steward was wearing a tie; Kick wondered if he'd gone home to change for the meeting. She couldn't be too critical about it, since she herself was wearing a pale blue summer dress. It was the first time she'd worn anything but cargos or jeans in months. She'd had to borrow a razor from Johanna for her legs.

"I thought that Mr. Kilbride should be here," Steward said.

When Raney stood to greet her he wore the same contented smile as he had on their last visit there, an expression that suggested he'd enjoyed his life and that these little sidebars of late were the ice cream on the pie. Kick shook hands with the accountant, whatever his name was, and then sat down. The accountant had an open laptop on the table in front of him.

"I've being looking at your horses, Blaine," she said. "And I'm here to make you a deal. You allow me to cull the herd a little, and I'll get out of your hair and let you carry on, unfettered and free."

"Cull the herd?"

"We dump two imprints," Kick said. "You've got some dead wood here. Cookbooks on tape? This thing hasn't made a dime in three years. And this other gig you've got going with TVO, this history tie-in. Not exactly hotcakes."

"Well," Steward said. He didn't appear particularly happy, yet he didn't seem to be upset either. Kick guessed his mood had been buoyed by her saying she was going to leave him alone.

He was now looking at the accountant, who was typing on his laptop. "You're talking about two popular imprints," Steward said while he waited.

"Bullshit," Kick said.

Steward walked around behind the accountant and stood frowning at the screen of the laptop for a moment. Kick could hear the accountant's fingers clicking away; for a moment she amused herself with the notion that the guy was playing a video game while Steward pretended to be in deep thought.

"There would be some downsizing, personnel-wise," Steward said after a moment.

"But it's doable?" Kick asked.

"There would be some downsizing."

"I heard you the first time," Kick said. "How many jobs?"

Steward looked at the accountant.

"A couple at least," the man said, considering. "Maybe three."

"Anybody here who might be amenable to early retirement?" Kick asked.

Raney raised his hand. Kick laughed while Steward frowned.

The accountant did some more considering. He was a deliberate type. "Possibly."

"There you go, Blaine, old sport. I think we can do this. Nobody's going to miss this stuff."

Steward sat down, nodding behind his hand on his chin, as if he and only he had the required business acumen and just plain intuition to declare the plan a viable one. Kick could see that he was all for it, though. He'd be a lousy poker player, she thought.

The accountant was looking at Kick like a man regarding a used car dealer. Now he turned to Steward. "This wouldn't free up any capital. To speak of, anyway."

"Fine with me," Kick said. "I'm just trying to help the bottom line, as you guys say. If I'm gonna own this company, I'd like to see a little profit come my way every once in a while."

That appeared to please Steward even further. He had the expression of a nervous kid who'd just been informed by his dentist that he didn't have any cavities. "We'll have to put some numbers together," he said after another contemplative moment. "Talk to the editorial staff. See what options we have vis-à-vis the payroll situation." He craned his neck and then nodded emphatically. "But yes, I think we can work with this."

Kick spread her arms in a gesture of magnanimity. "See? That wasn't so hard."

Steward was fairly beaming now.

"There *is* one more thing," Kick said.

Raney raised his eyebrows and smiled, as if he'd known all along that there would be one more thing.

"And what would that be?" Steward asked.

"This record label, KEB," Kick said. "It seems to be a separate entity."

"Named for you and your brothers, by the way," Raney interjected.

"I'm aware of that," Kick said. "I'm also now aware that the last recording KEB made was a Christmas CD that sold roughly seven hundred units. A CD that cost … let me see, was it thirty thousand to make?"

"At this point in time, we are nearly out of the music business," Steward said.

"I don't want to pull rank here," Kick said. "But at this point in time we are *completely* out of the music business. I told you I was here to make a deal, Blaine. Maybe you haven't noticed, but so far, I'm getting nothing out of this. Well, guess what? From what I've read, it appears that each of these eleven—soon to be nine— imprints has basically enough money to function from quarter to quarter. However, KEB Music has—for reasons that I can't fathom, and frankly, don't care to try—has a tidy sum of $250,000 in its accounts. Hey, we could make another seven or eight Christmas albums, kids."

"Well—" Steward said.

"Let me finish, Blaine. This is gonna be a slam dunk. As of this moment, KEB Music ceases to exist and will be replaced by Great North's new documentary film division. We'll call it … hell, I don't care what we call it. All I know is that it's going to finance the film I'm making right now. So there's your deal, Blaine. I get my financing, you get to keep your books on tape and I'm taillights, buddy. We'll send each other Christmas cards."

She noted that Steward's smile was in full retreat. But she also saw that Raney had now leaned back in his chair, his hands clasped behind his head, and he was grinning at her like she was a precocious two-year-old that he was not responsible for.

"Um—" the accountant said from behind the laptop, although he was looking not at the screen but at Steward. "That money is not exactly accessible. It's been designated to the NIC project."

"What's the nick project?" Kick asked.

"Has anyone suggested to you that you read the will, Kathleen?" Raney asked innocently.

Kick looked at him.

"NIC is an acronym," Steward said. "It stands for Nothing Is Certain."

"Benjamin Franklin said that nothing is certain but death and taxes," Kick said, joking. "That's the only nothing is certain I know."

"That's the one," Steward said.

"Has anyone suggested to you that you *read* the will, Kathleen?" Raney asked again.

She was about to tell him that he sounded like a broken record but she realized it would come off like a bad pun. "All right, what the fuck is going on here?" she asked instead.

"It's in the will," Raney said.

"Stop saying that."

"We have a contract to produce an album with Jonah Peck," Steward said.

"Jonah Peck," Kick said. "The country singer?"

"Yes."

"All right, I'm gonna need more info here," Kick said. She saw Raney open his mouth to speak. "Don't say it," she warned him. "I'll read the goddamn will when I get home."

"Jonah Peck owes the United States government about twelve million dollars in back taxes," Steward said then. "You probably read about it."

Kick raised her palms. "I don't know," she said irritably. "Maybe. Some information just kind of slips under the radar."

"Well, your father read about it. He decided he would try to help this Peck out, by signing him to a record deal."

"Wait a minute," Kick said. "My father was a country music fan? I never saw him listen to so much as a Christmas carol. He didn't know the words to Happy Birthday, for Chrissakes."

"He's not a fan of the music," Steward said.

Raney took over. "This was just after Everett's battles with the IRS over the parts plant in Ohio. Battles that he lost, for the most part. In typical Everett fashion, he developed an intense hatred for the U.S. tax department. When he heard about this singer's problems he stepped in and offered him a record deal. At this point your father was giving money away by the truckload anyway. The added attraction of skewering the U.S. government was all the incentive he needed. Peck had no idea who Everett Eastman was, but he accepted, of course. And $250,000 was earmarked for production costs."

"And so it became the 'nothing is certain but death and taxes' project," Kick said. "NIC, for short. I get it. My, what a heartwarming tale. Multimillionaires helping one another out. And me without a hanky."

"Jonah Peck hasn't made a record in years," Steward said. "Word is, he quit the business. The theory is that Peck's fans will buy the album—CD, actually—in droves, to help him out of a jam. The average fan, presumably, is not going to side with the tax department."

Kick put her hand to her forehead. "Okay. So where does the project stand? Do they have a release date?"

"Well, they, um ... they haven't actually recorded anything yet," Steward said.

"What's the holdup?"

Steward turned toward Raney, who was watching him expectantly. "We've been in pre-production," he said after a moment. "We've had ... well, trouble coming up with songs that meet Mr. Peck's approval."

"I thought these guys wrote their own material," Kick said.

"He used to," Steward said. "Apparently, he's somewhat ... blocked. With his recent troubles and all."

"And how long has this been going on?" Kick asked.

"A little over a year."

"Over a year," she repeated. "And you're telling me that there's been virtually no progress on this thing. Not a single song recorded. Is that it?"

Steward sighed. "That's it."

"And the $250,000 is just sitting there," Kick said.

"Not exactly," Steward said. "We've hired this producer in Nashville. A top producer. The money is tied up, you could say."

"Watch me untie it," Kick said. "The project is scrapped."

"You can't do that, Kathleen," Raney said.

She looked at him for a long moment. "And if I ask you why I can't do that … I know what you're going to say." She glanced at the others as she got to her feet. "So I guess you all know what I'm gonna do now."

"What's that?" Steward asked.

"I'm gonna go home and read the will."

BEN WAS IN THE MIDST of a thirty-minute-long email exchange with Lynn that had her, if she was to be believed, on the threshold of orgasm, when Louise buzzed him and told him that Teddy Brock was there. He typed a final message for Lynn.

—duty calls. finish without me—your dog—

When Teddy walked in Ben was sitting with his feet up, his keyboard on his lap to conceal his hard-on. He lowered his reading glasses onto his nose and looked at the lawyer, his expression that of a working man interrupted, which was almost the truth. Teddy was wearing one of his expensive suits, white shirt, silk tie. Clothes that indicated he was either going to or coming from court. He pulled a chair up opposite Ben and sat down, flopping his briefcase on the desk top as he did.

"How are you, Ben?"

"Working like a dog."

"Right."

"What can you tell me?"

Teddy reached into the case and pulled out the will then tossed it onto the desk, where it landed with a thud. "It's the last will and testament of a lunatic."

"Didn't I tell you?"

"That's the good news. The bad news is—there's nothing here to challenge. I didn't expect there to be. Raney Kilbride has been doing this since the dark ages. This thing's bulletproof. Eccentric as a frog riding a bicycle, but bulletproof."

"Eccentric?" Ben repeated. "There's a fucking clause in there that says I'm not allowed to *stop* making the KL19 throttle sensor."

"I know what's in there," Teddy said. "Believe me, I spent some time on this thing. It actually says that you can't stop making that sensor as long as there's a market for it. It seems your old man was sentimental about carburetors."

"Nice to know he was sentimental about something."

"Hey, you got off easy compared to the others. It seems as if all you have to do is carry on. Ethan, for instance, is required to drag that distillery into the black if he wants his inheritance."

"He does? No fucking way."

"You didn't read this thing yourself?" Teddy asked.

"That's what I have you for," Ben said. "That place hasn't showed a profit in five years. The old man let it run at a loss because he liked the idea of owning a distillery. Jack Dutton is old school and he's dead against progress. He'll chew Ethan up and spit him into a whiskey vat. What about Kick?"

"Among other things, she has to make a record with the country singer Jonah Peck. What the hell is that about?"

Ben smiled. "My old man. What a fucking nut. And you're telling me he was competent?"

"I'm telling you that nothing jumps out of this document that says it could be overturned. And certainly no coercion on anybody's part."

"What about Johanna?"

Teddy shrugged. "She was his housekeeper for thirty years. None of his wives lasted five. Why wouldn't he take care of her?"

Ben, his penis back to normal and no longer requiring cover, put the keyboard on his desk and leaned forward in his chair. "What happens if Ethan and Kick don't meet the challenges? Is that what they're called?"

"Then the companies go up for public sale. All the profits go to charity, including, for some reason, a large percentage to Ducks Unlimited."

"So you're telling me this is all I get."

"Yeah, this thriving parts manufacturing plant is all you get," Teddy said. "My old man died, I got a bill from the undertaker."

"Still ... you can see how I might be disappointed, can't you?" Ben asked. "I mean, I was under the impression that my daddy was worth somewhere between fifty and a hundred million dollars. I've been dividing that variable by three for a lot of years now. And it turns out that I'm left with a factory that I'm not even allowed to sell!"

"Life is full of little drawbacks. What can I tell you?"

"You can tell me that I have options."

Teddy looked at his watch. "You could talk to Johanna. Could be she doesn't want to stick around. You could offer her a lump sum, call it a retirement payment. Then the three of you would get the house and the farm. It's worth a few bucks."

"A few." Ben was doodling on his desk top now. "What if ... what if Ethan isn't competent?"

"We can't challenge his competency. Your father could've left the distillery to his cat, if he wanted. Is he that bad?"

"He's oatmeal from the eyes up. Pharmaceuticals is my guess." Ben looked at Teddy a moment. "Could be that Kathleen isn't exactly residing in the real world either. She makes documentaries for a living, for fuck's sakes. Nobody ever made a dime making documentaries."

"Ever hear of a guy named Michael Moore?"

"She's not Michael Moore. She made a film about the Inuits. Fucking Eskimos." He gestured toward the bulky document on the desk. "Okay ... what about this? What if we say these challenges aren't practical? That they're detrimental to the bottom line of the distillery and the publishing house? Is there some way I can step in? You know, to save the day."

"The will doesn't say anything about you stepping in anywhere, Ben. But if Ethan isn't up to things, maybe you could get power of attorney. But that's a different matter altogether."

"Shit."

"You'd have to talk to the people in charge at the distillery, and Great North. Might be something there. It would be tricky." Teddy reached for his briefcase. "There's still the house. Maybe Johanna dreams of sandy beaches and fancy rum drinks."

"Who doesn't?"

Teddy stood up. "Well, let me know. With regard to Ethan's competence, I know some doctors who handle this type of thing. It could get expensive. Not to mention what I'm gonna charge you just for reading the will."

When he was gone, Ben stared at the door for a moment. He considered driving out to Crooked Pear to talk to Johanna, if nothing else to put those notions of sun-drenched beaches and piña coladas in her head. But first he turned to the computer to see what Lynn was up to.

THE MONTGOMERY FARM was on a crest above the river valley. In fact, the old-timers in the area maintained that the property was the highest point in the county, although Verne Wagter, who had a chicken operation on the third line, had long disputed the claim. Verne was a mean drunk who would, under a few drinks of hard liquor, argue the issue most vociferously. Will Montgomery didn't really care one way or the other, and his indifference to the matter aggravated Verne even further, to the point that he challenged Will to a fistfight at a dance at the community center one night, a fight that would, in Verne's words, "settle the matter once and for all." When Will had declined, adding that a topographical survey would be required for such a resolution, Verne had taken offense to that obvious truth and thrown a punch anyway. Will, clipped on the ear, had then knocked the drunken chicken farmer out with one punch. He felt bad about it for a week, or at least several days, afterward.

But, all such bragging rights aside, Will's farm was on a hill and as a result the acreage drained more quickly than did the surrounding properties. The sun finally came out for a few days and by Tuesday afternoon the big field on the south side of the farm was dry enough to plow. Will walked the field late in the morning then went back and hooked the five-furrow plow to the Massey tractor. He was on the field shortly after lunch. He started where the river road met the old mud lane, made one pass down the field, and one back. There, he crossed the headland and dropped the plow to start again and blew a hydraulic line, spewing fluid everywhere. Without the hydraulics he couldn't lift the plow, so he had to walk the quarter mile to the machine shed by the barn to retrieve a set of wrenches.

He was back in the field and removing the line when he heard a car and looked up to see the Jetta pull into the house drive. Kick got out of the car, but spotted him immediately and got back in and drove over. She parked on the shoulder of the road and walked through the ditch and climbed over the fence. At least she could still climb a fence like a country girl. She was wearing jeans and a hooded sweatshirt, hiking boots. The day of the reading was the first Will had seen her in a few years but she hadn't changed much. At least not outwardly. Her hair was longer now, falling to her shoulders. She was lean, like the athlete she had been, and she moved in a long-legged stride that was sexy in a purely uncalculated way. Will could see her square shoulders and the swell of her breasts beneath the hoodie. Kick's mother, he remembered, had been a fashion plate—one of those women who would never be seen, even at home, without full makeup and jewelry and coiffed hair, a silk scarf or two hanging from her somewhere. Watching her now, it occurred to Will that Kick had purposely chosen an opposing tack when it came to fashion. The last time he'd seen her in a dress had been at her wedding.

"Hey," she said, approaching.

"Hello, Kick." He had a wrench on either side of the fitting and he reefed on it, freeing it with a snap.

"Looks like you've got hydraulic problems."

Will straightened up, the ruptured line in his hand. "That's what I was thinking. Always nice to get a second opinion though."

"Hey, no charge."

He examined the split in the line. He hoped that Mowat's Farm Supply in Fergus would have a new line in stock. "Sit on my ass for two weeks," he said, "waiting for the weather to clear, then I plow for ten minutes and break down. Never fails."

"Funny how that always happens," Kick said. "It's inevitable, like … I don't know, death and taxes."

He laughed, shoving the wrenches in his hip pocket.

"Oh, so you're aware of the infamous NIC project," Kick said. "I wasn't sure. I don't recall you mentioning it to me in the ice shack the other day. You know, when I was telling you of my plan to scuttle the record label."

"Of course I know about it. There was kind of a splash when it was announced a year ago or so. Made all the papers. I'm surprised you never heard."

"I must have been out of the country. As a rule, I try to keep abreast of the comings and goings of irrelevant hillbilly singers."

"Well, it's also mentioned in Everett's will. And I remember you saying that you'd read the will."

"I have now," Kick said. "And you're right. It seems I'm required to honor this dumb-ass record deal."

"You are."

"As executor, I might have assumed it was your job to point this out to me."

"As executor, I advised you to read the will. I was thinking that your reading abilities would be at least on a par with mine."

"What the hell? Are you mocking me?"

"No, ma'am."

She put her hands up. "Don't start with that ma'am shit either. Okay, let's get past this. I have now taken the advice of you, and pretty much everybody else on the planet, and read the goddamn will. And in that great document, we find a condition that guarantees the NIC project. Now I'm here today to ask you, again as executor, if we can't somehow circumvent that condition."

"On what grounds?"

"On what grounds?" She hesitated, ran her forefinger along her nose. "On the grounds that it's not moving forward. On the grounds that nobody involved seems to have any interest in it. On the grounds it was a dumb idea to begin with."

He began to loop the hydraulic line into a coil, holding it away from his body to avoid the dripping fluid. "I'd have to talk to Raney Kilbride. I'd have to ask him if the conditions of the will can be ignored based on—" Now he hesitated, and he matched her fingertip to the nose move. "What are we basing it on? The fact that you think it's a dumb idea?"

"For a reluctant executor, you're having a lot of fun with this, aren't you?" Kick said. "Look, it's been a year and nothing has happened. The money can be used elsewhere."

Will pulled a rag from his pocket and wiped the oil from his hands. "I don't think we can go against Everett's wishes. I don't think it's legal. And I don't think it's right."

"Playing the ethical card," Kick said. "You should be ashamed of yourself. Okay, smart guy, what about this? Great North is a viable company that operates in the black every year. Isn't it my responsibility to see that it continues to do so? My argument is that throwing money at this record deal will destroy that profit margin. And *that* is a violation of the will. In spirit, at least."

He smiled. "That's pretty good. You're kinda proud of that, aren't you?"

"I thought it was okay. You know, for spur of the moment."

"How do you know that the record won't be a success?"

"I'm thinking more along the line that the record will never be a record."

"I guess that's possible."

"So," she said. "What are you going to do?"

"Head into Fergus for a new hydraulic line. Finish plowing this field."

"In other words, you don't want to talk about this."

"I've got ground to plow," Will said. "Hell, last week we could have sat around and talked about it all day long."

"Would it have changed anything?"

"Nope. It's what your father wanted, Kick. Maybe it doesn't make a damn bit of sense, but it's in the will. There was an agreement between Everett and Jonah Peck. So long as Peck himself is on board with this project, it goes forward."

SIX

Jonah, wearing an ancient Comanche print bathrobe and slippers, watched the news from the satellite feed, flipping from one network to another while drinking a pineapple smoothie. A suitcase containing a hundred pounds of low-grade plutonium had been found in a locker in an airport in Cairo and the individual news agencies were treating the discovery with wildly varying degrees of alarm and speculation. By the eight o'clock hour, however, the panic had apparently abated since most networks had reverted to fluff interviews and concerts on the plaza. Jonah clicked to the weather channel and watched the forecast move west to east until it reached Tennessee. Then he turned the set off. He went into the bedroom and put on the same cotton pants and T-shirt and sandals he'd worn the day before. He got a green apple from the fridge and put it in his pants pocket as he walked out to the barn.

Billy had already fed the horses and turned them out. Jonah walked through the barn and out again to find the two animals standing in the corral, the mare against the fence, watching him as she was always watching him, her mind—he was convinced—one step ahead of his and everybody else's. Four legs, two legs, it didn't matter; he'd never met a smarter animal. Her tail was switching methodically over the spotted blanket of her rump, chasing away the flies that had just in the past week or so begun to be a nuisance. The bay gelding was in the middle of the paddock and, as Jonah stepped out of the barn into the bright sunlight, the horse decided to roll, dropping down to his side and then attempting three times to roll over in the dust of the corral. The mare walked past the gelding, heading straight for Jonah, and as she did Jonah was sure she gave the gelding a look of derision. He'd never seen the mare roll in the dirt.

"Hey Patsy," he said when she came close and he made her look for the apple in his pocket. She found it quick enough and he pulled it out before she could tear his pants trying to get at it. He broke the apple in half and gave her one piece and then waited for the dusty gelding to arrive, looking for his.

"Pancho," Jonah chided as he offered it. "You're a mess. And Billy just brushed you out, didn't he?"

He slapped the dust from the animal's flanks. The gelding stood for it only until he realized there was no more treat to be had, then he walked across the corral and went back to his rolling. Patsy, who loved Jonah for more than just apples and carrots and sugar cubes, followed him to the fence, where she leaned her forehead against his chest and just stood there.

The Appaloosa mare had been a gift from a film director he'd auditioned for a few years earlier. She'd been prepping a miniseries on the history of Texas, and had initially offered Jonah the role of Sam Houston. Later, when a name television actor became interested in the role, she'd rescinded the offer and hired the name. Jonah had not been particularly upset. This was before his tax problems and besides, he knew it was just business, and the movie business to boot. The mare had arrived in a trailer a month later, with a brand-new Mexican saddle and a note of apology from the director. Jonah had toyed for a couple of days with naming the horse after the woman, whom he'd gone to bed with in the course of auditioning, but in the end called her after Patsy Cline, with whom he'd had a more intimate relationship, having listened to her for forty years.

The mare was out of a Texas stallion named El Guapo and a Tennessee dam called Maxine. Jonah had developed a habit of referring to the horse as the love of his life. The assertion was brought up during a *Sixty Minutes* profile, by the interviewer—not Ed Bradley or Safer or the woman, but a different guy—who had shown up at Jonah's farm decked out in new blue jeans and a western shirt with stitching on the shoulders and pearl snap buttons. He and Jonah were standing in the middle of the corral at the time, surrounded by a camera crew, sound people, lighting technicians and makeup people as well as various producers and gofers. The gelding Pancho was having none of the spotlight and had retreated to the corner of the paddock, where he had stood looking longingly over the fields that stretched up into the hills. Patsy though, in true country and western fashion, was standing by her man, and had even allowed one of the crew to give her mane a quick brushing.

"Some would think it ironic," the interviewer had said, "that a man who has in his lifetime penned hundreds of beautiful love songs and who has, in fact, been married four times, would refer to this little filly as the love of his life."

"She's a mare," Jonah had said.

"Duly noted," said the man. "But still—"

Jonah had put his hand under the mare's chin and raised her face to blow softly into her nostrils. "Well, I do get mad at Patsy here from time to time, but when I do I just lock her in the barn and don't speak to her for a couple days. Try that with a wife and you'll sure as hell end up on the television, trying to explain yourself to that Oprah woman."

Now the gelding gave up trying to roll over. He lay on his side for a while, as if contemplating the futility of it all, then got to his feet and gave himself a shake. Patsy wandered to the trough for a drink. When Jonah turned to leave, Susie Braddock was walking out of the barn.

"I said hey," she said. "You getting deaf?"

"I might be," Jonah said. "Too much honky-tonk. Look at you— you hear I was throwing a party?"

Susie was wearing a short black dress with a full skirt cut tight at the waist and low in the front where her breasts were pushed together like a couple of fat puppies in a hatbox. Her blonde hair was piled in a carefully arranged swirl on her head and she wore stiletto heels, both conceits designed to enhance her diminutive stature.

"Shave her head and shuck them shoes off her, and you could slip that girl in your pocket," Jonah's buddy Clark had once said.

"Stay where you are," Jonah told her. "You walk out here in those shoes, you'll get stuck in the mud. I'll have to put a harness on old Pancho to pull you out."

She was lighting a cigarette when he got to her, one of the foul-smelling French sticks she favored. Jonah couldn't figure why.

"Did you get a moment to look at the songs?" she asked.

"A moment was all it took."

She had a long pull on the manure stick and looked away. He could tell she was angry. There was a mark on her neck that she'd attempted to hide with makeup. Jonah recalled hearing that she had a new boyfriend. Some public relations guy, he thought.

"Are you gonna pout now?" he asked.

"No," she said, pouting.

"Then what's the matter? We got ourselves a real stalemate here, Susie. We can't make a record without songs. I thought maybe you'd given up on the whole deal. That's the first I heard from you in months. You ever look at those songs Clark wrote?"

"I looked at 'em. I don't know what the hell I would do with 'em. One was about a fucking farm co-op or something, wasn't it?"

"It was meant to be allegorical," Jonah said.

"Shit."

She took another draw on the cigarette and then dropped it in the dirt and put her pointy toe on it. Jonah suspected she couldn't stand the smell any better than he could.

"I got a phone call from Kathleen Eastman," she said then.

"I don't know who that is."

"Everett Eastman's daughter. The Everett Eastman that's bankrolling this record."

"How is old Everett?"

"Dead."

As she said it, she was absently adjusting her breasts in the tight constraints of the dress, pushing them into some semblance of symmetry with the heels of her hands while she tucked in her chin and looked down her nose at her efforts. Jonah turned toward the mare, who was now standing by the water trough, having drunk her fill, and was watching either him or Susie. More likely Susie. The last time she'd been at the farm, Jonah was walking the mare out after a run, and when Susie tried to pet the animal like a dog, the mare had bitten her.

"When did this happen?"

"I don't know," Susie said as she finished her alignments. "I never asked. Recent, I would say. Sounds like the kid has taken over the record label."

"She was looking for a progress report?"

"She was looking to get out of the deal. Woman's got more fucking nerve than Jesse James. I told her so, in a polite sort of way."

"You don't have a polite sort of way, Susie," Jonah said and he walked into the open doorway of the barn, knowing that she would be obliged to follow. There was a walkway that ran through the center of the building, with stalls on both sides, six in all, although four were unused now. There were hay lofts above, on either side, and the tack room at the far end. The walkway opened onto the drive on the far side, a hundred yards or so from the house.

Jonah came out of the barn and stopped by Susie's Mercedes convertible with the RECORD GAL vanity plates. She was on his heels now, and if she was aware that she was in the process of being dismissed for the day—and she most certainly was aware—she never let on. She had the skin of an alligator, Jonah thought. He was surprised that the new boyfriend had managed to plant a hickey on that hide.

"So how did it end up, with you and the daughter?"

"She was asking questions that were none of her beeswax, far as I'm concerned," Susie said. "I told her that I'd been given a free rein on this thing, as producer. She doesn't know jackshit about the record business but it's pretty obvious what she's got on her mind, Jonah. She's after the money ... probably got her eye on some fancy new snowshoes or whatever it is they wear up there."

"I'm sure that's it, Susie."

She walked to the car and opened the door. Jonah could see the ermine seat covers inside.

"Why don't we just do an album of covers and be done with it?" she said then. "I had a great idea driving out here. We do a concept album. The record's about the taxman blues, so we use songs from the Great Depression. Jimmie Rodgers, Woody Guthrie, railroad songs, hobo songs. Hey, we put you on the cover in an engineer's outfit, at the throttle of an old locomotive, blowing that horn. Casey Jones Peck ... whoo, whoo!"

As Susie imitated the train whistle, Jonah was watching down the lane, where he could see Clark Van Zandt's Dodge pickup approaching at a crawl. Clark never drove any more than forty miles an hour, even on the highway, and when he could slow it down to a bug's pace he would, happy inside with his eight-track tape deck and his thoughts and his chaw.

"I made a deal with Everett Eastman for an album of original songs," Jonah said.

"Yeah, well he's dead," Susie said. "Far as I'm concerned, that part of the deal is null and voided. Was it written in the contract?"

"I don't recall whether it was or not," Jonah told her. "Don't matter to me one way or the other. That was the deal."

She was back in full sulk as she turned the convertible around and drove out, meeting Clark as he pulled up to the barn and stopped. Clark had a straw cowboy hat that he'd owned for most of his life and he put it on as he got out of the truck and reached into the back for his shotgun. He looked at Susie as she drove past him without a glance and then he walked over.

"Hello, Jonah," he said.

"How are ya, hoss."

"She was here last time I came out. You got something going on with that girl?"

"I'd rather stick my pecker in a spool of barbwire," Jonah said. "Come on up to the house. You want something to eat before we start?"

"I already ate."

Clark sat on the back deck looking up into the piney hills while Jonah went into the house to change into his hunting clothes. There were blue jays and cardinals and grackles in the branches of the cottonwoods, the jays squawking loudly at the interlopers whenever they drew near. The lawn, which needed mowing, ran right to the edge of the woods. The bush was thick with old-growth oak and ash, a few scattered pines. The narrow trail they would take in a few minutes ran into the forest.

Jonah came out of the house, wearing jeans now and boots and carrying his black powder rifle in a doeskin cover. He had a canvas bag over his shoulder and he'd pulled a baseball cap over his long, graying hair that he'd tied in a ponytail at the back of his neck.

"You heard anything?" Clark asked.

"Nothing," Jonah said. "I been up since dawn. Not so much as a horny jake."

They walked across the lawn and, with Jonah leading the way, they took the trail up into the hills. The turkeys were to be found a couple of miles into the woods, Jonah guessed.

"Least, that's where they used to be found," he said as they walked.

It was the first he'd used the trail this spring and it was overgrown in places, with new saplings trying to get a foothold in the rotted pine needles and maple leaves on the ground, and branches from existing trees grown enough in the past months to impede their passing. These they pushed aside or twisted until they broke off. Jonah had meant to bring the machete he'd picked up at the army surplus but he'd forgotten it.

The going was slow and it took them the better part of an hour to reach the tree stand in a grove of red oaks by a rocky-bottomed creek. Clark held the guns while Jonah climbed up to the platform, then Clark handed the weapons up and followed. There was raccoon shit on the plank seat and Jonah brushed it aside before sitting down.

Jonah opened his bag and took out his powder and shot, then he laid out his calls and his scratches and, finally, his stash. Clark loaded the shotgun, and then produced his own calls, although he carried everything in a multitude of pockets in his coat. After Jonah loaded the rifle they both leaned back against the rough limb of the oak and waited, each trying a hen's scratch from time to time.

"She look at them songs I wrote?" Clark asked.

"Yup."

"She don't like 'em."

"You don't write the type of songs Susie's gonna like," Jonah said. "That's about the biggest compliment I'm ever gonna give you."

"She looks at me like I'm a spittoon."

Jonah reached forward and gave his gobbler a shake. "Well, you ain't never won a Grammy or a Country Music Award. You ain't worth knowing."

"Well, fuck her."

"You might have to get in line for that, hoss."

They sat for an hour with no sign of a bird. Clark had a new call he'd made from a hollowed-out turtle shell and a piece of slate, which he scratched with a tine from a deer antler. Not once did they hear as much as a faint reply, other than that of crows and the odd wood duck.

"They're out there though," Clark said. "Don't know why it's so damn quiet."

Jonah was rolling a joint. "Don't knock the quiet. That's the reason I come here." He licked the paper and folded it over the grass. "But yeah, they're out here. We're out here. Just a matter of interconnecting."

"Life's like that," Clark said.

"Sweet Jesus," Jonah said. "You're not gonna turn into a goddamn philosopher, are you?"

"I don't intend to, no." Clark removed his hat and hung it on a broken limb. "There's good songs around. Why not just pick ten or twelve and make the damn record?"

"Susie," Jonah said. "Those people up in Canada hired her to run the show. I guess I let 'em so I got nobody but myself to blame for that. I don't know where my head was at. She does have a reputation for making records that sell."

"I've heard 'em."

Jonah sighed. "I know."

It was sometime later, although after smoking the joint neither one of them could say how much later, that they heard the hen and then saw her stepping lightly through the trees. The big tom was maybe fifty yards behind her. Clark had his rifle across his lap and he started to raise it, but Jonah put his hand out.

"Lookit that old boy," he whispered. "Lookit the colors on that bird."

"You want him?" Clark asked.

Jonah watched as the tom followed the female bird across the clearing in a cock bird strut, the tom's wings elevated, his chest puffed up. "Let's just let 'em be," he said softly. "We don't want to disturb the quiet."

WILL MANAGED to get the south field plowed before the rain arrived again. But arrive it did and once more it overstayed its welcome, coming down steadily for two days, filling the streams and creeks, sending torrents of brown water through the ditches and furrows, swelling the Grand River well up over the road in places, churning the water into a boiling foam in the shallows below the farm. Will was once again relegated to standing in his machine shed with Dalton, looking on with frustration as the sodden hours passed. Behind them, the cultivator, seed drills, tractors and discs were greased and oiled, belts and lines replaced, tires checked, chains lubricated.

"You might as well go on home," Will told his hired man, mid-morning of the second day. "You must have things to do."

"Sit at the window and watch the weather," Dalton said. "No, the wife'll think of something needs doing. She'll have me tearing up the kitchen floor or something. Woman's got more crazy ideas, things to do than … I don't know what."

"You ought to send her to Ottawa," Will said. "Put her to work on the unemployment problem."

"I like the part about sending her to Ottawa," Dalton said and he took a bite from a plug of tobacco. "What the hell we gonna do about this rain?"

"Everybody talks about the weather but nobody does anything about it," Will said. "Least that's what Mark Twain said."

"Is he related to that country singer?"

After Dalton left Will decided to drive over to see what Kick was up to. He hadn't heard from her and he was surprised. She may have given up on any notion of putting a stop to the record deal, but from what Will remembered of Kick that was highly unlikely.

Her Jetta wasn't in the drive when he pulled in but Ben's Corvette was there, parked half on the lawn. The rain had actually stopped, for the moment at least, and Will found Ben and Johanna out by the vegetable garden at the bottom of the slope behind the house. Johanna was dressed in a T-shirt and jeans and a nylon jacket, an old fedora for a rain hat. She was leaning on a shovel; there were fresh trenches dug on either side of the garden in an effort to drain the ground and save the plants from drowning.

Ben, standing back from the digging, wore crisp khakis and a striped dress shirt. Johanna was wearing rubber boots, black with orange piping, and she was muddy up to her knees. It was apparent who had been trenching and who had been watching. When Will rounded the corner of the house and started down the slope, Ben gave him a look every bit as dirty as Johanna's boots.

"Are you winning, Johanna?" Will asked.

"I should be building a boat."

"We all should."

"I've never seen anything like it," Ben said. "I was on the golf course when it started yesterday. Came down so hard it washed a pot bunker completely away. I thought the greens keeper was gonna have a nervous breakdown, right there on the spot."

"That's the saddest thing I ever heard, Ben," Will said.

Johanna smiled and ducked her head to hide it, busying herself by scraping the mud off her boots with the shovel. The wind gusted then and as it did the rain started again; it seemed to go from not raining at all to absolutely teeming in a flash, as if a dam had burst in the sky. The three of them ran for the cover of the back porch. Will and Johanna got there first, and Will turned to see Ben doing a fat man's waddle up the slope, his shoes kicking up streams of dirty water, soiling his pant legs.

On the porch Johanna took off the fedora and shook the water from it. Will guessed that the hat had once belonged to Everett, who had favored old-fashioned headwear, especially after he began to lose his hair. Occasionally, playing the gentleman farmer, he would drive his Ford Jubilee tractor around his acreage while wearing a snap-brim hat and a cashmere overcoat. Not accomplishing anything in particular, unless looking a part could be considered an accomplishment.

Ben came up the steps, panting and wheezing from the fifty-yard run, although Will would be hard-pressed to describe what he'd been doing as running. Ben stood dripping on the pine planking of the porch, running his fingers through his hair, which was, Will noticed now, spiked with blonde highlights.

"Well, I got a pot of coffee on," Johanna said.

She pulled off her muddy boots outside the French doors and went inside. Will left his own boots beside Johanna's. Ben walked right in, his Topsiders planting perfect muddy prints across the tiled floor. The two men sat at the counter while Johanna poured the coffee.

"Kick's not here?" Will asked.

"I haven't seen her, not since yesterday," Johanna said. "She had a meeting in Toronto. Something about financing for her film."

"Where's Ethan?" Ben asked.

"Upstairs. He and the girl Janey."

"She still around?" Ben said. "Should've known that. I can't put my finger on it but there's something not right about her."

Will regarded Ben for a moment. "What're you doing out this way, Ben?" he asked. "Looking for a dry place to golf?"

"Very funny. I happened to be in the area and I thought I'd stop and see how things were."

Johanna set the coffee down. "He came here to ask me what I thought about vacating the premises."

"That's not true," Ben protested.

"Sorry," she said. "I must have misunderstood you when you asked me if I ever thought about moving to Florida."

"Isn't that just like a woman, Ben?" Will asked. "Take something you say, twist it around and then … well, repeat it word for word."

Ben looked at Will darkly, started to speak then seemed to think better of it. He turned to Johanna, who had removed the nylon jacket, and his eyes went directly to her breasts. Her shirt was soaking wet and, even though she wore a bra, her nipples were clearly visible under the thin fabric. Ben gawked at her like a teenager.

"I'll be right back," Johanna said.

When she was gone Ben looked at Will and shrugged, then had a drink of coffee. Will was familiar with the shrug; it was Ben's standard response to himself acting the ass. As if it excused the behavior.

"I'm glad you're here, Will," Ben said, putting his cup down.

"Yeah?"

Ben glanced in the direction Johanna had gone and lowered his voice. "We have to make the best of a bad situation here. Kick and Ethan and I took a royal screwing on the will. If I'd have known the old man had lost his marbles, I'd of taken power of attorney five years ago. That fucking Raney Kilbride should be held accountable for that but I don't know there's anything we can do now. But this house and property has got to be worth—what? A million and a half?"

"Couldn't say."

"Whatever it's worth, there's no reason for Johanna to be here anymore. I suppose she helped out with the old man the last couple years but I've got a feeling she helped herself to his bank account in the process. I'd be surprised if she hasn't got a few hundred grand salted away somewhere. Point is, it's time for her to go." He paused. "She might need some convincing."

"Yeah?"

"She might listen to you, Will. You're not part of the family. You could, you know, suggest to her that she'd be happier in a smaller place, for instance." Ben glanced again toward the stairs that Johanna had taken. "And I know what you're thinking. What's in it for you? Well, I'll see to it you get first crack at the acreage. No realtor fees, just a straight deal. Maybe even go ten percent under the market price. Will you think about it?"

"I'm thinking about it right now," Will said.

They could hear Johanna as she started down the stairs. "This is just between you and me," Ben whispered urgently.

"Absolutely," Will agreed.

Johanna came back into the kitchen and sat at the counter. She now wore an aged sweatshirt with Mariposa Folk Festival across the front. She gave Ben a look and then turned to Will.

"How's the coffee?"

"Fine," Will said and to demonstrate he took a drink, smacked his lips in satisfaction. Then he said, "Ben wants to run you out of here, Johanna. He figures you've got no right to be here anymore. And he's pretty sure you embezzled a big chunk of money out of Everett's account. He wants me to convince you to leave, promised to cut me a deal on the farmland if I did."

Johanna turned to Ben, whose mouth was hanging open. Then she smiled at Will. "And what did you tell him?"

"Said I'd think about it."

"You're a fucking asshole," Ben said, getting to his feet. He looked at Johanna. "I was talking about down the road, years from now."

"Were you?" Johanna said. "And the embezzling?"

Ben had no answer for that. He turned on Will. "Don't make the mistake of thinking you're smarter than you are, Will. Being named executor doesn't change who you are. You're still just a farmer. I'll be leaving now. I can get a fresh cup of coffee at Tim Hortons," he added pointlessly.

Johanna reached beneath the counter and came up with a tea towel. She flung it at Ben, who caught it awkwardly against his chest.

"Wipe that floor before you go," she told him. "Clean up your mess."

Ben, unhappily, did as he was told.

"YOU REALLY DON'T have to say anything," Janey told him.

They were driving along the river in the rain, Janey behind the wheel, Ethan looking out through the trees at the passing, swollen current. The rental car's wipers were worn; one of them was making a high-pitched squeaking sound that was driving Janey crazy. She turned the switch to intermittent but then she found herself anticipating the squeak, which was just as bad and possibly worse.

She'd called Jack Dutton that morning, and said that Ethan, having fully recovered from whatever malady she'd invented for him previously, wished to tour the distillery. Dutton's tone suggested that he'd been expecting the call; he was cooperative in the extreme over the phone.

Ethan had been spending most of his time on the internet, downloading information about the planting of organic vegetables. He had a large quantity of pot seeds he'd brought along from the island and she knew he was sowing them somewhere on the farm. As for his prescription drugs, he had evidently decided that he was through with the pharmaceutical industry. If he was going to medicate, he'd do it the old-fashioned way.

After calling Dutton, she'd walked into the upstairs family room that they'd taken over and found him at the computer. She passed behind him in order to look at the screen, which was filled with information on natural fertilizers. She told him about the trip to the distillery; when he made no comment, she asked him what he was up to.

"If my thought-dreams could be seen," he said, "they'd probably put my head in a guillotine. But it's all right, ma, it's life and life only."

"Food for thought," she'd said.

The receptionist this time was somewhat friendlier to Janey, now that she was actually with the heir himself. With nary a single whoa she provided them both with name tags and white hard hats while they waited for Jack Dutton, who presently came charging out of the back in a gust of goodwill.

"Well, well," he said. "Good to see you again, Janey. And you're Ethan. Jesus, I wouldn't have recognized you. Last time you were here you were … well, not much taller than a whiskey barrel. How are you, Ethan?"

Ethan smiled. "Well, you can tell everybody down in ol' Frisco, tell 'em Tiny Montgomery says hello."

"What?" Dutton said. He looked at Janey. "Who's Tiny Montgomery?"

"Um … Ethan's making a joke," Janey said. "That's a nickname he uses sometimes."

Apparently that was good enough for Dutton and his mission of benevolence. He turned to lead them into the plant and when he did Janey rabbit-punched Ethan in the rib cage. He grunted in pain and looked at her in admonishment, but said nothing.

Dutton gave them an extensive tour of the place, from the docks where product was loaded and unloaded to the vats, the aging barrels and the bottling plant. From time to time he would launch into a detailed description of the more technical aspects of the distilling process, tutorials designed, Janey guessed, to overwhelm rather than educate.

Janey took mental notes and asked a few questions. Ethan endured the tour in silence; Janey suspected that he was remaining mute not because she'd requested it in the car, but because he was sulking about being slugged in the ribs. If that was the case, it was something she would put on file for future use.

They basically toured the plant in a large counterclockwise circle, and although the showing was comprehensive enough, Janey had the feeling that Dutton had them on a stopwatch. Back in the reception area he thanked them for coming and then presented them with a case of Royal Highland Reserve.

"It is an old facility," Janey said.

"I suppose it is," Dutton said guardedly.

"I hear there are plans for a new distillery," she said.

"We don't have money for a new distillery," Dutton said. "We're barely keeping our heads above water as it is."

"But you are?" Janey asked. "Keeping your heads above water? I thought you were operating in the red."

"It's a complicated business," Dutton told her. "There are certain carry-overs—grain inventory, for instance—that skew the numbers. I can't explain it to you in a nutshell. I could show you the books but I doubt you'd be able to make head nor tails of them."

"I've got an MBA from the University of British Columbia," Janey said. "Why don't I give it a shot?"

AFTER BREAKFAST Johanna went into town for groceries and shortly after that Kick saw Ethan and Janey drive off in the Taurus. She retrieved the canvas bag from under the bed where she'd stowed it, and then went down to the liquor cabinet in the dining room and filled Everett's flask with some of the sixty-year-old Dalmore scotch he had favored. She put the flask in the bag. She didn't know whether she was ready to face him. It was something she'd avoided while he was alive. Now seemed like a hell of a time to break with tradition, but she knew that if it wasn't now, it just might be never.

The ducklings that Everett had spent his last days defending were now three-quarters grown. They'd lost their pin feathers and the males were already taking on the colors of their adulthood. They glided noiselessly along the creek and a few ventured bravely out into the current of the river. Kick sat in the broken Adirondack chair and watched them, envious of their idyllic existence, their oblivious lives. After a long while she pulled the unloaded Colt from the bag and placed it on her lap. She unscrewed the cap from the flask and had a taste of the single malt, allowing it to rest on her tongue, the sweet peaty scent of it in her nostrils, before swallowing.

For the moment there were no snapping turtles to be seen, but Kick remembered them well from her childhood. During mating season the turtles would wander from the sanctuary of the river and each spring she and Ben would manage to catch one and keep it in a box in the barn until its inevitable escape. Until that happened Kick would attempt to feed the thing dead flies or chunks of wiener while Ben would pass his idle hours tormenting the creature, ramming sticks in its mouth until the turtle, in a fit of rage, would strike out with its fearsome jaws and crush the wood with amazing force, the act both scaring and exhilarating Ben at the same time. In Kick's memory, the turtles were mean and fierce and totally indestructible.

Kick lifted the flask and had another drink. It was not the first time in her life she'd experienced confusion over how she was supposed to feel about significant events, as opposed to just feeling whatever she was feeling. Her wedding day had been such an instance, when she'd found herself in the curious act of walking trance-like down the aisle while a voice inside screamed for her to run like hell in the opposite direction. Of course, there'd been plenty of times when she'd heeded that voice—that shrill advocate of cut and run—and inevitably regretted the heeding as much as the ignoring. Damned if you do and damned if you don't.

Which was where she'd always stood with Everett, it seemed. She'd stayed away even when she'd known that his health was failing, arguing to herself that there was still time. Time for what was another matter. She was always able to make the case that she was too busy to fly home, and besides, she wasn't convinced that anything could kill him anyway. And it wasn't as if there were things unspoken between the two of them. Of course, the truth of the matter was that there were many things unspoken between them but it was also true that they would remain so. Proximity had nothing to do with that.

She wondered if he was lonely in those final days. It seemed unlikely, as loneliness was not a word she could associate with her father. If he was lonely he would have done something about it. And he was not the type to surrender to such a human frailty in any case. He was mean and fierce and almost indestructible.

She heard the crunch of boots on the gravel behind her and turned to see Will Montgomery standing there.

"Hey," he said.

"Hi, Will."

He walked around beside her. He was carrying a round-mouthed shovel in his left hand and had a pair of worn leather work gloves stuffed in the hip pocket of his jeans.

"Clearing ditches?"

"Seems like it's all I do these days," he said.

She offered the scotch over. "You want a drink?"

He took the flask and drank, then wiped his mouth. "That thing's not loaded, is it?"

"I wouldn't know how."

"Thought maybe you were gonna take up with those snappers."

She took the flask back and screwed the cap on. "I'm not sure what possessed me, but I did a little research on those turtles last night. You know they don't care for their young? And they are, in general, a particularly unsocial creature. The females can carry sperm for several seasons, procreate without a male. Talk about commitment phobic. Their favorite pastime is to lie in the muck with just their eyes and noses exposed, waiting to ambush. Remind you of anybody, Will?"

"You might be reaching a little. If Everett was a snapping turtle, then why would he want to kill his own kind?"

"I've been wondering that. Maybe in the end he was killing himself. Exorcizing his inner turtle. Or maybe he decided he would rather be a duck. All that philanthropy and uncharacteristic kindness." She handed the gun and the canvas bag to him. "Load it for me, Will. Just one bullet."

"They're not bullets," he said but he took the powder and a single ball from the bag and did as she asked. "You see a turtle you want to shoot?" he asked as he worked the rod, pushing the powder and ball into the cylinder.

"I have no quarrel with *Chelydra serpentina.*"

Will took a cap from the bag and pushed it on the nipple of the chamber. He aligned the cylinder and handed the Colt to her. "You have to cock it."

Kick stood up and held the heavy revolver out from her at shoulder height. She cocked it back, two distinctive clicks, and held it in steady aim at the far shore of the creek. After a moment she lowered the gun and handed it back to Will.

"Unload it," she said. "And take it home. I've got no use for guns."

"Only one way to unload it," Will said. He held the gun out from his side and fired the ball into the mud bank of the creek.

"Take it," Kick said. "It's yours."

The next day she left for Nashville.

SEVEN

The flight was expensive and Kick was broke. After playing a futile game of solitaire with her credit cards in her bedroom at Crooked Pear, she'd had an epiphany and called Blaine Steward at Great North. His voice had by now taken on a decidedly cautionary tone whenever talking to her.

"I'm going to Nashville."

"Well," he said and then there was a pause so long that Kick thought they'd been disconnected. "I don't know what you expect to accomplish."

"Me neither."

"Well," he said again, and again he paused. "Good luck then."

"I need Great North to pick up my expenses."

"Oh, I don't think we can do that." It was the quickest she'd heard him speak yet.

"Why not?"

"I just don't know how we would do it. Where the money would come from."

"You're the general manager of the company, right?" Kick had asked.

"Of course."

"Are you telling me that if you wanted to fly to Nashville to check on the status of a quarter-million-dollar project, that Great North couldn't foot the bill?"

"Under those circumstances, I suppose it could."

"So all I have to do is install myself as general manager," Kick said then. "Question is—where would that leave you, Blaine?"

The mother of all pauses followed. "I'm going to have to call you back."

When he did, it was to tell her that the flight was already booked and that she could pick up her ticket at Pearson. Round trip, although Kick was certain Steward would have been happier to make it one way.

She landed in Music City shortly after five in the afternoon. There was a shuttle from the airport and, mindful of her financial state, she took it instead of a cab. At first blush, Nashville looked exactly like she might have thought it to look, if she'd ever given the matter any thought. She hadn't.

She'd made a reservation at the Sheraton on Union and Seventh and the shuttle dropped her out front. When she got to her room she felt grungy after the day's travel, so she had a shower then changed into pants and a light V-neck sweater and went for a walk around the downtown area. She headed over to Broadway, then made her way down to the banks of the Cumberland River. The river was slow-moving and murky and dotted here and there with cruising power boats. Across the water the football stadium dominated the landscape.

She went back into the town and walked up and down the streets that represented the commercial core. Music City could just as well have been named Souvenir Town. She'd never seen so much junk for sale in her life, pens and lighters and playing cards and swizzle sticks. As well as cowboy hats, and boots and fiddles and mandolins and wigs and sequined everything—from shirts to pants, scarves and socks. One store offered a special—buy one pair of boots, get two pairs free. Kick decided they were making a lot of money on that first pair of boots.

She ate dinner in a restaurant called Hobb's, which overlooked the river, opting for the roasted chicken special. The walls of the place were covered with autographed pictures, everyone from Gene Autry to, surprisingly, Pee-wee Herman. At least half of the photos—and there were literally hundreds—were of people Kick had never heard of, the more obscure the personality, the less prominent the point of display. Some were actually hung at knee height. Kick decided that she herself would be relegated to somewhere down around the baseboard.

After eating she walked back to the Sheraton where she stopped in at the hotel bar for a drink. The place was moderately busy and the clientele on the conservative side, not a rhinestone Stetson or snake-skin boot to be seen. Kick had one scotch and headed for her room. She watched a bored David Letterman poke fun at an oblivious young actor with three first names and then she went to bed.

Susie Braddock had offices and a studio on 17th Avenue, better known as Music Row, just a five-minute cab ride from the hotel. The building was of stucco, positioned between the Sony building and Nashville Sound. The street out front was tree-lined and immaculately clean, as befitting a boulevard that presumably brought great wealth to the city's coffers. Opposite the studios were attractive older homes, most converted into commercial properties.

Kick was arriving without an appointment. Her phone conversation with Susie Braddock earlier in the week had gone rapidly south, and as a result she was pretty sure she would be denied an audience. She went up the front step, past a sign set in a concrete slab that read simply SUSIE BRADDOCK in letters five feet high. Two minutes later Kick found herself standing in the reception area inside, in the presence of the woman herself, who was in fact not much taller than the letters on the sign.

The encounter was at least as awkward as Kick had anticipated. She was obliged to stand patiently while the petite record producer circled around her, looking her up and down in the most obvious way. Kick endured the scrutiny in amused silence; she half expected the woman to sniff her, one stray dog meeting another.

"How'd the hell you get down here?"

"On an airplane."

"Ha. I just bet."

Susie had come out of her office while Kick was attempting to explain her presence to the receptionist, a skinny blonde woman with tattoos covering both arms and multiple piercings in her ears, eyebrows, nose, lips and—Kick had to assume—many other, less public, places. Susie wandered out in her stocking feet and came upon Kick unexpectedly. She wore tight black leather pants and a form-fitting red satin top, unbuttoned enough to reveal her substantial cleavage. Her blonde hair was pulled back from her face and tied at the back of her neck.

"Well, you're here," she said unhappily and she indicated her office. "Y'all might as well come in." She added, "For a minute."

Kick followed her into the office. The room was big enough to park three or four Cadillacs inside. The walls were covered with photos of Susie with various luminaries from the music world as well as a handful of actors, comedians and other assorted riffraff in general. Kick thought it might be fun to do a cross reference with the pictures in Hobb's restaurant but then suddenly realized that it might be time to redefine her notion of fun.

There was an enormous desk in the center of the room—everything in the place was outsized, in fact, like a film set for *Gulliver's Travels*—and on the desk were a pair of new boots of buttery leather with stiletto heels that had to be at least five inches high. Susie walked around to sit at the desk, and then she picked up a cloth and dipped it into a jar of viscous yellow goo, which she began to rub vigorously into the toe of one of the boots.

"Ostrich," she said to Kick. "Set a minute, will ya? Ostrich skin, you have to take care of it. Keep it lubricated, you want it to last."

Kick sat. "Nobody likes a dry ostrich."

"I get it," Susie said. "So you're a Canadian?"

"I am."

"What the hell happened to k.d. lang? I mean, I can live with the lesbian thing, but the jazz? What a waste."

"It's considered a national tragedy, back home."

"Ha. I bet." Susie had moved on to the other boot now. "I hope to hell you've got other business in town. I hope you didn't fly down here just on my account. Because if you did, you're gonna find out that was a waste of money."

"Funny you should mention money," Kick said.

"You get right to it, don't you?" Susie said.

"I've been told there's $250,000 kicking around somewhere. I'd like to inquire as to its whereabouts."

"The money's safe, if that's what you're worried about." Susie scooped more goo from the jar, landed it onto the boot with a splat.

"I'm more interested in the progress of the recording," Kick told her.

"We're in pre-production, honey. We'll record when we're ready to record."

"I assume that money is spent in pre-production."

"That's right."

"How much?"

Susie used the cloth in her hand to indicate the wall behind her. "Those are gold records, honey. Go ahead and count 'em. What I'm saying is that I'm a music-making, multitasking she-wolf from the Texas hill country. I can't give you numbers from every project I've got on the go at the drop of a Stetson hat."

"What kind of hat would you have to drop to get me those numbers?"

Susie quit rubbing the boot for a moment and smiled. "Careful now. You might be the biggest bullfrog in the pond up north but you ain't nothing but a tadpole down here."

"I was never any good at biology," Kick said. "Let's try this. Seeing as I came all the way down here, I think I'll just stick around until you can get some accounting together for me. Now I appreciate that you're a busy woman—lubricating ostriches and making hit records and all that—so maybe you can put someone else on it. What about that receptionist out there, the one who looks like she was ravished by a porcupine?"

"Easy now, tadpole."

"Could you call me ma'am?"

"What?"

"Nothing," Kick said as she got to her feet.

Susie had been smiling. She put down the cloth and took a moment to pull on her newly oiled boots. When she walked around the desk, she was now just a couple of inches shorter than Kick.

"When I take on a project," she said, "I assume full control. That's the only way I work. I told that peckerwood up in Canada that. What's his name—Stewart or Steward or whatever? The only people who have any say over this record is me and Jonah Peck."

"Then I'd like to talk to Mr. Peck. Does he live in Nashville?"

"No, he doesn't."

"And you're not going to tell me where he lives?"

"Nope. The man is an artist. He doesn't like to be harassed."

"Did I say I was gonna harass him?"

"I'm telling you that you're not gonna get the opportunity. I'm the one Great North hired."

"Well, I'm the new owner of Great North, so I guess it's me and you, Susie," Kick said. "And what you need to know is that you're working for me, not the other way around. And I'm going to need to see what you've been doing."

Susie shrugged. "You don't have to get all hard-ass about it. How long did you say you were in town for? Because it might take me a few days to put this together. It might take me a week. I'm due in the studio this afternoon, cutting a disc with Kenny Butternut. I'm sure you've heard of him."

"Sorry."

"You will. He's the next big thing, a talent we see once in a lifetime. Now that I think about it, it might do you some good to stick around this town a few days. I don't think you appreciate what it is I do."

"Susie, I'm just dying to appreciate what you do," Kick said. "Get me the fucking numbers."

BEN WAS LATE FOR WORK the next morning. The transmission was making a noise in the minivan and Meredith had made an appointment to take it in to the dealership. Ben had to follow her into town and then pick her up.

"They wouldn't give you a car for the day?" he asked, driving her back home.

"I didn't ask. I hate to."

"It's part of the deal," Ben said. "The money I throw their way."

"If I needed a car, I would've asked," Meredith said. "I planned on spending the day on those flowerbeds anyway. I don't need a car."

As he pulled into the drive Wilson was just rounding the corner of the house, pushing a wheelbarrow filled with topsoil. "That's something else," Ben said. "You don't need to be working in the damn garden. That's why I hired Jamaica Joe there."

"Don't call him that," Meredith said. "I hate that expression. I don't mind getting my hands dirty. I seem to remember a time when you weren't averse to a little yard work yourself. You used to have a contented look on your face, pushing that mower."

"I don't remember that."

"Well, I do. Maybe you should try it again, might improve your mood, which has been a little less than joyful of late. You could use the exercise too."

"I golf for exercise."

"Driving around in a cart drinking vodka is not exercise."

Ben slapped the shifter into park. "Okay, I'm sorry I insulted our friend from the Caribbean. Are you happy now?"

She shook her head at him and got out without another word. He watched as she walked across the lawn in her jeans and cotton jacket. Her ass was getting bigger, almost imperceptibly so but bigger, in spite of her workouts in the gym, in spite of everything she did around the house and yard. It was something unavoidable, he guessed. After all, she was thirty-eight.

As he backed out onto the street he saw her stop to talk to Wilson, putting her hand on the gardener's shoulder as she pointed something out in the hedge. Ben felt a sudden twinge of jealousy; he'd wondered in the past if his wife could possibly be fucking the old boy. He was probably twenty-five years older than her but Ben knew about those guys. They loved to fuck white women and who knows what kind of weird herbs or whatever they took to keep themselves going. He had an image of Meredith and the old black man going at it in the shed, with her bent over the wheelbarrow, him giving it to her from behind. He bet Wilson would have no problem with the size of her ass.

It began to rain as he hit the ramp for the 401 and in minutes it was pouring. So much for Meredith's gardening plans with the old boy. He knew that he had no reason to suspect anything was going on between the two of them. It was his own distrustful nature. He'd seen a shrink a few times in his twenties; he'd dropped out of university during his third year and after a couple of years dedicated to getting stoned every day, had begun to suffer a crisis of self-esteem. One day the doctor, a beanpole Frenchman with a thick accent, had the audacity to suggest that people who distrusted everyone around them were quite often disloyal in their own dealings. Ben had blown up at the comment and walked out of the office. Never paid the fucker either.

He parked the Vette in his spot. As he walked through the glass doors to the outer office Louise was giving him a strange look that he couldn't quite qualify. Then she shifted her eyes to her left and Ben turned to see Lynn sitting on the couch there, wearing a short white skirt and heels and a T-shirt with Puerto Vallarta across the front.

"Miss Hoffman," Ben managed to say. "Oh, of course. You're here to pick up the files for … that other matter."

"Miss Hoffman?" she said when they were in his office.

"You surprised me," Ben said. "I had to cover, didn't I?"

"Nice job. I'm here to pick up the files on the other matter."

Ben took off his jacket and tossed it toward a chair in the corner. It hung on the arm for a moment then slid to the floor. He sat down at his desk. "Give it a rest, Lynn. Why are you showing up here anyway?"

"Because you won't answer your cell."

"Shit," Ben said. His cell phone was at home in the charger. "So there's an emergency, is that it?"

She walked over and picked his jacket up and draped it neatly across the back of the chair. She sat down and crossed her legs. "Jose's Fitness is closing its doors. The place I go to, on Dundas?"

"Well," Ben said, looking at the V where her thighs met the short skirt. "Then this really is an emergency."

"Don't be a smart-ass. My girlfriend works there. They're closing down at the end of the month. I want to buy the place."

"And the only thing stopping you is the fact you don't have the price of a cup of coffee?"

"Things haven't been the way you promised. I put my career on hold for you, Ben, and all along I been hearing how things would be once the old boy was gone. Well, the old boy is dead and buried."

"Remind me what career it was you put on hold."

"You want to get smart with me, then don't do it while you're trying to look up my skirt. If we're going to have a future together it has to be on more than one level. A relationship has to, like, grow."

"I wish you'd stop watching those shows."

"I want to buy Jose's. I can make a go of it, Ben, and if you quit being a dickhead I'll tell you how. Co-ed gyms don't work but women-exclusive places do. Women like to work out on their own. Guys are always gawking."

Ben was gawking when she said it. He turned in his chair and looked out the window. The rain had stopped but there were puddles, mini lakes actually, everywhere. The parking lot was awash and the Eastman banners above it were torn, hanging loosely.

"What're they asking?"

"I don't know," Lynn said. "They haven't even announced that it's closing yet."

When Ben swung his chair back to her, he looked down at his stomach. "Do you think I'm out of shape?"

"No," she said at once.

"Meredith made a comment this morning."

"She's probably just pissed cuz you don't fuck her anymore. You don't, do you?"

"No," he said at once.

"Then don't worry about it," Lynn said. "I like a man with some meat on him."

She smiled and Ben felt himself getting aroused. He glanced involuntarily toward the door; Louise was on the other side, not twelve feet away. "I'll get Teddy Brock to make some calls about the gym. Keep in mind I'm not exactly rolling in it for the time being. I might be able to help you out with the down payment, something along those lines."

"All right," Lynn said and she got to her feet. She smiled. "You wanna fuck?"

"Here? Jesus, Lynn."

She walked behind him and began to close the blinds. "Yeah. Here."

Ben's voice dropped to a whisper. "Louise is just outside."

Lynn walked to the door. "You are such a pussy, Benjy." She locked the door with one hand while unzipping her skirt with the other. She turned to him and let it fall to the floor. She was wearing nothing beneath. She pulled the T-shirt over her head and unsnapped her bra.

"Clear your desk, big boy. Miss Hoffman is here to pick up those files."

Ben cleared it.

THE RAIN FINALLY STOPPED overnight and the day dawned fresh under a cloudless sky and, more significantly, a clear forecast from the plastic RCA radio atop the toolbox in the machine shed. Will spent the morning walking the muddy fields once more with a shovel in his hand, clearing the ditches again where they were clogged with branches and debris. The heavy clay clung to his boots as he moved from field to field and he was forced to stop several times to scrape the excess off with the shovel. By the time he had his ditches and those of the Eastman farm running freely, it was noon. He finished up at Crooked Pear and walked home along the grassy riverbank, the shovel over his shoulder.

He ate a can of soup and a couple of slices of toast and then, at loose ends again, he decided to do some vacuuming. He found the old upright in the back closet where he'd pushed it after using it last a month or two ago. He vacuumed the carpet in the living room and the hallway. He didn't do a very good job but the upshot was that it didn't take him very long. When he shut the machine off, he heard a noise and looked up to see Denise standing in the doorway to the kitchen.

"Who showed you how to run a vacuum cleaner?" she asked.

"I took a correspondence course."

She smiled. "How are you, Will?"

"Never better. You?"

"I'm okay."

"Why are you here?"

She exhaled, her body language suggesting that she'd hoped things could be cordial between them. She'd perfected a martyred look long before Will had ever met her and she could turn it on like a light.

"Thought I'd pick up some things," she said. "See how you were."

"Never better."

"You said that."

He saw now that there was a carry bag on the floor behind her. He picked up the vacuum by the handle and walked past her. "Everything's where you left it," he said.

She moved out of the doorway to let him pass and watched his back for a moment. He could feel her eyes on him as he stuffed the vacuum back in the closet. When he turned to confront her, though, she was headed for the stairs and their old bedroom.

When she came down a few minutes later Will was sitting in the kitchen drinking a cup of coffee. She set the bag on the floor. He glanced at it, in that moment deciding that he couldn't care less what she'd claimed as hers.

She pulled a chair back from the table and sat on the edge of it, as people do to demonstrate they won't be staying long. Her hair was shorter, he saw now, and it was blonder than usual, puffed up to frame her face. She wore black jeans and a down vest that he'd bought her for Christmas a couple of years ago. She looked fit but then she'd always been a fanatic about working out, at least when it came to the gym. Throwing hay bales or grain bags was another matter. Apparently such activity didn't qualify as exercise and she'd always avoided it, even back in the days when she had proudly referred to herself as a farmer.

"I suppose this weather has got you in a holding pattern," he heard her say.

"Yeah," he said. He looked at her for a moment. "There's coffee on the stove."

"I had one on the way out. Thanks."

He got up and poured more for himself.

"We're having the same problem at work," she said. "I mean the weather. The excavators can't get in."

"You have a job?"

"Why ... yes." She seemed surprised by his ignorance of the fact.

"And I'm supposed to know this?" he asked.

"I'm working for Carlton Homes," she said. "I thought you would know."

"Why? Was it published somewhere?"

"No," she said flatly. "I just thought you would know. We do have mutual friends, you know. I assume that you talk to Dean and Lori, Sean and Linda."

"Not about you," he said. "So what're you doing for Carlton Homes—framing, roofing? Laying a little brick?"

"I work in the office. I basically coordinate with the contractors, interface with the local realtors, handle permits, stuff like that."

Will sipped the hot coffee. "Sounds fascinating, all that interfacing and coordinating. I had no idea you could do that."

"Well, I can," she said defensively.

"Where did you learn? You take a correspondence course?"

"Jeff's been teaching me. Jeff Carlton—he's the youngest of the brothers. And it's been amazing. I mean, to take a piece of empty farmland and create a neighborhood with families and ... I don't know ... there's a real sense of fulfillment I get from it."

"I'm getting goose bumps just hearing about it."

"All right," she said and she shook her head. "I don't know why I thought I could talk to you about this. But I'm doing something worthwhile with my life. And I love it. I absolutely love it."

"Well, you're always in love with something," Will said. "Did you get what you came for?"

"I got more than I came for, as usual," she said and she got to her feet. "What you've never been able to understand is that I need to be passionate about life. That's who I am. My life is exciting now."

"Sure. What could be more exciting than turning good farmland into instant yuppie ghettos?"

"Okay, you and I are never going to agree on this. You're stuck in the past, Will. That was always going to come between us. I can see that now. Let's not beat each other over the head with it. I got a few things from upstairs, my jewelry and stuff. My lawyer says you need to sign off on that document he sent you. Then I'll come back for the furniture and the rest."

She walked to the back door, carrying the bag.

"You're not getting the Mustang."

"My lawyer says I shouldn't discuss any of the specifics with you."

"You're not getting the Mustang."

She exhaled heavily. "This isn't a contest between us, Will. This is about what is fair. We have to be responsible people. There were promises made with regard to the car, and you know that. My lawyer says—"

"Is it necessary for you to begin every fucking sentence with 'my lawyer says'?"

"Forget it," she said. "I refuse to do this. I won't stoop to your level."

"So you draw the line at being a car thief? That's good to know."

"Fuck you, Will. I have to get back to work."

He stood up and followed her outside. She was driving a BMW that he'd never seen before. The buckskin mare was in the front pasture field and the animal came over to the fence as Denise walked to her car. Denise got in and never so much as glanced at the horse. The horse he'd bought her as a filly the year they'd been married. The horse she'd once loved as much as she now loved the construction business.

AFTER LYNN LEFT Ben put his pants back on and then fell asleep in his chair for an hour. When he woke up he was hungry so he grabbed his jacket and left, telling Louise that the GM dealership had called and told him there were complications with the transmission problems in the van. As soon as he said it, he realized that the call would have had to come in through Louise.

"They called me on my cell," he added, and he left.

He went to the drive-through at McDonald's and ordered a quarter pounder with fries and a Diet Coke. He ate behind the wheel of the Corvette, sitting in the parking lot, watching the high school kids from across the street descending on the fast-food joint like locusts. He was lucky he arrived when he did; ten minutes later and he'd have been waiting in line. The school was Roman Catholic and the boys wore gray slacks and white shirts with ties. The girls wore the classic uniform, now favored by certain strippers as well, of a white shirt, tartan skirt and knee-high socks. Some of the skirts were so short they barely covered the girls' crotches. Ben doubted that it was a look the school board had in mind when they decided to make the uniforms uniform. It worked for him though.

After he ate he took a drive to Dundas Street and headed east. He found Jose's Fitness near the intersection of Hurontario, wedged between a travel agency and a discount shoe store. There was a vacant parking spot out front. He pulled over and turned the motor off.

He really had no frame of reference for fitness centers so he didn't bother going inside. From the car he could see the front desk and a few workout machines in a room behind. There were a number of people there walking around in sweats and shorts and T-shirts. And most were women. Watching them, he began to think of Lynn on his desk a couple of hours earlier, her knees up, wearing only her high heels.

After a while he started the car and drove north to the 401, and then headed west to Waterloo. The sun was out now and the highway

was dry, although the ditches ran full and the fields beyond were
submerged in the low-lying areas. Ben set the cruise control and
cranked up the oldies station out of Toronto. The Cowsills were
singing.

Unlike Kick and Ethan, Ben had kept in contact with Jack
Dutton and the gang at McDougall's over the years. He'd looked
forward to the rare visits to the distillery when he was a kid. For
him the place had an excitement about it that the auto parts plant,
which stank of oil and grease and paint fumes, did not. Having no
interest in books, audio or otherwise, the offices at Great North
held even less appeal. But there was something satisfying, almost
magical to a ten-year-old, about the transforming of water and
grain into the clear amber liquid that was McDougall's rye. Ben
had not been athletic as a child and in general he wasn't much of a
fan of outdoor activities. But he'd been given a chemistry set one
Christmas and he'd loved the simple experiments he could do with
it. To him the distillery was a large-scale chemistry set, and for that
he kept coming back. That, and the fact that he got his whiskey
wholesale.

Ben had always felt a kinship with Jack Dutton. When he and
Kick and Ethan would be running around the plant, it was clearly
Ben whom Dutton favored. He would allow Ben to drive the tow
motor, or pretend to let him decide which rye grain was suitable
for which mix. It occurred to Ben, even then, that Kick was too
acerbic for Dutton's tastes, and that Ethan was just too young to
bother with. Dutton was a simple guy, largely uneducated, and he
was distrustful of anything he didn't already understand. He'd
decided, early on it seemed, that Ben would be his ally. And he
would be Ben's.

Today he was having a late lunch at his desk when Ben found him.
Dutton had an office, if it could be called that, off the end of the
bottling plant, a wood-and-glass-partitioned cubbyhole that

featured a few slat-back chairs and a number of antiquated oak filing cabinets. Ben had never seen the office door closed; to even attempt such a maneuver would mean the rearrangement of the cabinets and the desk itself.

"Ben," Dutton said when he saw him. He had what appeared to be a balogna sandwich in his large hands and he took a bite. There was a brown lunch bag lying open on the desk and a bottle of apple juice alongside.

"How are you, Jack?" Ben said and he sat down across from him.

Dutton nodded around the mouthful. After he swallowed he took a drink from the apple juice and then leaned back in his chair. "What are you up to, boy?"

"I won't beat around the bush, Jack. I'm concerned about Ethan and this place. I don't think he can cut the mustard."

"Muster."

"What?"

"You cut the muster. It's a military term." Jack opened the face of his sandwich. "*That* ... is mustard."

Ben dismissed the condiment with the back of his hand. "Whatever the hell it is, he can't cut it. Raney Kilbride should've put some sort of qualifier in the will. You can't just turn an operation like this over to someone without knowing what their capabilities are."

"You don't have a lot of faith in your little brother, Ben."

"That's not it, Jack. I'm here to help him any way I can." He glanced out the office door as a forklift rolled by. "By the way, he's my half-brother."

Dutton put the last of the sandwich in his mouth and then took a moment to neatly fold the lunch bag up and set it aside for, Ben had to assume, future use. "He was here yesterday," Dutton said then.

"Who was here?"

"Ethan. Who are we talking about?"

"He was *here*?"

"He was. Had a girl with him. It was the second time for her. Being here. She seems to be the brains of the outfit, for whatever that's worth. Does the talking anyway."

"What did they want?"

"To tour the plant. Least that's what she wanted. Ethan didn't say more than two words the whole time. The girl had questions. Lots of questions, about how much we produce, sales numbers, things of that nature." He had another drink of the juice. "She was asking about the bottom line too."

Ben hesitated as Dutton fished a toothpick from his shirt pocket and plopped it in his mouth. "Ethan is required to get the place turning a profit," he said. "As a condition of the will. If he doesn't get it done, he doesn't get ownership."

"Who does?" Dutton asked.

"Nobody. The company is sold, the proceeds go to charity."

"Jesus."

"Even he won't save us then, Jack."

A young woman wearing blue coveralls and a hard hat appeared in the doorway. She was carrying a walkie-talkie. "We've got a problem in shipping, Jack," she said.

"What kind of problem?"

"Truck broke down on the way to Montreal. Cornwall."

Dutton nodded to her and when she was gone he looked thoughtfully at Ben for several moments. "I got a lot of years in here, Ben."

"I wouldn't get too worried just yet," Ben said. "I think maybe the thing to do is to give Ethan and his little friend a little rope. They might use it to build a bridge to the future."

Dutton got to his feet and reached for his hard hat. "Or they might use it to hang themselves?"

"Gee, you'd hate to see a thing like that," Ben said.

EIGHT

If Susie Braddock wouldn't tell Kick where Jonah Peck lived, there was no shortage of people who would. It was common Nashville knowledge, she learned, that Peck lived on a farm about an hour east of the city.

The bartender at the Sheraton lounge knew, as did the cabdriver who had driven her back to the hotel from Susie's office. Carl also knew. Carl was a songwriter she met while having lunch at a tiny café tucked in the shadows of the Sheraton. The place was called Swing A Cat, presumably because the space was too small to do so. Kick struck up a conversation with Carl after banging elbows with him several times while both were eating. He was boyish in a way that suggested he would still be boyish in his fifties, and he had beautiful long eyelashes that marked him as an artistic type, whether he was or not. She ended up talking to him for over an hour. Carl was not a successful songwriter; he'd been trying for three years and hadn't placed a single song. He had come to the conclusion, given the current state of the genre, that his songs were either way above the bar or way below.

"I'd just like to know which," he told Kick, and then he told her that he'd be playing at a songwriters' showcase that night at Dooley's on Fifth Street. Kick decided she would stop by and check it out.

She hadn't intended on sleeping with him, right up until she did. She was doing all right until the last song of his short set. It was a simple poem about days gone by in an unknown valley in an unknown place. There was a stream and a barn full of sweet-smelling hay and a brown and white mutt named Bob. A girl in a thin cotton dress. Carl's phrasing was such that Kick wasn't sure if the song was meant to be reverential or mocking. And that—along with a persistent horniness on Kick's part of late, going back to and preceding the young cowboy in Casper—had done the trick.

They spent the night in her hotel room. The sex had been fine, swell even, and when she woke up next to the young songwriter, Kick thought that he was either one of the sweetest humans she'd ever met or the smoothest operator in the state of Tennessee. It was a question she didn't need answered. If the latter was true, his motives were probably no less noble than her own. Sometimes she simply felt like a battery that required charging.

They had breakfast in the same café where they'd met. Kick, in spite of her meager cash supply, said that she would pay.

"Oh no," Carl said. "It's on me."

"That wouldn't be right," Kick said. "You're a struggling artist."

"Actually, I have a pretty substantial trust fund," Carl told her.

Had she allowed it, the confession could have tarnished any lingering romantic emotions about their encounter. But she didn't. What the hell—even rich kids need to get laid from time to time. She let him pay and then she set out to find a car to rent for the day. It was only later that she admonished herself for not asking him if he and his trust held any interest in investing in the world of documentary film.

She discovered that a vehicle could be had pretty cheaply in Nashville, as long as the vehicle was a 1993 Fiesta with torn upholstery and a four-cylinder engine that clattered like a Singer sewing machine. The car cost twenty-nine dollars for the day. Kick had to supply the gas.

Jonah Peck's place was on the unlikely named Tater Peeler Road, about fifty miles from the city. Kick got the general directions from the big-city bartender, and the specifics from a man she found lounging on a bench near the traffic circle in the center of the little town of Lebanon.

Ten minutes out of town and she was in the hinterland, farm country and forest, the soil a startling rusty red, the fields planted in corn and oats and hay. Horses and Holsteins grazed side by side in pasture lots flecked with blue and gold wildflowers. Following directions, she turned north onto a gravel road along a rail line which itself ran parallel to a rocky creek. There was forest on either side; every now and again she would come upon a trailer in the woods, propped up on blocks, a junked car or pickup alongside. The road snaked to the east. She crossed the railroad and the stream and was soon on a narrow lane, dark as a cave from the overhanging limbs above. Chugging along in the noisy Ford beneath the ominous branches, she began to have doubts about the directions she'd received from the local in Lebanon, a man with squinty eyes and an unusually large head. Then, on the verge of entertaining an unhappy Wizard of Oz fantasy, the forest relented, the lane widened and she found herself on a newly paved road that dissected a sun-drenched meadow. A mile farther, she came upon Tater Peeler Road. The sign was a relief in itself; Kick had suspected that her leg was being pulled when she'd first heard the name.

The farms she passed were modest to the eye, the barns distinctive, high peaked, with wide doors and disproportionately large lofts above. The country grew hillier as she drove. She kept watching down the road in anticipation. She fully expected Peck's place to be some sort of hillbilly mansion with impenetrable fencing surrounding the grounds and security at the gate. Maybe a handful of feral Dobermans roaming the perimeter. When she found the place, easily enough (there was an RFD mailbox with the man's name scrawled on it), there were no guards at the gate. In fact, there was no gate, just a lane that ran through a patch of spindly pines to a farmhouse and barn on a rise.

The house looked to be a hundred years old or more, a solid two-story frame building with fading white paint and green shutters. The roof was shingled with cedar shakes. The barn was newer than the house, much newer in fact, and it was covered in steel-ribbed siding of slate gray. The barn roof was red. There was a split-rail corral off the side of the building.

A number of vehicles—pickups and station wagons and an older, rusty SUV—were parked at different angles in the drive and on the lawn. Kick parked beside the SUV, where the Fiesta would not, she reasoned, look too out of place.

When she got out of the car she heard a horse whinny and she turned to see an old man riding an Appaloosa horse at a trot around the corner of the barn, heading straight for her. The man had his head down, adjusting the stirrup, and when he looked up and saw her he quickly reined the spotted horse to a stop.

Kick, thinking she might be run over, had retreated behind the open door of the car. The man on the horse was maybe seventy. He had long gray hair tied at the back of his neck and tucked up beneath a dirty cowboy hat. He wore jeans and running shoes and a tank top that showed his gray chest hairs and his thin arms. He had a tattoo on his right biceps, a heart with someone's name etched within. The man's face was covered in gray stubble.

"Easy," the man said and Kick realized he was talking to the Appaloosa, which was fidgeting, obviously not happy with the sudden halt. "When did you get here?" the man asked. This time he seemed to be talking to her.

"Two seconds ago. Is this the Peck place?"

"It is."

"Would, um ... Jonah Peck be here?"

"Maybe," the old man said. He looked at her a long moment. "I myself haven't seen him today. You have business with him?"

Kick walked over now. She reached out to pat the Appaloosa on the withers and as she did she glanced up to get a better look at the man beneath the hat. "I do have business with him."

"What kind of business?"

"That's something I need to discuss with Mr. Peck," Kick said. "You say you haven't seen him today?"

"I have not seen Jonah Peck today."

The horse turned its head suddenly and tried to nip at Kick. The man pulled the reins as Kick moved back a step. She looked at the man again. "You haven't shaved today, have you?"

The man's hand went automatically to his chin. "Guess I haven't."

"If you had," Kick said then, "could you still say you haven't seen Jonah Peck today?"

The man took the cowboy hat off and hung it on the saddle horn. "You're a pretty smart gal. For a Yankee."

"I have my moments," Kick told him. "And I'm not even a Yankee. I'm Kathleen Eastman. My father was Everett Eastman." She reached her hand up and the man shook it, albeit reluctantly. "People who like me call me Kick," she added. "I wouldn't say the club has a huge membership, but—"

"But what? It's growing?"

She smiled. "I wouldn't say that either."

He nodded at that, as if he was taking the matter quite seriously. She saw now that his eyes, beneath craggy eyebrows, were the bluest of blues. He had a boxer's nose, although not that of a particularly successful boxer. The skin hung loosely on his neck. His forearms and shoulders were thin, his chest sunken.

"I reckon I know why you're here," he said then and he put the hat back on and pulled it low over his brow. "And I reckon I should tell you that Susie Braddock is the woman you need to talk to. But then you're gonna tell me you already have. How am I doing so far?"

"Right on the money."

He nodded again, rather unhappily this time, she thought. He reined the horse around so he faced the barn. "Billy!" he shouted.

The horse jumped when he yelled and so did Kick.

"I'm about to take Patsy here for a run," he said then. "My hired man will show you around while I'm gone and when I get back you and I can set on the porch there and talk. You ain't gonna learn nothing you don't already know but you found your way out here in that little rattletrap of a car and you at least deserve some courtesy. That and the fact that I have an agreement with your father, Miss Eastman."

"You can call me Kick."

"No thanks."

Billy, the hired hand, was in fact a hired boy. No more than thirteen, Kick was to learn that he lived at the farm next door and came over a couple times a week to muck stalls or throw bales. He was a stocky kid and about as verbose as Harpo Marx. He gave Kick a ten-cent tour of the barn and the grounds and finally, the house itself. There was hardly any furniture inside and, aside from a high-ceilinged room on the ground floor that housed a grand piano and about two dozen guitars, the place was hardly the opulent palace that Kick had expected of a country music legend. Of course, the fact that the legend was bankrupt might have been a factor in these dashed expectations.

After the tour, Billy said that he had work to do at home and he left Kick in the music room. After a while she sat down at the piano and began running scales. Soon she moved on to Strauss, a little of which she remembered from her childhood lessons. Strauss made way for whatever Mozart she had retained. She grew bored with the classical, though, and was soon tapping out "Itsy Bitsy Spider" on the keys, and singing it to boot. Kick had no voice, and even if she did it was not a song that would serve as much of a showcase. As such, she was dismayed to look up and see Jonah Peck standing in the doorway.

"We'll go to the porch," he said.

He led the way through the house and out the front door. There were rocking chairs on the porch, and a wicker settee with cushions of tartan plaid. Peck looked at his watch as Kick sat down in one of the rockers. "Well, it's got to be noon somewhere. How about a beer?"

"I'm fine," she said.

"I didn't ask how you were. I asked if you wanted a beer."

"No, thank you."

"Oh, come on. One beer ain't gonna hurt."

In the face of his determination, she shrugged. "Why not?"

He came back with a longneck Coors and a glass for her and a diet soda for himself. "I though *we* were having a beer," Kick said.

"I haven't had a drink in nine years," he said.

"Let me guess," Kick said. "One was too many and a thousand weren't enough?"

He shook his head. "Wasn't that so much."

"As what?"

"I was a real prick when I was drunk."

Kick put the glass on the floor and drank from the bottle. "Well, I guess the important thing is that you came to that realization."

"There were quite a number of people kind enough to point it out to me. Mostly wives, at first, and hell … I could divorce them. Then everybody else got in on the act. I quit drinking to shut 'em all up."

Kick smiled and had another sip. Across the yard, the Appaloosa was trotting back and forth along the railing of the corral, head up, watching them intently. There was another horse, a bay, standing along the fence, looking off in the direction of Tater Peeler Road.

"Look at her," Peck said, watching the mare. "She's jealous."

"Of what?" Kick asked.

"You. She don't like another woman around the place. She took a bite outta Susie Braddock the other week."

"Well, I'm not going to hold that against her," Kick said.

He turned in the chair to look at her, his head pulled back. "How'd you find me anyway? Susie didn't tell you."

"Found this talkative dude in a place called Lebanon, sitting on a bench near the roundabout in the center of town."

Jonah's eyes narrowed. "Old buzzard, in bib coveralls? A head like a punkin?"

"It might have been in the gourd family. You know him?"

"Jem Newhouse. Got it in for me. Tells everybody who'll listen that I'm in breach of promise. Stemming over a situation with his daughter."

"Maybe you'd rather not talk about it," Kick said.

"The only thing I ever promised the woman was that she'd have a good time. I never heard any complaint on that account." Jonah took a drink of the pop. "So why are you here?"

"Looking for a progress report."

"Way I heard it, Susie gave you a progress report over the phone. You showing up here makes me think you might be suspicious about something. Or somebody."

"I own Great North Music," Kick told him. "Now I'm not gonna pretend that I know anything about the music world." She paused and took another drink, still watching the fitful mare. "But I do know a little bit about the real world. And in the real world, you spend a quarter million dollars on something, there should be something to show for it."

"What are you talking about?"

"I'm talking about NIC," Kick said. "You guys are calling it the Nothing Is Certain project? Well, I'm thinking about renaming it the Nothing Is Happening project."

"Back up the truck, lady. What's this about a quarter million?"

"That's what Great North has invested so far. You're not aware of this?"

"I ain't aware of it … and I don't believe it," Peck said. "We haven't bought a single song, or as much as stepped foot in the studio yet. What did Susie tell you?"

"She told me she would—at some point—show me the numbers on the expenditures to date." Kick tipped the longneck back. "She also told me I was a tadpole."

"That sounds like Susie."

"Oh yeah, she's a pip."

Peck leaned back in the rocker, in an effort, Kick suspected, to conceal the fact that he was looking at her legs. She crossed them and turned toward him. "So where is the $250,000?"

"Sitting somewhere, would be my guess," Jonah said. "It's likely you've got yourself all worked up about nothing."

"No offense, Mr. Peck," Kick said then. "But this whole project came into existence because my father heard that you owe something like twelve million dollars in back taxes to the U.S. government. Is that correct?"

"Give or take a million."

Kick nodded and looked out at the horses in the corral again. "Well now. In light of that, a cynical person might find irony in the suggestion that I should trust your bookkeeping instincts on this. A cynical person might suggest that your bookkeeping instincts are a tad inconsistent. If you can consider twelve million dollars a tad, that is."

Saying it, she was fully prepared to suffer the old man's wrath. Instead, he laughed. In fact, he actually removed the cowboy hat and slapped it on his knee a couple of times. Kick waited, assuming that he would have something to say when he finished laughing and slapping. He never did.

"I can see that the mention of staggering debt just tears you up inside," Kick said.

"Well, what're you gonna do? Sometimes, there ain't nothing to do about life but to sit back and laugh at it."

A kindred spirit, Kick thought. Just what she needed. "Tell me something, Jonah Peck. I once owed the city of Toronto eight hundred dollars in unpaid parking tickets. I don't know how that happened. It just did. But how the hell does a man fall behind twelve million dollars' worth?"

"I hear what you're saying," Peck said. "And I'll tell you it really shook my faith in my government. What the hell are those boys in Washington doing, that they let a country picker like me run up that kind of bill? I had half a mind to sue those bastards for incompetence."

Kick smiled in spite of herself. If she'd had a hat, she'd have slapped it on her knee. "Seriously though."

Peck drank the rest of his pop and placed the can on the porch railing. "I just trusted the wrong people," he said. "They claim it was bad investments, but I know for certain that people were stealing from me. But that ain't nobody's fault but my own. I'm the one hired them."

"And you really owe twelve million?"

"I paid some of it off. I sold pretty much everything I owned at auction. Including this place. I got money coming in from royalties every month so I'm keeping ahead of the interest, if nothing else."

"You don't own this place?"

"No, ma'am. The government forced me to hold an auction." He gave her a narrow look, as if deciding if she could be trusted. "We kinda pulled a fast one on 'em. My friends bought most everything up and are holding on to it for me. I'll pay 'em all back eventually. But I don't own a hell of a lot these days."

A phone began to ring inside the house. Peck put his hat on— apparently he wasn't a man to answer a phone bareheaded—and went inside. Kick stood and walked to the top of the stairs that led to the front walkway. She leaned against the post there and looked out over the farm that didn't belong to Jonah Peck.

Beyond the barn was an open pasture field through which a shallow creek meandered. Past the field was a rocky area, from which the stream sprang, and beside it was a meadow spotted with evergreens and shrub. There was a small herd of what appeared to be beef cattle gathered in the shade of the trees. The herd looked fat and contented on their graze. Kick wondered if Peck didn't own them either.

A moment later she heard the screen door swing open and close behind her. "I'd say we got a little off topic," Peck said as he approached. "That was Susie Braddock on the phone. She tells me you're looking to pull the plug on the record deal."

Kick turned. "Who'd she hear that from?"

"She claims you."

"She's a liar."

Peck nodded slowly. "You're not the first one to suggest that."

"What's her story anyway?"

"I don't know the woman very well. It was your guy Steward hired her. She's a successful producer, been the big dog the last couple years, I'll give her that. And I guess it's country music but it ain't exactly my country music."

"Just so you know, I'm not about to renege on my father's deal," Kick said. "I'd just like to know why it's spinning its wheels. I make documentary films, Mr. Peck, and I'm in need of a little capital myself these days. Now it seems to me that the intent of this record is to make you a lot of money. If that happens, then it's going to make Great North a lot of money too, so I'm all in favor of that. But apparently to do that we're going to need a record. Where is it?"

"I signed to do an album of original songs," Peck said. "Can't do it without songs."

"I was checking you out on the internet," Kick said. She smiled. "That's how I recognized you when you were pretending to be somebody else. There's a consensus out there that you are one of the greatest songwriters in the history of country music."

"*Was*, I'm afraid."

"You've got writer's block, is that it?"

Peck took his thumb and his forefinger and squeezed the crease in the brim of his hat. He had a pained expression on his face. "Susie's gonna supply the songs. Taking longer than I figured."

"If there's anything I can do to help speed that along, let me know," Kick said.

"Don't take this the wrong way, but I believe Itsy Bitsy Spider's been recorded to death." He pointed a thin finger at her. "But don't look down your nose at country. Who do you listen to anyway?"

"I'm kind of partial to the Gershwins, and Cole Porter. Nat King Cole does it for me sometimes too, depending on my mood."

"They're all dead," Peck said. "But if you can figure out a way to get one of 'em to write you a song, I'll be glad to give it a listen."

Kick started down the steps. "I'll see what I can do. Maybe I'll hold a séance. But I do have other things on my plate."

Peck walked to the edge of the porch. "Like what?"

"Like finding out what happened to my $250,000."

BLAINE STEWARD, like most people, never really considered how smoothly his life was humming along until he found his rails suddenly greased. And as of late, they had been most thoroughly greased. Everett Eastman effectively engineered the lubrication by breathing his last and, in doing so, handing the oil can over to Kathleen. Now, with his production scaled back and Kathleen on the loose in Nashville, Steward was feeling, for the first time in twenty-odd years, that he was no longer in control of what had been a cozy little existence at Great North AudioBooks. The call from Ben Eastman that morning, saying that he was stopping by for a visit, did nothing to alleviate that feeling.

Ben had put on at least thirty pounds in the years since Steward had seen him last, and he carried himself with a careless, lumbering confidence that Steward, who'd always remembered him as a mouthy yet insecure brat, did not recognize. And neither did Ben bother with small talk these days.

"I won't beat around the bush, Blaine," he said. "I'm worried about Kathleen and this place. Frankly, I don't think she can cut the muster."

"I'm not sure I know what you mean by that" was Steward's slow response.

"It's a military term. What's Kick know about audio books?"

"She hasn't actually indicated that she intends to run it."

"No? What has she indicated?"

Steward walked around his desk and sat down. "I don't know that I'm at liberty to discuss this with you." He nodded toward a chair. "Sit down, Ben."

"I'm not here to sit down," Ben said. It seemed he was assuming the unlikely guise of a man of action. "And I think it's in your best interests to discuss this with me. I might just be the one to pull your fat out of the fire if this thing goes sour."

"Why would it go sour?"

"You tell me. Tell me what Kathleen is up to, because I know Kathleen. She's definitely up to something."

"Well," Steward said uncertainly. "I can tell you that she's in Nashville."

"What's in Nashville?"

"Great North has that record deal with Jonah Peck, remember? That's where the producer is. Peck too, I guess."

"Sorry. I don't subscribe to Cornpone Monthly magazine. So Kick's down there to try to get the record made."

"She, um—" Steward began. "I have a feeling she's going to try to stop the deal. She thinks the money earmarked for the record would be better suited for her, uh … endeavors in documentary filmmaking."

"Is that what you think?" Ben said. "You're wrong. Kick wants to make the record."

"She does?"

"She has to. Question is—can she do it? Has Great North got the money?"

Steward shrugged. "Your father set this thing up, and he supplied the money out of his own pocket. So it's never really mattered to me one way or the other. I could care less if it ever gets made."

"What if they come to Great North for more money?"

"They're not going to get it. They know that, or they should. They'll either make the record for the $250,000 or they won't. I suppose if your father was still alive, they could go to him for more money. But he's not."

"I'm aware of that. Kick could give it to them. She's the boss now."

"I can't see that happening. I still think she'd like to kill the thing off."

Ben moved to plop his bulk into the chair offered earlier. "Don't be too sure about that. She gets down there with those celebrity types and she might forget all about making boring documentary films about fucking dog sleds and starving Africans. She's probably already bought cowboy boots and a ten-gallon hat."

"What are you saying?"

"You know what she's like. Fucking Bohemian kook. She gets her mind set on something and there's no stopping her. Like when she went to South America to shoot that rain forest movie. She spent every last nickel she had on that thing. When it comes to growing up around money, there are two kinds of people, Blaine. I'm the first kind—I understand money. I know how to make it and I know the proper way to spend it. Kick's the other kind—money to her is like sand on a beach. She has no concept of what it is. I'd be worried, if I were you."

"What the hell can I do?" Steward asked. "All of a sudden, I'm just another employee around here."

"All I'm saying is I'd be worried," Ben said. "Kick could go on a spending spree down in Kentucky with Great North's money."

"What's in Kentucky?"

"Nashville," Ben said. "You forget where she is?"

"Nashville's in Tennessee."

"Kentucky, Tennessee ... doesn't fucking matter. You want to listen to me on this or you want to give me a geography lesson?"

"I want things to be the way they were."

"Of course you do," Ben said. "You've done a good job all these years too, Blaine. This isn't right, what's happening. But you know— I think the thing to do is to give her a little rope."

"Really?" Steward asked. "You're thinking she'll come around?"

"Probably not. But we have to give her the opportunity. I mean, I want to be fair here."

"Oh, so do I," Blaine said quickly.

Ben got to his feet and walked to the doorway before looking back. "In the long run, though, I'm afraid it's going to be up to you and me to save this place."

THE RAIN FINALLY STOPPED, as everyone knew it would, even the people who'd spent the past month or so asking, "Is this rain ever going to stop?"

The days that followed could not have been more beneficial for the farmers. The temperature went up sharply and a drying wind came out of the southwest. The creeks and streams subsided, leaving a tangled debris of leaves and twigs and branches scattered where the water had risen. The Grand River began to slow, and then to drop, and finally to clear.

Will got on the ground Thursday morning and worked for five days straight, sowing corn and barley on his own farm and then putting in a hundred acres of soybeans on another farm he leased on the third line. He finished up with the acreage at Crooked Pear, planting the entire two hundred acres in beans as well. He and Dalton worked through the weekend, running the seed drill by moonlight, and by late Monday afternoon the planting was done. It was getting dark as Dalton drove the bean compacter off the Eastman farm, heading for Will's, while Will ran the last of the ditches with the little Massey Ferguson.

Running the V-blade across the headland by the bush, he scared a half dozen turkeys out of his wheat field to the east and then, while cutting a trough toward Willis Creek, he saw Ethan kneeling in a clearing in the brush. Will ran the ditch to the creek then turned around and headed over. Despite the noise of the tractor, Ethan was absorbed enough in his task that he didn't look up until Will was practically on top of him. There was no fence to separate the two farms at this point and when Will stopped, he stood up in the tractor to determine just whose property they were on, his or Everett Eastman's. Then he looked at Ethan, who was now standing, his hands plunged in the pockets of his dirty-kneed cargo pants. Will looked past him to where a dozen or so scrawny sprouts were stuck in the dirt.

"I got nothing against a little marijuana for recreational purposes," Will said. "But it appears that those sorry-looking plants might be on my farm. If I get busted on a cultivation rap I'll cut your nuts off and feed 'em to my barn cats, Ethan."

"Businessmen they drink my wine, plowmen dig my earth," Ethan replied. "None of them along the line know what any of it is worth."

Will nodded. "Just so you know."

"Hey," Ethan said as Will reached for the ignition switch. "What's the pH factor of the soil here?"

"*High Times* magazine doesn't have a help column?" Will asked. He hesitated when Ethan didn't reply. "It varies along the valley. Sometimes I have to spread lime to bring it up, but it's usually about six. I'm not sure I should be telling you this."

Ethan smiled and flashed him a peace sign.

Heading back to the home farm, Will saw the girl Janey wandering around behind the big barn at Crooked Pear. Looking for Ethan,

Will decided, probably worried about him with nightfall coming. Well, it had nothing to do with him and he kept going. A couple hundred yards along, he turned back. She was heading toward the ice shack when she heard him coming, and she stopped and waited for him in the freshly tilled field.

"He's in the back forty," Will said.

"Oh?"

"Planting dope by the bush."

"Oh."

She was wearing a skirt and a T-shirt with a denim jacket over it. Some sort of clog things on her feet, not exactly ideal for traipsing around a farm. Her hair was hanging loose to her shoulders. He hadn't noticed the day of the reading how small she was. Her wrists were thin as reeds, her skin almost translucent. A slip of a girl. She didn't want to look at Will, it seemed. She seemed shy and out of place, not knowing what to say or where to cast her eye. He shut the tractor off.

"So how's it going?" he asked. "I heard you and Ethan had a tour of the distillery."

She looked at him now. "How did you hear that?"

"Jack Dutton called me."

"Why would he do that?" Her tone was sharp and Will considered that she might not be so shy after all.

"He had questions about the will. He thought I might be able to help him out. I'm the executor."

"I know that."

She looked toward the bush as she said it and Will turned in the tractor seat to see that Ethan was now making his way back, wandering languidly along the old lane, hands behind his back, his face lifted upward toward the setting sun. He looked like a child in an old-world painting, carefree and happy, safely cocooned from the big bad world out there. Will thought for a moment that, at heart at least, maybe that's just what he was. On the other hand, there was ample evidence that he was an addled pothead.

"What kind of questions?" he heard her say.

"Ethan-related questions," Will said.

"That your polite way of saying none of my fucking business?" Janey asked.

"I had no idea I had such a mouth on me," Will said. "Dutton wanted to know exactly what's required of Ethan with regard to the will. He said he didn't get a lot of information out of him the day you guys were there."

"We were just looking around." She shrugged. "Did you tell Dutton that Ethan has to turn the place around?"

"Not in so many words," Will said. "I figure that's between Ethan and Dutton. Did Ethan tell him?"

"Ethan didn't have a lot to say."

"And sometimes he does?" Will looked at her profile until she turned to him. "Have a lot to say, that is."

She smiled at him. She had a wonderful smile that seemed to change her. It expanded her features, made her sexier, more substantial. It took Will off guard. "You have to be able to … interpret. He's been going through some changes."

"Yeah?"

She hesitated. "He's been on and off prescription drugs for over ten years. Prozac and lithium and all the rest. He's decided to go it without for a while. You go ten years without anything positive happening, it's time to change tactics. Don't you think?"

Will nodded. "So the two of you thinking of going into the whiskey business?"

She shrugged her thin shoulders again, holding the smile, as if she knew its effect. "Might be interesting. I've been researching a little on the net. The liquor business has got a lot going for it. For one thing, it's not about to go out of fashion anytime soon."

Will glanced at the slowly approaching Ethan. "Does your boyfriend feel the same way?"

"Boyfriend. Haven't heard that one in a while."

"What's the preferred term these days?" Will asked. "Partner? Sounds like you're rounding up cattle."

"It does. What about significant other?"

"Really?"

"Fuck it. Call him my boyfriend if you want. Ethan doesn't know what he wants to do. He's a musician at heart. That doesn't mean he can make a living from it. I figure he can be a musician and a distiller too. I can help out."

"With the music, or the distilling?"

"Having fun, aren't you?" Janey said. "You think I'm an opportunist, is that it? Let me tell you this—I've been with Ethan for almost two years. Until a couple weeks ago I didn't know anything about his family. He didn't talk about them, I mean not one fucking word. Now all of a sudden he's got family coming out of his ears. There's an obnoxious brother and a gorgeous filmmaker sister and a dead eccentric dad. Oh yeah, and a cool housekeeper with melt-in-your-mouth cookies coming out of the oven. And of course, it turns out that the father already gave away his millions. So if I'm an opportunist, Mr. Executor, I'm not very good at it. If I was, I'd have shown up here when the big money was still around. Make sense to you?"

"I guess so. As much as anything." He gestured toward Ethan. "What's with the gibberish?"

"He's just goofing," Janey said. "I think it's his way of keeping the world at bay until he gets straightened out. There is a story behind it though. Do you know the Dylan song 'When the Ship Comes In'?"

"No. I was more into the headbanger stuff, back when I was planting my own dope by the bush."

"Well, we were on this little pontoon boat crossing the Georgia Strait about a month ago. Maybe two dozen people, on a party run.

Heading home, and a storm blows up suddenly. One of the pontoons sprang a leak and it got very scary very quickly. I thought we were going down and so did everybody else, including the guy operating the thing. He was actually crying. All of a sudden Ethan starts strumming his guitar and singing the Dylan song." She hesitated, then began to sing—"*Oh, the fishes will laugh as they swim out of the path, and the seagulls they'll be smiling. And the rocks on the sand will proudly stand, the hour that the ship comes in.*" She smiled up at Will as she finished. "And man, he's playing the shit out of that guitar and he's singing the song and when he finishes—it's a long song too—he starts again. And I swear, everybody kinda chilled out and got their shit together. One guy took over from the operator and it seemed like the storm eased up a little too. Anyway—next thing you know, we're pulling into shore."

On the tractor, Will tugged at his ear lobe. "He saved you with the song?"

"All I'm saying is that we're here. Don't knock it, man."

"I'm not knocking it."

"He's coming around," she said. Ethan was close now, probably close enough to hear her, which was what she wanted, Will suspected. "I think he realizes that there's life to live beyond Mr. Zimmerman. Hey honey—how was your walk?"

"It's all just a dream, babe, a vacuum, a scheme, babe, that sucks you into feelin' like this," Ethan told her.

Janey looked at Will. "But then you just never know," she said. "Come on, Ethan. Johanna was baking something when I left."

They walked away, arm in arm, through the gate and up the back lawn to the house as the sun fell to the horizon. Will watched them for a bit, and then started the Massey and headed home. Dalton was waiting for him in the machine shed, drinking a beer while he removed the front tire from the big John Deere. Will ran the Massey inside and parked beside the John Deere.

"Got a bearing barking," Dalton said, removing the lug nuts with the impact wrench. "Thought maybe you broke down yourself."

"I stopped to talk to Ethan's girlfriend," Will said.

"Little blonde girl, walking around the barn?" Dalton asked. "I wondered who that was. Looked like she was lost."

Will stepped in and the two of them lifted the heavy wheel off the hub. They rolled it over to lean against the wall.

"Well, was she?" Dalton asked.

"Lost?" Will asked. "No. Ethan maybe. But not her."

BEN SPENT MOST OF THE DAY in the sand or in the water. They were playing twenty-dollar Nassau with automatic presses and standing on the eighteenth tee, and he knew he was down two hundred and forty dollars. There was a pond along the left side of the fairway about two hundred yards out. Ben hadn't hit a good drive all day, so he figured he was way past due. He took the oversized Taylor Made driver from the bag.

"What am I down?" he asked. "Hundred and eighty?"

"Two-forty," Teddy Brock said. "Nice try."

"Fuck it, double or nothing," Ben said and he pulled the club back and hit a screaming hook into the middle of the pond.

Teddy put his driver back in the bag and hit a long iron off the tee. He knocked his second shot just short of the green and then got up and down from there for a par. Ben's double bogey ran his debt to a little under five hundred dollars. In the clubhouse afterward, Teddy bought the drinks.

"I don't know why I play this game," Ben said. They were sitting at a corner table.

"I don't know why you play it like you do," Teddy said. "Pay up."

The waitress brought the drinks. She was new to the club, a blonde of ample proportions and shy manner. Watching as Teddy signed for the round, Ben had a thought. "Bill me for it."

"What?"

"Send Eastman Technologies a bill for the four-eighty," Ben said. "I'll pay you out of the company funds. Call it legal costs for whatever."

"Fuck you. Then it's on *my* books. It's income."

"It is income."

"It's golf income and I'm not paying tax on it. Get your wallet out."

Ben paid, but he waited until the waitress brought the second round before he did, peeling off the five hundred-dollar bills in front of her and then sliding them across the table to Teddy Brock.

"Keep the change," he said and he smiled at the waitress. "Lawyers. Always got their hand in your pocket."

Teddy tucked the bills away and then flipped a twenty back as the waitress departed. "You're pathetic, you know that?"

"See the rack on her?" Ben asked. "Whoever does the hiring around here deserves a pat on the head."

Teddy got up and grabbed the remote control from the next table over and turned on the big screen television at the far end of the room. He flipped through the channels until he found the PGA tour stop of the week. He watched maybe a minute of golf, then three minutes of commercials. He hit the mute button.

"Speaking of racks," he said then. "Did you move on that gym you had me check out for your girlfriend?"

"She's not my girlfriend," Ben said. "She's just a friend."

"Really? She told me you paid for her boob job. That's pretty generous. You know, for a friend."

"What? Jesus, I can't believe she told you that."

"She didn't," Teddy said. He smiled as he picked up his fresh rum and Seven. "I just had a hunch, the day you introduced us. You're like the sun coming up in the west, Ben. What'd that run you?"

Thinking of Lynn's breasts, Ben could sulk for only so long. "Less than my plasma flat screen," he said smiling. "And, entertainment-wise, a much better investment. Worth every penny."

"So you buying her the fitness place?"

"I'm not buying her anything."

"So the tits are rentals?"

"You're a fucking riot. I'm taking care of the down payment. She needed twenty-five percent, because it's commercial. So I'm helping out."

"You're a heck of a guy, Ben."

"Hey, I do what I can. And I expect so little in return."

"Just sex."

"I prefer to call it companionship. My wife doesn't understand me." He sucked at his vodka and tonic like it was mother's milk.

Teddy caught the waitress's eye and held up two fingers. "Does that mean you're still getting a divorce?"

Ben shrugged. "Oh, yeah. The question is when. It's a tough call. I'd do it today if Meredith would consider a buyout, lump-sum type of deal. And she might. She's not into money that much. She didn't even care that the old man gave all his away. Imagine that. What I'm afraid of is what happens if she gets to talking with her girlfriends, especially the divorced ones, and they start telling her you gotta do this, you gotta do that. You know how fucking bitter divorced women are. Next thing I know she's got some asshole top-gun lawyer and I'm strung up by my thumbs in the town square with my pockets hanging inside out."

"Have you ever discussed this with her?" Teddy asked.

"Oh no. She thinks everything's cool."

Teddy shook his head. The drinks arrived and he signed for them again while Ben smiled up at the waitress.

"What's your name?" he asked.

"Vanessa."

"You a farm girl?"

She frowned. "No. Why?"

"Just wondered." He watched her walk away, then turned to Teddy. "On the other hand, if things work out with the distillery and Great North, I might be further ahead to get out of the marriage now. I'd rather give her half of right now than half of down the road."

"What do you mean—if things work out?"

"The way I see it, Ethan's got as much of a chance of making McDougall profitable as I have of winning the Masters. He couldn't run a lemonade stand. And the only thing Kick's interested in is her whacko liberal documentaries that nobody ever sees. There's a chance she could meet her challenges, but the thing is, she doesn't want to. She'd just as soon take what cash she can get her hands on and vamoose."

"Where do you come in?"

"You tell me. I'm thinking that all I have to do is tell the both of them that these conditions are impractical. And if they let me, I'll challenge the will on that basis."

"What basis?"

"That the old man wasn't competent. Thing is, for me to step in and save the day, I'm gonna want fifty-one percent of the distillery and Great North. Think about it. If you were Ethan, wouldn't you love to hear you get half of McDougall and you don't have to do squat to get it?"

"Maybe," Teddy said. "If he's as out of it as you say. But Kick doesn't have his problems. How would you convince her?"

"Kick has her own problems. According to Steward, there's some question about the money for this stupid country album. Questions about just where the fuck it is. And there's no more money to follow. Kick might jump at the chance to get out from under it."

Teddy watched the golf on the screen while Ben talked. "Disregarding for the moment the daunting task of having a dead man declared mentally incompetent," he said now, "what would you do with the companies? If this worked, that is?"

"That's the easiest part. I just revert back to the status quo. Tell captain Jack Dutton and blubbering Blaine Steward to carry on."

"But the distillery is losing money."

Ben smiled. "Is it now?"

"All right, I don't want to know," Teddy said. "So you get controlling interest in all three companies, and the companionship of Miss Implants, and live happily ever after."

Ben took a drink of vodka. "Hey, it's not the thirty million I was counting on from the old man, but it's the best of a bad situation. Get the numbers running consistently and sell off everything in a few years. I'll put the run on that fucking Johanna too, then I can sell the house and the farm." He leaned back in his chair, fingers interlocked behind his head, a man of leisure. "Then I buy a place on Hilton Head, devote myself to my golf game so I can kick your ass at Harbortown when you come to visit."

Teddy lifted the remote and, weary of the ads, clicked the golf off. "It's a wonderful dream you have, Ben. Heartwarming, in fact. If only you had some nuns to torture or some orphans to evict—I'm sure the folks at Disney would be interested."

"Tell 'em to give me a call," Ben said.

He was half in the bag as he drove home from the course. It was rush hour on the highway, but rush hour around Caledon never really amounted to much. For Ben, the town itself had never really amounted to much either. They'd moved there after Ben Junior was born eleven years earlier, right around the time that Ben had convinced his father to make him CEO of the automotive plant. Until that point, they'd lived in a high-rise north of Oakville, near Glen Abbey, where Ben had been a member. With the new baby, and the new responsibilities at work, Ben had persuaded his father that he needed a house with a yard and a swing set. Everett, the absolute world champion of absentee fathers, had for some reason agreed with him, and had paid for the place in Caledon. Looking back now, Ben could see that that day marked the beginning of his father's change in attitude toward his family. The change never extended to any actual displays of affection from the old man—he would have had to live a hundred and fifty years for that—but that was okay as far as Ben was concerned. He'd never shared a single intimate moment with his father and he would have been horrified to start at the age of thirty. He was perfectly content to have the old man plunk down four hundred grand for the Tudor-style house on Brant Road. Who needs intimacy when four baths and a three-car garage are available?

But the town was a disappointment. It was a place of money, of tight-ass retirees and film people and high-end horse farms. Ben had never felt welcome. He'd joined Caledon Golf and Country Club his first year there and had never been received by the membership as anything other than an outsider. He'd tried to organize an Eastman Technologies golf tournament early on and was told that the club would rather not entertain such activities, the suggestion being that he should take his scramble to a public course somewhere, where blue-collar duffers would feel more at home.

Meredith, on the other hand, had managed to fit right into the community. She was an outgoing woman by nature, but more than that she was a woman who quite instinctively saw past an individual's shortcomings to discover something worthwhile in everyone. After all, she had married Ben. She'd made dozens of friends over the years. Ben suspected that her success in social situations was due, even more than her generous nature, to her willingness to spend time with people who passed hours discussing fascinating topics like gardens and schools and the placement of traffic lights. And of course, children—the raising of snotty miniature millionaires seemed to be the sole reason for existence for most of the women he'd met in the area. Meredith had also served on a grassroots committee that had managed to chase a proposed landfill out of the area. Ben would be damned if he'd go to those lengths just to make a few friends. He had plenty, or at least enough, friends.

Junior was in the front yard when he pulled in, playing catch with Wilson, who was wearing Ben's own ball glove, the brand-new Rawlings he'd bought last year and never actually used yet, although he kept promising Junior that they'd go to the park and toss the ball around. He felt a twinge of ire seeing the old black man using the glove, and then one of jealousy. He thought for a moment of taking over from the gardener but then knew better than to try. Ben had never been any good at baseball—he threw underhand as a rule— and after the six or seven vodkas he'd downed at the club, he'd be lucky to hit the side of the house, let alone Junior's mitt.

"Dad," Junior said when he got out of the car. "Wilson can throw a curveball."

"Good for Wilson," Ben said. He made a point of smiling at the old voodoo man to deflect any implied sarcasm.

"He's gonna teach me, when my hand gets bigger. Then I can teach you."

"Sounds like a plan," Ben said and he walked through the garage and went into the house. Meredith was in the front room, flipping through a magazine and drinking a bottle of water. "Hey," she said. "What's new?"

"Wilson can throw a curveball," Ben said.

"So I heard. Pretty exciting."

"Isn't it though?"

"Louise has been trying to get you. Where's your cell?"

"It was off." Ben was standing by the French doors, watching the game of catch in the yard.

"Interfere with your putting, does it?"

"Matter of fact, it does. What's your problem?"

"It was just a joke."

"Right. Good one."

"I don't have a problem, Ben," she said. "But apparently Louise does. With a contract? Something about the Toyota contract. Ignition something, is that it?"

He turned to her. "I have no idea. I'll take care of it in the morning." He walked through the archway into the kitchen and began to make himself a drink. There was no tonic in the fridge; after searching noisily through the cupboards, he found a bottle in the space below the island.

"Oh, not much," he heard Meredith say from the other room. He thought for a moment she was talking to someone else. "Dropped Benny at school, did the grocery shopping. Had lunch with Nicole. We're thinking of taking the kids to Manitoulin Island this summer; her family has a cottage there. Then Wilson and I dug up the old rose bushes out back and planted the new Sir Edwards. Tomorrow we're thinking of car-bombing Queen's Park."

Ben came out of the kitchen carrying his drink. Meredith was still sitting on the couch, looking at the fireplace while she talked. Now she turned to him.

"You know, same old stuff." She smiled. "I assume you were going to ask."

She let the smile fade and when she did he took his drink into the room she referred to as his den. He sat down and kicked his shoes off and then turned on the TV. The golf was still on but it was raining now. The players were sloshing down the fairways under umbrellas, looking miserable and put out. Ben watched them, feeling a kinship, as he sipped his drink. Before the glass was empty, he was asleep in the chair.

NINE

Kick had anticipated being in Nashville for a day, or maybe two at the most. She should have known better. She was certain there'd been times in her life when things had gone off without a hitch. She was also certain that she couldn't name such a time if someone were to hold a gun to her head.

She should have considered that when packing a bag back at Crooked Pear. Now she found herself running out of clean clothes rather quickly. With her cash supply dwindling and little inclined in any event to splurge on zircon-encrusted Faith Hill T-shirts, she was soon washing things out in the sink in her hotel room.

Oddly enough, though, the city was growing on Kick. Like most tourist towns, Nashville had a very specific and genuine heartbeat beneath the cheap veneer. One needed only to retreat a few blocks from the glitzy downtown to find it. Not to say that there wasn't a certain perverse charm to be found in the souvenir shops and the merchandise therein. Kick had lived with a guy during her second year of university at McGill, a journalism major who was, ironically enough, almost illiterate. One of his prized possessions had been the classic print of dogs playing poker. When they'd split up that summer he'd bequeathed the art to Kick, perhaps in apology for being a first-class shit. Kick, who had always hated the picture, had found herself unable to throw it away.

She was beginning to feel that way about Nashville. Of course, when she graduated and left the apartment, she had no qualms about leaving the card-playing dogs behind. She had a sneaking suspicion she would feel that way about Nashville too.

She waited for Susie Braddock to get back to her and while she waited she checked out the museums and the art galleries, the ones that offered free admission anyway. She paid to tour the Country Music Hall of Fame where she became fascinated with A.P. Carter, even buying a CD of his songs, despite the fact that she had no way to play it. She ran along the Cumberland River. She ate catfish at the Crab Shack.

She had her laptop with her, and every morning she went online and searched for developments on the situation in Wyoming. The *Casper Star* had a website, as did the *Gillette Citizen*. There wasn't a lot to be learned. Stanley Dawe's case was not yet scheduled for trial. Kick was certain that the drilling was ongoing. The filmmaker in her hoped that things would remain quiet for the time being. Maybe the story had slipped beneath the radar to the extent that she could still be the first to get Dawe on tape once she extracted herself from the situation at hand. There was a part of her, however, that would delight in hearing that another rancher had reached for his Winchester.

She'd called Blaine Steward after resigning herself to the fact that she was going to be there for a few days and told him that she needed a credit card in the name of Great North. Judging by his reaction, she might just as well have asked for one of his virgin daughters to sacrifice. After being reminded again who was in charge he had very reluctantly agreed to make whatever changes were needed at the accounting end to afford her signing privileges and then to forward the card to the Sheraton. Kick didn't mention that the hotel room would be the first thing on the card. Waiting for Blaine Steward was a little like waiting for Susie Braddock. Kick was pretty sure that they both wished she would just go away. The truth was, she was all in favor of the idea herself, but only on her terms. She hadn't asked for any of this. If her mother had had the good sense to sleep with somebody else thirty-five years ago, then Kick would right now still be in Wyoming, trying to come up with enough cash to shine a klieg light on AmCom and the indiscriminate drilling. Of course, she didn't know that to be true either. If her mother had allowed a different man to impregnate her it would follow that Kick would be a different person. She hadn't gotten much from Everett, but she was certain she was whoever she was as a result of being his daughter. Growing up in that particular dysfunctional family had pretty much guaranteed that she would either become her own person or a head case.

But hopefully not both.

Each morning after breakfast—which she ate in the hotel restaurant and charged to her room, now that she knew the card was on its way—and a half hour on the laptop, she called Susie Braddock's office and asked for the woman herself.

"Who's calling?" the receptionist would ask. Kick presumed it was the porcupine lady.

"Kathleen Eastman."

"Ms. Braddock's in a meeting. Can she call you back?"

Kick would go along with the charade, giving the receptionist her cell number and her number at the hotel. On the fourth day, she decided to change the routine.

"You got a fax over there?" she asked, after hearing that Susie was yet again in conference.

"Why ... yes."

"I need the number."

When she got off the phone she called Raney Kilbride in Waterloo. She could imagine him in his study, wrapped in a heavy cardigan, reading the paper and reluctantly digesting his daily bowl of All-Bran.

"Nashville?" he repeated, surprised but just slightly. "Yes, that is where you would be."

Kick gave him an abbreviated version of her adventures to date with Susie Braddock, and of the cloudy circumstances surrounding the financial status of the NIC project in general. She could hear him chuckling into the line from time to time; apparently her misfortunes were a source of great amusement for the old man.

"What can I do?" he asked when she was finished with the telling. "Or did you just call to cheer me up?"

"Yeah, that's it," Kick said. She was in her room, sitting on a windowsill and looking down on the street below. "I thought you could fax her a letter on Great North's behalf, threatening her cracker ass if she doesn't comply with my request to see some accounting on the NIC thing. Tell her she's in violation of some international music doctrine, the Lawrence Welk Accord or something like that."

"You'd have me lie to the woman?"

"Tactfully," Kick said. "I wouldn't want you to get disbarred at your age."

"I would love to be disbarred at my age," Raney said. "Do you have the fax number?"

Susie herself called at four that afternoon, her voice so sweet that Kick thought molasses would run out of the phone and into her ear. She insisted that she had tried to call Kick several times but couldn't get through. Then she invited Kick to accompany her to a recording session that evening at someplace called TSA.

"I can pick you up at six," Susie said. "Oh, and I have that information for you."

Kick had to guess at the proper attire for a country recording session. She decided on jeans and a white cotton shirt, and was waiting on the sidewalk out front when Susie pulled up in a garish Mercedes roadster. Kick got in, settling on what appeared to be genuine fur seat covers as Susie, smoking a brown cigarette, pulled into traffic without looking. Horns blew and Kick watched as Susie gave someone the finger in the rearview mirror.

"How you doing there?" Susie asked. She was wearing a short skirt and a tight ZZ Top T-shirt, a blazing red Z centered perfectly on each of her breasts.

"I'm okay," Kick said.

There was a plastic glass filled with ice and an amber liquid in the cupholder on the console between them. Shifting the cigarette to her hand on the wheel, Susie reached for the glass and had a sip.

"Listen," she said, putting the glass back in the holder and glancing at herself in the mirror. "I'm sorry it took so long to get back at you, but I been busier than a one-armed switchboard operator with the crabs." She laughed and took a pull on the cigarette. "That's from my old man."

"I could've sworn it was Noel Coward."

Susie shrugged. "Maybe the old man stole it. Anyway, I been tied up."

"It's all right," Kick said. "I hope you didn't take it personally, getting Great North's legal team involved. I just thought that a letter might expedite things."

"I never got a letter from no lawyer," Susie said.

Kick watched her eyes when she said it. The lie, although not particularly skillful, was automatic, told without a moment's hesitation. It was a trait that Kick could hardly see working in her favor.

"You're in for a treat tonight," Susie said then. "You a fan of Kenny Butternut?"

"You asked me that the other day. Sounds like a gourmet coffee."

"He's gourmet all right." She had another drink from the cup. "In more ways than one."

"I can hardly wait."

They soon took a ramp to a freeway and within minutes were out of the city proper. Susie predictably kept to the fast lane and juggled the steering wheel, the cocktail and a succession of brown cigarettes with an ease that was paradoxically unsettling. When they reached the thruway, Kick decided to fasten her seatbelt. She couldn't decide whether or not the woman was drunk but it seemed the prudent move either way.

The recording studio was in a shining new building of brushed aluminum and brick on the edge of the town of "Historic Franklin." There was a parking space with Susie's name on it near the main entrance. She wheeled the roadster into the spot and then finished the drink with a gulp while she flicked the cigarette butt out the window. Kick suspected that Susie's life was full of such synchronization.

"You don't own this place?" Kick asked, looking at the building.

"I sure as hell do," Susie said. Getting out of the car, she reached into the back to retrieve a leather briefcase. "The Tennessee Sound Authority. It's a play on the Tennessee Valley Authority. You ever hear of that?"

"I've heard of it."

The place housed what Kick had to assume was a state of the art recording facility. The studio itself was on the ground floor, and took up most of that level. When they arrived there were three guitarists in a glassed-in isolation booth. One was bald and paunchy, maybe fifty-five, and the other two were twenty years or so younger. Both of the younger men wore their hair long and both sported bandanas on the wrists of their picking hands. They were dressed in jeans and T-shirts. Susie looked at the trio with transparent irritation and then went directly to another glass booth off the studio, where two men, one sitting, the other standing, were in front of a board that had, Kick guessed, a couple hundred switches and lights and dials on it. Large speakers dominated the room and the walls and ceiling ran at odd angles. The standing man turned when Susie and Kick entered. He wore shorts and a Hawaiian shirt and had a set of headphones dangling around his neck.

"Hey," he said.

"What the fuck are they still doing here?" Susie asked.

"Just finishing up," the man said. The other man, sitting, did not look up at all. He was adjusting something on the board in a most meticulous manner. It was obvious that Kick wasn't going to get an introduction.

"They were supposed to be out of here by five," Susie said then.

"We weren't done at five," the standing man said. "I was under the impression that you wanted them to record all the tracks, Susie."

"I don't need sass from you," Susie said. "I'm saying I don't like paying overtime. You know what that fucking bald-headed rhythm player is costing me? Shit—where's Kenny?"

"Down the hall. Makeup."

"Get those pickers out of there quick as you can," Susie told him. "We got vocals to record."

She left. Kick smiled pointlessly at the standing man and then followed Susie down a long corridor.

"Did he say makeup?" she asked, catching up. "He wears makeup to record an album?"

"No such thing as an album anymore," Susie told her. "It's a CD. CMTV is filming the recording sessions. We share the footage, use it later to promote the record, maybe incorporate it as part of a video. It's all about marketing, tadpole."

They entered a large, well-lit room where the rising star Kenny Butternut was indeed in makeup, leaned back in a chair while a woman in a blue smock plucked his eyebrows with the steady hand of a bomb squad expert. Another woman, standing at a counter on top of which was scattered an assortment of blushes and hair care products, watched the plucking critically.

Kenny Butternut winked at Susie when they entered and jumped to his feet as soon as his eyebrows were groomed. He was a skinny kid, maybe twenty-one, Kick estimated, and he had unlikely jet black hair and pointed sideburns. He wore skintight jeans, faded to the palest of blues, and black cowboy boots. Before embracing Susie, he pulled off the makeup apron to reveal a sleeveless white T-shirt. The shirt, apparently from the Stanley Kowalski designer label, was torn here and there in an artistic manner.

The kid put Susie in a bear hug. "There's my girl," he said, actually lifting her off the ground before planting a wet kiss on her neck. Susie's skirt rode up as he hoisted her, revealing skimpy pink panties. The kiss left a mark; apparently the kid was wearing lipstick. Kick saw the makeup women exchange unhappy glances.

"Look at you," Susie said when her high heels were back on the ground. "You're a star. You're my fucking Alabama jubilee star."

The kid turned on Kick then. Fearful of a similar embrace, she stepped back. But he just extended his hand. "How are you, ma'am? I'm Kenny Butternut."

"This here's Kathy Eastman," Susie said. "She's down from Canada, looking to learn about the music business. She asked me to teach her how to make a record. I said, shit, you might as well ask Lassie how to be a dog. It's just what I am."

As the nonsense gurgled out of Susie Braddock, Kenny Butternut's eyes never left her, his powdered face set in a huge grin, his expression bordering on the reverential. His hand, when Kick shook it, was as soft as a baby's.

"Okay, star," Susie told him, patting his cheek. "Let these gals finish you up, although I swear, you get any better looking, I'm gonna get me a spoon and eat you alive. I'll see you out there. We're gonna make some magic tonight."

"Wait," the kid said. "You didn't see the hat yet. It just come in from Houston." He crossed the room to where a huge hatbox sat on the floor. Out of the enormous box came an enormous cowboy hat—pearl white, with a large crown and a curling brim. The kid plopped it over his dark hair and pulled it low over his eyes.

"Star," Susie said, putting her hands out toward him. Her eyes were suddenly wet. "Alabama jubilee … you're breaking my fucking heart, kid. You are breaking my fucking heart. I'll see you in there."

Out in the corridor again, Susie's eyes dried up almost immediately. She led Kick up a flight of stairs. "Let's get a drink," she said. "Gonna be a while till they get those session players out of there. You want to get rich, tadpole? Buy yourself a Martin guitar and become a picker in Nashville. The money I pay those fuckers, good Lord."

They went into a room on the second floor that appeared to be a lounge. There was a pool table and a jukebox and a bar, as well as several tables and chairs. Susie tossed the briefcase on a table and went behind the bar to open the cooler door. "I believe I'm gonna have a Corona. Might be a long night, better stay out of the hard liquor for the time being. You having a beer?"

"Sure," Kick said and she sat on one of the stools.

"So you make documentaries, that it?" Susie asked as she opened the beer.

"Yeah."

"What about?"

"I'm working on something right now about industrial pollution in Wyoming ranch country." Kick thought about the missed opportunity with Carl. "Say—you looking for an investment?"

"You got the balls of a Texas Longhorn," Susie said. She handed Kick a beer across the bar. "There any money in it?"

"Sure," Kick lied. "Might make you feel good to boot. You're a country girl, right? Well, this company GreenPower Gas and Oil is a division of AmCom and they're making a royal mess of things up there. Sucking the aquifers dry, killing all kinds of fish and game, giving the ranchers a screwing that could put them out of business. It's a travesty."

Susie smiled mysteriously and took a long drink of beer. "A travesty. Let me think about it. I'm always on the prod for a good investment."

Kick nodded at the unlikelihood and had a drink herself. "Those guitar players—so they're playing on a different record?"

"Nope. This one."

"Then why are they leaving?"

"Because they're finished. Or they fucking well better be ... toot sweet." Susie had another large swig. "You're just as green as alfalfa, aren't you? Everything's done separately these days—the percussion, the rhythm, the strings. We lay all the tracks down and then those two techno-geeks you saw in there mix it all together like a big old pot of jambalaya. Then we bring the singer in—the talent, I like to call it—and he does his thing."

Kick took another drink. "So Kenny Butternut doesn't have any musicians with him while he's recording?"

"Nope. And that's the way I want it. Musicians have opinions, too many fucking opinions for my liking. They want to try this, they want to try that. Next thing you know, we're not making the record I set out to make. We're making a *concept* record, or an *experimental* record, which to me are records that some pointy-headed fucker from *The New York Times* will say is the greatest thing since canned peaches but that nobody buys. I'll tell you the truth, tadpole—I was real close to making this record with no musicians at all. Just synthesizers and computers. I got talked out of it, for now anyway."

"You decided to let the musicians live?" Kick said.

"You're a sassy one too, aren't you?" Susie said and she lit another cigarette. "Musicians are fine in the philharmonic, or for concerts in general. In the studio though, they're just another aggravation. And I got enough aggravation in my life, if you know what I mean."

"You talking about me?" Kick said. "Why don't you show me what you've got in that briefcase?"

"Don't rush me. I'm gonna tell you a little story first. Now I don't know how things are where you come from and I don't need to know. But I'm gonna tell you about this town, and this industry. It's all about family. Tennessee is what you call a red state and what that means is that we hold family values over and above everything else. Now this industry is one big family and that's the way I look at it."

She paused to take a long pull on the cigarette. Kick reflected on the fact that moments earlier Susie had been all in favor of booting the musicians out of her one big family. She decided not to mention it.

"Now you have become part of this family," Susie went on. "This just isn't some business transaction. This is something bigger than that. Your father, and now you, and Jonah Peck and me—we've all come together to create something. Do you understand that? It's not just about money. Hell, if all I cared about was making money, I could go back to Florida and sell Cadillacs to rich retired people ... which is what I used to do, before I found my God-given talent to make records. Are you getting this?"

"I think so," Kick said. "Red state, family values, not about the money."

Susie regarded her narrowly but got up and walked around to retrieve the briefcase from the table by the door. When she brought it back, she flopped it onto the bar and placed her hand on it in a solemn manner. At the moment of benediction though, she noticed that her bottle was empty; she went into the cooler for two more Coronas.

"Next you're gonna learn about the Songwriters' Syndicate," she said, pushing the beer toward Kick. "Because for the past year, you've been part and parcel of the Syndicate. And you're about to benefit from that association."

Kick's first beer was barely half gone. She realized that it might be a bad move, trying to drink with Susie Braddock. Aside from the woman herself, everything about Susie, from her boobs to her hair to her ego, was oversized. It stood to reason that her liver would be as well.

"Tell me how that's gonna happen," Kick said.

"I've got the top twenty-five songwriters in the business working for the Syndicate," Susie said. "And we just now are in the process of selecting ten or twelve songs for Jonah Peck's record."

"Who is in the process?"

"Myself, and Jonah."

"He told me there were no songs yet," Kick said.

"See, that's what happens when you get to nosing around something you don't know anything about," Susie said. "I'm sure you misunderstood Jonah. He would have told you we didn't have all the songs yet. I think we do now. I sent three or four out there just this morning. You haven't talked to Jonah today, have you?"

"No."

"See? You go pretending you know things you don't, you get yourself in trouble," Susie said.

"Well, that's one way," Kick said. "I've got others. How much of my money goes to the songwriters?"

"Well, they don't work for free. Lucky for you, I've got these people all under contract. Project like this, they get a flat rate, plus royalties."

"You saying you haven't spent any of my money yet?"

"I'm not saying any such thing. I've already paid for studio time, I've got the graphics in the works, the musicians have been signed, I'm laying out a marketing scheme. Distribution plans. These people are in demand—you want 'em, you have to lock 'em up. This is a go project. It's not some hograssle I'm running here."

Kick couldn't decide to be worried or relieved at what she was hearing. For all her rough edges, Susie—here on her home court—did appear to be a model of efficiency. Capable of spouting more bullshit than a roomful of drunken senators, but a model just the same.

"You're saying you're ready to make the record?"

"That's right."

Kick indicated the briefcase. "And these contracts are in there?"

"Nope. I don't carry contracts with me. I'd need a damn Humvee."

"I thought you had some accounting for me," Kick said. "What's in there—your lunch?"

"Songs," Susie said.

"For Jonah Peck?"

Susie finally opened the case, revealing scores of pages of sheet music. "I don't know if I have any of Jonah's songs with me or not." She shuffled the pages in an unconvincing manner. "No, just some other songs we've been working on. You might be interested in having a look." She handed over a couple pages.

Kick handed them back without a glance. "I'm interested in seeing where my money is."

Susie's eyes suddenly changed. For a brief moment she took on the expression of an inbred dog, a mongrel quite capable of unchecked mayhem. With what appeared to be considerable effort she dismissed the animal. "You'll see it, tadpole. First off, I'm gonna show you how to make a record."

Two more Coronas and forty-five minutes later they were in the control booth, watching and listening as Kenny Butternut began to lay down the vocals for the new record. There were two Betacams in the booth with him; one still unit on a tripod in the corner, operated by a heavyset kid in baggy shorts and a ball cap worn backwards, and another shoulder-held camera, the shoulder holding it belonging to a striking black woman in faded khaki pants and a T-shirt.

Kick leaned against the side wall of the control booth while Susie donned headphones and a tiny microphone and took a seat front and center. The kid who was the focus of all this attention seemed well at ease in the booth, propped on a stool beneath his giant hat, his boots gleaming, his makeup picture-show perfect. Throw in a photogenic horse and a wise-cracking sidekick and he could have passed for a matinee cowboy from a 1930s western.

"Okay, jubilee," Susie said into the mike. "Let's do one to check the levels. You're just gonna hear the piano for now. This one's to get the juices flowing, baby."

Kenny Butternut began to sing. Kick had a buzz on from the beer; she watched him for a moment, then she looked over at Susie, who was suddenly all business, her eyes shifting from the dials on the soundboard to the earnest kid behind the mike. Kick wondered again if she was, her cartoon excesses aside, the real deal after all. After all, Lassie was indeed a dog. In the end, it was all that Kick should care about. As far as the existence of the songs went, she decided there was really only one place to check that story out. And that place was about an hour east of Nashville.

Kenny Butternut was singing the chorus now. The song was a moribund ballad, a boast of manhood and a plea for understanding and a tip of the hat to God and country all rolled into one over-cooked soufflé. The kid was selling it as best he could:

"You know, baby, I'm a God-fearin' man
But I know, baby, I got to take my stand
'Cuz I can't be your lover,
If first I'm not a man"

The kid sang with his eyes closed, his head back. He was feeling the music, or something. Listening to the drivel, Kick stumbled into eye contact with the camerawoman. Kick arched her eyebrows and the woman looked at her for a moment and then shifted her attention back to the singer. It seemed to Kick that she smiled, just slightly. Kick looked back at Kenny Butternut. She had a feeling she was in for a long night. She was a half hour out of the city. She wondered how much a cab back to the hotel would set Great North back.

AFTER BREAKFAST Johanna ran the tiller over her garden a couple of times to open the ground up to the sun and the breeze. Then she drove into Miller's Garden Supply and picked up a couple dozen bedding plants—tomatoes, zucchini, butternut squash and several kinds of peppers. She also bought string bean seeds, carrot, onion sets and leeks. She had seed corn and various herb seeds from last year's crop in the root cellar.

When she got back to the farm she had lunch and then changed into her overalls and hauled several wheelbarrow loads of rotted horse manure from the barnyard and dumped it beside the garden plot. By late afternoon the ground was dry enough to till properly. Johanna had a forty-year-old Tecumseh rototiller she'd bought at an auction when the kids were small and it became evident that she was going to be responsible for their nutritional health. She'd changed the oil and the spark plug before firing it up that morning and now she lowered the depth bar and then went over the plot a half dozen times, breaking the soil down. Stopping, she shoveled the black manure on top of the tilled ground, and then adjusted the bar and worked it again.

When she shut the tiller off for the second time, she turned to see Ethan crouched in the grass a few feet away, hunkered down like a hunter on the stalk, watching her. Johanna, peeved at the voyeuristic nature of the situation, took a moment to remove her gloves and stuff them in the pocket of the overalls. Then she looked back at him.

"Why are you watching me?"

He smiled. "All along the watchtower, princes kept their view. While all the women came and went, barefoot servants too."

"That's interesting, Ethan," she replied. "But the last I looked, you were not a prince. And I'm not your servant anymore. Barefoot or otherwise. So if you want to talk to me, talk straight."

His eyes showed instant hurt and he looked down and began to tug at the grass at his feet, pulling loose blades from the ground and tossing them aside. She regarded him a moment longer, then pulled her gloves on and picked up a rake and began to level the freshly tilled soil. When she glanced up, he was standing beside the plot.

"Why do you use manure?" he asked. "They make chemical fertilizers."

She went back to her raking for a moment, considering the reasons for such a question. She straightened and leaned her chin on the rake. "I don't know if I should be educating you on the fine points of home gardening, Ethan."

"You gotta get up close to the teacher, if you wanna learn anything."

"I told you to stop that."

He shrugged away her complaint. "I've been reading about organic gardening on the web. I'm interested in it."

"You've been planting marijuana all over the farm," she said.

"That's purely recreational."

"It's purely illegal too."

"Liquor was illegal at one time," Ethan said. "Eventually the government will come around. Marijuana's been here for centuries."

"So has war and syphilis," Johanna said. "If you want to make bathtub gin, I am with you all the way. We can plant some juniper trees."

He smiled broadly then and she saw in him, for the first time since his return, the little boy he'd been. The guileless child, lacking Ben's clumsy manner or Kick's razor instinct, always floating above the wind-blown confusions that marked life in the Eastman family. His only constant had been a lack of anything consistent, and that detachment, strangely enough, had been his salvation back then. It was quite probable, though, that it hadn't served him well in adulthood. Still, Johanna was overjoyed to see the child, if even for a moment.

"I might dig up a plot of my own, behind the barn," he said. "I was thinking I'd like to try my hand at some organic vegetables."

Johanna knew he was being honest. There remained in him too much of the fry for her to think otherwise. She began her raking again, but she stopped. "I prefer manure because I know what it is. It's manure. With chemicals, I don't know, and I have no desire at this point to learn. I'd be worried about long-term effects. But I've been eating tomatoes fertilized with horse poop for thirty years now and I haven't grown a third eye yet."

Ethan, looking at the black soil, nodded somewhat absently and she could see the child slipping away. He turned and began toward the house. She watched him walk away and went back to her raking. It was the closest she'd come to an actual conversation with him since he'd returned to Crooked Pear, and she decided, in this case, to accentuate the positive. It was her nature to be an optimist.

And then she heard him ask, "Would you like some help?"

There were times when optimism paid dividends quicker than others. She didn't look up because for some reason she didn't want him to see her smile. "I would love some help," she said.

APPARENTLY SOME OTHER LUCKY-DAY renter beat her to the Fiesta. Kick got a Sunbird this time, black, with flames along the dented front fenders and three mag wheels out of four. There were cigarette burns in the upholstery and a large crack across the windshield, but it ran well enough to get her back to the Peck farm on Tater Peeler Road.

She pulled up to the house at about ten-thirty. To amuse herself, she'd counted dead possums on the drive out and come up with a baker's dozen. Roadkill. The usual array of vehicles was parked on the property, angled every which way in the drive and on the lawn. There was no answer when Kick knocked on the front door and after a while she gave up and walked out to the barn.

"Hello!" she called as she entered but got no response. The barn was neat and clean; there were several horse stalls and a tack room with a couple western saddles on stands, along with bridles and blankets and a martingale on a hook. The barn smelled as it should, sweet and pungent, a mixture of hay and manure and animal sweat. She walked out to the corral then and found the two horses standing in the shade along the wall of the building, looking at her. The bay approached her immediately but the Appaloosa mare hung back. Kick reached out to rub the gelding's forehead as he arrived and the horse began to nose around her pockets, looking for a treat.

"Well, I guess he didn't go riding, did he?" Kick said, looking around. She turned back to the gelding. "I'm not sure why I'm telling you this."

She went back to the house and knocked again in vain. She was backing the Sunbird up to leave when she saw the front door open and a head poke out. Seeing Kick, a thin woman with long dark hair stepped out on the porch. She was barefoot and wore a large T-shirt that reached almost to her knees. Kick shut the ignition off and got out and walked up to the house.

"Hey," she said from the lawn.

"What can I do for you?" The woman had obviously just awakened. Her hair was a tangle and as she spoke she used the heel of one hand to push away the sleep encrusted in the corner of her eye.

"I was looking for Mr. Peck."

"*Mister* Peck?" the woman said, blinking. "Well, he's bound to be around here somewhere. That's his truck. Who are you anyway?"

"I'm Kathleen Eastman. Great North AudioBooks. We're doing a record with Mr. Peck."

"Would you quit calling him that? Besides, he hasn't made an album in years." The woman gave her stomach a vigorous scratching while she scrutinized Kick. "I need a cup of coffee. You might as well come in, seeing as you woke me up."

"I thought you country folk got up early," Kick said as the woman turned away.

"Country folk my ass," she said as she went inside.

Kick entered and followed her down a hallway and into the kitchen. A calico cat was dozing on the counter there. Kick sat down at a scarred harvest table while the dark-haired woman stood at the sink, filling a carafe with water. "My brain is nonfunctional without caffeine." She was gazing out the window as she said it. "I think that's Clark's truck," she said after a moment.

"Okay."

The woman turned. "If that's Clark's truck, they're out turkey hunting."

"Turkey hunting."

"Yeah." The woman poured the water into a coffeemaker then spooned the grounds in and turned it on. As the brew began to gurgle she looked on top of the fridge and in several drawers before turning to Kick. "You wouldn't have a cigarette?"

"Sorry."

The woman left. The weekend edition of a Nashville paper was on the table and Kick began to leaf through it. In the entertainment section she came upon a picture of Susie Braddock, hanging out with Kenny Butternut and a half dozen other local luminaries at a night spot called Del Rio's. Susie was glassy-eyed in the shot and her breasts were spilling out of her top. Kick tossed the paper aside when the woman returned. She had a cigarette in her mouth and one tucked behind her ear and was now apparently looking for a light.

"Do you have a name?" Kick asked.

"Of course I have a name. Do you know people who don't have names?" The woman found matches above the stove and lit up. She closed her eyes in orgasmic pleasure with the first deep pull on the smoke. "I'm Paige."

"Hello, Paige," Kick said. "And you are ... Jonah's wife?"

"Are you fucking nuts? I'm twenty-eight years old."

Kick would have guessed thirty-five, maybe even forty. "Sorry."
She tried to make amends. "These big stars often marry women half
their age, you know."

"Jonah's my daddy."

"Oh."

"They'll be gone all day, if they're turkey hunting."

The coffee was ready now and the woman named Paige took
down cups from a cupboard overhead and poured. Shooing the cat
from the counter, she slid one over to Kick and then went into the
fridge for milk. There was sugar in a bowl on the table. She sat down
and added four heaping spoonfuls to her cup. Kick used a little milk.

"Why are you here again?" Paige asked.

"Making a record with Mister … your daddy."

"You really believe that, don't you?"

"I pretty much have to, at this point," Kick told her. "So do you live
here?"

"Naw, I'm just passing through." She yawned hugely. "I just got
out of rehab and I'm heading to New York. Thought I'd stop and
check out the old man's attitude."

"And how is it?"

Paige pulled fiercely on the cigarette while she considered this. "I
don't know. He's just drifting along. Got no focus anymore, it
seems." She exhaled expansively. "I think he needs a woman in his
life. That's why I got my ass out of bed when I looked out the
window and saw you leaving. Thought you might be the new love of
his life. You're a little young for him, but you know how these big
stars like to marry women half their age."

"That coffee works pretty quick."

"I might be a little more pharmaceutical-sensitive than the
average person. I'm not saying that's a good thing." She had another
sip. "You're not from around here, I'm guessing."

"Nope. Canada."

"All right," Paige said. "I know who you are now. This is that back-tax album. What the fuck are they calling it?"

"Nothing Is Certain."

"Yeah," she snorted. "Dumb fucking name that is. The rich dude from Canada is putting up the money. So it's actually going to happen?"

"I guess. The rich dude was my father. I sort of inherited the project."

"You're not in the business?"

"Nope."

"But you want to be."

"Not in the least."

Paige laughed. "Welcome to Nashville. So who's producing this thing?"

"Susie Braddock."

"Oh Christ. What's my father doing with that Texas skank?"

Kick took a drink of coffee for the first time. It was good coffee. "I'm told she's the hot producer," she said after a moment. "That not true?"

Paige had already burned the cigarette to a nub; she dropped the butt in a pop can on the table. "Oh, she probably is. You're not naive enough to believe that you have to make good music to sell a lot of records."

"I might be that naive," Kick said. "So what's her story?"

"Susie Braddock? Depends on which version you want to believe. She rolled into Nashville a few years back. With a shitload of money and more nerve than a toothache. She supposedly owned a Cadillac dealership in Miami. Sold out, that's where the money came from. The dealership got busted, afterward I guess, part of a ring shipping stolen luxury cars to the Mideast." Paige laughed. "You know how they launder money? Well, I guess they were laundering Coupe De Villes."

"And she became a record producer?" Kick asked. "Just like that?"

"She got lucky first time out of the box. Made a bad record with some country singer turned actress. Single had a movie tie-in and sold like ten million copies. Like I said, you don't need taste to make hit records." Paige took a noisy slurp of coffee. "Is Jonah writing the songs for the record?"

"No. He says he doesn't write anymore."

"That's why he needs a woman in his life. He wrote his best stuff when he was either falling in love or getting his heart broken. You know how it is with artists."

In truth Kick knew a fair amount about the subject. Enough that she chose to drink her coffee and hold her tongue.

"So Susie's supplying the songs," Paige said then.

"Yeah, and that seems to be the holdup so far. You know, coming up with good songs. But she told me last night that the songs were done, the musicians hired, studio booked. Everything's a go."

Paige took the cigarette from behind her ear and lit it. "And so why are you here today?"

"To ask your father if any of it's true."

WHEN SHE GOT BACK to the city she dropped the flamed Firebird at the rental place and then decided to walk the mile or so back to the Sheraton. Driving in from Jonah Peck's farm, she'd had time to consider just what it was she was accomplishing here. If the record really was on track, then Kick was nothing more than a bystander in all of it, asking stupid questions and spending Great North's money. She might be better off back in Ontario. Maybe she could pry enough money out of the publishing company to finance a week or two's shooting out in Wyoming. She'd love to get the rancher on film, the guy who'd shot up the rig. His trial was probably months away. By that time a lawyer would have him calmed down and walking a line; it would be nice to get him talking while his blood was still up.

But first she had to make certain that the Nashville picture was as rosy as Susie Braddock was painting it. She'd left her cell number with Paige, who promised to have Jonah call when he got back from hunting.

"If he can't get through on the cell, have him try me at the Sheraton downtown," Kick had added.

"If he can," she'd said. "Chances are he'll be high as a pine when he gets back from the bush. There's no turkeys around for some reason and when my old man gets bored he has a tendency to get into the ganja."

Back in her room Kick called the airport to check on a flight north. Her return ticket was open. She was told she could leave either that evening or first thing the next morning. She booked the morning flight, depending now on Jonah Peck to come through.

She had lunch at a Thai place near Music Row and then afterward was feeling so logy she went for a run along the river. She ran in her hiking boots, which were not ideal for the job, and she might have attracted a few stares but she was certain that she was a long way off from being the strangest sight in town.

Back in her room she read the papers and flipped through the channels on the television before turning it off. She sat there for a while, bored. She wondered if a turkey-less Jonah Peck was out in the bush, feeling the same. With no ganja to get into herself, she lay down on the bed and fell asleep. She dreamed of Crooked Pear, and in her dream it was the Crooked Pear of her childhood, the quasi-magical kingdom that protected her from any number of stepmothers and familial discombobulation. As was often the case, she appreciated in mid-dream that she was having a dream. In her semiconscious state, though, she decided not to allow that realization to ruin the diversion.

When she woke up it was past six. The kingdom was gone and Kick was left wondering if in fact it had ever really been there. She checked her cell and the hotel phone for messages but there was nothing from Jonah Peck, or Paige either. She suddenly realized that the woman's name was Paige Peck. No wonder she was in rehab. She turned the TV to the news and let it play while she went in to shave her legs and have a shower. She threw on jeans and a blouse and went down for dinner.

Walking off the elevator into the lobby, she was more than a little surprised to see Jonah Peck himself, sitting in a plush wingback chair and reading a newspaper. He looked like a man who had indeed spent the day in the bush. In fact, he looked like a man who had spent several days in the bush. He wore dirty tan pants and a Jerry Jeff Walker sweatshirt and the same creased cowboy hat he'd worn the first time she'd met him. When Kick started across the carpet, a stout woman in an orange muumuu cut in front of her.

"You're Jonah Peck," the woman said as she reached the singer.

"Yes, ma'am."

"Gimme your autograph." The woman thrust forward a scrap of paper.

Jonah obliged the woman, who walked away without a word, examining the signature as if she was afraid it was forged. Kick, as if in line, stepped forward.

"Mr. Peck."

"Well, there she is."

"What the hell are you doing?"

"Waiting on you."

"They have telephones in the rooms here."

"I figured you to pass through, sooner or later."

Kick gestured toward the departing woman. "Or maybe you just enjoy the attention?"

"Yeah, I crave it. That's why I come to town every three years."

"You haven't been to Nashville in three years?"

"Nigh on to four. You ought to be flattered, young lady." He got to his feet and pulled down the brim of the hat. "Well, let's get going."

"Where we going?"

"To find Susie Braddock."

Jonah's battered pickup was double-parked in front of the hotel. The doorman was protecting it like it was a brand-new Bentley.

"Let me get that for you, Mr. Peck," he said, opening the door. "So nice to see you, Mr. Peck. Have a nice evening."

"You got ass-kissers up in Canada?" Jonah asked as they drove off.

"You wouldn't believe it," Kick said.

He had no idea where Susie's office was so Kick, suddenly the home girl, directed him. She thought it odd that he'd be the stranger, but not as odd as the fact that she was being chauffeured around Nashville by a man considered to be a living legend, in a truck that was worth about seventy-five dollars.

"My guess is she ain't gonna be there," the legend said as they drove. "But it's as good a place as any to start."

Susie wasn't there but the multi-punctured receptionist was, although she was standing on the front step when they arrived. Just locking up, she said when she saw them, and to prove it, she locked up. Jonah, after taking in all the piercings, asked after Susie.

"She's gone to dinner."

"You wouldn't know where?"

"Try Casey's." She tried the door to be sure it was secured, then put the keys in her pocket.

"Would you have her cell phone number?" Kick asked.

"Yup."

"Can I have it?"

"Nope."

She turned on her heel and walked away.

"You'd think she'd get an infection," Jonah said.

Neither one of them knew where Casey's was. Kick's stint as the knowledgeable one was short-lived. They drove back downtown and got directions from a cop on a horse. As it turned out, the place was just a block from Susie's office, on a side street. They parked and walked inside. Susie wasn't there. The bartender told them that she hadn't been in but that she'd been frequenting the place.

"Might as well have a drink and wait a bit," Jonah said.

Kick had a rye and water and Jonah a glass of orange juice. Sipping at the whiskey, Kick thought that now might be the ideal time to ask just why they were looking for the record producer. Then she remembered a song—John Prine, she thought—that suggested that a question wasn't really a question if you already knew the answer.

So instead she asked, "You shoot any turkeys?"

"Nary a one."

"My neighbor's been shooting plenty of them. Back home."

"Up in Canada?"

"Yeah."

"I didn't know they had turkeys that far north."

"Oh yeah. Big ones."

They waited for an hour or so. Kick had another drink and then they asked the bartender where else they might find Susie.

"Try Grimey's Basement. Lot of musicians hang out there." He'd been watching Jonah all along. "You're Jonah Peck, aren't you?"

"Yes, sir."

"I wondered what happened to you."

"I wonder that myself sometimes," Jonah said and they left.

Grimey's Basement was crowded for a Sunday night. There was a rumor floating around that Bobby Bare was going to appear to try out some new songs. They stood at the bar and Kick had another rye while Jonah switched to tonic water. Word soon got out he was there and he was obliged to sign a few autographs. Nobody had seen Susie Braddock that night, although everyone seemed to know who she was.

Kick watched as Jonah signed a dollar bill for a young guy, after explaining that it wasn't he who had written "Me and Bobby McGee." The kid had insisted on an autograph anyway.

"What was it you wrote again?" he asked when he had it.

"Last thing I wrote was a grocery list," Jonah told him.

"I don't know that one," the kid said and walked away.

"I've never hung out with a genuine celebrity before," Kick said.

"Exciting, ain't it?" Jonah said. "It's even better once everybody gets drunk. Then people stop telling you you're a genius and start reminding you of all the times you screwed up in your life. That can be a real treat—especially when the times you screwed up outnumber the times you were a genius by about ten to one."

"I'm looking forward to it," Kick told him. She waved the bartender over.

"Besides, I thought you said you made films for a living," Jonah said. "You must know lots of so-called celebrities."

"I make documentaries," Kick said. "I know an Inuit man named Iti Kut who once killed a polar bear with a hunting knife. And I'm on speaking terms with a Caraca Indian from Brazil who saved a hundred thousand acres of rain forest from the clear-cutters. Neither of them has ever made it to the cover of *People* magazine."

"They got nobody but themselves to blame for that," Jonah said. "They don't want to go that extra mile—you know, snort a little cocaine, shoot a wife or two—then they ain't never gonna be famous. Not in today's world anyway."

"You don't come to town too often, but you're pretty funny when you do," Kick told him. "You should try it more often."

"Maybe I would, if I had more pretty girls visiting me from Canada." He smiled at her as he said it, but not to suggest that he wasn't flirting. It seemed rather that he intended her to know that he was.

Kick took a drink of rye. "I might have to switch to tonic water myself," she said. "I have a feeling you're a dangerous man, Mr. Peck."

"These days I'm just an old turkey hunter," he said and showed her the smile again. "But there was a time—"

Kick was saved by another autograph seeker. This one wore tight blue jeans and a Grand Ole Opry T-shirt that appeared to be brand new. She had come prepared, offering an elaborate gilded autograph book and requesting that Jonah sign under the section reserved for the P's. Looking over the woman's shoulder, Kick could see that Ray Price and Dolly Parton had already obliged.

"I think you're one of the greatest country singers ever," the woman said, watching Jonah make his mark. "But as a guitar player, you're well down my list."

"I appreciate your opinion," Jonah said, handing the book back. "I been thinking of taking lessons."

"Wouldn't hurt," the woman said and she was gone. Jonah watched her walk away, then drank off his tonic and rattled the ice in the glass. The bartender nodded.

"So they call you Kick," Jonah said, turning to her. "What are you—a karate expert?"

"Well, I've dabbled in the martial arts," she said. "But no. My father was a project-oriented guy. Now that I think about it, his parental involvement was basically a series of projects, most of them ill-conceived. Well, one summer he decided that my brothers and I needed nicknames. So he started calling me Kit. Short for Kathleen, right? My brother Ben had a slight speech impediment. A not-so-slight moral impairment too, but that's another story. Anyway, I became Kick."

"And it stuck," Jonah suggested. "Probably because it fit."

"Where Ben was concerned, it did. I used to kick his ass on a regular basis. I'm probably not done yet, where that's concerned." She shrugged. "But I can always say that my name is a noun and a verb at the same time. How many people can make a claim like that?"

Jonah watched the bartender as he poured the tonic over ice. "Oh, I don't know. Bob, for one. Jack. Mark."

"Okay, okay," Kick said. "That's something I say that you're supposed to accept at face value. You damn writers."

"Lever."

"Lever?"

"Yep. I knew a old boy built banjos, name of Lever MacDonald."

"Now you're just making shit up."

"I'd do better than that, if I was making shit up," Jonah said as he picked up his fresh glass. He had a drink. "He called me once. Your father."

"Yeah?"

"Yep. Just the once. That's when he made the offer to bankroll this record. It was well after midnight that he phoned, I recall thinking that he was a night owl, like me. We shared IRS stories, like a couple old GIs talking about the war. It was just the once though; after that I always talked to that Blaine character. Our conversations were a tad shorter ... I always got the feeling he was frettin' about the long-distance charges."

"That would be Blaine."

"Well, whatever the case, him and me don't seem to have a lot in common."

"You and Everett wouldn't either," Kick said. "The two of you might as well have been from different planets."

"Sounds like he was a rich man who ignored his family. I'd say him and me were two peas in a pod, at one time anyway."

As he spoke he was watching the woman in the Opry shirt. She had returned to her table and was now enthralling her friends with what was undoubtedly her account of her exchange with the legendary Jonah Peck.

"About time for us to make a move," Jonah said.

"Is there a snowball effect with autographs?" Kick asked.

"Yep."

Kick had a drink of the rye and then a thought came to her. "Del something," she said.

"What?"

"I was reading a newspaper in your kitchen this morning and there was a picture of Susie in a place called Del something. A Spanish-sounding name."

"Del Rio's," the bartender said. He glanced from Jonah to Kick, then shrugged. "I was listening."

"Good for you," Kick said. "Where is it?"

Del Rio's turned out to be next door to the Thai place where Kick had had lunch. It was on the ground floor of an old warehouse that had, from the looks of it, recently been rejuvenated. On the drive there Kick was feeling the effects of the rye and she remembered she hadn't eaten dinner. She wondered if owning a record label was turning her into an alcoholic. It seemed like a bit of a cliché if she was.

Del Rio's could fall under the same category. The bar was overly familiar to Kick. Upscale, style over substance and probably the place to be. In fact, had she not been with Jonah Peck, she was sure she wouldn't have been allowed past the doorman. Looking around while she and Jonah stood in the entranceway, she sighed heavily.

"What's wrong?" he asked.

"We've got places like this in Toronto," she told him.

"Like what?"

"Places like this, where all the posers hang out," she said. "You know—twenty-two-dollar martinis, thirty-dollar hamburgers, people pretending to be something they're not." She glanced at him. "Put it this way—if Susie isn't here, I don't know where she'll be. This place was built for her."

"They sure got pretty waitresses," Jonah said, looking into the bar.

"Well now, that's a consolation."

"There she is."

Susie was at a large table that sat above, rather than beside, the dance floor. She had with her a dozen people or more, including Kenny Butternut and a dark-haired man who wore a string tie and a black Stetson. The man must have been Susie's boyfriend, Kick reasoned, as there would seem to be no other explanation for his hand to be that far up her skirt.

The table was covered with beer bottles and drink glasses as well as several bottles of Cristal champagne, some empty, others half full. Two girls, obviously still in their teens, sat together at the end of the table; they wore embroidered shirts and thick mascara and slightly bewildered, or possibly stoned, expressions. Kick recognized one of the men as the bass player from the recording studio.

Susie didn't see them until they were standing at the table. Then she let out a whoop that frightened her boyfriend into retrieving his hand from its explorations.

"Jonah Peck!" Susie shouted and she pushed herself to her feet. "Would you look at this? The man doesn't come to town but once every ten years and when he does, it's to see Susie. Come here, gimme some sugar, Jonah Peck."

She made her way around the table and reached up on her tiptoes to put Jonah in an embrace. Kick saw Kenny Butternut get to his feet and respectfully remove his cowboy hat. "Let me introduce you to some people," Susie said, and only then did she notice Kick. "Hey, tadpole! Jonah, you caught yourself a tadpole. And here I thought it was Jonah and the whale. Shit, you sure went from one big fish to one little one."

"A whale's not a fish," Kick said. She'd seen the wariness in Susie's eyes when she first spotted Kick. "Neither's a tadpole, come to think of it."

"Fucking Canadian know-it-all," Susie laughed, dismissing her. "Come on, Jonah. You're gonna sit with me. I want you to meet Kenny Butternut, he's a big fan. Big fan. Put the tadpole at the end with the jailbait. She can tell 'em about fish and whatever else she wants."

"We need to talk," Jonah said to her.

"We're gonna talk, honey. Soon as I fix you up with a drink. We already decided, we're not leaving here till we clean this place outta champagne."

"I don't drink," Jonah said. "Is there somewhere we can talk?"

Kenny Butternut stepped forward then. "Mr. Peck, it is a pleasure to meet you, sir."

"How you doin', son?" Jonah shook the kid's hand without looking at him. "Susie, we're gonna talk."

Susie watched the kid go back to his chair, his shoulders slumped. She turned to Jonah. "Well, let's talk," she said sharply. "Seems like you got something on your mind that's affecting your manners, Jonah. People like to say hi, pay their respects. These young people look up to you, you know."

"That's unfortunate for them," Jonah said. He indicated Kick. "Why don't the three of us go somewhere quiet?"

"I'm not going anywheres," Susie said. "I'm here with my friends. Tell me what's on your mind, Jonah."

"All right," he said, resigned. "Did you tell this girl that this recording was ready to roll? Songs selected, pickers hired, studio time booked?"

"I never said anything of the sort," Susie said.

"Wait a minute," Kick said.

"You wait a fucking minute," Susie snapped. "What're you trying to pull?"

"That's *exactly* what you told me," Kick said.

"You're a fucking liar." Susie turned to Jonah. "You know damn well we're not that far along, Jonah. You see what this is—she's trying to squash this thing, Ray Charles could see that. I was you, I'd put her skinny ass on a plane." She glared briefly at Kick, then turned back to Jonah. "But I do have some new songs for you to look at. Why don't we talk tomorrow?"

"Why don't we back up to where you called me a fucking liar?" Kick asked.

"You still here, tadpole?" Susie asked. "You're out of your element. Fuck off, honey, and leave the music business to the people that know it. We'll talk tomorrow, Jonah." She started back to her seat, dismissing them both.

"Hold on," Jonah said. "I got a problem, Susie."

Susie, executing a slow burn, did a turn to match. "I *said* … we'll talk about your problems tomorrow. You hear me?"

"I hear you," Jonah said. "Problem is, I don't believe you. And I do believe her."

Kick smiled. "Why, thank you, Mr. Peck. You know—just today, someone asked me why anybody'd want to get involved with this Texas skank anyway."

It was then that Susie pulled back and punched Kick squarely in the face, knocking her over an empty chair and into the lap of Kenny Butternut.

And it was just after that when all hell broke loose.

TEN

Johanna called Will Montgomery from Crooked Pear first thing Monday morning to tell him that her goat had died during the night. Will, who hadn't been particularly close to the animal, was a little surprised at the call. Then Johanna asked if he could come over to Crooked Pear sometime that morning, as there was a favor she wanted to ask. He fed some grain to the cattle and did some paper-work, then drove over in the pickup, arriving just before noon.

Johanna was behind the barn when he got there, in the corral, wearing a cotton shirt and jeans tucked into a pair of rubber boots. The black goat was lying there in the dirt. Johanna's Belgian mare was standing a few feet away, a sheaf of untouched hay by her feet. Johanna's eyes were red.

"Hey," Will said when he walked around the barn. He climbed through the fence and as he did he noticed a plot of ground, maybe thirty feet square, worked up along the edge of the pasture field beyond the fencing. He looked down at the goat. "What happened?"

"He just got old. It was probably his heart; he's been moving pretty slow the past few weeks. He got so he couldn't even climb on top of that little hill anymore." She wiped her eyes. "I don't know what the heck is wrong with me. Just a little goat."

"You get attached to things, Johanna."

"Well, I needed a companion for this one," she said, indicating the mare. "After Buck died. I wasn't about to train another horse. She's going on thirty, you know that? She'll be the next to go."

She picked up a handful of hay and, as she offered it to the disinterested mare, Will saw that her hair was wet, pushed behind her ears, as if she'd just got out of the shower. He'd never known her to wear much makeup; she probably considered it frivolous. Her cropped hair was as blonde as it had ever been. There were tiny lines crowfooting out from her eyes but aside from that she could easily pass for forty or younger, Will thought. In her jeans and the thin cotton shirt and her grief, she looked incredibly sexy this morning. It had been a while. A year or so before his marriage, he remembered, which would make it eight years this fall.

"You want some help with him?" Will said, looking at the goat.

"No, I called the livestock removal. They'll be here this afternoon."

"We could bury him, if that would make you feel better."

She gave up on the idea of feeding the mare, tossing the hay to the ground. "No. They'll pick him up. That's not the favor I wanted." She ran her hand along the big horse's flanks, then slapped her lightly on the rump, raising a little cloud of dust in the air. "Would you take her, Will? She'll die of loneliness without that little guy around. You know how horses are. You've still got the butterscotch, right?"

"Buckskin."

"I always get that wrong. Right color, wrong name." She hesitated. "Oh, I never thought … that was her horse, wasn't it?"

"She's mine now, apparently."

"Well then, what do you say? I can pay you for board."

"I'll take her," Will said. "And you don't have to pay me anything. I'll turn her out with the mare and the cattle for the summer. And I've got an extra box stall she can have for the winter."

"She might not last that long."

"You never can tell."

She turned and walked into the barn then, where she sat on a bench along the wall just inside. Will followed her, stopping in the doorway and reaching up to grasp the lintel overhead. She looked at him, and then past him.

"There's been a lot of changes lately," she said. "Funny how that is. Seems like nothing happens for years on end and then ... well, Everett dying, and your marriage ending. And the kids coming home. Those kids ... where did I go wrong there?"

"First of all, they're not kids anymore," Will said. "And where did you go wrong? Without you, the three of them would have been living out here with the cats. Most of the time, you were all the mother they had."

"It sure seemed like it, most summers. I was only twenty-one when I first came here. Ben was ten, Kick was six. And Ethan was just a baby, he couldn't talk yet."

"He's not exactly a chatterbox now," Will said. "You hear from Kick?"

"She's in Nashville, that's all I know." She smiled. "I think you're a little bit sweet on her, Will Montgomery."

"Kick? No. Come on, I've known Kick since she was a kid."

"What's that got to do with it?"

Will shrugged. "What about the other two? What're they up to these days?"

Johanna pointed through the open doorway to the tilled plot of land. "Did you see that?"

"Yeah," Will said. "Thought maybe you were starting a second garden."

"It's Ethan's. He wants to try organic vegetables."

"You believe that?"

"We'll see," Johanna said. "He's been using my internet connection. I'm not sure what he's researching but he has questions from time to time. Garden questions. They both took off this morning though."

"What's he going to do with the distillery?"

"What do you think he's capable of doing with the distillery?"

"Not much," Will said, considering it. "What about Ben—he still trying to nudge you into retirement?"

"He hasn't been back. Who knows what he's up to. I'm sure he has convinced himself he was cheated on the estate."

"Ben could have gotten every penny and he'd still find a way to claim he got screwed."

"Oh, he was a hateful little bugger when he was little," Johanna said. "I must have taken the yardstick to his backside a hundred times."

Will turned to look at the Belgian mare, and the little black goat in the dirt. The flies had just discovered the carcass. Will wondered when the livestock truck was coming.

"How are you getting along?" he heard her ask.

"Good." When he spoke, the horse turned to look at him.

"We never really talked about Denise," Johanna said. "It was one of those things—it was unexpected but not a surprise. If that makes sense."

"As much as anything."

"Was she—" she began, then stopped. "Maybe you'd rather leave it alone."

"No. Go ahead."

"Was she the love of your life?"

Whatever Will had been expecting, it wasn't that. He turned back to her. "No, she wasn't," he said in realization. After a moment he added, "Thanks."

"Don't mention it," she said smiling. He watched as she pulled off one boot, revealing her ankle and calf where the jeans rode up, and dumped a pebble from inside onto the barn floor. He thought about her comment regarding his feelings for Kick.

"And now you're looking at my leg," she said.

"I guess I am."

"Would you know how long it's been?" She put the boot back on.

"You know I was just thinking about that. I'd say about eight years." He looked at her a moment. "Surprised that I know? You figure that men don't think about that stuff."

"Sometimes I'm surprised that you guys think at all," she said as she stood up. "But you're right. Eight years this fall." She took a step toward him. "And you were just thinking about it, were you?"

"I was."

She reached up to take off his RedLine Seed cap, then brushed his hair back. She kissed him on the side of his mouth, then full on. "I don't know what's got into me today. It's just this ... feeling of melancholy."

They kissed again and he put his hand under the cotton shirt. She was wearing no bra and when he cupped her breast she ran her tongue inside his mouth.

"Oh my," she said after a moment and she glanced around. "You'd better take me to the house. I'm too old to be doing it in a hay mow."

"You and me both," he said.

JANEY SET THE MEETING UP over the phone. Jack Dutton agreed to Friday, then called at the last minute and changed it to Monday. That was fine with Janey as it gave her the weekend to bolster her case, and to convince Ethan, who'd been reluctant to attend. She sat him down and explained to him that he had to make an appearance. Since starting his garden he'd been sleeping less than twelve hours a day, which she took as a good sign. She wasn't convinced he was ready to take on Jack Dutton and the situation at the distillery, but the fact that he was accomplishing a task like tilling the ground, without the use of antidepressants, was encouraging. He'd told her back in Victoria that he wouldn't go back to the drugs and she was in agreement with him on the matter. Of course, on Monday morning she watched as he smoked a fat joint in the car on the way to the distillery. She said nothing about the ironic nature of the act. Whatever would get him through the day at the distillery. In truth, she'd expected it.

What she didn't expect was to find Ben Eastman there, sitting in a room off the front foyer with Jack Dutton, smoking a cigar and acting like he was exactly where he was supposed to be. Janey stopped short when she saw him.

"Hey kids," Ben said. "I hope you don't mind me crashing your meeting."

Ethan walked to the window to look at the river passing outside. Dutton was on his feet, his hand extended; when Ethan didn't notice, he offered it to Janey. She shook it and then looked at Ben.

"I'm sorry. Why are you here?" she asked.

"I was thinking I might ask you that," he replied.

The room was furnished more like a living room than a board-room of any kind. There was a couch and several stuffed chairs, and a large glass-top coffee table in the center. Janey was carrying a folder and she set it down on the table, then took a place on the couch, sitting forward, her elbows on her knees, hands within reach of the folder.

"Ben happened to stop by this morning," Dutton said. "I told him about our meeting and suggested he stick around. After all, he is family. I have coffee here. Anybody want a cup?"

"Sure." Janey spoke to Dutton but she was still looking at Ben.

Dutton poured from a stainless-steel carafe on the table. Ben declined, content to puff on the cigar. Janey looked at him a moment longer and then began.

"Ethan and I have had a chance to look at the books. We're trying to find a way to move McDougall out of its ... moribund ... state. And we're under the gun a little bit, time-wise. Obviously."

"Did she say moribund?" Dutton asked Ben.

"I believe she did," Ben replied.

Janey waited until it was apparent that no further comment would follow. "So, what do you think the problem is?" she asked Dutton.

"I don't know that we have a problem."

"You're losing money."

"I like to think we're in the trough of the wave," Dutton said. "We'll bounce back."

"What if the wave is bigger than you think?" Janey indicated the folder. "Looks to me like a tsunami."

"Moribund," Ben said. "Tsunami. Wow. This girl's got you in her sights, Jack."

"I shoulda brought my dictionary," Dutton said.

"You should've," Janey said. "You could've looked up the word 'image.' Because you have a problem with yours. There's nothing wrong with your product. You just don't know how to sell it. There's a generation of drinkers out there that don't know you exist."

"You're just an old traditionalist, Jack," Ben said.

"Call me what you want. Just don't call me late for dinner."

"This vaudeville act is about as old as your marketing plan," Janey said. "But you do believe in growth, don't you?"

"I believe in growth," Dutton replied. "We have grown. For the past hundred and fifty years, in fact. This business is cyclical."

"You're saying you won't help Ethan out on this," Janey said.

"I'm sorry. Is Ethan asking for my help?" Dutton asked. He looked at Ethan, who was still watching the river. "I must've missed that."

Janey let it pass. "Fine. We're gonna move on this. First thing I'm gonna do is find a market analyst with some expertise in this field."

"Did you try the yellow pages?" Ben asked, smiling.

"Did we ever establish why you're here?" Janey asked.

"Hold on now," Ben said. He put his hands up. "I'm just having a little fun. I'm on your side. Well, I'm on Ethan's side. I assume you're speaking for him. Because you—on your own—have no claim on any of this."

"Ethan and I are in agreement," she said.

"That right, Ethan?" Ben asked.

"I'm gonna sit out on this bank of sand, and watch the river flow," Ethan said and he turned to smile at them.

Janey saw the amusement on Dutton's face now as well. She was of a mind to tell Ben to go fuck himself, but then he had somehow supported her, although in an insulting, passive-aggressive manner that she assumed was his way. And then Ethan decided to walk out of the room. They watched as he passed through the foyer and into the plant itself. Dutton stood up when he realized where Ethan was heading.

"Hey," he said.

"Hey what?" Janey asked. "He can go where he wants." She smiled. "Can't he?"

Dutton looked at Ben in protest. Ben watched the door where Ethan had departed for a long moment, then shrugged his shoulders, his attitude suggesting that Ethan was harmless. Let him wander. Dutton seemed to arrive at a reluctant agreement to this. He turned to Janey.

"I wish you luck with your plans," Dutton said. "If there's anything I can do—"

"Right," Janey said.

"Come on, Jack," Ben said. "Let's give these kids a chance. You're willing to look at any marketing scheme Ethan comes up with, aren't you?"

Dutton smiled, then turned to Janey. "Absolutely," he said. "Tell Ethan to give me a call. Anytime."

"There you go," Ben said. "Teamwork."

On the drive home Janey considered what had happened. She sure as hell hadn't expected Ben to come to their rescue, if indeed that was what had occurred. Of course, she hadn't expected Ben at all. She realized now that Dutton had probably canceled the Friday meeting to arrange for Ben to be there today. But she'd received a reluctant nod of cooperation from Dutton, which wasn't much, she had to admit. What was clear to her was that she couldn't go on dragging Ethan around like he was an idiot savant. Especially when the idiot was running rings around a largely absent savant.

"You think Ben showing up was a coincidence?" she asked as they made their way back north. She'd found Ethan in the loading area, wearing a conspiratorial smile.

"When you got nothing, you got nothing to lose," Ethan said. "You're invisible now, you got no secrets to conceal."

"That's what I thought."

They turned onto the river road a short distance from the farm. The stream there was narrow and still high with the rains. Two boys, ten or twelve years old, were pushing a raft down the slope to the water. When they got near the shore the raft took off on its own down the last few feet, plunged into the water and was pulled away by the current. The boys raced along the shore after it but it was gone. Just like that.

When she looked back at Ethan, she saw that he was holding a handful of grain. He was examining it as they drove, rolling it between his fingers, holding it to his nose. She'd seen him do the same when buying grass. Now Janey caught a whiff of it, an odor that was musty and stale.

"What's that?" she asked.

"Rye grain," he said and he poured it from one hand to the other, watching the cascade with fascination. "That's what it is."

"It smells old."

"It is old," Ethan said. "They don't use it anymore. They don't use rye to make rye whiskey anymore."

THEY BOTH FELL ASLEEP in Johanna's big bed on the second floor. Later, Will speculated that it was probably the first time either of them had taken an afternoon nap in years, but then they'd had a pretty vigorous workout beforehand. When he woke up Johanna was standing on the balcony that overlooked the farm. The bedroom had once belonged to Everett and Margie, Ben's mother, and it was she who'd insisted on the balcony. It was only after Everett's third attempt, and subsequent failure, at matrimonial bliss that Johanna took over the room. It had been a practical move, if nothing else. She could watch her horses from the deck.

Waking, Will needed a moment to remember where he was, and why. Seeing her naked on the balcony, standing with her breasts resting on the railing, her back to him, refreshed his memory, and then his desire. He propped himself up on his elbows.

"If I had a camera," he said.

She didn't say anything at first, and then, walking toward him, she said, "You'll be taking no nude pictures of me. However, flattery just might work in your favor." He pulled the covers back and she got in beside him. "We were both sleeping. They came and took the goat away. I didn't even hear them."

He drew her up to him and kissed her. She put her arms around him and they lay quietly like that for a moment.

"Why did you stay here all this time?" he asked.

"Funny how people will ask questions when they're naked that they might not ask otherwise."

"Come on. There must have been things you wanted to do."

"I made a good life here," she said. "Everett was a difficult man, but when he got older he developed a generous side. It surprised me. Funny, just the other day I told Kick that people don't change and now I'm telling you that he did. But early on, I just felt like those kids needed me. It was a sad thing that none of their mothers was cut out for motherhood. You need a license to own a dog in this country, but anyone can have a child. Does that make sense?" She moved closer to him. "So the kids needed me and then Everett needed me, these last few years. And in between—well, I don't know where the years in between went. Does anybody?"

"I guess not." Will ran his forefinger down her nose, then across her lips.

She smiled around his fingers. "But I think I'm just about finished here now. I'll leave, even though I know my leaving will make Ben happy. But I won't stay just to spite him. What's the saying about cutting off your nose? I have no idea what Ben's vision of a happy life might be."

"What's yours?"

"I guess that's something I should try to discover," she said. She kissed him again. "I might head to the southwest. Arizona or New Mexico. I don't need snow in my life. I might find a cowboy who treats me right. I've always had a thing for you cowboys." She reached for his cock then. "Golly, the feeling is mutual."

She got on top of him, and just as they were getting into rhythm they heard car doors slam and then the front door open and close. She smiled down at him and shook her head.

"Ethan and Janey. They won't come here." She smiled. "I might."

Twenty minutes later they were lying side by side again, catching their breath and smiling like a couple of teenagers sneaking a moment under their parents' noses. She had her leg hooked over his. The phone on the nightstand began to ring.

"The machine will get it," Johanna said. "Or Janey will. She's all right, you know, that girl. I'm still not sure why she stands by Ethan, the way he is these days."

"I talked to her the other day," Will said.

"About that?"

"About a lot of things. I think she believes in him. Believe it or not, I think it's as simple as that."

The words were barely out of his mouth when someone tapped lightly on the door and then Janey's voice asked, "Johanna, are you in there?"

"What is it?"

"Kathleen's on the phone. She wants to talk to you."

"Take a number and I'll call her back."

"Okay."

They could hear her move away. Will looked at his watch. "Well, I got chores to do anyway. I'll walk over after supper and put a lead on that mare."

She pulled him to her and kissed him as he made to get out of the bed, and then Janey was back, tapping again. "Johanna ... um, she says it's kind of urgent. Apparently she's in Nashville."

"I knew that," Johanna said.

"Apparently she's in jail."

ELEVEN

Due to the impending bankruptcy the deal to purchase the fitness place went through quickly. Lynn bought the gym as a turnkey operation and even arranged to keep most of the staff, including the manager, Mandy, which was in itself a good thing, as Lynn really didn't have a clue how to run a fitness center, or anything else for that matter. Mandy knew the business side and was a freak when it came to fitness. She had the body fat of a steel post and she knew more about nutrition and muscle groups and general health than anyone Lynn had ever encountered. She was, in fact, a little frightening.

Lynn, for her part, knew how to shop and she went out and dropped a couple grand on a new wardrobe, including workout ensembles, power suits, track pants, designer sweats—in short, an outfit for every occasion. The day that Ben and Teddy Brock showed up she was wearing pleated cotton shorts, white Nike trainers and a golf shirt with the new logo—Get Fit—stitched above her impressive left breast.

"You remember Ted," Ben said.

"How are you, Ted." She extended her hand. "Welcome to Get Fit For Women."

Teddy shook her hand and then Lynn gave them a tour. "Ordinarily, there are no guys allowed in the workout areas," she said. "But I'll make an exception. Just this once."

"Hey, I happen to be the owner," Ben said. "If I want to, I'll lie in the middle of that floor naked, eating a cheeseburger and singing 'Stairway to Heaven.'"

"Maybe save that for the membership drive," Teddy said.

"You're a co-owner, Mr. Eastman," Lynn said. "But that still doesn't mean you get to use the facilities. This place is all about pussy power. You don't have a pussy, do you, Ben?"

Teddy smiled. "Do you, Ben?"

"The two of you can fuck off anytime now," Ben suggested.

They ended the tour in Lynn's office, which had been renovated for the new ownership. There was a leather couch along one wall, with two matching chairs, and a new desk, bar fridge, glass shelves and an array of entertainment equipment—big screen TV with surround sound, CD and DVD players, and a small kitchen counter adorned with various mixers, juicers and a number of other shining aluminum devices Ben couldn't name.

"What do you think?" Lynn asked. She was standing in the middle of the room, on the new beige carpet.

"I think the local Sears must have had a good week," Ben said.

An office intercom sounded then and Lynn reached for it. Teddy sat on the couch and patted the cushions on either side, arching his eyebrows at Ben as he did. A voice on the intercom was asking Lynn to come out to the reception area.

"I'll be right back," she told them.

When she was gone Ben walked around the room, looked at the new computer on the desk, the video and audio equipment, and then finally checked out the contents of the fridge. He glanced over at Teddy. "Lot of liquor in here for a fitness place. Grey Goose … holy shit."

"Make yourself a martini," Teddy said. "I have a feeling you paid for it."

Ben walked over to sit in one of the leather chairs. "Don't you worry about that, Teddy boy. I did my homework on this. These places make money."

"Come on, Ben. What've you got invested here so far?"

Ben sighed. "It was supposed to be about forty thousand. I have a feeling it's more like fifty now."

"Is this office included in that number?" Teddy asked. "Because you can add another ten if it's not."

Ben was getting irritated. "Just ... don't. Okay? Whatever the number is, it is. I told her she has six months to get this thing rolling. If it isn't, I can sell it for what I've got into it. Probably even make some money with all ... this." He gestured at their surroundings.

Teddy grinned. "This chick's an expensive piece of ass."

"Well, she's worth it," Ben said. "So watch what you say. You might be interested to know that I'm gonna marry this woman."

"How's your wife feel about that?"

"You're hilarious today," Ben said. "This is a very sensitive move to make. It has to be timed just right. It all depends on the situation at McDougall and Great North. Things are getting interesting at the distillery, by the way."

"Yeah?"

"Ethan and his girlfriend—whatsername—have apparently decided that they can turn the place around."

"Maybe they can."

"Bullshit. However, I'm encouraging Jack Dutton over there to accommodate them. It's going to take a little time but I'm thinking all I need is for them to run up against a few obstacles and they'll come to the realization that they're in way over their muddled little heads. But I need to get Ethan involved."

"How you gonna do that?"

"I'm just gonna drag him into the real world. What I've got going for me at McDougall is that Jack Dutton hates the fucking sight of Ethan and that little blonde dipsy. Jack doesn't want change. He's afraid of it. You gotta remember, the guy's a high school dropout. He figures new ownership means change. And change means new people. I can play on that a little too. Jack and I go way back. He'll play ball with me."

"You're a devious man, Ben." Teddy had his head lolled back on the couch, his eyes closed.

"Give me a break. Fact of the matter is, this is all for the greater good. Ethan would run that place even further into the ground, and Kick's got no more interest in Great North than I do. Speaking of which, I have a question about that situation too. If they need more money for this stupid record, how far can she go? Technically, she only owns the place in trust. Can she bankrupt the company?"

"I have no idea," Teddy said. "Might depend on how it was budgeted. I thought your old man bankrolled the thing out of his own pocket."

"But it's still on Great North's books. I know that, because Blaine Steward told me to my face when I went to see him last week."

"You've been there too? You're a busy boy, Benjamin. Spend any time at the plant lately?"

"The plant is humming along like a Swiss watch. There's a little delay with the Toyota contract but it's just a bump."

"Ever wonder why your father let you off so easy?" Teddy asked. He got to his feet and walked across the room to look at a print on the wall. "I mean—he left Kick and Ethan each a concern that neither knows anything about. He's challenging them, Ben. But then he turns around and leaves you a prosperous automotive plant you've been running—more or less—for ten years. I'd feel a little … slighted … if I were you."

"Well, I don't," Ben said. "The way I look at it, the old man knew I was the only one taking care of business. So don't throw that shit at me. Back to this record deal. If Kick wants more money, Blaine Steward is gonna pop a vein. He's like Jack Dutton. He'd love for me to step in and stir things up. He'd like nothing more than to show Kick the door and go back to making boring books on tape that show a six percent profitability rate."

Teddy turned on a ceiling fan, watched it as it picked up speed. "You bring joy to so many."

"You've got it," Ben said. "And that's where the timing comes in on the divorce. If I come riding to the rescue, and suddenly become owner, or at least part-owner, of these companies, then I'm gonna need make it appear as if they're all in the red. Is Meredith going to take me to court to try and claim half of my debts, or will she accept the lump-sum offer I make to her?"

Teddy stopped looking at the fan, shifting his attention to Ben. "Do you feel no remorse about any of this?"

"Remorse ... what's that?" Ben asked. "The fact of the matter is, I'm doing everyone a favor here. I'm a big picture guy, Teddy. If it wasn't for—" He stopped as his cell phone began to ring from his pocket. He held a finger up—as if Teddy had been hanging on his every word—and he answered it.

"Yeah?"

Teddy walked over to look through Lynn's CDs while Ben talked on the phone. There was a lot of hip-hop—Macy Gray, Alicia Keys, Nelly. Teddy was a Billy Joel man.

"For what?" he heard Ben say. Then, a few moments later, "Unbelievable. Keep me posted. Right."

When Ben put the phone back in his pocket he was smiling like a kid with a new pony. "It couldn't get any better than this."

"What's going on?"

"That was Blaine Steward. Kick's in jail in Nashville."

"What?"

"You heard me."

"What for?"

"Apparently she beat up some record producer in a bar." Ben walked to the fridge and helped himself to an apple juice. "You know what I'm gonna do now, Teddy? I'm gonna drop you at your car, and then I'm gonna come back here and fuck my girlfriend on that brand-new leather couch. And then I just might go home, tell my wife that I love her and then toss the ball around in the backyard with my son." Walking out the door, he began to sing. *"Life is but a dream—"*

A DUSTUP in a pretentious midtown Nashville bar wouldn't have garnered much interest except for the fact that Country Music Hall-of-Famer Jonah Peck was one of the combatants. With that, the story made news across the city the next morning, and then spread from there, breaking on tabloid TV that evening and eventually to the networks. In short order, the tale became increasingly tall. Jonah was said to have fallen off the wagon and it was suggested that his return to the bottle precipitated the brawl. Kick was cast as a mysterious Canadian and depicted variously as Jonah's girlfriend, groupie or stalker. Susie Braddock came off fairly well in the reports, possibly as a result of her reputation as a producer who contributed significantly to Nashville's greatest export, but probably because she was so willing to feed her creatively edited version of the incident to the media. What was not disputed, for the most part, was the fact that Susie had gotten her ass kicked by the girl from the north country.

Kick might have been better off losing the fight, although she really didn't pause for any such rationalization when she came out of Kenny Butternut's lap to answer to Susie. If she had lost, then maybe the judge would have looked upon her with some clemency. As it was, he released industry fixtures Jonah and Susie, both charged with causing a disturbance, on their own recognizance and set bail for Susie's boyfriend, who'd decked Jonah, at two hundred dollars. For Kick, a rank outsider who was looked upon as a foreign citizen, a risk to flee and in all probability a rabble-rouser to boot, the charge was aggravated assault and bail was set at five thousand dollars.

The only person she could think to call was Johanna. When she did, Janey answered the phone. If Kick hadn't been preoccupied with the fact that she was sequestered in a Tennessee holding cell with a less than savory group of Nashville whores, thieves and crack addicts, she might have considered it odd that Johanna was, in Janey's opinion at least, having an afternoon nap. She gave Johanna a condensed version of her misadventure in the bar, mentioning in the telling that Susie Braddock was a lying weasel who had apparently misappropriated the money budgeted for the record.

"Are you all right?" Johanna asked, always the maternal figure.

"Yeah."

"And the Braddock woman?"

"I gave her a whupping, Jo."

"Kick."

"I know. I feel bad about it. And now I need five grand for bail. I'm guessing they're gonna want it in American currency too."

"I can send you the money."

"I don't want it to come out of your pocket," Kick said. "I was wondering about the money Everett left for the house—the taxes and upkeep and whatever. Can I borrow it from there?"

"Will Montgomery might have the answer to that," Johanna said. "As executor, I mean. He's here right now. He stopped by."

"He's there? Put him on."

While she waited for Johanna to bring Will to the phone, Kick was left wondering why he just happened to be there and, furthermore, why he happened to be there when Johanna was purportedly having a nap. She was still studying the possibilities when Will came on the line. "Seems like all I do is bail you out of jail," he said.

She hesitated, then laughed. "Hey, I'd forgotten all about that." The summer she was eighteen she'd rolled her Camaro over in the ditch along the river road, driving too fast on the curves above Crooked Pear. The police had taken her to the station and charged her with careless driving. Neither of her parents was around at the time and it was Will who had come down to the station to get her.

"How's the facilities?" he asked now.

"I've slept in worse places," she said. "And I'm developing friendships here that I'm sure will last a lifetime."

"Right."

"You gonna bail me out?" Kick asked. "I'll pluck your turkeys. I'll plow your wheat."

"You don't plow wheat," he told her. "I'd have to ask Raney Kilbride about that account. I can send you the money myself, Kick."

"I'd rather you didn't. It wouldn't feel right."

"What about Great North?"

"I thought about that too. I figure just my asking would give Blaine Steward good old-fashioned apoplexy. Wait'll he sees my room service bill at the hotel. Besides, this recording deal down here is about as fucked up as a thing can be. Using Great North cash for bail money doesn't feel right either."

"All right," Will said. "We'll get it to you one way or another. Where do I send it?"

Kick had the information on a card she'd been given and she read it off to him while he wrote it down. When he told her twice to slow down, she realized she was still a little wired from the fight. She was also a little preoccupied with Will's being there, and Johanna's alleged nap.

"Okay," he said when he had it. "Sit tight. And Kick—try to behave yourself."

"Hey, she started it."

It was a woman officer who'd escorted Kick to the room where the phone was and now she led her back to her cell. Kick really had no idea where she was. It seemed the holding center was somewhere in the city, in the basement of the central police station. Kick wasn't in the cell more than five minutes when the officer came back.

"Your bail's been paid."

"By who?"

The woman smiled. "I'll give you a hint. I just got his autograph."

THERE WERE A FEW REPORTERS hanging around the lockup, tipped off, it seemed, that Jonah Pike was in the building and in the process of springing an international felon. When Jonah reasoned that they should get out of the city, Kick was agreeable to the suggestion, thinking the farther the better at this point.

"I thought you were broke," Kick said as they drove east in the rusty pickup. "Where'd you get five thousand dollars?"

"Hell, nobody's that broke."

"I am."

They pulled up to a red light. She saw him looking at her hands; the knuckles were skinned and beginning to bruise.

"I thought you were joking about the karate."

She shrugged. "I had a lot of unharnessed energy when I was young. The doctors called it aggression. Somebody suggested to my father that karate would be a good outlet for his … rambunctious child. Typical Everett—he went whole hog, bought me books and videos and the gis. Hired this hotshot instructor. Then forgot all about it, never once mentioned it to me again." She sighed and looked out the side window of the pickup. "Tell you the truth, though, I was never very good at it. I didn't have the self-control."

"I noticed."

They were moving again now.

"You got a bit of a shiner," she said.

Jonah was wearing an old cap with a RedMan Chewing Tobacco logo on the front. He pushed it up on his forehead to look at himself in the rearview. There were a half dozen stitches below the left eyebrow. He touched the side of his eye gingerly. "That's the first fight I been in since I quit the booze. I've lost a lot of fights in my day. I always blamed it on the liquor. Another one of my theories shot to hell."

"I could show you a couple of moves."

"I believe I'll pass on that."

When they pulled up to the farmhouse it was already dark. Paige's truck wasn't in the drive. He shut the engine off and looked at her. "What're you going to do now?" he asked.

"If you mean *now*, I'm gonna take a shower. I've been wearing these same clothes for two days. I'm surprised you didn't make me ride in the back. I was gonna borrow some clothes from Paige."

"She's off somewheres. Borrow away."

She stayed in the shower a long time. She was stiff from the fight; she seemed to have pulled a muscle in her right shoulder and tried to work it out under the hot spray. Her lip was swollen where Susie's sucker punch had landed. After drying herself off she went into Paige's closet and found a pair of cotton pants and a T-shirt.

When she came downstairs Jonah had a platter of sandwiches on top of the piano, along with a bottle of pop and a cool Texas longneck. She didn't realize she was hungry until she saw the food. She opened the beer and took a sandwich as Jonah tinkered with the keys. Kick sat on a stool and listened. When he stopped, he looked at her.

"I asked what you're gonna do now."

Kick's mouth was full and she swallowed. "I know you did. I'm still thinking about it. Waiting for an epiphany. I'm not holding my breath though."

"I guess the first thing is to figure out where the money went," Jonah said. "And how much of it is left. I could try and talk to Susie about the songs. Though I got a feeling she might be done talking."

Kick had a drink of beer and wiped her mouth. "I'll call Blaine Steward. I'd rather have a root canal. There must have been some sort of accounting on his end. He didn't just hand Susie a quarter million." She looked at Jonah. "Did he?"

"I wouldn't know about that."

"Well, I'm gonna find out."

"I can't believe I'm about to advise this," Jonah said. "But if you intend to go after Susie Braddock in the courts, you're gonna need a crackerjack lawyer."

"You know any?"

"Lawyers? Hell yeah, I know lots of 'em. They're the ones got me twelve million in the hole. You want their names?"

"I believe I'll pass on that."

"Finish them up," Jonah said, indicating the sandwiches. "You want another beer?"

Kick shook her head but reached for another sandwich. "Why are things so fucked up?" she asked.

"I might be the worst person on the whole damn planet to ask that question to," Jonah said and he began to play the piano. The tune was vaguely familiar to Kick. She ate the last sandwich and then leaned back against the wall and drank the beer while Jonah played. After a while he began to sing:

"There's a church in the valley by the wildwood,
No lovelier spot in the dale,
No place is so dear to my childhood,
Than the little brown church in the vale"

Jonah glanced up at her, then resumed, looking at a spot above her head.

"Come to the church in the wildwood,
Oh, come to the church in the dale,
No spot is so dear to my childhood,
As the little brown church in the vale."

"I know that song from somewhere," Kick said.

"First song I ever learned," Jonah said. "On a piano my grandmother had sitting on the front porch not two miles from here. House was so small there was no room for it inside. Weather played hell on the tuning, I'll tell you." He noticed that Kick's bottle was empty. "You might want something a little stronger. Help that swolled lip go down."

He got up and went into the kitchen and came back moments later with a bottle of sixty-year-old Dalmore and a juice glass. He put them both on the piano.

"Now that's just spooky," Kick said. "The only person I've ever seen drink that vintage of Dalmore was my father."

Jonah poured the scotch. "It ain't near as spooky as you think. Your father's the one sent me this. In return I was gonna make him a record. Guess you could say I've been a little slow holding up my end."

Kick drank the scotch and as she did she thought about sitting in her father's broken chair along the creek bank a few days earlier. Of snapping turtles and whiskey flasks and archaic pistols. Of words never spoken. Of opportunities forever lost.

Jonah walked around to sit at the piano again, played a couple of notes, then stopped. "Been a long and twisty road from granny's back porch to here. Maybe it's getting old that does it, but there are times when a man looks back and wonders what it was worth. Being famous sure ain't what it's cut out to be. You hear pickers say they never wanted to be famous, they just wanted to make their music. But that's bullshit, 'cuz if all you wanted to do was make music, you'd a stayed on granny's porch with that old tinny piano. No, there's more to it than that. Once you start making music, you want some-body other than your friends to tell you it's good. You want *strangers* to tell you it's good. Ain't that an odd thing? To care about the opin-ions of people you don't even know? But you do. And if enough strangers are of the opinion it's good, then stand back. You got your-self a tiger by the tail, just like Buck said. And it'll catch you up."

"What will—the money?" Kick asked.

"The attention. Crowds and limousines. Fancy hotels. TV shows. Women. Oh, the women. All that nonsense that's got nothing to do with the music. When in the beginning it was all about the music. Being famous ain't nothing but a curse. Look at Hank. Look at Patsy. Good Christ—look at me. I'd have made better music if I never set foot off that porch."

"You saying you haven't made good music?"

"From time to time. I've made some shit too."

"Well, here you are today," Kick said. "Maybe you've come full circle."

"I started out broke and I'm back to being broke, if that's what you mean."

"Maybe you're back where you started with the music too. Metaphorically speaking."

"Too big a word for a country boy like me."

"Bullshit," Kick said.

He began to play again:

"There, close by the church in the valley,
Lies one that I loved so well,
She sleeps, sweetly sleeps 'neath the willow,
Disturb not her rest in the vale.
Come to the church in the wildwood,
Oh, come to the church in the vale,
No spot is as dear to my childhood,
As the little brown church in the vale—"

THEY SAT on Raney Kilbride's front porch, drinking Raney's twenty-year-old scotch and talking about the alleged outlaw Kathleen Eastman. Will had called the old judge earlier with the question of the bail money and then, when he'd called back to say that Kick had made bail on her own, Raney had suggested he drive in anyway. For a drink and a talk, he'd added.

"The scotch is the carrot," Raney had said over the phone.

"That means there's a stick," Will said but he drove in anyway.

It was early evening when he arrived in Waterloo. He was still wearing jeans and a work shirt but he'd traded his manure-caked rubber boots for a pair of slightly cleaner work shoes. Raney looked every bit the retired sage in an ancient navy cardigan and brown corduroys. They sat in padded wicker chairs. There was about an hour of daylight left and there were kids on bicycles and skateboards out in the street. Occasionally a couple walking a dog would pass by, and they would wave to Raney.

"You know all these people?" Will asked.

"I don't know any of these people," Raney said. "Seems like I'm the last of my generation left in the neighborhood. I was still in my twenties when we bought this place. Those sugar maples were no bigger around than your wrist. It's nice, though, having these young people around."

Will tasted the scotch. It was very smooth and very good and for that reason reminded him of Everett Eastman and his last days, sitting along the creek with his flask and his cap-and-ball Colt, turtle annihilation his intent. It was the first Will had thought of the old gun since the day when Kick had insisted he take it home.

"This is nice stuff," he said to Raney.

"I look forward to this time of day, these couple of ounces of single malt. I'd hate like hell to have to decide between this and my dear wife, Will. I'm so fond of them both."

Will smiled and had another drink. "So what's this about? Unless you just invited me in to sit on your porch and drink your scotch. Because I'll have you know I'm all right with that."

"Help yourself. There's more where that came from. Besides, we're waiting for Blaine Steward."

"We are?"

"Yes. I think we need to discuss just what it is Kathleen has gotten herself into down south. I'm hoping that this little donnybrook was a minor occurrence and will be looked upon as such by the courts. But you never can tell about these things. If an overly zealous judge decides to make an example of our girl, he could lock her up for a year or so. I don't think that's what Everett was hoping for when he handed her the keys to Great North."

"What's Steward in all of this?"

"Blaine Steward might be the one person who would be happy to see Kick incarcerated," Raney said. "So I intend to make it clear to him that I don't share those feelings. Furthermore, I think we need to know the ins and outs of this recording contract. That *is* what started the fight, is it not?"

"It sounds as if there was a spirited debate on the subject."

Raney chuckled into his hand. He looked at his watch and then poured more scotch for them both. "You live twenty miles from here and you were five minutes early. Blaine Steward lives a mile away and he's half an hour late."

"There he is," Will said as a GMC minivan pulled up behind his truck.

Steward extracted his bulk from the car and came moping up the walk like a fifth-grader coming home with a bad report card. He wore baggy jeans and a golf shirt and sandals and a floppy Tilley hat. Upon arriving on the porch, he declined a drink, an act that seemed to peeve Raney even more than the tardiness. Steward himself seemed determined to display a put-upon front. Will had met the man a couple of times over the years but Steward did not seem to recall the fact. He shook Will's hand like it was the first time and then sat down.

"What's going on, Raney?"

"You tell me what's going on," Raney said sharply. "Kathleen's in jail somewhere below the Mason-Dixon Line, there's a large sum of money missing, and apparently nobody knows anything about anything. If this is the way you conduct your business, I suggest you get out of publishing and go into politics."

"I told her not to go down there," Steward said.

"She's your boss. You don't tell her anything."

"Who ever could?"

Raney gave Steward such a look of contempt that Will thought for a moment the elderly judge would reach across and slap the man. But then the look passed. Raney settled for more scotch before continuing.

"If you're in the telling mood, then try this," he said. "How has Great North been monitoring this record deal? Who's holding the purse strings?"

One look at Steward's florid face and Will could see that there hadn't been much in the way of monitoring anything.

"There were no ... purse strings," Steward began in his deliberate manner. "This whole thing was very unconventional from the get go. Everett provided $250,000. It didn't come from Great North. Heck, you think we could finance something like that? It really had nothing to do with Great North."

"The money never went through you?" Raney asked.

"The money went through us," Steward admitted slowly. "But Everett came up with this producer, this Braddock woman. Seems to me he read about her in the newspaper or something. We did a contract with her."

"And you sent her the $250,000?"

"Well ... that's what Everett wanted."

"And since then, you haven't requested any kind of accounting on that money?"

"It was Everett's deal!"

"Everett is dead," Raney said. "Are you clear on that?"

Steward straightened in the chair. "Then I guess it's Kathleen's deal now. Isn't it?"

Raney slowly rotated the glass of scotch on his knee. "It's Kathleen's deal now. If the money is gone, and there's no record album to show for it, no return revenue on the investment, then Great North is going to suffer."

"That's right," Steward said.

It was one thing for Steward to admit to that, Will thought, watching him. It was another that he didn't seem particularly dismayed by the possibility. In fact, he seemed to welcome it, maybe as a vindication of sorts against Kick's involvement. Maybe something else altogether.

"Somehow I don't think that's what Everett had in mind when he made his will," Raney said then. "I think you've handled this whole matter like a bear cub playing with his prick, Blaine." He stopped to take a sip of the liquor and he held it in his mouth a moment, as if to cleanse his palate of the bad taste that was Blaine Steward. But then he said, "And that's why we're sending Will to Nashville."

"What?" Will asked it first but Blaine Steward was close behind.

"You heard me, both of you," Raney said. "In accordance with the conditions of the will, Kathleen is required to get this record made. To do that, the money has to be found. And, as the guy who's had his head in the bloody sand on this little project, Blaine, I'm saying it's your responsibility to allow Will to go there on Great North's behalf to help try and find it."

"I resent that comment," Steward said.

"You think I care what you resent, you dunderhead? Will, when can you leave? You got your crops in?"

"Well … yeah."

"Then you can leave tomorrow. Is that what you're telling me?"

Will smiled. "You seem to be doing all the telling here, Raney. I'll need a couple days to square things around."

"That's fine. The estate will pay for your expenses. That's how an executorship works. Now, you are going to have to figure a way to straighten this thing out."

"Sounds simple enough," Will said. "Hell, I should be home for supper."

The judge looked at him. "You'd better hope you're home in time for harvest."

Steward got to his feet. "Can I go?"

"You can go."

They watched as Steward lumbered off the porch and down to his van. As he was driving away, Raney turned to Will. "Never trust a man who turns down a glass of good whiskey."

TWELVE

It seemed to her that the incessant squawking of the grackles in the cottonwoods outside awakened her. When she came to, she was immediately aware of problems more pressing than noisy birds. Her temples were pounding and her mouth was as dry as dust and sour with the aftertaste of the expensive scotch. And then she heard him snore.

She turned and her hangover became secondary. He was on his back, his mouth open. They were both as naked as the grackles in the trees. Kick lay there for a time and then quietly slipped out from beneath the covers, gathered Paige's clothes from the floor and went downstairs. She sat down at the kitchen table.

"Fuck," she said.

After a while she found a phone book. A taxi back to Nashville cost her sixty-five dollars. She bought aspirin at the hotel convenience kiosk and went up to her room and fitfully slept the day away. Every time she woke, it would take a moment to remember what she'd done. Her conscious self would inform her semiconscious self that she was an idiot and then she would take more aspirin and go back to sleep.

She hung around Nashville that day and most of the next. She had a strained telephone conversation with an obtuse Blaine Steward. Eventually her head cleared and she realized that someday her conscience would do the same. Exile was going to accomplish nothing at this point. When Paige called to invite her to the farm for dinner, she was almost relieved.

"Jonah's cooking chicken," Paige said over the phone. "And he said to tell you that the scotch is locked away. What the hell does that mean?"

"No idea," Kick said. She would have kissed Jonah for his discretion but that was how the whole thing had started.

Paige picked Kick up in front of the Sheraton late that afternoon. Kick, with fresh regrets to nurture, had pretty much forgotten about the fight with Susie Braddock. Paige reminded her.

"You don't look any worse for wear," Paige said when she got in. "Jonah looks like he called Mike Tyson's mama a dirty name."

"How'd you get stuck with being chauffeur?" Kick asked.

"I volunteered." They were in traffic now. Paige took a moment before elaborating. "I love my father but he drives me fucking nuts. I guess it's a cliché but it's true. Parents."

"I wouldn't know about that."

Paige glanced over. "You saying your father never drove you crazy when he was alive?"

Kick considered it a moment. "You know, this might sound strange, but my father never started to drive me crazy until he died. Leave it to Everett to come up with a twist, even on that."

Paige was lighting a cigarette. They were headed for the thruway but before they got there she took a right and started out of town on a side street.

"So how does Jonah drive you nuts?"

"He just—" Paige said. "He might have this rebel image from his younger years, but the man is Ward Cleaver with a ponytail. Nowadays, anyway. I swear, the questions he asks. What are your plans? What do you intend to do with your life? Why aren't you married? Like he's a fucking expert on marriage."

"So what do you tell him?" Kick asked.

"I don't tell him anything. I cut and run. That's my strong suit."

"I can relate to that."

They drove in silence for a time. In ten minutes they were out of the city. They passed a series of subdivisions and then drove through the town of Mount Juliet. Beyond it was farm country, the vivid red dirt, lazy grazing horses, the smell of hay, fresh-cut and lying in windrows. Kick watched the countryside pass for a time, then she turned to Paige.

"So what do you do?"

Paige had just finished her cigarette and she reached for another. "So far, I've been a singer, an actress, bartender, movie gofer, clothing designer and a barrel racer. Oh, and a drug addict, but that was recreational, not vocational." She laughed hoarsely. "Going in, anyway."

"Barrel racer?"

"Yeah. That's my quarter horse in the corral at the farm."

"The Appaloosa?"

"The Appaloosa is Jonah's horse. She's a fucking head case, like every other female he's ever been involved with."

Kick fired her a look but the remark seemed to be innocent enough. Still, it was cause for more of the self-analysis she'd been undergoing these past few days. Getting lumped in with a legion of unnamed fucking head cases did little to alleviate her doubts about herself and her actions.

They were driving through the town of Lebanon now. Kick looked for old pumpkin head as they circled the town center but his bench was empty. Driving east out of town, they passed the high school. The football field was ringed with bleachers and had an electronic scoreboard that was lit up with "GO BADGERS! FALL '07."

"My alma mater," Paige said.

Kick glanced at the brick building. "And were you a good student?"

"Not even close," Paige said. "What about you?"

"I had a guidance counselor tell me I was an underachiever."

Paige pulled the cigarette down to the filter before tossing the butt out the window.

"Did they mention to you in rehab that nicotine is a drug?" Kick asked.

"A *legal* drug," Paige said. "They don't mind you doing the legal drugs. Keeps the economy humming." She shot Kick a look. "And that's enough about me. Jonah said you make documentaries. When you're not in the music business. Which you're not."

"Correct. On both counts."

"So how does an underachiever become a filmmaker?"

"Anybody can shoot a doc. All you need is a camera, a subject that gets your blood pumping and a stubborn streak. Oh, and the willingness to go ass over tea-kettle in debt."

"Shit, all I'm lacking is the camera." Paige reached for the cigarettes on the dash, and then, looking at Kick, tossed them back without taking one. "You telling me your rich family doesn't help you with financing?"

"My father is the one person I never approached for money. Not sure why. He did put me through school, but that was about it. I worked for a newspaper in Montreal for a few years, then I ended up in Germany one Christmas, with a guy I was about to marry. We started snooping around his family history. His ancestors immigrated to New Jersey in the early 1700s, and then moved north to Canada with the United Empire Loyalists. Anyway, we ended up making a little film about his family tree. It was more a vanity project than anything. But it got me hooked. My first real film was about a guy from Hamilton who made goalie pads for all the pros, starting back in the thirties."

"What happened to the hubby?"

"Marriage wasn't nearly as addictive as filmmaking."

"Where is he?"

"Toronto. He teaches school."

"So he's smart?"

"Smart enough to divorce me. I have a bad habit of maxing out credit cards with absolutely no notion of how I'm gonna pay them off."

"We all have our little vices, don't we?"

"Can't imagine life without them," Kick said.

They slowed and turned onto a side road. Kick could see the Peck farm in the distance. They were approaching from a different direction this time. Paige must have sensed Kick's unease in arriving.

"The homestead," Paige smiled. "Lots of history here, girl. I bet those dusty Germans are looking pretty good right about now."

When they got to the farm Jonah was on the rear deck, wearing a Foghorn Leghorn apron and cooking chicken over a bed of coals in an old oil drum that had been sliced in half lengthwise and mounted on four steel legs. He smiled at Kick when she walked out on the deck and then he nodded. After a second, she nodded back. And that seemed to be it. Kick sat down at a large redwood picnic table and accepted a beer from a cooler. Jonah was drinking tonic water.

"Did you make the potato salad?" Jonah asked.

"I made the salad, Jonah," Paige replied. She was having an iced tea and another smoke. "You sat there and watched me."

"Oh yeah, I did."

When he turned back to the fire, Paige glanced at Kick and pantomimed pulling on a joint. Then she arched her eyebrows and laughed. Kick got up to have a look at the fowl on the grill.

"That's not wild turkey, is it?"

"Wish it was," Jonah said. "I don't know where them birds have got to. They were plentiful last year. I blame it on all these damn yuppies moving out here to build homes in bush lots. Our forests are gonna be all gone before you know it. We got plenty of open land. It ought to be a law that you can't cut down a single tree to build a house."

"You cut down a dozen trees to build that barn," Paige said.

"That's different," Jonah said, but it was evident that he wasn't about to explain why. He looked at Kick. "Well?"

"I made a call," Kick said. "I now know twice as much as I knew before. Problem is—I didn't know anything before."

"Is the money gone?" Jonah asked.

"It doesn't sound good," Kick replied. "Apparently the money was handed over to Susie and she was told to run with it. Great North is now taking the position that the contract was a separate entity between you and my father. It's pretty obvious that Blaine Steward is only interested in this thing if it doesn't cost Great North any more money. He claims that any problems would have been handled by Everett. Well, we've got all kinds of problems, and no Everett. He was always good at disappearing at inopportune times."

The fire flamed up in the drum, and Jonah splashed his tonic water in to squelch it.

"I called Susie's office today, but she didn't call back," he said. He looked at Paige. "You want to get those songs?"

Paige got up and went into the house. When she came back she put another longneck in front of Kick and then tossed a sheaf of loose papers the size of a manuscript on the redwood table. She sat down across from Kick.

"There's about fifty songs there," Jonah said. "And that may be all you're gonna get for your quarter million. I'm guessing Susie's gonna claim she spent all kinds of money trying to put this thing together. Even if you take her to court, it's gonna take years to convict her—if you can—and then you'd still have to collect. And I have no intention of making this record five years down the road. I intend to make it now."

Kick was looking through the stack of papers. Now she glanced up. "You still want to make the record?"

"I made a deal with your father," he said. "Paige, did you get a chance to look at those songs?"

"Don't I always do what you tell me, daddy?"

"No."

"Well, this time I did."

"And?"

"There's about forty I wouldn't let my fucking dog sing, if he could." Paige leaned forward to pick up some of the songs. "The others … I don't know. Might find five or six worth working on, you want to rewrite 'em." She turned to Kick. "The music itself isn't necessarily a problem, you get the right pickers. We got the best musicians in the world around here; they can snatch a melody out of the air. But the lyrics … they seem to be lacking in—" She looked at her father. "What am I trying to say, Jonah?"

"They suck like a howlin' wind."

"That's it."

They ate at the big table on the deck. Along with Paige's salad and Jonah's chicken, they had bread and peas and tomatoes. The chicken was very good.

"That's because it was raised right," Jonah said. "My friend Clark raises them on his farm out near Franklin. Rhode Island Reds, feeds 'em nothing but corn and grain, lets 'em run around his barnyard as they please. He treats 'em all like little pets. Right up to the moment he lops their heads off."

"I was in Franklin the other day," Kick said. "With Susie."

"You were in Franklin, Tennessee," Jonah told her. "I'm talkin' about Franklin, Kentucky. Ain't nothing in Franklin, Tennessee, but a bunch of brand-new millionaire so-called country stars. And people like Susie."

It was getting dark by the time they finished and they moved into the kitchen to get away from the mosquitoes. Paige said she would make a fresh pot of coffee. Kick and Jonah sat at the harvest table marked by the years, Jonah still wearing his apron. He had carried the stack of songs inside. Kick lifted a few of the pages and began to read.

"You're a songwriter of great acclaim, Mr. Peck," she said after a minute. "Can't you just take these songs and make them better?"

"Hell, a monkey could do that," Paige said from the counter. "Be easier to write your own, Jonah."

"I don't have any of my own," he said sharply. "You gonna make the coffee?"

"Yeah, you need caffeine," she said sarcastically.

"Is it my imagination," Kick asked, "or are these songs all the same?"

"Now you're getting it," Paige said. She brought the coffee over. "The songwriter is in love with God, country and himself. Not necessarily in that order."

Kick looked at Jonah, who sat staring morosely at the floor. She poured milk into her coffee. "There's nothing personal about them."

"You manufacture the emotion nowadays, the same as you manufacture the singers," Paige said. She was speaking to Kick but looking at her father. "Isn't that right, Jonah?"

He refused to look at her.

"All the songs sound the same, and everybody looks like a fucking fashion model," Paige continued. "It's all about image. Steve Earle called Shania Twain the world's highest paid lapdancer. That about sums it up."

"Are you telling me there are no good songwriters around?" Kick asked.

"They're still out there," Paige said. "The man that raised that bird we barbequed is one of the best."

"Why don't we hire him?"

"Because he's not in Susie's stable," Paige said. "This is a Susie Braddock project."

"All right, that's enough," Jonah snapped and he sat up. "Where we gonna get the money to record this thing? I can put some pickers together but we're gonna need studio time, and production money."

"Don't look at me," Paige said. "I'm a bankrupt. I might add that I come by it honestly."

"I'm broke too," Kick said. "But first generation."

Jonah glanced from one to the other as if he suspected them of conspiring against him. "Maybe I can track down Susie Braddock," he said. "Appeal to the better angels of her nature—"

"Good one," Paige said.

Jonah looked at Kick. "She told you she had studio time booked."

"And she told you she didn't," Kick said.

Jonah sighed. "Well, if that girl squandered your money, then she's got to feel some obligation to you."

"Beating the shit out of her in the bar might just work against you in that regard," Paige said to Kick.

"Gee," Kick said. "And it seemed like such a good idea at the time."

WILL MONTGOMERY WASN'T ONE to dwell on such matters but he would, if pressed, admit to having few fears in this life. Those that he had, however, were substantial. Rats, because they were rats. Yellow jackets, because he was allergic to them and he usually left his EpiPen on the kitchen counter. Once, cutting timber in the bush behind Crooked Pear, he'd run into a nest of them and was stung maybe a dozen times. He swelled up like a beach ball before he got home to the antidote.

He was also slightly leery of lightning, because his grandfather had been killed by it while walking the fields behind the farmhouse one July afternoon when Will was seven. Death by lightning was an extremely random thing though, and it wasn't a fear as much as a minor concern.

But flying was a different matter. Back when he was playing hockey, there had been no way to avoid it. So he would routinely steel himself with vodka or beer and endure it the best he could. When he washed out of the NHL he could've wrung a few more years, and a few more dollars, out of his career by playing in Europe. But the thought of all that flying was too much. He came home to the farm and had managed to avoid airplanes ever since.

So he drove his pickup to Nashville. If the matter had been more urgent, he might have considered getting on a plane. But the situation as he saw it—Kick out on bail, the record deal up in the air, the money possibly gone—while not encouraging, was not one he would qualify as life or death. Furthermore, although he hadn't mentioned it to Raney Kilbride, he really didn't have any idea what he was going to do when he got there. It was about seven hundred miles to Nashville, he estimated. He was hoping that something would come to him along the way.

He left the farm at five in the morning and drove straight through, crossing the border at Buffalo and then swinging southwest, angling down through the Ohio Valley, skirting Cleveland and Columbus, passing through Cincinnati before heading south to Bowling Green. He'd followed the route once before. When he was in his late teens and determined that he was going to be anything in this life but a farmer, he and a couple of high school friends had headed for Texas in Will's four-door Chevy Biscayne. Then, as now, they had been lacking in anything resembling a real plan, other than to visit the Alamo and party along the way. They'd ended up in Fort Worth, both car and passengers broke. The frame was rusted out on the Biscayne and the car essentially snapped in two on the freeway. Their juvenile dreams similarly broken, the trio had to wire home for bus fare back to Ontario.

This time Will was behind the wheel of a Ford F150. He had a thousand dollars in traveler's checks in his pocket, courtesy of Everett Eastman's estate, and the chance of a broken frame on the five-year-old truck was practically nonexistent. And although it wasn't the Alamo he was looking for this time around, reports indicated it was a battleground just the same. He wondered if he'd find Kick wearing a coonskin cap.

The farmland he passed through must have suffered the same spring weather as had home; he was well into Kentucky before he saw any noticeable progress in the corn or the beans over his own. The Ohio River was over its banks even yet in places.

It took him thirteen hours to reach Nashville, which was roughly what he'd estimated. It took him another twenty-four to find Kick. He tried her cell number from Bowling Green and every couple of hours after that. He kept getting her voice mail. In Nashville he went directly to the Sheraton downtown but was told she wasn't registered there. There was another Sheraton out on the McGivock Pike but again he was disappointed. He went back to the downtown hotel and asked that they check again.

"I was told she was here," he said to the same desk clerk.

"I'm sorry," the woman said after looking.

"And she wasn't here at some point?"

The woman hit a few keys. "Yes. She was here. Checked out yesterday."

"You couldn't have told me that before?"

"You didn't ask before."

Kick had left no forwarding address. That made sense; knowing Kick, she was probably heading for home and jumping bail in the process. Bail-jumpers rarely left forwarding addresses. At this point Will was fresh out of ideas and hungry to boot. He walked to a restaurant called Hobb's and had a steak. The walls of the place were plastered with photos of people he'd never heard of but the beef was first rate. After he ate, he phoned Johanna on his calling card.

"Kick's not there, is she?" he asked when she came on the phone.

"Kick's in Nashville."

"So am I."

"Really? And you can't find her?"

"It's a good-sized city."

The only other number Will had received from Blaine Steward was for Susie Braddock's office. The message on the answering machine said that they were closed for the day, but would be back in the office at ten the next morning. He was told he could leave a message after the yodel. Will hung up before the yodeling commenced.

He drove to the north edge of the city and got a room at a Super 8, figuring to conserve money where he could. He didn't know what else Kick may have gotten herself into, if indeed she was still in Tennessee. Steward had informed Will, rather brusquely—the man was a lot tougher over the phone than he was in person—that Kick would receive no more money from Great North with regard to the NIC project. Apparently Steward was still having trouble grasping the fact that Kick—right or wrong, in jail or out—owned the company.

The next morning he had breakfast at Denny's and then sat in his room waiting for ten o'clock to arrive so he could call Susie Braddock's office again. As he waited, he began to anticipate more answering machines, receptionists, and in general a major runaround in trying to find the woman. The wait-for-the-beep kind of stuff that he and virtually everybody else he'd ever known despised. At nine he looked the company name up in the phone book. The address was there. By quarter to ten he was parked across the street from the place.

Five minutes later a Mercedes with license plates reading RECORD GAL pulled into the driveway. A blonde woman wearing tight black jeans and a sequined satin shirt got out and tottered on stiletto heels to the front door. Will got out of the truck and walked over.

"Hello."

She turned as she was unlocking the front door. When she saw him, she actually looked him up and down for a moment. "Good golly," she said. "Is it my birthday?"

"Beg your pardon?" Will stopped on the lawn below the front step, next to the giant sign bearing the name SUSIE BRADDOCK.

"Honey, if you're that Carolina boy Geraldine's been bragging on, I don't care if you can sing or not. I'll find something for you to do." She opened the door. "Come on in, I've been expecting you. You were supposed to be here yesterday."

Will had no idea who it was he was supposed to be, but it appeared as if the misunderstanding was going to get him in the door.

"So you're Susie," he said as he stepped into the outer office.

"I am," the woman said. She had her back turned to him as she said it, her hand in front of her. When she turned back, it seemed as if she'd undone a button, or two, on the form-fitting shirt. He noticed now that she had a slightly swollen lip and three tiny stitches high on her left cheekbone.

"I should explain why I'm here," Will said.

"Let's go into my office," she said. "I'm here alone today. My receptionist has a nasty infection from a navel piercing. They've got her on an antibiotic IV. Can you believe that?"

Will followed her into an inner office. The room was big enough to shoot skeet in, and the walls were decorated with blowups of album covers and commemorative records. Susie walked over to sit on a sectional corner couch that appeared to be covered with the hide of a dappled steer. She patted the cushion next to her.

"Geraldine tells me you're the next Toby Keith," she said. "And that kind of talk just gives me goose bumps. I think she might be fibbing me a little on your age—I'd say twenty-six has come and gone for you, handsome—but you look like you spend some time in the gym. Tell me, Carolina boy—you like Toby's music?"

"I might. I've never heard it."

"Yeah, right. Tell another. Would you get over here and set?"

"Hold on," Will said as he moved to sit in a leather chair beside the couch. "We've got our signals crossed here. I'm not from Carolina and I don't know who Geraldine is. Or Toby either, for that matter."

"Then just who the fuck are you, honey?" Susie asked sweetly. "Are you a singer?"

"Nope. I'm a farmer. I'm looking for Kathleen Eastman."

Susie's eyes narrowed at this, but her smile stayed in place and the syrup never left her voice. "You sonofabitch," she said after a moment. "I ought to throw your ass outta here."

"I'll leave if you want," Will said. "I was hoping you might know where Kick ... Kathleen, might be."

"You talking about that little bitch who sucker-punched me in the bar the other night? That who you're talking about?"

"Well, she's not that little."

"Far as I'm concerned, she couldn't get any littler. She's in jail, last I heard. And I intend to do whatever I can to see that she stays there for a good long time." She was getting worked up now. "I'm with people—important people in the industry—at one of this city's finer dining establishments, and suddenly I'm attacked by this ... drunken fucking lunatic. She's lucky the cops showed when they did. And I know what you're thinking ... you look at me and you see this sophisticated woman, but I'll have you know I grew up hardscrabble. I dusted a few people to get where I am today."

"She made bail," Will said.

"She made bail? Well, good for her. I have no idea where she is. Anything else I can do for you? I have work to do."

"Well, actually—"

"Are you the boyfriend?" Susie asked suddenly. "Is that what's going on here?"

"I'm not the boyfriend."

"You're just some farmer wandered on the scene, that what you're telling me?"

"I'm here," Will said, wondering if he knew himself, "I guess I'm here representing Great North. It's kind of complicated, but I was hoping to find out what's going on with the recording deal."

"Okay, now I am gonna throw your ass out of here," Susie said. "I got no time for you or the tadpole or any of this. I will *not* discuss this matter any further."

Will got to his feet. "I thought it was worth a try. What's this about a tadpole?"

"Goodbye."

As Will turned toward the door, Susie walked over and sat behind the huge desk in the center of the room. He went through the reception area and had his hand on the door handle when she called to him. He turned and stepped back through the doorway and stopped. She had her feet up on the desk now, and was leaning back in her chair, tapping a felt pen on her chin as if in the act of determination.

"You got a name, farmer?" she asked. "Jesus, are all the farmers in Canada as good-looking as you?"

"Just me," Will said. "You don't want to see the rest. My name's Will."

"Sit down, Will." When he was seated, she swung her legs off the desk and leaned toward him. "I'm real reluctant to tell you what I'm about to tell you. But the tadpole has fucked this situation up to the point I have no choice. What you have to realize is that this city, and this industry, is one big family, Will. And Jonah Peck is part of that family. He's had his troubles in recent years but we've stood by him and at times we've covered for him. You see, he contributed a lot to the industry for a long time. And that's why it breaks my heart to tell you this. But the fact is, he has sabotaged this record deal from the start. I couldn't begin to calculate how many hours I've put into this thing. I've had my writers on it, my musicians, my sound guys at the studio. Hell, we did a demographic survey to try and figure out what people might want from Jonah Peck at this point in his career. This would've been a done deal months ago except we were missing one thing—Jonah Peck. It appears that he has no intention of doing this record, and he never did."

"Why would he agree to do it then?"

"It could be—" she said hesitantly. "It could be that his judgment is clouded. Everybody knows he's drinking again. He was definitely liquored up the other night. He took a swing at my boy—er ... one of the people at our table. It's sad, really."

Will regarded her from across the desk. She actually did appear saddened. "How much of the budget has been spent?" he asked.

"Practically all of it. I don't know what you're gonna do now. I fulfilled my obligation to this project. Matter of fact, I'm out of my pocket for expenses I'll never see. But that's the risk I took. Hell, I just wanted to make a record with Jonah Peck."

"Who's the tadpole?" Will asked again.

"The tadpole's your girlfriend." The phone rang and Susie reached for it. "On top of everything else, I gotta answer my own phone today." She barked into the phone like a drill sergeant. "Susie Braddock! Tell me something good."

Will watched as her eyes hooded over, then she caught herself and smiled across at him.

"Mr. Peck," she said coolly into the phone. "We were just talking about you. How was your head the other morning?" She listened a moment. "Yeah, I just bet. Listen, I got a handsome gentleman sitting here, he's looking for that psycho-bitch you been running with. You got something going on with that girl, Jonah?"

Will really didn't want to hear whether Jonah Peck had something going on with Kick. He got up and took a walk across the room to examine the records on the wall. He'd always wondered what gold records were actually made of. It appeared that they were ordinary records just spray-painted gold.

"Well, I'm sorry it has to be this way, Jonah," he heard Susie say. "I hope you can work something out. I've given you some quality songs. What you do with them is up to you. My involvement with this project ended with the mayhem in the bar the other night. There's no room for mayhem in country music."

Will heard her hang up. He turned to see her watching him.

"The tadpole's out at Jonah Peck's farm," she said, rolling her eyes at some unspoken implication. "That was Jonah. Now he's talking out of the other side of his mouth, says he wants to make the record. He's all hat in hand, looking for free studio time. Did you happen to see a sign out front says I'm running some kind of charity here?"

She was staring at Will as if actually expecting a reply. "Could I have a look at that demographic survey you mentioned?" he asked instead.

"It's not here," Susie said quickly.

"No? Where do you keep your demographic surveys?"

Susie leaned back in her chair. "For a farmer, you think you're pretty smart, don't you? Better watch your step. I'm pretty smart myself."

"That's good," Will said. "We get all these smart people together, we should be able to figure this thing out. Great North is going to want to see your books on this project. They're going to want to know where the money went."

"I told you where it went," Susie said. "And I'll show you, honey. I can provide you with enough receipts to fill a fucking boxcar. What you have to realize is that I'm the only one here doing her job. I'm the one being taken advantage of."

Will nodded, then turned back toward the wall. "What're these gold records made out of?"

"Gold. You make gold records out of gold," she said defiantly. "And hard work. And sweat. And integrity."

She was still naming ingredients as Will walked out the front door and headed for his truck across the street.

BEN BOUGHT A BUCKET of chicken at the Colonel's, thinking he'd have a couple of pieces for lunch, then take the rest back to the office and leave it in the fridge for snacks. He ended up eating the entire bucket on the drive to Waterloo, as well as the fries and the slaw and the giant diet cola that came with it. He was fully gorged by the time he pulled into Great North's parking lot and he sat there behind the wheel for a moment, a little sheepish at the sheer gluttony of what he'd done.

There was a rap on the passenger window, and Blaine Steward opened the door. Ben moved the red and white bucket from the passenger seat and put it on the console. Steward squeezed himself into the car.

"I was out for lunch and saw you pull in," he said. "We might just as well talk out here."

Ben glanced at the front of the building, where the plate-glass windows were every bit as transparent as Steward's story. It was fine with Ben though; it probably wasn't a good idea for him to be seen too often at Great North. He knew nothing of the other employees, where their loyalties might lie.

"What's going on?" Ben asked. "Louise said you sounded a little frantic."

"Will Montgomery's in Nashville."

Ben put his fist to his mouth to suppress a belch. "That's a popular destination these days," he said when it passed. "What's he doing there?"

"That's a darn good question," Steward said. He was pouting a little. "One you'd have to ask Raney Kilbride. It was his big idea; seems he's all worried about Kathleen. And get this—Will is there on behalf of Great North, looking into this messed-up record deal. I had no idea that being a farmer qualified a person as an expert in the music business."

"Take it easy now," Ben said. He thought about it for a moment. "This is just Raney pretending he's still in charge. Senile old fucker. It doesn't mean it's a bad thing though. Have you heard from Montgomery?"

"He called this morning. Apparently he had a meeting with the record producer."

"Yeah?"

"She's quit the project. She says that Peck is impossible to work with; they spent all this money and nothing has come of it."

"Isn't she the one Kick beat up?" Ben asked. "Shit, I'd quit the project too. Question is—where do they go from here?"

"That's what I wanted to see you for. Montgomery says that Peck still claims he wants to make the record. What does that mean?" He hurried to answer his own question. "I'll tell you what I think it means. They're going to come to me for more money."

"That's probably what it means," Ben said. "Okay, Blaine—what would *you* do? I mean, if Raney had decided to send you down there, which he should have done to begin with."

"Thank you very much. I was wondering if anyone else would realize that." He straightened in the uncomfortable bucket seat. "I mean, we've held up our end and we've received nothing in return. I say we sue Peck, and this producer, for the money they've spent, and make them produce the darn thing as originally planned."

There was a little pop and ice left in Ben's paper cup, and as he sucked at it through the straw he nodded, as if in full agreement. "Get the project back on board. Get tough with the whole dirty lot of them. Yes, sir. Then Kick can come home, take over the company, and take a huge load off your shoulders. I can see exactly what you're thinking."

He watched Steward's Adam's apple bounce. "I'm not sure that's what Kathleen would want," he said after a long moment.

"Oh, you know Kick. I'm sure she's got big plans for Great North. Wouldn't surprise me you're out of the audio book business altogether in a couple years." Ben laughed. "You might be turning out porn films, Blaine. Oh relax—I'm just having a little fun."

Ben counted to ten as he waited for that to settle in. He felt his belt cutting into his stomach and wished he'd settled for the ten pack of chicken. "On the other hand—" he began and then stopped.

"What?" Steward asked at once. "On the other hand what?"

Ben shrugged. "Maybe Great North should just pull the plug. You've done your part. They haven't. I want you to know that I support Kick all the way on this. Hundred percent. But I can't see her getting this thing done. Not without sucking the company dry." To make his point, he pulled on the straw again. "If it doesn't work out, and I'm guessing it won't—what the hell does Kick know about making a record—then I'll be willing to step in and help right the ship. You're gonna need an escape hatch here. And if that happened, I would ask you, Blaine, to resume control of the company. I'd say you've done a pretty fair job of it so far."

"I think I have. What about Will Montgomery?"

"What about him?"

"Well, he's in Nashville. And Raney's given him authority."

"The only thing Will's qualified to do is shovel manure. And the only reason Raney sent him down there is because Kick got tossed in jail. He's nothing but a fucking babysitter. No, the more I think of it, it's in your best interests to put the brakes on this thing. Lock the cash drawer. Kick has got to learn to sink or swim on her own."

So they left it like that, two fat men crammed into a Corvette, a bucket of stripped chicken bones and a tacit agreement between them.

AFTER BREAKFAST they sat at the harvest table and came up with twelve songs that Jonah thought might have possibilities, or at least "didn't make him puke," as he put it. They bundled the twelve songs in a shoebox and Jonah took the box into the music room and sat down at the piano. Kick followed him, stopping to lean against the wall just inside the French doors. Behind her she could hear Paige in the kitchen, rinsing the breakfast dishes. Jonah opened the keyboard lid, then looked at Kick.

"I was thinking those horses could use a brushing," he said. He paused purposefully. "If you two girls were looking for something to do."

Paige walked in as he said it. "Aren't you a subtle old bastard?" she asked.

"I never claimed to be."

Paige looked at Kick. "You ever brushed a horse before?"

"Lots of times," Kick said. "Belgians."

"Well then, this ought to be a snap."

Paige was still in the T-shirt and pajama bottoms she'd slept in and she went to change. Kick was already wearing a pair of Paige's jeans and a faded cotton shirt and, taking Jonah's hint, she walked out to stand on the porch to wait. She'd moved out to the farm from the hotel the night before. All her own clothes were dirty and at some point that day she intended to find out if the bankrupt Jonah Peck owned a washer and dryer.

The two horses were in the corral, the Appaloosa mare standing hipshot near the water trough and the bay gelding wandering along the fence, stopping every now and then to tug at the sparse grass beneath the bottom rail. Paige suggested that they tie the two in their stalls in the barn, where it would be easier to brush them out.

"I'll take her," Paige said, nodding in the mare's direction. "You can have the old boy."

The spotted mare didn't look in need of a brushing at all. The gelding, Kick saw approaching him, was absolutely filthy. His mane was tangled and there was mud from forehead to hoof.

"How come I get your horse?" Kick asked.

"Patsy might take a chunk out of you," Paige said. She indicated the bay. "What's wrong with him?"

"He looks like the Joad family just rode him in from Oklahoma." She took the gelding by the halter and slapped his dirty shoulder. "Come on, Woody Guthrie."

Kick worked the better part of the morning cleaning the bay. Paige brushed the mare out quickly and then passed the time smoking and offering encouragement to Kick. There was no smoking allowed in the barn, so she alternated between outside and in.

"When you headed to New York?" Kick asked once, when she was in.

"I don't know. Thought I'd be gone by now, tell you the truth."

"What're you going to do there?"

"I got a boyfriend, or ex-boyfriend, or something. Living in SoHo."

"I didn't ask who was there. I asked what you were going to do." Kick was trying to remove some dried mud from the gelding's mane. There was a large puddle by the trough in the corral and it appeared that the horse had been lying in it.

"Maybe see if I can get some auditions. Theater work."

"You have an agent?" Kick asked.

"Not at the moment. Agents aren't scrambling to sign unknown actors coming out of rehab."

"I suppose not," Kick said. She looked over the horse's back. "Substance abuse being so rare in the arts."

"You've heard."

Kick went back to the untangling. "Maybe you ought to stick around a while, see what happens with this recording deal."

Paige had climbed onto the top rail of the stall to watch Kick work. She was wearing a straw cowboy hat and a pair of torn overalls. "I'm not so sure about that," she said. "Jonah and I are already getting on each other's nerves."

"Maybe a little friction in his life would be a good thing," Kick suggested. "Fire up his creative side."

"Do I look like a martyr?"

The bay sidestepped then, pinning Kick against the side of the stall. She shoved him over forcefully and then reached for the currycomb and began to brush. She was hoping that Paige would stick around, and not necessarily for the sake of any recording that may or may not happen. It had appeared, at first, that Jonah had put their encounter the other night in the past. Now Kick wasn't sure. Going to bed last night, she'd given him a hug and he'd attempted to kiss her. She'd slipped away and that had been it. She hoped. All she needed was a complicated situation to get more complicated. She figured that Paige would make a good chaperone. Besides, Kick liked her.

"You think Jonah will get any of those songs to work?" Kick asked, finally removing the last of the dust from the horse's hide.

"Nope. But then I never thought you'd get that horse clean either. So I guess we'll just have to see how it goes."

Kick led the gelding out of the barn and turned him loose in the corral, where the mare was waiting. The bay trotted all around the perimeter of the enclosure twice, then went to the center of the ring and flopped down in the dirt for a roll. Kick watched him, then turned toward the barn, where Paige was standing in the open doorway, a smile on her face.

"Ain't he a peckerhead?" she asked.

"You knew all along he was gonna do that, didn't you?"

Paige shrugged. "Come on, let's get some lunch. Watching you work made me hungry. We can check out Jonah's progress." She laughed. "Jonah's progress—there's a concept I haven't considered for a while."

As she said it they could hear a vehicle come down the lane and then stop. Walking through the barn and then out into the noonday sun, they came upon the sight of Will Montgomery, climbing out of his pickup truck that was parked beside Jonah's. Not seeing them as they emerged behind him, he started for the house.

"Ontario plates," Paige said, looking at the truck. "You know this dude?"

"Yeah," Kick said.

"Nice ass in those jeans," Paige said.

"Hey," Kick called.

Will turned and saw them, and then waited as they walked over. Kick wasn't sure whether to embrace him or shake his hand, so in the end she did neither. She introduced the two of them. When Paige shook Will's hand she stepped so close Kick thought she would knock him over.

"Nice to know you, Will Montgomery," Paige said.

"Hello," Will said and he looked at Kick.

"This would be where I ask what the hell you're doing here," she said.

Before Will could reply they heard the creaking complaint of a screen door swinging on rusty hinges. All three turned to see Jonah stepping out onto the side porch, carrying the shoebox.

"Well, he's still got the songs," Kick said. "That's a good sign."

Jonah came down off the porch and walked over to a stump about twenty feet away. He put the box on the stump.

"That's not," Paige said.

Jonah disappeared back into the house and in a moment returned, this time carrying a double-barrel shotgun. He fired both barrels. There was a deafening roar and the perforated shoebox jumped crazily in the air, its lid flying off and the bits and pieces of the papers within scattering like confetti across the lawn, where they began to float and drift with the breeze.

Only then did Jonah notice them. He looked their way for a moment, nodded curtly as if agreeing upon some trivial matter, and went back inside. Paige turned to Will, who was standing, wide-eyed, watching the paper debris as it traveled on the wind.

"What's the matter?" she asked. "Don't they have music critics where you come from?"

THIRTEEN

Ben called Teddy Brock's office on his way back to work from Waterloo. Teddy's secretary told him that he was in court for the day. Ben left a message on Teddy's voice mail and then went back to the plant.

All that southern-fried chicken had rendered him groggy and he almost ran off the road several times on the drive there. He had Louise fetch him coffee when he got back to the office and, thus revived, he actually did a couple hours' work. Eastman Technologies was trying to set up a subsidiary plant to build the Toyota ignition module in Indiana. They could make the component at home, but the tariff situation made it much more profitable to do it in the States. Ben had found a suitable building in the city of Gary, and a realtor with his own fine sense of walking the line when it came to zoning laws, and spent most of the afternoon on and off the phone with the man, trying to buy the property for half the asking price.

He called Lynn from the car on the way home but got her voice mail as well. He left a message saying he'd see her for dinner the following night. He'd told Meredith he was going to a banquet at the club after his Saturday golf game. He was pulling in his driveway when his cell rang. It was Teddy Brock.

"Where are you?" Ben asked.

"Just leaving the courthouse parking lot," Teddy said.

"Shit," Ben said. "If you'd called five minutes ago, I could've met you for a drink. Now I'm sitting in my driveway and my wife is looking at me out the living room window."

"Your life is nothing but hardship, Ben," Teddy said.

"I need to talk to you about something," Ben said. "I'll call you back in about ten minutes, when I'm by the pool with a vodka in my hand."

"Why don't I come by?" Teddy asked. "I'm heading your way as it is."

"Sure. You can stay for dinner if you want," Ben said, still watching Meredith in the window. "Give me somebody to talk to."

It was warm enough to sit outside, even though Wilson hadn't actually opened the pool yet, a fact that Ben thought to mention to Meredith when she brought him his Stoli's and tonic.

"It's still early June," she said.

"What does he do all day?" Ben asked.

"Yard work. He's here one day a week." She went back inside.

Ben changed into baggy shorts and a Hawaiian print shirt. He was reclined in the chaise lounge, his face angled toward the falling sun, eyes closed, when he heard a car door slam. A moment later Teddy came walking around the side of the house.

"The great man in repose," he said.

Ben sat forward. He looked toward the house. "I'll get you a drink. Meredith!"

"She's not a waitress," Teddy said. "I can get it myself."

He went inside, where Meredith met him with a hug. They stood and talked in the kitchen for five minutes while Ben watched and waited impatiently. Finally, Teddy came out with a bottle of beer and a pilsner glass. He sat in a deck chair by the covered pool.

"What's up?"

"Kick's time at Great North," Ben said and he laughed. "Things are in an advanced state of disarray over there. Blaine Steward is this close to pissing his pants and running home to his mommy. If he ever had one."

Teddy poured the beer into the glass. "Obviously a situation that makes you very happy. But not one that you need to talk to me about."

Ben raised his eyebrows, nodding emphatically. "I need to talk to you about the distillery. Great North is on the fast track to ruination because of this fucked-over deal with the country and western star. But I need McDougall on the same road. I'm thinking I'd like the whole thing to happen at once. Especially with regard to the situation—" Ben jerked his head toward the house.

"With Meredith?" Teddy asked.

"Keep your voice down," Ben said.

"With Meredith?" Teddy said in a stage whisper.

"Yuk it up," Ben said. "What I'm thinking is this. I stopped out at the farm yesterday. I like to keep an eye on things, you know, with Johanna and this little blondie Ethan's hooked up with. No telling what they might try to pull."

"People can be so duplicitous."

"Tell me about it. I had an idea on the way home. Ethan is a fence post; you can hardly get anything out of him that makes any sense at all. How hard would it be to have him declared incompetent? McDougall is a million-dollar industry, I don't care if the bottom line is a little iffy these days. You can't have someone like that in charge."

Teddy regarded the beer in his glass. "Have you thought about how this is going to make you look? Trying to have your brother ousted?"

"I'm going to look just fine," Ben said. "Because I'm not going to be involved. I'll get Jack Dutton to do it."

"You're pulling a Pontius Pilate?"

"You're quoting the bible to me? Don't you have any modern references?" Ben asked. "All Jack has to do is say that Ethan doesn't respond to any sort of corporate decision making that needs doing." He paused, then pointed a finger at Teddy. "And just so you know— I'm behind Ethan all the way on this. Hundred percent. I'm going to tell Jack to give him every opportunity to step up to the plate and score a touchdown."

"So to speak."

"But if that doesn't happen, then something has to be done. This is for the good of the distillery, Teddy. This is the family name we're talking about."

"Your name's not McDougall."

"Okay, the family business."

Meredith came out of the house then. "You guys okay?"

Ben held his glass out. "I could use another vodka. Bring Teddy another beer."

"Have a drink with us, Meredith," Teddy said. "How long has it been since I made you a Manhattan?"

Ben shot Teddy a look. "Okay," Meredith said. "I'm going to check on dinner, you make me a Manhattan."

"We were in the middle of something," Ben said when she was gone.

Teddy stood up. "What did you want from me?"

"You told me you knew doctors who had background in this stuff. Incompetency."

"We can talk about that," Teddy said hesitantly. "If we have to. But give the kid a chance, Ben. For Chrissakes, give him a chance. You got any sweet vermouth?"

OTHER THAN A FEW HOCKEY PLAYERS, who really didn't count, and the time that he'd taken a leak beside Martin Short in a restaurant washroom in Orillia, Will had never really been in the presence of anybody famous. So he had no idea what to expect on his drive out into the Tennessee countryside to the farm of Jonah Peck. And if he had, it was likely that those expectations would not have included a twelve-gauge Browning blowing a shoebox full of songs to smithereens. In contrast, Martin Short had just pissed and zipped up.

Will had received directions to the Peck farm from the owner of a hunting and fishing store near Mount Juliet. Driving by, Will had seen turkey decoys in the window display and gone back to have a look. When he mentioned the singer's name, the store owner had said that he himself hunted near Peck's farm and then drew Will a map. Will bought a tom turkey call that the man's father had made and then headed for Tater Peeler Road.

He'd given up trying Kick's cell number and he wasn't at all sure that she was even at the farm. He was going on Susie Braddock's word, and he had a suspicion that Susie was not the most reliable person in the state, especially where Kick was involved.

But Kick was there. She called to him when he got out of the truck and he turned to see her walking toward him, looking both sexy and lean in jeans and boots and a man's shirt, the sleeves rolled up to the elbows. Her hair was tied loosely at the back of her neck and she was slightly dirty and unkempt, the dishevelment making her even more attractive. With her was a thin dark-haired woman, wearing a cowboy hat and overalls, smoking a cigarette and looking a little like a wasted fashion model.

There was barely time for introductions when the cold-blooded execution of the shoebox interrupted things. The dark-haired woman, whose name was Paige, offered Will a rather cryptic explanation of the motives behind the shooting, and then the three of them went inside.

Jonah Peck was in the kitchen, carelessly shuffling through some dozen or so loose pages that were scattered across a pine table. He glanced up at them when they came in. His eyes flickered on Will for a moment, then he went back to the papers.

"Picking your next victims?" Paige asked.

Her comment seemed to trigger within him a sense of futility. He shoved the pages away, some falling to the floor, and then he slumped into a chair. He pushed his long gray hair back from his face with the fingers of both hands.

"This is Will Montgomery," Kick said to him. "A friend of mine from home."

Jonah looked at Will without enthusiasm but managed to half-raise himself to shake hands nonetheless. Will tried to read the name inside the tattooed heart on the man's arm, but it was faded and illegible.

"I'll tell you why Will's here as soon as I find out myself," Kick said pointedly. She turned to Will. "I have a feeling that Raney Kilbride is behind it. Trying to save me from myself."

"It was Raney, all right," Will said. "But not to save *you*, necessarily. The record deal is part of the will."

"Aw, it's not about *you*," Paige said, smiling at Kick but approaching Will. "You want some lunch, cowboy? I'm going to whip something up, I don't know what. Jonah, you eating?"

Jonah, now regarding Will narrowly, said nothing.

"Will's the executor of my father's estate," Kick explained. "Raney Kilbride was a friend of my father's. He's also a meddler. And a judge."

"You figure you can fly down here for a day and straighten this thing out?" Jonah snapped. "That it?"

"I drove down here," Will told him. "And no, that's not it at all. I figure if it was that easy to straighten out, you'd have done it yourselves by now."

"Kind of a smart aleck, ain't you?" Jonah said.

"I like him," Paige said. "I think I'll treat him to some homemade soup. If I could find the goddamn can opener."

Jonah didn't stick around for the soup. He went into the other room, and by the time Paige had the Campbell's chicken noodle bubbling in the pan, they could hear him playing something on the piano. It sounded closer to a Bach sonata than George Jones.

After they ate, Kick said that she would show Will around the place. Paige gave her a look that suggested she herself should be giving the tour but Kick ignored it. Will suspected that showing him around had nothing to do with showing him around.

"What the hell are you doing here?" she asked a few minutes later. They were standing in the tack room in the barn. Will, avoiding Kick's accusatory glare, was looking at the tooled western saddles on the stands.

"I told you. Raney wants to know where the money went. Blaine Steward doesn't seem to know, and doesn't seem to want to know."

"So you're down here to check that out?"

"Well, yeah."

"Remind me again," Kick said. "What am I doing down here?"

"Besides getting thrown in jail?"

"Fuck you."

"I can't imagine how you ever got into a barroom brawl," Will said. "With that attitude."

"My attitude isn't the issue here," Kick said. "It makes me look bad, you showing up. It makes it look as if I can't handle the situation. You can see that, can't you?"

"What have you done so far, to handle the situation?" Will stepped back when he saw the look in her eye. "I'm not being smart. I'm asking."

"I've spoken to the principals," Kick said. "I even went to a recording session with Susie Braddock. This was early in our relationship, when we were still Thelma and Louise. She told me that the Nothing Is Certain project was all hunky-dory. Then Jonah Peck told me that everything she said was bullshit."

"She told me that he's a drunk. And that's the problem."

"Who told you?" Kick asked. "Susie Braddock? You talked to her?"

"Did you ever wonder how I knew you were here? By the way, I tried your cell a couple dozen times."

"I lost it in the brawl," Kick said. "How the hell would Susie know where I was?"

"Peck called her while I was in her office. Trying to get things back on board, I gathered. But she's out of it. She says you guys are on your own."

"And she said Jonah's drinking?"

"Yup. Said he was pie-eyed the night of the fight."

"She's lying," Kick said. "I was with him the whole time, he never had a drop." She turned back from the window. "I myself had a couple cordials."

"Kinda figured that."

"Jonah says he hasn't had a drink in years. And I believe him. He's a bit of a pothead, but I'm told that the use of marijuana is becoming quite popular in the music world." She paused. "So that's how she's gonna spin it."

"That's what it looks like."

Kick walked out of the room and into the barn. She stood in the big double doorway leading outside to the corral a moment, her hands plunged in the pockets of the jeans, looking out at the farm as if the acreage might tell her what to do. Will watched her, and as he did he tried not to think about how terrific she looked. He was reminded of Johanna's remark the other day, suggesting he was harboring feelings for Kick. Wasn't that something he'd have picked up on himself? He had to admit he'd been a little on the oblivious side since Denise had left. Not that oblivion was a bad thing when it came to certain matters.

After a moment she turned back. "And now you're here to save us all?"

"I doubt that."

"Then what?"

"The way I look at it, there are two possibilities. One, you get the money back, and call the whole thing off. Which gets Great North off the hook financially. Two, you make the record, and recoup the investment that way. There's just one problem with both these scenarios."

"Neither one of them is likely to happen," Kick said.

"You got it. Plus, the first violates the conditions of the will. You'd lose your claim on Great North."

"Oh, darn."

"And as for Plan B—it doesn't look to me like anybody's gonna record anything. And, in case it's slipped your mind, there's something else to consider here. You've been charged with criminal assault. Raney's concerned they might lock you up for a few months, Kick. That's the real reason he sent me here, if you ask me."

Kick exhaled heavily and sat down on a bale of straw along the wall. "If Everett was alive, I swear to God I'd shoot him, Will. I got half a mind to skip out of here, tell Blaine Steward to take a flying fuck at the moon and just forget about Great North and the whole goddamn bunch. I was doing all right on my own."

"You skip, and you're gonna lose your border-crossing privileges, you know that. So much for the Wyoming project."

"Yeah, I thought of that too. And that's not an option. I'm gonna finish that film, I don't care if I have to sneak across the Saskatchewan border in the dead of night. Hey, it worked for Sitting Bull." She sat quietly for a moment, her back against the wall, legs crossed. She looked up suddenly. "So what'd you think of Susie?"

"I thought for a minute she was gonna take a bite out of me."

"I don't doubt it," Kick said. "And I think Paige might be entertaining the same thoughts. I guess these southern gals like you Gary Cooper types."

When they got back to the house Paige was sitting on the porch, her feet in cowboy boots propped up on the railing. She was wearing a skirt now, and she had brushed her hair and put on a little lipstick. She had an unlit cigarette in her mouth.

"Going to town?" Kick asked, climbing the steps.

Paige smiled at her and lit the smoke. Kick sat down in the chair next to her. Will stayed at the bottom of the steps.

"You gonna stay the night?" Paige asked him. "There's plenty of room."

"My bag's at a motel in Nashville," Will said.

"Get it," Paige said. "I'll go along for the ride."

Will saw Kick fire Paige a quick look. Paige smiled again and blew smoke in the air above her head.

"Well, the room's paid for," Will said. He looked at the screen door that led inside the house. "I'd like a word with your father before I go."

"He's gone hunting," Paige said.

"I thought he was looking for songs to record," Kick said.

Paige flicked her ash over the railing into the flowerbed. "He's not gonna find them on that kitchen table. Besides, what's the point? There's no money to record anything anyway. By the way, I read the Nashville paper while you guys were making out in the hay mow."

"Please," Kick said.

"There's a little follow-up to your scrap at Del Rio's the other night. Susie's quoted as saying that Jonah was three sheets to the wind. Said she feels sorry for him. Fighting his demons, as she put it. Lying little whore."

"Shit," Kick said. "She went to the papers with that stuff?"

"Woman's a skank," Paige said. "I told you that, first day I met you."

Will looked at the pair of them as he listened to the exchange. A week ago he'd been working day and night, trying to get his crops in, and now he was here. A lot of guys would love to be in his shoes. Pristine farm country. Sun shining overhead. Not one, but two beautiful women. On the surface it would seem to be a pretty nice arrangement. That was the problem with veneer, though. It always looked real nice on the surface. If a man was smart, he wouldn't scratch too deep.

"What's he hunting?" he asked.

"Wild turkeys," Paige said. "But he won't get one."

"How can you be so sure?" Kick asked.

"Well, for one thing, there's no turkeys around." Paige tossed her cigarette butt away. "For another—he left his gun on the back porch."

BY THE TIME he got to the tree stand, he'd calmed down a little. At least he'd relaxed to the point where he realized that he was on a hunting trip without his gun. He had a buck knife on his belt, but Jonah had never in all his years in Tennessee heard of anyone bagging a wild turkey with a buck knife.

"Doesn't mean I won't be the first," he said to the breeze in the trees.

He sat in the stand and laid out his calls and his scratches on the limb in front of him, just as he normally would. He had a joint in his pocket and he placed it on the limb too, along with his lighter. He didn't light it right away though. He knew that if he got high he wouldn't be inclined to think about the situation back at the house and he wanted to think about it, at least for a while.

He knew that he'd let it go too long. He'd let Susie Braddock run with it because he really wasn't of a mind to get involved in all the nonsense surrounding the thing. The truth was, he wasn't of a mind to make a record at all. He'd told himself that that would change, once he had the songs to do it, but in his heart he'd known all along that Susie would never come up with them. Jonah knew there were good songs out there, but he was just as sure that they wouldn't find their way into Susie's hands. Besides, she wouldn't recognize them if they did.

There were producers he could've approached himself. Cowboy Jack Clement or Rick Rubin. He could've asked Willie for help. Or Kris. Or Merle, or any number of people. But he didn't. He sat back and let Susie run the show. Well, she ran it right into the ground by the looks of things.

As far as the money owed the IRS was concerned, most of Jonah's royalties went toward paying the interest. The government didn't seem real interested in throwing him in jail, not so far anyway, and Jonah knew that his being old and famous was helping him out in that regard. The government wanted the money but they didn't want to look bad getting it. Of course, that would change eventually. He wouldn't get less older but he was getting less famous by the day.

The whole thing could have gone on indefinitely, if it wasn't for Everett Eastman up and dying when he did, thereby introducing a whole new cast of characters to the mix. And Jonah had to admit that he had a crush on one of them. And it wasn't because Kick was beautiful, although she was. There were more pretty girls in Nashville than a man could shake a Gibson twelve-string at. She just had a way about her. Jonah couldn't find a word to describe it and then he did. She was uncivilized, in the best possible manner. It wasn't a trait that was real popular these days, which made it even more appealing to Jonah. Maybe it was something she'd developed as a defense mechanism or maybe it was a genetic thing. Wherever it came from, it wasn't an act. And Jonah was pretty damn sure it had gotten her into more trouble than it had gotten her out of. It sure as hell did the other night at Del Rio's. It was part of her. How she walked, and how she talked with that Canadian accent. How she handled Susie, in more ways than one. She was probably half his age, Jonah realized, but only the brain could recognize a thing like that, or give it any significance. A man's heart knew nothing of years.

And then today the friend had shown up. Jonah didn't know what to think of him. He was pretty damn sure of himself, whoever he was. Jonah could only speculate on his relationship to Kick, and it was a speculation he'd rather avoid for the time being. He was an executor, she'd said. Jonah wasn't even sure what it was an executor did but it didn't seem like much of an occupation. Of course, there were those who might place burned-out country singer a little low on that list too.

There was one other consequence of Kathleen Eastman's arrival. It had been years since Paige had spent more than a day, or two at the most, at the farm. When she arrived more than a week ago she'd said she was heading to New York the next day. She was still here and Jonah had to believe that the hullabaloo surrounding Kick and the aborted record deal was the reason why. Whether that was it, or something else, he didn't care. He was just happy to have her on the premises. She was his youngest child, and undoubtedly his last. And she was the one who everybody had always claimed was exactly like him. It was little wonder they didn't get along.

Thinking of Paige, he took the notebook from his pocket. He flipped to a place where he had done several sketches of her face. As he looked at the faces he'd drawn, each one a little different in temperament, he took the pencil from the book's binding and began to sharpen it with his knife.

It was starting. He'd felt that way for a while now and he'd particularly felt it the night before, when Kick had gently pushed him away, like the grandfather he was, and he'd ended up staying up half the night at the kitchen table. She'd rebuffed him with a little kiss on the cheek. Thinking back, it would have been more flattering if she'd shoved him harder, slapped him even.

After a while he lit the joint and took a couple of long tokes before stubbing it out on the limb and putting it carefully in his shirt pocket. The wind was picking up and above him the branches of the evergreens and the cottonwoods stirred but it was still quiet in the clearing. He looked about the woods for a while. He could smell the white pine trees and the heavy loamy aroma of the forest floor. There were squirrels, both black and gray, chasing each other pell-mell along the limbs of the hardwoods. Squirrels had been a steady part of his diet growing up, although it had been years now since he'd eaten one. Bushy-tailed rats, Clark called them, although Clark still ate them in abundance. Jonah had no desire to shoot the squirrels. No gun either, for that matter. He went back to the notebook.

With the grass, and whatever inspiration had followed him to the tree stand, it seemed that the gobble-gobble of the tom was in his ears for several moments before it actually registered in his mind. When it did, he jerked his head around toward the sound. The bird was off to his right and sounded at least a couple of hundred yards away. Jonah got his hen scratch and worked it softly. The tom replied at once. Jonah waited for him to call again and when he did, the bird was definitely on the move. Jonah's hen beckoned him now, flirting with him. The tom came closer.

"Wish I had my goddamn gun," Jonah said. "Least I'll get a look at you, you bastard."

The tom came on steadily, gobbling intermittently as he did. Finally Jonah set the scratch aside and watched through the heavy branches of the evergreens. He heard a noise, then another. By the sound of the approach, the bird had to be huge.

And then Will Montgomery stepped into the clearing. He had a homemade gobbler in his right hand and after a moment he looked directly up at the hunt stand.

"What in the hell?" Jonah said and he stood.

Will smiled and shook the gobbler one last time.

"You're lucky I didn't shoot you," Jonah said.

"With what?" Will asked. "Your gun's up at the house."

"That's because I'm not huntin', I'm scoutin'," Jonah decided to tell him. "So you figured to play a joke on me, is that it?"

"How the hell else was I going to find you?" Will asked. "Your daughter told me to follow the trail. I never did find any trail. I could've walked all the way to the Mississippi River."

"The Mississippi's thataway," Jonah said, pointing back in the direction Will had just come. "Who taught you how to call a turkey?"

Will showed him the call. "Not bad, eh? Paid seven dollars for it in a little town down the road this morning."

"Shit. Didn't sound nothing like a turkey."

"Fooled you," Will said. "You gonna let me come up there?"

"I guess," Jonah said unhappily. "Stand down there, you're gonna scare all the birds away."

"Yeah, there seems to be quite a flock of them around," Will said and he began to climb.

Jonah moved over when he arrived and let him sit. He noticed now that the man's hands were calloused and nicked with cuts here and there. One thumbnail was blackened, as if it had been hit with a hammer.

"Why you looking for me anyway?"

"To talk." Will hunkered down on the cramped platform.

"What'd you do to your thumb?" Jonah asked. "Pinch it in your briefcase?"

"I pinched it in a springtooth," Will said. "I don't own a briefcase."

"That's a first. I never met a lawyer didn't own a briefcase."

"I'm not a lawyer. I'm a farmer."

Hearing that, Jonah hesitated. "The girl said you were a lawyer."

"She didn't say anything of the kind. She said I was an executor."

"What the hell is that?"

"I'm not exactly sure. But if I ever figure it out, I'll let you know." Will put the turkey call on the limb beside Jonah's belongings. The notebook was there, lying open. Jonah picked it up and slipped it into his coat pocket.

"You went to a lot of trouble to find me," Jonah said. "To *talk*. You coulda waited at the house. I'd of come back sooner or later. I always have."

"I wanted to talk to you alone," Will said. "I'm assuming Kick hasn't told you everything you need to know about this situation. This will of Everett Eastman's has some odd conditions attached to it. One of them is that this record's got to get made. Otherwise, Kick will lose ownership of the company. She tell you that?"

"Nope."

"Well, she wouldn't. Kick's spent her entire life thinking she can handle everything on her own."

"You sweet on her?"

"What?"

"Never mind," Jonah said. "What do you need from me?"

"Susie Braddock told me you have no intention of making a record for Great North. If that's true, then Kick has a right to know it."

"You got a lot of goddamn nerve," Jonah said. "Talking to me like that. You don't want to get on my bad side, farmboy."

"What're you going to do—shoot me with that pencil?"

"I just might," Jonah said. "But first off I'm gonna set you straight. You ain't gonna get very far, hoss, listening to the likes of Susie Braddock. I'll make the record. I just don't know how we're gonna go about it now. Takes money to make records."

"What about the songs?" Will asked. "I watched you rejecting a few of them earlier. You and your double barrel."

"That's what you call a Tennessee shredder. Good for all kinds of paperwork."

"No wonder you're twelve million in debt."

There was an uncomfortable silence, and then Jonah laughed. "You're right, farmboy. I was shootin' my accounts when I should've been shootin' my accountants."

"My name's Will. Kick's brother used to call me farmboy."

"And you didn't care for it?"

"I didn't care for him. Still don't."

"He anything like her?"

"He's nothing like her," Will said. "And he'd like nothing better than to see her fall flat on her face where Great North is concerned.

It could work to his advantage. That's part of the will too, but it's complicated and I don't feel like explaining it to you. Makes my head hurt."

Jonah looked at the sky as he considered this, and then he began to gather his calls and scratches and put them in his canvas rucksack. "If I had the dough-ray-me, I'd make the damn record," he said when he finished. "I'd find the songs somewheres. I always have before."

"Then it's just about the money."

"It always is," Jonah said and he nodded toward the ladder. "We better head back, we got some weather coming."

They climbed down from the stand and walked through the clearing toward the trail. The sky was completely overcast now, making the way even darker. The wind was still on the rise.

"Let's get a move on," Jonah said over his shoulder. "We're gonna get wet."

They walked single file through the cottonwoods. In a short while Jonah heard thunder from the west. He looked back at Will, who wore just a faded cotton work shirt, rolled up at the sleeves. Jonah thought the man would have owned a coat, coming from Canada.

"You saying you got the dough?" he asked when the trail opened up and they were walking side by side.

"Afraid not," Will said. "I just wanted to know where you stood."

"Well, now you know. What do you intend to do with the information?"

"Raney Kilbride sent me down here to stick my nose into this thing," Will said. The rain started then, just a few drops, and he looked up to where the dark clouds rolled above the branches. "Sticking my nose into things is something I like to avoid, but here I am. And if making this record is the best thing for Kick and Great North, then I guess we have to figure out some way to do it."

"There ain't no way to do it," Jonah said. "If the money's gone."

The downpour hit at that moment. Jonah stopped and unslung the rucksack from his shoulder. He took out a camouflage poncho for himself and handed a hooded jacket to Will, who hesitated and then took it and put it on.

"I can see why you don't bother with a gun," Will said as they set out through the rain. "I tramped around in here for an hour and never saw any turkey sign at all."

"Shit," Jonah said. "What would you know about wild turkeys?"

"I know there's none around here."

Jonah stopped. "Wait a minute. Kick told me she had a neighbor been shooting wild gobblers up north. Would that be you?"

"That would be me."

Will had the hood up and tied at his throat; he looked like a snapping turtle. Jonah regarded him skeptically for a moment, then started off again. "Wild turkeys in Canada. They got any size to 'em?"

"I shot one this spring, weighed out at twenty-seven pounds. They eat well, at my expense."

"And vice versa, I'm guessing," Jonah said. "I might just have to make a trip up there sometime."

"You're more than welcome," Will said. "They're nothing but a damn nuisance to a cash cropper."

They were walking through a thicket of cedars now, the sweet sharp smell of the wet needles hanging in the air. The trees gave them partial cover from the downpour. Jonah stopped again.

"I like that girl," he said. "She's got some sand. I don't know if she got it from her old man or where, but she's got it. I don't want to let her down."

"She's pretty headstrong," Will said. "Whatever happens, she'll survive. She's always made her own way in life."

"See, that there's just something that looks good on paper," Jonah said. "But it don't cut it with me. Every little defeat in life takes its toll. Every damn one."

FOURTEEN

The packages from the courier came mid-morning, two days in a row. Johanna signed for them both days and then left them on the kitchen table for Ethan, who, in spite of his fledgling agricultural interests, was still sleeping more than an adult should. She went to town the first day and when she returned the envelope was gone. The second day she was in the kitchen, washing her breakfast dishes, when Janey came downstairs. She poured coffee for herself and then sat down. When she saw the envelope, she picked it up and began to open it.

"That's addressed to Ethan," Johanna told her.

"He won't open it. He didn't yesterday."

"So you've got power of attorney?"

"Something like that," Janey said. "Would you prefer nobody open it at all?"

Johanna said nothing as Janey read the contents, then tossed the pages aside. "Do you want to know what it is?" she asked.

"No," Johanna said. "It's none of my business."

Janey shrugged and took a drink of coffee. The morning paper was on the table as well and she picked up the front section and began to read the headlines. Johanna finished the dishes and began to dry.

"You want the frying pan left out?"

Janey shook her head. "I'm just going to have toast."

Johanna put everything away and then hung the tea towel on the handle of the oven.

"I'm going to plant some more garden," she said and started for the back door.

"It's from McDougall," Janey said. "There's something strange going on. They want Ethan's input on … well, nothing, to tell you the truth." She picked up the pages and read. "For instance, they want his okay to ship fifty cases of rye to Vancouver. Yesterday, they wanted the go-ahead to change the filters in the water purification system at the distillery. All this, out of the blue. Would you say that's a little odd, Johanna?"

Johanna was standing at the French doors that led onto the deck. Down the hill, her garden waited, the soil lying black and fertile in the morning sun. She'd planted half of it earlier in the week, with Ethan's help. Today she would put in the sweet corn and mound up the hills for squash and pumpkin. "I'd say that it smells," she said.

"What's it smell like?"

"It smells like Ben," Johanna said, and she walked out.

Janey drove over to McDougall after breakfast. Ethan was up when she left. He'd eaten a bowl of cereal and was at the computer, reading Mary Jane Butters's website. She told him what she intended to do and he waved at her over his shoulder as he read from the screen.

Janey was by now resigned to the fact that her arrival at the distillery was never going to bring a smile to the face of Jack Dutton. She would have settled for something neutral though, something less than a scowl. She wouldn't get it today. She carried both envelopes with her, and she and Dutton sat in the little room off the foyer again.

"Ethan asked me to respond to these," she said.

"Well, that's good of you," Dutton said. "But you don't have the authority to do that."

"Let's say I'm his secretary."

"We can say that," Dutton said. "You still don't have the authority."

"No, but I can pass on messages," Janey said. "Ethan is busy and for the time being he wants you to handle the day-to-day operation of the distillery."

"I thought he wanted to run things."

"Did he tell you that?"

"Does he tell anybody anything?" Dutton asked. "I guess it was you who told me that."

"That's not altogether true, either. For the time being, though, you can carry on with things the way they are. But Ethan and I are looking at ways to turn this thing around. There's some interesting market research information out there."

"Good for you," Dutton said smiling. "You kids have a lot of fun with that. I can lend you a hammer if you'd like to build a new loading dock. But right now, I have a distillery to run and if I have questions for ownership, I'm going to send them over. Ethan can respond or not, that's up to him. Okay?"

"Yes sir," Janey said and she got to her feet. "But you should keep in mind who's in charge here. If you require all this input to run a place that's in a habit of losing money, we might have to conclude that you're not the man to help us turn it around."

Dutton stood now too. "I didn't know that secretaries were allowed to make threats. You'd better double-check your job description. As for running this plant, I was doing it before you showed up and I have a feeling I'll be doing it long after you go chasing the next shiny thing that catches your fancy."

This time he didn't bother to show her out.

WILL WAS ASKED TO STAY to dinner at the Peck farm. Kick noticed that he was asked by Paige, rather than Jonah, who still wasn't showing Will much down-home hospitality, despite the fact that the two of them had walked out of the woods together, drenched to the skin. Will had to sit around looking uncomfortable in a robe while Paige put his clothes in the dryer for half an hour.

Dinner was burgers and tortilla chips, and they sat out back by the barbeque drum. Kick and Will drank beer, while the Pecks stuck with soft drinks and cigarettes.

"These northerners are going to think we're nothing but a bunch of drunks down here," Paige said, looking at her father.

"They're the ones drinking," Jonah replied.

At one point, shortly before dinner, Paige disappeared inside for something and Jonah went to feed the horses. Will and Kick were left alone on the deck. The rain had stopped now but it had brought a drop in temperature. The barbeque gave off enough heat to warm them.

"So when's your court date?" Will asked.

"End of the month. You gonna stick around and defend me?"

"Raney said you wouldn't take this seriously."

"Raney doesn't know everything in the world. Just because he's old." She took a drink of beer. "So I had a difference of opinion with a woman in a bar. That really doesn't seem to be much of a crime, not when you look at the larger picture. All the horrors in the world today."

"That gonna be your defense? You think the judge will let you off if you remind him there's people starving in Africa?" Will watched her but she was staring off into the brush. "Do you know the cop's name, the arresting officer?"

Kick indicated the house with her thumb. "I got a bunch of paperwork they gave me when I made bail. With my stuff. Did you bring your trench coat, Sam Spade?"

Will took a drink from the longneck. "That razor wit should come in handy. In the big house."

"The big house," Kick scoffed. "You know, I think it's kind of fascinating that all of a sudden people have come to the conclusion that

I need looking after. Where the fuck was everybody when I was five, back when I was trying to figure out how to tie my shoes, who my parents were, stuff like that?"

"You resent the fact that people are concerned about you?"

"No," she said, looking into the dying coals. "Just takes some getting used to."

Later, Jonah brought a guitar out and played a few songs, with Paige occasionally joining him on vocals. After each song, Jonah would make a point of saying who had written it. None of the songs were his own. Guy Clark, Townes Van Zandt, Johnny Cash, Hank Williams, but no Jonah Peck.

"So what is the problem with country music these days?" Kick asked after a while. "Can't just be Susie Braddock."

"It's a whole lot bigger than Susie," Jonah said.

"She's not the problem," Paige said. "She's just the poster child for the problem."

"It's the *marketing*," Jonah said. "I hate that goddamn word."

Paige took the cowboy hat from Jonah's head and plopped it on her own, then imitated her father's scowl. "These newcomers don't have no appreciation for the *history* of it all."

Jonah didn't rise to the bait. He played a couple chords and then he looked up. "History has something to do with it," he said. "But so does geography."

"Here we go," Paige said.

"Red River Valley," Jonah said. "Rose of San Antone, My Old Kentucky Home." He began to sing—

"Oh, the sun shines bright on my old Kentucky home"

"There ain't no geography in songs anymore because everything's what they call generic. Songs today got no location to them." He strummed the guitar wildly.

"I got a dog, you got a truck,
Whatdya say we get drunk and fuck"

"Now there's a Susie Braddock song," Paige said.

"Ain't it the sad truth?" Jonah said. He tuned the guitar before singing—

"'Tis the song, the sigh of the weary,
Hard times, hard times, come again no more.
Many days you have lingered all around my cabin door.
Oh hard times, come again no more."

"What's that from?" Will asked.

"Hardscrabble, son," Jonah told him. "That's what it's from."

"Like you remember hardscrabble," Paige said.

"You live it, you remember it," Jonah told her. "You're the one doesn't know the meaning of the word."

"It's not a country song anyway," Paige said.

"If it ain't country, there's no such thing as country," Jonah told her.

"Sing us one of yours," Kick said.

"I would, if I could think of one didn't bore me to tears," Jonah told her. He slipped the pick through the strings and set the guitar aside.

"Aw, come on," Paige said. "I was hoping for another chorus of I've got a dog, you've got a truck."

"Turn on the radio," Jonah told her.

WILL DIDN'T SPEND THE NIGHT at the Peck farm, although Paige pushed him to. He took the particulars of the arrest from Kick and he went back to the motel. The next morning he ate breakfast and then went back to his room and called the downtown police station and asked for the arresting officer. He was surprised when the cop called back, less than half an hour later. He was on patrol and he agreed to meet Will in the motel coffee shop.

"I want to talk to you about the charges against Kathleen Eastman," Will said when they were seated in the diner.

They were waiting for coffee. The cop was very large, maybe thirty or so, with a rectangular head and sagging jowls, like a bulldog. The restaurant was nearly full, mostly truck drivers and construction workers having breakfast. Their waitress looked well past retirement age. She wore a gray wig that had shifted slightly off center.

"Remind me who that is," the cop said.

"You charged her with aggravated assault," Will said. "A few nights ago, a bar called Del Rio's."

"I thought you had information about a meth lab," the cop said. He pulled a notebook from his pocket. "Shit, I musta called the wrong guy. Who are you again?"

"I'm a friend of Kathleen Eastman's."

"You're her *friend*? And you think I got time to talk to you?"

"Hey, I'll buy the coffee."

The cop deliberated, clearly put out. "You got about two minutes."

"How hard are they going to push this? It seems to be a pretty minor thing."

"Breaking the law is never a minor thing." The coffee arrived and Will watched as the cop heaped several spoonfuls of sugar into his cup, then topped it off with enough cream to overflow the rim.

"I suppose not," Will said. "I'm just thinking there must be room for compromise. She could plead no contest and get off with probation, something like that."

"At this point in the investigation, I can assure you that no such consideration would be made without the consent of the victim."

Will laughed.

"I say something humorous, sir?" the cop asked.

"I'm guessing that's the first time anybody's ever referred to Susie Braddock as a victim."

"You're entitled to your opinion. But I can assure you that the city of Nashville considers Miss Braddock to be a victim in this investigation." The cop slurped his coffee noisily.

Will nodded. "The story I got is that Susie sucker-punched Kathleen and took a shit-kicking for her trouble. Then she lied about throwing the first punch. She also lied about Jonah Peck being drunk. The man hasn't had a drink in years. And she's your victim?"

"That's what the report says."

"Can the victim drop the charges?"

"Only the district attorney can dismiss a charge," the cop said. "However, he would usually do that, if the victim indicates to him her desire to … not go forward." The cop paused, apparently dismayed over his verbal stumbling. He quickly drank more coffee.

"I guess I need to talk to Susie Braddock."

"You can do as you please," the cop said. "I will advise you that Miss Eastman is, upon condition of bail, not to contact Miss Braddock."

"Right," Will said and he stood. He hadn't touched his own cup. "One more thing: do you guys have a fraud department?"

"I beg your pardon?" The cop was hurrying to finish the syrup he'd made of his coffee. He'd been the one to point out his pressing schedule earlier and he seemed determined to be the first to leave.

"Who would I talk to if I'd been defrauded?"

"Have you been a victim of fraud?"

"Nope."

The cop got to his feet slowly, keeping a close eye on Will, who was reaching for his wallet to pay for the coffee.

"I'm going to have to ask you for some identification, sir," the cop said.

Will handed over his driver's license. The cop gave it a long look then passed it back. "I didn't think you were a local citizen. I don't know what this is about, but Woodrow Hoskins is lead detective on the fraud squad." He paused for effect. "I wouldn't play games with the man."

"I don't intend to," Will said. He placed a five-dollar bill on the table and then put his wallet back in his pocket. "Why would you say a thing like that?"

"It seems to be your MO. Good day, sir."

"Ten four," Will told him.

SUSIE BRADDOCK AGREED to meet with him for a drink that afternoon. Will was a little surprised that she didn't require much convincing. He'd had visions of himself chasing the woman all over a town he didn't know. On the phone she was flirtatious, as she'd been on their first meeting, and she said she was looking forward to it.

They met at the Boone Hotel downtown. There were two bars, one upstairs and one down. The upper bar was the fancier of the two and of course that's where Susie wanted to meet. She showed up in a bright yellow dress with black stockings and her standard high heels. Will was in jeans and a leather jacket and he waited in the lobby for Susie, thinking he would have a better chance of entry with the fancy record producer on his arm.

They sat at a table near a window that looked down over Broadway. Susie had some sort of martini that arrived pink in color and garnished with things not readily identifiable to Will. He had a Budweiser, which he recognized at once.

"I was wondering if I'd hear from you," Susie said. "I am real curious to know what kind of tales you been hearing from Mister Jonah Peck."

"And here I thought it was because I look like Tony Keith," Will said.

"*Toby* Keith. I swear, you are a lost cause, honey. But do tell—what is Jonah claiming these days?"

"He'd still like to make the record."

"I just bet he would," Susie said and she took a drink of the oversized martini. "The old boy shoulda thought about that before, when he was doing everything in his power to sabotage the thing. Funny how he changes his tune when you and the tadpole show up."

"There must be a way to get it done."

"Good luck with it." Susie took more of the martini. When she drank, her eyes above the glass grew as wide as saucers, giving the appearance that she was amazed at the very act of imbibing.

"Getting back to the tadpole for a second," Will said. "That little misunderstanding the two of you had the other night. You don't want to see this thing go to trial, do you?"

"I most certainly do."

"It's going to be a circus," Will said. "And you know who the media's going to focus on. Kathleen Eastman is nothing to these people. But look at you—you're rich, you're powerful, you're a celebrity. Top it all off, if you don't mind me saying—you're gorgeous—you'll look great on the evening news, coming out of that courtroom every day. Day after day."

Susie leaned back in her chair and smiled at him. "Well, aren't you the slippery one? I had you pegged for a simple country boy."

"Hey, I'm just describing what I see."

"And you pretty much hit that nail square on the head," she said matter of factly.

"Letting it slide might be good for your image," Will said. "Show the two sides of Susie Braddock—classy southern lady, taking care of business, always dressed to the nines. But cross her and you've got this hellcat in a bar fight. Thing is—she takes it all in stride. She's a going concern—she's got no time for court cases and lawyers and all that nonsense."

As he talked, Susie was looking out the window to the street below, and pretty soon she was nodding at the image he was painting. Will could see that she was embracing it, flattering as it was.

But admiring a picture and buying it were two different things.

"She broke my fucking bridge," she said when she turned back to him. "I'm not cutting that little bitch any slack."

"Well then, have fun at the circus," Will said. He looked at his watch as he took a drink of beer.

"You got a heavy date, sugar?"

"No, I just have to be over to the police station before five o'clock."

"You gonna go begging on that girl's behalf?" Susie asked. "I hate to see a good-looking man beg. Well, depending on the circumstances, that is." She raised her eyebrows and smiled but just briefly. "Fuck her … she made her bed."

"Oh no, I already talked to the arresting officer about that," Will said. "I'm heading over to find a detective named Woodrow Hoskins. You heard of him? He's with fraud."

"Aren't you the busy beaver?" Susie asked. She looked toward the bar, feigning disinterest. She sipped again from her glass. "Why would you have to see him?"

"Because there's a quarter million dollars missing on this record deal. And you can bet that Great North is going to want to sue somebody. I've been sent down here to try and find out who."

"No need to go running to the police, I can tell you who's responsible," Susie said. "Jonah Peck. And you might just as well sue that beer bottle in front of you as sue him. The man doesn't have a pot to piss in, which is how this all got started to begin with."

Will smiled. "You telling me I should find someone a little more solvent to sue?"

Susie glared at the implication. "I'm telling you that you'd be smart to forget the whole damn thing. You find a lawyer who can get blood from a stone, you hire him. Otherwise, you're wasting your time and your money. You'd do well to let it be."

"I can't do that, even if I wanted to." Will drank the last of his beer and looked again at his watch. "I gotta go. One more thing. The cops took Peck to a hospital for stitches after the fight the other night. Would you know where that was?"

"I got no idea. Why you want to know that?"

"Well, with the police involved, and the charges and all, there's a good chance they did a blood alcohol test. You're telling people he was drunk."

"I never said any such thing."

"It was in the newspaper."

"I was misquoted."

"You told it to me too," Will said. "In your office. Were you misquoting yourself? Never heard of that before."

"Well, what's it matter anyway?" Susie snapped. "It was the tadpole that attacked me."

"I hear you lied about that, too," Will said. "But getting back to Peck—you're saying this record deal fell through because of his boozing, and he's saying he hasn't had a drop in years. So it matters to me which one of you is the liar, when it comes down to trying to figure out where the money went." Will got to his feet and took a twenty from his pocket. "Will that cover a beer and a shot in a place like this?"

"Don't worry about it," Susie said glumly. "I'll get it."

Will put the twenty on the table. "No thanks. Don't take this the wrong way, but you people down here seem to have a hell of a time handling money. I'll see you around."

WHEN KICK GOT UP there was nobody else around the place. She'd been given a large bedroom that overlooked the back of the house, and the woods beyond. There was a tarnished brass bed, with a mattress and no box spring, a burled oak dresser and a single pressed-back chair. Getting out of bed, she glanced at her watch and saw that it was nine-thirty. She almost never slept in, unless of course she'd been out half the night, and those times weren't nearly as frequent as they had once been. She pulled on jeans and a tank top and went barefoot across the hall to the bathroom. She washed her face and brushed her teeth and then went downstairs to the kitchen. There was coffee in the brew machine on the counter. It was fresh, and of the half dozen butts in the ashtray on the table, one was still smoldering, so she knew Paige hadn't been gone long. She poured a cup and carried it out onto the front porch. The SUV Paige had been driving wasn't in the yard. She sat in the wicker rocker and pulled her knees up as she looked out over the farm. It was a sunny morning and there wasn't a breath of wind. There were robins hop-stepping across the lawn and blue jays raising a racket in the lower branches of the cottonwoods along the lane.

She felt she was in some weird sort of limbo, with the court case pending and the record deal apparently as dead as the man who had dared to initiate it. And here she sat, stuck in Tennessee, not knowing which way to turn. Moving forward was something she'd always been good at. The moves hadn't always worked out; in fact, there had been times when they seemed to never work out, but she'd always looked upon inertia as her natural enemy. It bred complacency, and while complacency was all right for some, to Kick it represented the slippery slope to apathy and ennui. Which was why she wasn't used to sleeping in. And she definitely was not accustomed to sitting on her ass all day, waiting for the world to come to her. The problem was, here on this calm June day, on this backwoods farmhouse porch, with all pertinent matters at a screeching standstill, she couldn't think of a thing to do.

And then, looking across the yard, she did.

After she drank her coffee, she put on socks and her hiking boots and made her way across the yard to the barn. She got the brushes and the currycomb from the tack room and went out to the corral, thinking that this time she'd stay out in the sunshine, at least get some color while she worked. She caught the gelding by the halter and tied him to the gate post.

"Okay, pigpen, it's me and you," she told him and went to work.

The Appaloosa mare watched from a distance for a while and then came over and stood so close to the gelding that Kick had to push her away. "You get," she told the horse. "Too late to come kissing up now."

The gelding stood calmly and let her work. From time to time Kick would look him in the eye and suspect a conspiracy there, that he was planning an even more spectacular roll this time than last. Other times, though, it seemed he was just a bored horse looking back at her. She wondered if she was growing paranoid. Worse yet, she wondered if she was growing paranoid over a horse.

But then who knew what anybody was thinking? Kick wasn't even sure what she herself had been thinking, coming here. It hadn't been a particularly fruitful trip so far. She had arrived with the intention of taking Susie Braddock to task over the issue of the production money. And while she'd easily outpointed the busty bantamweight in the Nashville bar, Susie had pretty much run circles around her the rest of the time. When she wasn't making Kick look like a fish out of water, she was badmouthing Jonah Peck to anyone who would listen.

It was evident that Jonah had dragged his heels on the record deal, but it was just as clear that he wasn't the villain Susie depicted him to be. He seemed like a nice guy who'd lost his desire, or his muse, or whatever it was that had made him a fixture in the music world in the first place. He seemed like a senior citizen, which was what he was.

And now she was obliged to shuffle Will Montgomery into the deck. She wasn't pleased that Raney Kilbride had sent him, no matter how protective or paternal the old man's instincts. And even though Kick had long considered Will to be a rock, he was not her rock. She had never thought about him in any world other than his own back home. He was a man who plowed fields and baled hay and harvested wheat. What did he know of crooked record producers and the music world in general?

Probably as much as she did.

Yet he didn't seem out of place here. He had a confidence, even in the face of Jonah's inhospitable behavior, that she'd probably taken for granted over the years. Of course, Paige was determined to more than make up for Jonah's attitude. It was obvious that she had carnal designs on Will, if he was amenable to the notion, and why wouldn't he be? Kick was frankly jealous of the possibility, and that was something else that puzzled her. To make things worse, every now and again she went back to the fact that Will had been with Johanna when she'd supposedly been having a nap. Of course, it was something she wasn't allowed to have an opinion on, since it had happened right about the time that the devil John Barleycorn had deposited her in Jonah's bed. Still, Kick had suspected that there'd been something between the two, off and on, for years. Why wouldn't it be on again, now that Will's marriage was over? They were a good match— both pragmatic, hard-working, smart. Neither given to wild flights of fancy, as a filmmaker might be. And both in possession of rather acute bullshit detectors. If anything, Kick should be encouraging such a connection.

She was working the tangles from the gelding's tail when she heard a vehicle come up the drive and park at the house. The mare trotted past the corner of the barn to see who it was, then turned and began to walk slowly along the fence there. Kick suspected that her indifference meant it was Paige, and not Jonah, who had arrived.

In the end, the only conclusion she could arrive at was that there was not going to be a record. And if there wasn't going to be a record, there was really no point in her sticking around. Let the lawyers fight it out over the missing money.

"I'll have you know I have unfinished business up in Wyoming," she told the gelding as she gave his mane one last tug with the currycomb and then untied him.

When she did, he stood there, stock-still, his head down as if he was dozing. He was still there when she walked through the barn and headed for the house. As she was climbing the steps to the porch she heard the heavy thud and turned to see the horse on his side in the corral, legs in the air, a thick cloud of dust above him as he rolled. Kick shook her head and then went inside. At least she'd found a way to pass the morning.

She went into the kitchen for a glass of water. She drank it standing by the window, watching the treacherous gelding, who was now back on his feet, trotting in tight triumphant circles around the corral, content once more in his sloth and his devious ways. After a moment Kick became aware that she was hearing a very familiar sound. She walked through the house to a room off the dining room that served as a den of sorts. Paige was sprawled on a couch there, eating potato chips and watching television. The familiar sound was coming from the set.

"Where'd you get that?"

Paige craned her neck to see Kick in the doorway, then she reached for the remote and paused the screen. "The Tennessee public library system. Turns out they have a pretty impressive documentary collection."

"They must have."

"I keep looking for you," Paige said. "I guess you stay behind the camera."

"It's not about me."

"I'm not so sure about that," Paige said. "I mean, I'm just getting into it, but it's obvious where your sentiments lie. You've got this tribe of Eskimos, and there's a shitload of oil beneath the ice. The old folks want to keep with the old way of life, and the young ones are all, Show me the money. Drill away."

"Inuit."

"You say potato," Paige said. "They look like Eskimos to me. But I like it a lot. You are a sure-enough filmmaker."

"You think I was making that up?"

"No, but some people believe they're something they're not. Like me—I may or may not be an actress. Or a singer."

"Barrel racer."

"Yeah, yeah. You gonna sit down and watch?"

"I watched it about five hundred times in editing," Kick said. "Now I'd just obsess about what I'd do differently. I think I'll have some lunch instead. You sticking with the chips?"

"Yup."

"Where's Jonah?"

"Went hunting again. Without his gun."

Kick thought about that. "Is he losing his mind?"

"I think he might be finding it," Paige said. She sat up now and when she did the crumbs from the potato chips fell from her shirt onto the floor. "He's writing songs. I think he has been for a while."

"How do you know that?"

"I can tell by the way he is. He gets this look in his eye at the weirdest times, like over coffee or when you're talking to him. I can tell he's working on a lyric. Yesterday I asked him what time it was and he nodded and said yup." Paige glanced over. "Besides, I snuck a look in his notebook when he was sleeping."

Kick was still standing in the doorway and now she came into the room. On the television was the still frame of Oka Anok, a woman of eighty-something who had made Kick a meal one day of seal-fin soup. Kick sat down in a leather chair.

"What's he going to do with them?"

"You'd have to ask him that," Paige said. "Maybe nothing, if the money's gone." She reached for her cigarettes on the table then hesitated. "My old man's a proud motherfucker, I'll have you know. Susie

Braddock may have spent all that money on ugly clothes and titty implants, but Jonah's feeling like he let somebody down here. You have to realize this is all speculation on my part. Jonah and I aren't much for father and daughter talks. But that's my take on the matter."

"So he's writing out of guilt?"

"I wouldn't say that. But he's writing. Who knows why people do what they do? Shit, you went up to the North Pole and made a film about Eskimos. I bet you froze your ass off. You could've went to the Bahamas and made a movie about … I don't know, conch fishermen. Why didn't you?"

"They're Inuit."

"Whatever they are, they don't live in the Bahamas," Paige said and she pointed the remote at the set and restarted the tape. "Stay here and give me a play by play. We'll have some lunch after. Who's that old girl anyway, with the fur hood? She looks tougher than a boot sandwich."

They watched the rest of the film together, with Kick giving background on the shoot, Paige asking questions and alternating between cigarettes and potato chips. When it was done, Paige insisted on watching the credits in order to see Kick's name.

"There's my girl," she said and she turned the television off. "What's it like up there? I think I might like being that far away from … everything."

"I shot a lot of footage I didn't use. Flora and fauna, a few polar bears. I'll show it to you sometime. You get to New York, you can come up and visit."

Paige reached for a cigarette, but made no comment.

"You *are* still going to New York," Kick said.

"I don't know," Paige said. "I'm a little bit afraid to."

"You lived there before, didn't you?"

"Not straight, I didn't." She lit the smoke. "I'm afraid I might get there, and if things don't go well, I might get discouraged. And then I'll want to get high."

"And you don't get that feeling here?"

"I get that feeling everywhere," Paige said. "It's just that the expectations are gonna be greater there. You know what I mean?"

Before Kick could reply, they heard the sound of the piano. She looked at Paige, who quickly held her hand up, then got to her feet. "Come on," she said softly. "I want to hear this."

They walked into the hallway and stood outside the door to the music room. From inside they could hear notes being played, a warm-up of random melodies and familiar tunes. And then they heard Jonah's sharp, distinctive voice—

"Tadpole, tadpole, so young and so strong,
Growin' like a weed, and soon you'll be gone.
Tadpole, tadpole, come sit with me a while,
You're the only one can make this old froggie smile."

He stopped singing then, and went back to playing with the melody. Paige smiled at Kick then nodded toward the kitchen, and the two of them moved quietly away.

"Didn't I tell you?" Paige said when they got there. "Sit. I'll make some sandwiches."

"And that's a new song?" Kick said as she sat at the table.

"Tadpole?" Paige asked sarcastically. She took a loaf of bread down from the cupboard. "Yeah, I would say that's a new song. Come on, it's pretty obvious what's got him writing. He's singing about you."

Kick laughed and Paige turned. "What's so funny?" she asked.

"And here all along, I've been thinking you were the intuitive one," Kick said. "Did you even listen to those lyrics? He's not writing about me."

Paige glanced in the direction of the sound from the piano.

Kick smiled. "He's writing about you."

FIFTEEN

Jonah was gone early again the next morning, and when he returned at noon he wasn't interested in lunch and he wasn't interested in having the two women around while he worked. It was Kick's idea that they take the horses for a ride. They saddled up in the barn and then started out along a lane behind the house, Kick on the again-dusty gelding and Paige astride her father's mare.

The lane turned into an old wagon trail that snaked through a forest of cottonwoods and oaks and old-growth white ash. It was another faultless day as they rode side by side along the narrow trail, the temperamental Appaloosa nipping at the gelding if it moved a step or two in the lead. From time to time they would come upon a clearing, the forest floor splattered with points of dappled light. There was fresh grass growing and the horses would constantly try to stop and graze.

They rode for two or three miles, Kick guessed, and then suddenly they came out of the woods, not five hundred yards from a hamlet of perhaps thirty or forty houses. There was a single main street with a gas station, a general store and a roadhouse with a hand-painted sign over the front door that said HARRY'S.

"Whoa," Kick said when she saw the village, and the gelding took the comment literally and stopped. Paige, looking back, reined in the mare too.

"Welcome to Stubbinsville," she said. "You feel like a beer? I could use an ice tea, wash away the trail dust."

Kick nudged the gelding into a lope and headed for the bar. There was actually a hitching post along the side wall of the building. They tied the horses and loosened the cinches and went inside. The place was tiny, four tables and a bar with a half dozen stools. There was a jukebox and coin-operated pool table, as well as a couple of pinball machines against the back wall. They took two stools at the front corner of the bar.

"Well, this is a convenient little place," Kick said, looking around. Four men were playing euchre at a table by the window, and one other patron, an older man, was sitting farther along the bar, staring at an empty glass in front of him.

"You don't know the half of it," Paige told her. "Back in the days when he was still drinking, Jonah had a habit of losing his driver's license on a regular basis. But that was never a problem for Jonah Peck. We always had horses on the place, so when he got thirsty he'd just saddle up and head for Harry's bar to whet his whistle. He even wrote a song about it—'Harry's by Horseback.'"

"Then he'd ride home drunk through the woods?"

"Well, the horse would do the navigating," Paige said. "Try teaching that to a pickup truck. Later on, my girlfriends and I used to hang out here, when we reached drinking age. Well, maybe before. We'd smoke a little dope in the woods then come here and flirt with the regulars. We were pretty obnoxious, but we didn't know it at the time."

"People who are obnoxious never know it at the time," Kick said. She took a drink of draft. "Was your mother around then?"

"No."

"So Jonah got custody after the divorce?"

Paige turned on the stool and watched the old man as he watched his empty glass. "There was no divorce. My mother died."

"Oh, shit. I'm sorry."

"Me too."

"What happened?"

"Car accident. The cops said it was alcohol-related, and nobody seemed too surprised by that. She, um … she liked her gin. I was twelve at the time." She took a drink of tea. "Okay, your turn. What's your sad family story?"

Kick shrugged. "Not so sad, I guess. I have one mother and two sort of stepmothers. They're all still around although I couldn't say where. My mother's in England. My father was a guy who *acquired* things. He was good at buying and selling. As far as I could see he kept marrying women he didn't much care for. Which is a rather curious habit."

"I'd say so."

"For the longest time I thought he completely lacked passion. I finally realized that he was only passionate about the things he hated."

"Like the IRS," Paige said.

"Yeah, like the IRS," Kick said. "I'm not saying he didn't love us. I'm just saying he wasn't very good at it."

"Where did you grow up?"

Kick took a drink of beer. "We had a place in Toronto, that's where I went to school, but we spent the summers out at the family farm, a place called Crooked Pear. My brothers and I were basically raised by a woman named Johanna Malden. She was from Holland but she must have grown up reading the Dutch edition of *The Saturday Evening Post* because she created this incredible Norman Rockwell life for us on the farm. She actually bought and trained two Belgian draft horses. We had sleigh rides at Christmas and hay rides in the summer. And, you know—camp fires, ice skating on the pond, snowball fights. And she could kick Betty Crocker's ass in the kitchen to boot. Of course, with all the assorted dysfunctionals lurking about, it was more like Norman Rockwell meets the Addams Family. I consider myself lucky that I remember the good stuff more than the bad."

"But your mother was always around?"

"I wouldn't say that," Kick said.

"So your dad was?"

Kick drank the beer. "I wouldn't say that either."

It was nearly dark when they got back to the farm. Paige turned the barn lights on and they unsaddled the horses and rubbed them down then put them in the box stalls overnight. Walking across the yard to the house they could hear the sounds of a guitar, and Jonah singing.

There was no sneaking a listen this time. They walked into the room and stood there while he played chords on the guitar. He looked up at them but kept on playing, a sort of a ragged up-tempo Merle Haggard melody. Then he sang—

"Too shy to write two words
For anyone to read
Too green to know that love
Was all he'd ever need"

He quit singing then and took a moment to tune the guitar. He sang the first verse again and then—

"And it's a big man
Coming down the road
It's a big, big man
Coming down the road."

"He's not singing about tadpoles now," Paige said later. They were in the kitchen and she was making coffee. "He's singing about himself, the first part anyway."

"Who's the big man?" Kick asked.

"I don't know," Paige admitted. "Could be it's not a man at all."

WILL HAD DINNER at the Cracker Barrel across the street from the motel. From there he could see the parking lot and the entrance to the front desk. He didn't want to miss Susie, if she decided to show.

He wasn't at all sure that she would, of course. There were any number of adjectives he could use to describe Susie Braddock, but predictable wasn't one of them. And neither was stupid. He had a feeling that the interstate between Florida and Tennessee was strewn with the bleached bones of those who had underestimated the woman. Will wasn't looking to add his own to the pile.

After he ate he went back to his room and sat on the bed, turning on the TV just in time to catch the start of *My Darling Clementine*. He'd bought a bottle of bourbon earlier that day and he poured a couple of fingers and leaned back against the pillows to watch the cowboys as they roamed the streets of Tombstone. Just as Henry Fonda was about to blast the Clantons into eternity, Susie made her appearance. She knocked once and walked in, wearing white jeans and a white leather jacket with red piping on the shoulders. With her was a man who practically had to turn sideways to get through the door. He wore a tight black T-shirt. His hair was cropped short and he had a goatee so thin it looked to be made of string. His arms were immense and covered with tattoos, some strange tribal designs. He was further adorned in gaudy jewelry, all of it gold. There were chains around his neck, earrings, bracelets, rings on his fingers.

Susie took a couple of steps into the room and made a show of checking out the sparse decor. "Lookit the fancy digs," she said.

"Hey, Susie," Will said. "Where'd you get the gorilla?"

Susie glanced at the bourbon. "Another Canadian can't hold his liquor."

There were six-guns blazing on the TV. Will hit the mute button, then indicated the table and chairs. "Have a seat."

Susie sat down, while the giant remained standing just inside the door. He'd had no reaction to Will's insult. Will moved over to sit opposite Susie, bringing the bottle and another glass with him.

"Sure," Susie said when he offered the bottle toward her. Will poured, then looked at the big man. "What about you, son? You old enough to drink?"

"You are fucking loco," Susie told him. "No, he doesn't want a drink. He's *working*."

Will shrugged and put the cap on the bottle.

"You know," Susie said, lifting her glass. "I sat there in that bar this afternoon after you left, and by God I swear I was catching flies, my mouth was hanging open so wide. I could not believe that you would walk in there and threaten me like you did."

"I threatened you?" Will asked. "Tell me how I did that."

"You are a cocky sonofabitch," Susie said smiling. She took a healthy slug of the bourbon, her lipstick leaving a bright red half-circle on the glass. "You and I coulda had some fun, you weren't running the wrong side of the range." She looked thoughtfully for a moment at the amber liquor in her hand. "But now it's come time for you to listen up, fuckstick. You don't come into this town and tell me you're gonna have me investigated for fraud. And you don't come into this town and question my integrity. It's just not gonna happen. So what you're gonna do tonight is pack your bags and head back where you came from. And that gentleman standing by the door … well, let's just say he's your new travel agent. He's gonna make sure you get outta town without a hitch. Or maybe with a hitch. Your choice."

"Hey, there's nothing I'd like better," Will said. He was trying not to look at the man by the door. Even without the gold adornments, he had to outweigh Will by a hundred pounds. "Truth is, I got plenty to do back home this time of year. I've got fertilizer to spread on my corn ground, and I'll be cutting hay before you know it. Problem is, I'm obligated to take care of this matter. You could say I gave my word."

Susie looked sadly at him and then shook her head. "I am real sorry you feel that way. I truly am."

Will's pulse was racing now. He wanted to take a drink but he was sure his hand would shake, giving him away. He had the sudden and disturbing notion that Susie rewarded the man by the door with a new piece of jewelry every time he maimed someone on her behalf. "Looks to me like you haven't thought this through, Susie."

"Oh, I'm real good at thinking things through."

"I don't know. I think there might be some middle ground here."

"Sorry, honey," Susie said and she turned in her chair toward the man in the doorway.

"Now wait," Will said. He put his hand up, a stop signal. "You have to take into consideration that I'm not too bright. That big guy comes after me, I might do something stupid. I might smash this whiskey bottle across his nose. I might hit him over the head with that big ceramic lamp with the swan on it. I might even club him with one of these chairs. Now, on the other hand, he doesn't look to me like he's any Mensa candidate either. He might try the same stuff on me. My point is, Susie, somebody could very well end up dead here tonight. And there you'll be … in a cheap motel room with a dead man. Add to that the barroom scrape the other night and the fact that Detective Woodrow Hoskins of the Nashville fraud squad is all of a sudden interested in you and you've got yourself a lot of negative publicity. Now how ironic would that be, seeing as your real goal in all this is to avoid bad press?"

While he talked, Susie kept her eye on the big man. He was awaiting her signal and while he waited he was staring at Will with a hatred that was almost incomprehensible, especially in light of the fact that they'd just met. Not that Will was in a position to analyze the curious nature of the fact. His heart was pounding like a pump with a thrown bearing and he was very close to hyperventilating. Waiting for Susie's next move, he felt like a Christian in the coliseums of old, holding his breath and trying not to look at the tattooed lion across the floor. On the screen Walter Brennan was screaming silently at Fonda, his face twisted with rage.

Finally Susie smiled and she reached for the bottle to pour herself more bourbon. She poured more for Will, too. And then she told the lion to take leave of the coliseum, to wait outside.

"But don't go too far," she added. He left reluctantly, like a kid who'd been promised a treat then disappointed.

"Well, he seems like a nice enough guy," Will said when he'd gone.

"You're either the bravest motherfucker I've ever met, or the craziest," Susie told him. "Neither one is going to save you."

"Maybe," Will said, "we can save each other."

KICK WAS SITTING on the front steps, eating a bowl of corn flakes, when Will Montgomery arrived the next morning. He parked his truck in the drive and pulled on a faded blue Quebec Nordiques cap as he got out. She watched him walk across the lawn, dressed in Levi's and a cotton shirt and worn work boots. By the time he reached the porch, Paige had come out of the house and was standing behind Kick.

"Mr. Montgomery," Paige said. "I declare. I was worried we scared you off."

"Not yet," Will said.

"Then come up on the porch and set a spell, as they say."

Will went up the steps. When he passed Kick he put his hand on her head and then gave the back of her neck a quick affectionate squeeze. She felt a surge of electricity go through her. She wondered at the gesture, and her response; it actually took her breath. She turned sideways on the step, her knees up, and leaned back against the newel post as Will sat down in a wicker chair beside Paige.

"Where you been?" Paige asked. "Thought I might have to come into Nashville and track you down. I was kinda looking forward to it."

"Oh, I had a wild old night on the town," Will said. "Had the catfish special at the Cracker Barrel. Slab of apple pie for dessert, with ice cream on top. Then I went back to my room and watched Wyatt Earp clean out the OK Corral."

"You're a party animal," Paige said.

Kick was watching Will closely. "He's a party animal who's not telling us something," she said. "I know a Cheshire cat when I see one. What else did you do?"

"Oh, let's see," Will said. "Might of drunk a little whiskey with a fancy record producer."

"All right," Kick said. "What's going on?"

"I think we reached a compromise," Will said. "Providing you approve, of course. But here's what we came up with. Susie will *not* confess to any wrongdoing. She will *not* admit to mishandling the money budgeted for the record. In fact, she will in no way admit that she was ever in any position of authority on this project."

"You sure you're on our side?" Paige asked.

"Keep talking," Kick said.

He went on. "However, she will give Jonah studio time for one week, along with whatever tape and technicians or sound guys or whatever is required. He'll have full use of—what's it called—the Tennessee Sound Authority? But Susie will not produce the record and she expects to be paid for any of her songs that Jonah might use. I didn't mention that he blasted them all to hell and gone with the shotgun."

The two women looked at him for a time before saying anything.

"So basically she's saying that she'll do what she should have been doing all along," Kick said. "Except she won't produce it."

"Hallelujah to that," Paige said.

"Why's she agreeing to this?" Kick asked.

Will shrugged. "Because she's a nice person and she wants to make this happen."

"No, seriously," Kick said.

"I don't know," Will said. "She may have gotten the impression that Detective Woodrow Hoskins of the Nashville fraud department is interested in knowing where the money went. She may have also heard something about Hoskins being further interested in Susie's past financial affairs with a certain Cadillac dealership in Florida."

"Is that true?" Paige asked.

"I couldn't say," Will said. "I tried to see this Hoskins yesterday but he's off in Argentina, trout fishing. Seems like a long way to go for trout."

"Well, now," Kick said, and then she looked at Paige, who smiled. "Looks as if we're going to make a record."

"Not so fast," Will said. "You're forgetting you don't have any songs."

"I've got the goddamn songs." Jonah's voice cut through the screen door like musket fire. A second later he stepped out onto the porch. "Don't tell me I don't have any songs."

"You used to give me hell for eavesdropping, Jonah," Paige told him.

"It ain't eavesdropping if it's my own damn business," Jonah said.

"You've got the songs?" Will asked.

"Did somebody put you in charge all of a sudden?" Jonah asked. "I'm still the big dog in this kennel." He made a move toward Will.

Kick got to her feet then. She stepped in front of Jonah before he could prove yet again that he wasn't much of a fighter. "Actually, if you'll all recall, I'm in charge. Great North and all that. So tell me, Mr. Peck, do you have enough songs to make a record?"

"I got two good songs that Clark wrote, and seven or eight of my own I'm working on," Jonah said. He looked a little sheepish now. "They're good songs," he added.

"You wrote all those songs in a week and a half?" Kick asked.

"Three of 'em are new. The rest I've had a while. I just been working on 'em a little, I just said that. I need a few more days."

"What about musicians?" Paige asked Will.

"You're on your own there, too," Will said.

"I can get the pickers," Jonah said.

Will got to his feet. "Susie wants this on paper, Kick. You know, that she supplies the studio and the rest and you absolve her of any wrongdoing."

Kick nodded. "I can come up with something. Maybe run it by Raney Kilbride."

"While you're at it," Will said, "you can tell Raney that she's dropping the assault charge against you, too."

"Jesus Christ," Paige said. "You slept with that little tramp, didn't you?"

Will smiled and stepped down off the porch. "I managed to retain my virtue. I'll be seeing you."

"Where are you going?" Kick asked.

"Home," he said, turning. "I've got a farm to run."

"You're going home? Now?"

"Good a time as any. I don't know much about making records."

"Did you have breakfast?" Paige asked. She had walked to the top of the steps.

"No. I came out here, soon as I got up."

"Stay to breakfast," she said. "I'll do ham and eggs. You country boys love that stuff."

Will glanced quickly at Jonah. "No, I'll be going. I talked to my hired man this morning. We're falling behind." He turned and started across the lawn.

"You'll stay to breakfast, goddamn it," Jonah said. He walked into the house.

Will stayed to breakfast. Jonah decided that he would cook and he shooed Paige away from the stove. Kick found some paper and sat at the harvest table and began to work on an agreement for Susie Braddock to sign. She wanted to get it down on paper while Will was there with the details.

"She said she'd phone the district attorney herself and ask that the charges be dropped," Will said. "But I'd double-check that if I were you."

"You sure you didn't screw her?" Paige asked Will.

"I'd remember a thing like that."

Jonah made a passable breakfast. While the others were finishing he left for a moment and came back with a long rifle wrapped in a deerskin sheath.

"You ever see one of these, Will?" he asked, pulling the weapon from the cover.

"Is that a Hawkins?" Will asked.

"It is."

"I've seen pictures, but never one in person."

Jonah handed it over to him. "Forty-two caliber. Made in 1856, in Bedford County, Pennsylvania."

Will was hefting the rifle, admiring the lock.

"Still shoots like a new gun," Jonah said.

Will looked up at Jonah. "You still shoot it?"

"Hell, yeah. That's my turkey gun."

"You hunt wild turkeys with a black-powder musket? Shit, I'm using a ten gauge."

"I like to give everybody a sporting chance," Jonah said. "Might be my one remaining virtue in life."

Will aimed the gun at a spot on the far wall, then ran his fingers over the walnut stock before handing it back to Jonah, who slid it into the deerskin.

"Well," Jonah said, as if suddenly embarrassed. "I just thought you might like to see it."

Kick walked Will out to the truck. Paige had said goodbye on the porch and when she did Kick was afraid she was going to kiss him, and it seemed like she would, but in the end she hugged him and told him to come back.

"How'd you pull that off with Susie?" Kick asked. They were standing by the open door of the pickup.

"I told her the story of Oney Brooks."

"Who's that?"

"A schoolteacher back home. My eighth-grade teacher, in fact. Real quiet guy, lived by himself. About, I don't know, fifteen years ago, one of his students accused him of molesting him. Screwed-up kid, took a dislike to Oney for some reason or another. But the cops charged him and he had to go to court over it. You can imagine the publicity, a small town. In the end the kid admitted that he'd made it all up. Oney was acquitted, got his job back. But you know, the community never really let it go. There were always whispers about Oney after that. And he was as innocent as the day is long. That didn't matter. In the end, he just moved away."

"You told Susie that story?"

"I did. I told her we'd bring her up on fraud charges, and even if she squirmed out of it there were always going to be whispers. I don't know what happened back in Florida but she sure got nervous when I mentioned it. She's a respectable woman these days and I get the feeling she'd prefer to leave her past right where it is. Besides, what's it going to cost her, giving you a week in the studio? Nothing, really. She's still getting off lucky."

Kick looked at the corral, where the bay was standing by the rail fence watching her. "If it was just me, I'd try to take her down. But this is Everett's deal. Might sound weird, but this is the last thing my father and I will ever do together."

Will smiled. "Maybe that's the way Everett saw it too."

"Maybe he did," Kick said. "Maybe one of us had to be dead before we could be father and daughter. Kinda sad, isn't it?"

"Not so sad," Will said. "Sometimes things are just the way they are."

Kick glanced toward the house. Paige had gone back inside. "You know, I thought she was going to kiss you."

"Who—Paige?"

"No, that horse over there," Kick said. "Who do you think?"

Will smiled.

"I'm glad she didn't," Kick said then.

"Why's that?" he asked.

"Because, if she did," Kick said and she stepped close and kissed him on the lips, "I wouldn't have done that."

She took a moment to enjoy the look on his face and then she turned and walked back to the house.

SIXTEEN

When Ben got to the sports bar on Highway 7 Blaine Steward was already there, sitting in a booth by himself. He had a bottle of Coors Light and a large plate of chicken wings in front of him, the wings heaped high and smothered in a viscous red sauce. Ben took his jacket off and tossed it into the booth before sitting down and helping himself to one of the wings. Steward gave him a narrow sideways look, like a dog whose food bowl has been threatened.

"Okay," Ben said. "What's this latest emergency? And is there any reason you can't tell me stuff over the phone?"

"Who exactly is Will Montgomery?" Steward asked. He wiped his mouth with a paper napkin.

"He's nobody," Ben said. "And if you had me drive a half hour just to ask me that, I'm gonna stick one of those chicken wings up your nose." He smiled and took another wing. "But not this one."

A waitress walked over then. Ben asked for a vodka and tonic and she left.

"Maybe you should order some food for yourself," Steward suggested.

"Maybe you should tell me why I'm here."

"I just wanted to know who Will Montgomery is," Steward said. "Because just when it looked as if this record deal was dead in the water, just when I thought things might get back to normal over at Great North, this Montgomery goes down there and smoothes everybody's feathers. They're claiming now they're going to make the record."

"Who told you this?"

"Raney Kilbride. Montgomery's there and back already. First thing he did was go running to old Kilbride to tell him the news. Now what I want to know is this—how are they going to make a record when the money's gone? I'll tell you how—Kathleen is going to want Great North to finance the thing."

"You can't let her do that," Ben said after a moment's consideration. "That's throwing good money after bad. Even if they make a record, who's gonna buy it? This Peck is a has-been. You know who buys CDs? Kids, that's who. Kids who've never heard of this guy."

"How do I say no?" Steward asked. "She owns the darn company."

"Not quite yet, she doesn't." Ben took another wing and gnawed on it as he thought. "This is the old man's deal," he said slowly. "The only reason Kick is even down there is because she has to honor that. Right? Then what about this—the old man put up a quarter mil for the project. That's it. Not $250,000 plus another hundred thou later on. Remind Kick that this was the old man's mess. Use him against her. She won't fight you on it. She's got that loyalty thing. Fucking annoying trait that is."

"And just shut it down?"

"Hey, you got things just where you want them. A significant loss on your books, and no recording to show for it. Once it becomes apparent what a disaster this thing is, I'll step in and you and I will restructure things. Don't worry about Kick. She'll pack up and leave. She always has. She doesn't care about this family, especially with the old man gone. Where was she when I was building Eastman Technologies into the force that it is? Traipsing all over the world making her fucking little movies."

"I thought your father built Eastman Technologies."

Miffed at the comment, Ben took two wings this time. "We both did. Okay?"

"Why don't you eat the whole plate?" Steward asked.

"I'm gonna, you don't start eating."

The waitress brought Ben's drink. When Ben allowed her to leave without his ordering food, Steward released a short exasperated puff of breath. Ben smiled at him and licked the sauce from his fingers before taking a drink of the vodka.

"I still haven't figured out just what miracles Will Montgomery performed to get this thing back on track," Steward said. He took a wing and as he did he slyly pulled the plate closer. "You're the one who said he was just a dumb farmer."

"That's exactly what he is," Ben said. "And what're we talking about here? Country and western music. More dumb farmers. He probably arm-wrestled somebody and won. But he's a little too fucking cozy with Raney Kilbride for my liking. I think he's after something, probably the farm. As far as Raney goes, I don't trust that old buzzard either. I wish he'd hurry up and die."

"That's an awful thing to say!"

"Is it?" Ben asked. "Sorry about that. Let's just pretend it never happened, okay?" He smiled and helped himself to another chicken wing.

JONAH WAS OBLIGED to act as go-between for Kick and Susie Braddock, as Kick's bail conditions restricted her from going near the record producer. Susie signed an agreement to the effect that she would provide everything required for the recording of the Jonah Peck album. And, as she said she would, she did talk to the courts. When Kick appeared before the judge on Thursday morning the charges were withdrawn, but only after the assistant district attorney and the judge engaged in some juvenile locker room banter about two women cat fighting in a saloon. For once Kick held her tongue and walked out a free woman.

Paige and Jonah had accompanied Kick to the courthouse, and after the dismissal Jonah collected his bail money from the clerk and they walked outside into a sudden rainstorm.

"Lookit here, I'm flush," Jonah said. "I can buy you gals lunch."

To get out of the rain they went to a place just across the street. It was only eleven-thirty, so they were the first to arrive. They sat by the front windows and watched the storm. People hurried by holding newspapers over their heads. Tourists in shorts, showing milky white legs, shoved their digital cameras up under brand-new Grand Ole Opry T-shirts and ran for cover.

"So Monday morning?" Kick asked.

"Monday afternoon," Jonah said. "Nobody ever made a record in the morning."

"Nobody?"

"Nobody I ever knew."

"Tom and Curtis driving up from Austin together?" Paige asked.

Jonah nodded, looking at the menu. "Matthew's flying in Sunday night. Whatever happened to menus that a human being could understand?"

"What about Joe?" Paige asked.

"Joe's fishing, but he'll be here."

"I assume," Kick said, "that you're talking about the band."

Jonah tossed the menu on the table. "Ask that waitress if they have such a thing as a roast beef sandwich in this place," he said to Paige.

"Ask her yourself," Paige told him.

"Jesus Christ."

"Stop it, you kids," Kick said. "Okay, I have one more dumb question. Actually, I probably have lots more since I know nothing about this. But, if Susie Braddock isn't producing this record, who is?"

"I assume Jonah Peck will be producing this record," Paige said, looking at her father.

"You're real close," he said. "Jonah Peck's daughter is."

"What? I've never produced anything."

"You telling me Susie can do it and you can't?" Jonah asked. "If we're gonna do this by the seat of our pants, everybody's gonna help.

You'll be singing backup, too." He looked at Kick. "Can you sing?"

"Itsy Bitsy Spider?"

"Oh, yeah. Forget it."

"I can make sandwiches," Kick said. "And sew the costumes."

"Costumes? What costumes?" Jonah asked.

"She's joking," Paige said.

"I thought jokes were supposed to be funny." He looked around the room. "Let's find that waitress and get some goddamn lunch. What's wrong with people? I want to work on those songs today."

Paige looked at Kick. "He's shifting into temperamental artist mode."

"You mind your mouth, girlie," Jonah said. "I should have turned you over my knee back when I had the chance."

"If you're looking for a producer you can spank," Paige said, "you should've stuck with Susie."

KICK AND PAIGE spent the weekend staying out of Jonah's way, although Jonah passed a good deal of his time back in the woods with his notebook and guitar. Jonah had a record collection consisting of hundreds of LPs and the two women listened to a lot of music, discussing what they liked about this record or that, and what they didn't. It was soon apparent to Kick that Paige knew more about the subject than Kick ever would. Paige understood the technical side but what she really knew was the other—less obvious—aspect of songwriting itself. The word she kept returning to was heart. Either a song had heart or it didn't.

"There's no faking that part," she told Kick. "And Susie fucking Braddock wouldn't know it if it bit her on the tit."

Jonah's pickers rolled into town one by one. Everyone arrived at the TSA studio Monday afternoon at about the same time. Jonah and the rest of the musicians began to unload their instruments while Kick and Paige went inside to make sure that the situation was as copacetic as they'd been led to believe. Susie was in the control room with a technician and Kenny Butternut was seated on a stool in the isolation booth, wearing a pair of earphones, a microphone a few inches away. The door to the booth was open a crack and they could hear him talking to Susie over the mike.

Susie glanced their way when they came in, curled her lip in an Elvis sneer, then made a point of ignoring them. Behind her, the technician held up the fingers of both hands and mouthed "ten minutes" to them. The two women sat in plastic chairs along the wall and waited. A moment later Kenny Butternut began to sing—

> *"Well, I'm a front porch picker*
> *And a real shit-kicker,*
> *I drink whiskey all night long—"*

"For fuck sakes," Paige said.

There were no video cameras around and Kenny, wearing a Crimson Tide ball cap and a sweatshirt, was dressed down for the occasion. As he sang he kept his eyes on Susie in the booth.

"I didn't expect her to be here," Kick said.

"Girl's a little marked up," Paige said. "That your handiwork?"

"I'm taking the fifth," Kick said. "You think she'll be hanging around?"

"Not a chance," Paige said. "Jonah won't allow her in the building, I don't care if she does own it."

They listened to the song for a moment.

"Any idea who the kid is?" Paige asked.

"Kenny Butternut," Kick said. "According to Susie, he's the next big thing. Susie seems inordinately fond of that expression."

When the kid finished the song, Susie said something into a mike and he began again. Paige lit a cigarette and took an empty pop can from a trash basket beneath a No Smoking sign to use as an ashtray. Kick watched through the glass as the earnest young singer gave it his all. She glanced at Susie, who was leaning forward, her eyes on the kid, her breasts straining the fabric of her satin shirt.

"Do you think these young singers get to sleep with Susie if they want to?" Kick asked.

"I think these young singers get to sleep with Susie even if they don't want to," Paige replied.

Apparently this take was a keeper, as Susie said something into the mike and Kenny Butternut, nodding happily, removed his headphones and walked out of the room. Paige and Kick stood up. He smiled when he saw them but then, undoubtedly remembering the incident at Del Rio's, he closed down the smile and walked past. Susie came out of the control room and embraced him. Keeping her arm around his waist, she turned to Paige, never giving Kick a glance.

"Who are you?" she asked.

"I'm Jonah Peck's record producer," Paige said.

Susie stopped just short of scoffing at the claim. "Never seen you before," she said. "What's your name?"

"They call me the breeze," Paige said. "And I'm the next big thing."

"Ha. I bet. Well, knock yourself out. You got one week." She looked up at the kid. "Come on, jubilee, you've earned yourself a little celebration."

That was the last they saw of Susie for the next seven days. Whatever her multitude of faults and vices, the woman at least knew when she wasn't wanted. Jonah and the band moved in and they began to rehearse the songs. Watching for a couple of hours on the first day, Kick had an idea. After bringing it up with Paige, who just smiled and nodded, she drove downtown and rented a Betacam, then bought enough tape to film the recording session. Jonah was not particularly happy when he realized what she was doing.

"What do you intend to do with the footage?" he asked as they were driving back home in the wee hours after the first day.

"Depends on you," Kick told him. "You better hope I don't make a doc called 'How to Piss Two Hundred and Fifty Grand Up Against a Tennessee Wall.'"

"Jesus," Jonah replied.

Things quickly fell into a pattern. They would arrive at the studio at around three in the afternoon and work until anywhere from midnight to four in the morning. For the first couple of days Kick took videotape of everything. She also made sandwiches, went for beer runs, ignored the occasional use of pharmaceutical supplements, from time to time availed herself of the occasional use of pharmaceutical supplements, and tried to keep out of the way the rest of the time. She even suggested a song for Jonah to record.

Paige worked with Susie's sound guys on the levels, talked to the musicians about arrangements, sang backup, and argued vociferously with Jonah. She didn't use Susie's assembly line style. The band played as a piece, with Jonah in the fore on vocals, guitar and—on a rollicking barrelhouse ode to a mysterious female named Patsy—on piano.

To Kick, the cutting of the record was a lot less interesting than was the transformation of Paige. She was suddenly in her element and she had very precise opinions on how the songs should sound, opinions that both surprised and aggravated Jonah, who'd written them. The resulting disagreements were significant, and sometimes loud. But Paige's fights with Jonah now had nothing in common with the get-on-each-other's-nerves bickering back at the farmhouse. She abandoned her slouching-toward-oblivion act for the pose that it was. In place of it was a genuine passion, backed by a confidence Kick hadn't seen in her before. Because she was singing backup, she actually cut back on her cigarette consumption. Even her skin looked better.

And she never gave her father an inch.

"The song's not a ballad," she told him when they were trying "Patsy" for the first time. Even Kick could tell the melody was stillborn.

"Don't tell me what the song is," Jonah said. "I wrote the damn song."

"It's not a ballad," Paige said again. "If anything it's a Texas two-step."

"I wrote it as a ballad."

"You wrote it for your horse."

At that point, the keyboard player, whom Kick knew only as Curtis from Austin, began to play an up-tempo version of the melody. The others took a moment, then joined in.

"Y'all gonna side with her?" Jonah asked. "Then fuck the whole sorry bunch of you."

He walked out of the studio. A half hour later he came back, sat down at the piano, and they cut the song as a Texas two-step.

For the first couple of days Kick was caught up in the excitement of it all, the creativity and the plain newness of the enterprise. But then—as in filmmaking—that feeling gave way to tedium. Being a fifth wheel on the project only added to her sense of discontent. On the third day she was sitting on the floor changing the lens on the camera when Paige approached her.

"Is it all you dreamed of?" she asked.

"Sure," Kick said.

"Bullshit. You're bored to tears."

"It's not like I'm adding much to the mix," Kick said. "No pun intended."

"You're filming," Paige said. "This is your thing."

"This is *your* thing, Paige," Kick said. "You might not know it yet, but it is. I got a feeling you've come home, girl."

"Shit. You gonna get all Hallmark on me?"

"Wouldn't think of it," Kick said. "This is gonna be your Pop Kenesky."

"Who?"

"Remember I told you about the first real doc I shot, about the guy who made goalie pads? Well, his name was Pop Kenesky. And I was greener than grass. Shot the whole thing myself on a shoulder-held sixteen millimeter. No crew. It's one rough piece of work. But it's my favorite, no question about that."

"Pop Kenesky," Paige repeated. "Well, I don't know what I expected when I came home this time, but I sure as hell didn't anticipate you."

"My point is," Kick said, "maybe you're finally doing what you should be doing."

"And what should you be doing?"

Kick fitted the lens on the camera and then pointed it at Paige. She didn't turn it on though, just watched the other woman through the viewfinder. "I should be in Wyoming, asking Stanley Dawe why he shot that drilling rig to kingdom come."

"That a fact?" Paige asked.

"That's a fact."

"Then what's stopping you?"

THE MEETING was in Teddy Brock's office on Tuesday morning. Jack Dutton and Blaine Steward were already there when Ben arrived, Dutton on the couch drinking a cup of coffee and Steward, already perspiring, pacing a trench in Teddy's expensive Persian rug. When Ben walked in he helped himself to coffee and a muffin, then sat down across the desk from Teddy.

"Sit down, Blaine," he said to Steward. "You're making me nervous. I can hardly eat my muffin."

"Is Raney Kilbride going to be here?" Steward said when he finally sat.

"This has got nothing to do with Raney Kilbride," Ben said. "Teddy, you want to start before Blaine here pisses himself and has to go home and change?"

Teddy had been leaning back in his chair and wearing a rather disagreeable frown, as if he'd encountered an offensive odor he couldn't quite identify. Now he seemed to shake himself from his malaise and moved forward to clasp his hands on the desk.

"This is … what are we going to call it?" He looked at Ben a moment. "This is a preliminary meeting to discuss the potential need to challenge the will of Everett Eastman," he said. "I guess that's what it is."

Ben was watching the others for a reaction; when he heard Teddy's lukewarm opening salvo he snapped a look at him. Teddy ignored it as he continued.

"You gentlemen are here to help assess the situation at Great North and the McDougall Distillery. As you may or may not know, Everett Eastman left codicils in his will, challenges that are to be met before any of the beneficiaries actually take ownership. Ben here is concerned that the challenges attached to McDougall and Great North are restrictive to the point of threatening the—um—well, the existence of the companies. So he's prepared to challenge the will, on the grounds that Everett Eastman was not of sound mind when he made it."

"This thing could get out of control," Ben said. "If we're gonna close the barn door, now's the time to do it."

"Okay," Teddy said. "We'll start with you, Jack. How would you assess Ethan Eastman's performance so far with regard to the operation of McDougall?"

"Hey, I don't want to talk against the kid," Dutton said. "But there's been nothing to assess. He doesn't exist, as far as the distillery goes." Dutton had been sitting back on the plush couch, legs crossed; now he leaned forward to pull a sheaf of papers from an envelope beside him. "I brought a sample of some everyday requests we've asked him to make decisions on. There hasn't been a single reply. All we've received is a couple of half-assed responses from his girlfriend. His girlfriend doesn't have the authority."

"Have you sent him anything by registered mail?" Teddy asked. "He might claim he hasn't received anything."

"Tried that," Dutton replied. "Not a word from Ethan."

"Is it your opinion that Ethan is not up to operating the distillery?"

"It's my opinion that Ethan couldn't operate a two-hole outhouse."

"Of course, you'd rephrase that in front of a judge," Teddy said. "But the company is losing money. Isn't that true?"

"We're about even this quarter," Dutton said. "We'll make money. We always have."

Teddy considered that for a moment then looked at Steward, who was gnawing away at the thumbnail of his right hand like a muskrat caught in a trap, seemingly oblivious to the problems of Jack Dutton. "Mr. Steward," Teddy said. "Tell us what's happening at Great North."

"What's happening is that things are screwed up royally," Steward said when he took his hand from his mouth. "We spent a quarter million dollars on a record that never got made. Now supposedly it will get made but where the money will come from to make it is a good question. I assume it'll come from Great North. Money we'll never get back in a hundred years, if you want my opinion."

"We do," Teddy said. "We just asked your opinion, remember?"

"Okay," Steward said. "The thing is—the quarter million is apparently gone. Kick's going to want more money. I'm just saying the woman has to be held accountable. She could put us under."

"Okay," Teddy said. "This is what I can make of this. I don't think you're going to convince anyone at this point that either of these companies is in imminent danger of collapse. But there is obviously reason for concern. What we're proposing is that Ben initiate a challenge of the will based on Everett's incompetence. The argument will be that these challenges are impractical to the point of counteracting the very intentions of the deceased. Ben will be granted fifty-one percent ownership of the distillery and the publishing house. That way we can return stability to the ownerships, and in the end protect Ethan and Kathleen. Protect them from themselves, basically."

"How you gonna do that?" Dutton asked.

"We'd have to get a judge to listen to the challenge," Teddy said. "The will itself, strange document that it is, would work in our favor there. In effect, we're trying to maintain Everett's wishes while at the same time insisting that they're not economically feasible. The idea is to get Kathleen and Ethan to agree to the challenge. We'd really like to avoid a competency hearing, especially with regard to Ethan. Ideally, they would see the logic in this. For instance, Ethan might be quite content owning forty-nine percent of McDougall. Whether the company rebounds or not, there's still a lot of equity there."

"Why would Kathleen agree to Ben taking over?" Steward asked.

"Because Ben's doing the heavy lifting here," Teddy said. "He's giving her an out."

"Kathleen will take her share and run," Ben said emphatically. "She doesn't want anything to do with Great North. If she sees an escape hatch, she'll take it."

"What about Jonah Peck?" Steward asked.

"If they can make the record, let 'em," Ben said. "But close the cash drawer. You've already financed the thing once." He had a thought. "Make Peck sign something though, in case a miracle happens and he gets it out there and it sells. Apparently, he used to be somebody."

"The next thing I need to know," Teddy said then. "Are the two of you comfortable with this, if we decide to go forward?"

"Absolutely," Dutton said. "I mean, especially if the kid gets looked after. We don't need any new blood. McDougall's has been alive and kicking for a hundred and fifty years. I'd hate like hell to see it go down because the old man lost his marbles at the end."

Teddy looked at Steward.

"I just want things to be the way they were," he said. "Is that what this is going to do for us?"

"That's exactly what it's going to do for you," Ben told him.

Teddy Brock told the two men that he would be in touch and they left. Ben helped himself to another muffin and more coffee. When he walked back to his chair, Teddy was watching him with his hands behind his head.

"In the movies, this would be where I ask you if you're sure about this," he said as Ben sat down.

Ben smiled and plucked the top off the muffin. "This has got to happen. My deal in Indiana fell through. Toyota's screaming they want their fucking ignition and I'm not set up to build it here."

"Hey, you have to build it," Teddy said. "According to the will."

"Not if I can challenge the codicils. If Kick and Ethan are off the hook, so am I. See how this thing comes together? I got everybody right where I want them. You mention the movies. I've been thinking this is like *The Godfather*. The first one, at the end where Al Pacino peels everybody's potatoes at once. That's what I'm going to do. The distillery, the publishing house. And then I'm gonna marry Lynn. Shit, that reminds me, I have to file for a divorce today. I had a meeting with the wolverine yesterday. I have to get that out of the way before this all goes down and my net worth escalates. You sure you don't want to handle it, Teddy?"

"I've never been more sure of anything," Teddy said. "I happen to like your wife. You're lucky I don't call her and tell her what you're up to, buddy."

"You won't do that," Ben said. "The reason I know that is that you just called me buddy. Plus, this little takeover action is going to be a very nice thing for you, Teddy. Stick with me."

"Because I'm stuck with you?"

Ben laughed. "That's pretty good, counselor." He put the rest of the muffin in his mouth.

SEVENTEEN

Stanley Dawe owned a half section on the old Canfield Trail, about seventeen miles northeast of Spotted Horse. The ranch house was small, one floor with three bedrooms, and it sat on a rise a few hundred yards back from the gravel road. There was a steel machinery shed along the lane leading to the house and an older barn of wood, weathered gray with the years, to the rear of that. The field beside the lane was dotted with sheep—three or four dozen ewes and nearly as many lambs. Their fleeces were a dirty gray-white against the green of the pasture. A rock-bottomed creek ran through the field at an angle. The creek was dry.

When Kick pulled into the driveway the sheep, with perfect choreography, raised their heads from their grazing. Some of the lambs came running toward her rental car and followed it along the fence as she neared the house. There was an older four-wheel-drive Dodge pickup by the barn and she parked next to it.

When she got out of the car she heard the heavy ring of wood striking wood, the sound repeated every few seconds. She followed the noise around to the back of the barn. There she came upon a wiry man of about forty-five, dressed in jeans and work boots and a faded green cotton shirt, driving a wooden wedge into a length of cedar log with a large mallet. The hammer looked like the type used in the old carnivals. Ring the bell and win a kewpie doll.

"Stanley Dawe," Kick said.

The man, intent at his task, hadn't heard her approach. He straightened now, looked at her and then looked past her, as if anticipating that she wouldn't be alone.

"Can I help you?" he asked when it was evident that she was.

"You are Stanley Dawe?"

The man nodded reluctantly. He had a bristly mustache that fell past the corners of his mouth, and his eyes were bright blue against a suntanned face. There was a caution about him that did not, however, suggest timidity.

"You're not a cop so you're probably a reporter of some kind," he said. "How'd you find me?"

"Well, the police in Spotted Horse wouldn't tell me," Kick said. "And neither would anybody else in town. So I looked in the phone book. There you were—124 Canfield Trail. All I had to do was find the road." She shrugged. "And I'm not a reporter."

Dawe raised the huge mallet and drove the wedge farther along the post. "Whoever you are, I'm not at liberty to discuss the case. My lawyer says it could work against me."

"I'm making a documentary about what's been happening here the past five years," Kick said. "The drilling. And the consequences of the drilling."

"Can't help you." He swung the hammer again.

"What are you making there?"

"Split rails. Building a fence."

"Don't they have barbwire in Wyoming?"

Dawe hit the wedge again and the length of rail broke away from the log. He picked it up and placed it with a pile of others to the side. Then he started the wedge again, tapping it lightly to gain a purchase in the log.

"We've got barbwire. This here's strictly for looks. I'm gonna run a split-rail fence along the lane from the road to the house. A surprise for my wife's birthday. She's gone to her folks for the week with the kids." He hammered a second wedge into the log.

"Isn't that how Abe Lincoln got his start?" Kick asked.

"So they say." He almost smiled beneath the mustache. "I got problems enough, I'm not looking to become president."

Kick watched him as he advanced the wedges along the log, then turned and had a closer look at the farm. It was a modest place but neatly kept. There was a large vegetable garden behind the house, lined with row upon row of sprouting plants. Kick thought of Johanna and her extensive garden back at Crooked Pear. Behind the machinery shed were two oversized water tanks of heavy green plastic. The tanks looked like a recent addition.

"Any chance we could talk off the record?" Kick asked then. "I know what's been going on here. I know about the aquifers, and the wells. I know about the contamination." She paused. "What I don't know is what made you do what you ... allegedly ... did."

Dawe swung the hammer back and then hesitated before bringing it forward with a smash. "Who did you say you were?" he asked.

"My name's Kathleen Eastman. I make documentary films. I give you my word that nothing you tell me will be made public until after your trial. And only then with your permission. We can put something on paper if you like."

"So I can trust you? That's what they said when they moved in. GreenPower Gas and Oil. Back when they were assuring us that the water table wouldn't be affected."

"Gee, a company like GreenPower wouldn't lie, would they?" Kick asked.

"Shit," Dawe said. "Of course, it runs a lot deeper than that. You pull back the covers and it's AmCom."

"I know it's AmCom," Kick said. "And that's who I'm after." She paused. "You made a joke about not wanting to be president. Well—for what it's worth—I'd vote for you, Mr. Dawe."

Dawe hesitated and then sat down on the log, as if succumbing to a great weariness. He extended the big hammer so the head rested between his boot heels. He looked to Kick like a child who was in trouble but who really wasn't sure for what.

"What happened that night?" Kick asked.

He continued to study the hammer a moment and then he began to talk. "What happened was I lost a lamb. We were right in the middle of lambing and we always lose a few. This little one came out snow white except for three black feet. My daughter Erin was out here, she's just eight, and she loves lambing season. Well, she took to this one right off. But I knew from the start it wasn't going to make it. Couldn't get it to breathe right. I tried to send Erin to the house but of course she wouldn't go. The ewe was with that little one in the pen, and when she was almost gone, I went to the pump to get the mother a drink of water. All I could think to do for her. And my well was dry. It'd been dry off and on ever since the drilling began. And it just—I don't know—it just made me mad." He looked at Kick now. "I know those bastards pumping the groundwater dry had nothing to do with that lamb dying. Nothing at all. But I couldn't even give that mother a drink of water. My own little one standing there, watching her daddy come up dry."

Kick didn't say anything for a long moment. Dawe turned the hammer over in his calloused hands. "People figure I got drunk and did what I did. I never had a single drink. Not one. I put my little girl to bed and then I grabbed my rifle and away I went. Didn't accomplish anything, did I?"

"It might be too early to say," Kick said. When he made no comment, she gestured toward the house. "I see you have new water tanks by the shed."

"Weeks we don't get rain, I'm spending two hundred dollars on trucked water," Dawe said. "Not enough money in sheep these days to support that kind of expenditure but I don't know what else to do. That creek running through the pasture is spring fed. Never ran dry in a hundred and twenty years. Well, it's dry now. Lot of ranchers around here are in the same boat."

"What's GreenPower say?" Kick asked. "Do they offer any compensation?"

"They claim it's got nothing to do with them. They blame it all on the drought conditions. Global warming. Of course, the government that's letting them drill claims that global warming doesn't exist. Isn't that a laugh? They're not about to compensate me anyway, not when they're suing me for two hundred grand for damages to their rig."

Kick nodded. She turned to look at the sheep in the field and the dry creek bed meandering through their midst. "You wouldn't want to tell me that story on camera, Mr. Dawe?"

"I don't know what good it would do."

"Maybe none," Kick said. "But I'd love to shine a light in some of AmCom's darker corners. Be nice to show them that there are people they can't trample."

Dawe looked up. "I'd like for my kids to know I'm not a nut."

"Anybody worth knowing is a bit of a nut," Kick said. "I'll draw something up for us both to sign. To protect you."

"To me signing something like that means that I can't trust you," Dawe said. "Can't I?"

"Well, I have a long list of faults," Kick said.

"Yeah?"

"But being untrustworthy isn't one of them."

KICK ARRIVED BACK in Nashville in time to catch the very end of the recording session. They finished the song "Tadpole" at three-thirty Monday morning. Kick, still wired from her trip to Wyoming, assumed the role of chauffeur and drove Jonah and Paige back to the farm in Jonah's truck. Before they were out of the city both father and daughter were asleep. At a stoplight in the east end of town, Kick glanced over; Paige's head was against her father's shoulder and his arm was wrapped tightly around her. She looked like she was ten years old. She looked happy. They both did.

But happiness would prove to be a fleeting thing.

Late Monday morning the three of them were having coffee on the front porch, watching the horses in the corral, and listening to the jays in the trees, and feeling pretty good in general about themselves and what they'd managed to accomplish over the past seven days.

"Don't get too puffed up," Jonah said after a while. "The same amount of time, God created heaven and earth."

"He didn't have to go through Susie Braddock to do it," Paige said.

They were still basking under their own collective light when the federal marshals arrived. There were two of them, a man and a woman, and they walked up to the porch and announced to Jonah that he had run out of continuances and delays with regard to his delinquent taxes. They had paperwork that detailed the imminent consequences of the situation.

"You've got no choice but to pay," the man said.

"With what?" Jonah asked. "I'm broke."

"You realize you *will* go to jail," the woman said.

"I realize it," Jonah replied. "How does that make me less broke?"

The two agents served the papers and left, after assuring Jonah they'd be back at the end of the month. To collect.

"What the hell they gonna collect?" Jonah asked as he watched them drive away.

"Either the money or you," Paige said. "And I don't think they care which one they get. They're going to make an example out of you, old man. Which means we better get this record finished. Maybe we can swing an advance on the distribution. Enough to keep your country ass out of the hoosegow."

The day was destined to get worse. They drove back to the TSA studio after lunch to make arrangements for mixing the tracks. A man they'd never seen before but who claimed to be the building superintendent led them into a waiting room near the front entrance. When Paige asked about a schedule for doing the mix, the man said he had to make a call.

"What's this about mixing a record?" Susie asked when she arrived half an hour later. "You're not mixing any record here."

Kick felt her stomach turn over. "That was the deal," she said.

"There's been a change of heart, tadpole," Susie said. "The Tennessee Sound Authority is finished with you. I told you, first time I met you, not to go sticking your nose into things that were none of your business. Well, it's come back to bite you on the butt."

"The deal with Everett Eastman was for the whole shebang," Jonah said. "That means finishing, and distribution too."

"You talking about the *original* deal?" Susie asked. "That rooster has flown the coop. I told you—things have changed. You got recording time and that's done. So am I, far as the bunch of you is concerned. And as far as distributing goes, I wouldn't distribute your record if Willie Nelson, Patsy Cline and Hank Williams himself sang on it. The industry has passed you by, Jonah."

Jonah started to speak, then he turned for the door. Kick could see the hurt in his eyes as he walked out.

"Where are the tapes?" Paige asked.

"I sent 'em out to Jonah's farm an hour ago," Susie said. "I was glad to be rid of them, you wanna know the truth."

"If I wanna know the truth, I'll ask somebody else," Paige told her and they left.

They drove back to the farm in silence, the euphoria of the morning replaced by confusion.

"What the fuck just happened?" Paige asked. They were in the kitchen, sitting around the table. "She plan this all along?"

"No," Jonah said. "She was talking about distribution just last week, when I set up the studio time. Something changed since then." He rubbed his eyes with his fingertips. "Maybe she heard the tracks and figures it's no good. Maybe it's as simple as that."

"No way," Paige said. "We just finished the thing a few hours ago. She wouldn't have had time. Besides, she doesn't know good music from bad anyway. It was something else. Something happened in the past few days. But what?"

"What was that about you sticking your nose in things?" Jonah asked Kick.

"The first time I met her she—" Kick began and then she stopped. After a moment, she shook her head in dismissal. "Shit, I must be getting paranoid."

"What?" Paige asked.

"Susie Braddock's a separate entity, right?" Kick asked then. "She doesn't work for anybody?"

"She's got her own label," Jonah said. "But she distributes through TSA. She doesn't own TSA."

"Who does?"

"National Music," Jonah said. "They've been around since the thirties. They have all kinds of smaller labels and distributors."

Kick got up and left the room. Paige gave Jonah a look. Kick was back a minute later with her laptop. She plugged it into the phone jack, went online and began to type into a search engine.

"The Tennessee Sound Authority is owned by National Music," she read, continuing to type.

"I just told you that," Jonah said.

"Well, you didn't tell me this," Kick said, reading on. "National Music has been owned since 1998 ... by AmCom. Which owns GreenPower Gas and Oil. Which is indiscriminately drilling holes all over the Wyoming countryside."

"Which is where you were this week," Paige said.

"Small world, isn't it?" Kick said and she logged off.

SHE FLEW OUT of Nashville the next day, landed at Pearson, drove to Waterloo, walked into the offices at Great North at about five o'clock, argued for thirty minutes with Blaine Steward, who kept whining that he had to be home for dinner, and then walked out. By six she was at Raney Kilbride's house, sitting at his kitchen counter, nursing a rye and water and telling Raney about the whole convoluted affair.

"Let me get this straight," Raney said when she was finished. "You made a record, or you didn't make a record?"

"Both," Kick said. "It's recorded but right now it's just a bunch of tapes. There's a lot to do yet, and no money to do it."

"What has to be done?"

"They have to mix the record," Kick said. "How can I explain the process—"

"I know what it means," Raney said. "I'm old, not misinformed. Why can't you mix it at Great North?"

"Because they don't have the facilities. They can make audio books but this is a different ball game."

"They have a studio," Raney said. "The place at the old train station. Will it not work?"

"I beg your pardon?"

"Come on, Kathleen. The place where they recorded their Christmas albums and the gospel stuff. I would've thought you'd been there."

"I've been there," Kick said. "Shit, we made forty-fives there when we were little. 'Santa Claus Is Coming to Town.' We sang Happy Birthday for Johanna. But Great North never owned the place. They just rented it, didn't they?"

"They've owned it ever since they came into existence," Raney said. "They rent it out now most of the time. This guy Stanhouse made a polka record over there last year. It won an award for something."

Kick reached for the rye, held it to her lips but didn't drink. She set it down. "This would be something Blaine Steward would be aware of?"

"Kathleen," Raney admonished.

"That motherfucker. Sorry, judge."

"Hey, if the profanity fits, let the motherfucker wear it."

Now Kick took the drink. "Well, I guess that means we have the wherewithal to mix it. Now comes the tough part. Apparently it costs a lot of money to distribute a CD these days."

"I would think so. How much?"

"To do it properly, I'm hearing a couple hundred thousand might be on the low side. Just to start. Unless we stand on a street corner, sell them one by one."

Raney was drinking scotch and now he got up for a refill. "This is past my limit but Alma's playing hoss at her sister's and I won't tell her if you won't," he said, pouring. He indicated Kick's glass but she shook her head.

"I've got to head out to Crooked Pear."

"Where will you get the money?" Raney asked. "I'm going to assume that standing on the corner will be a last resort."

Kick got to her feet. "We'll mix it first, then maybe take it to a bigger label, see if we can't convince them to help. You know, I'm no expert but it's pretty damn good, Raney. Jonah Peck is a cantankerous old bastard, but he … I don't know … he sings from the heart."

Raney walked her out to the front porch. "Was Will Montgomery of any help down there?"

"I still don't know exactly how he did it," Kick said, "but Will was the cavalry." She hesitated. "What did he tell you?"

"Just that you got things sorted out. Was there anything else he should have told me?"

"No," Kick said. "I just wondered."

JOHANNA WAS TAKING A ROAST CAPON OUT of the oven when Kick walked into the kitchen at Crooked Pear. She put the bird on top of the stove to cool then joined Kick at the table. Kick repeated the story for the second time in an hour.

"So Mr. Steward has a disclosure problem," Johanna said when she heard about the studio.

"He's gonna have employment problems, he keeps lying to me," Kick said. "Whether it's by omission or otherwise."

Johanna went to the cupboards and took down plates. Kick got up to help and the two of them set the table for four.

"Does this mean Ethan and Janey are joining us?" Kick asked.

Johanna shrugged. "They'll eat at some point. Hard to say when. You should know that Ethan's coming around. He doesn't sleep the day away anymore. He's been spending a lot of time on this little garden plot he has out behind the barn."

"Uh oh."

"No, it's not what you think. He's planted tomatoes and corn and pumpkins. Organic. He's been boning up on soil nutrients and pH indexes and things like that. By the way, he gets a courier package just about every day from the distillery, asking for his input on some trivial company business."

Kick stopped doling out the flatware. "Does he respond?"

"Never. She does, but I doubt that counts."

"Shit, Johanna. Somebody's setting him up."

"That's my impression."

"I'd better talk to him," Kick said after a moment.

"Well, I wish you good luck with that," Johanna said. She laid out potatoes and corn and a large salad. Kick went down into the cellar and came back with a bottle of Everett's French red.

"Hey," Johanna said when she saw the wine. "Do you know what that wine is worth?"

"Nope."

"Maybe two hundred dollars."

"Must be good wine then," Kick said. "Are you thinking there are people more deserving than us who should be drinking it?"

"The corkscrew's in the drawer by the sink."

Johanna hollered upstairs that dinner was served, and Janey yelled back thank you, but neither she nor Ethan appeared. Johanna and Kick drank the wine and ate the food. Johanna told Kick of the death of the little black goat, and of how Will had taken the big mare to his place. She left out the more intimate details of the story.

"Will came over yesterday and plowed that pasture field behind the barn," Johanna said when they'd finished. "Where I used to turn the horses out. I guess he'll seed it with corn or beans now. With the animals gone."

"Maybe you'll want another team someday," Kick said.

"No, I won't," Johanna said. She poured the last bit of wine in Kick's glass. "What will you do with the record?"

"Mix it and see what we've got."

"And do you know how to do that? Mix a record?"

"I got help coming on that front."

"And the distribution?"

"On that front, I got nothing," Kick said. "You wouldn't have a couple hundred grand lying around you're not using?"

"No. If I did, would you suggest I invest it in something like this?"

"Not on your life," Kick admitted.

Johanna got up to make coffee. "So you told me all about Nashville and Wyoming too but you didn't so much as mention one part. The last time I talked to you, you were in jail. What happened?"

"I don't know all the details but Will convinced the, um … the other party, to drop the charges. He didn't tell you that?"

"He didn't say too much. Just that things were back on track. He's a man of few words."

Johanna was leaning against the kitchen counter. The coffeemaker was gurgling behind her. "Did you know he drove all the way down there because he doesn't like airplanes? He just dropped everything and went."

"I knew that."

The machine stopped its noise. Johanna carried the carafe over to the table and sat down. She looked at Kick as she poured. "He's a good man, Will Montgomery."

Kick caught the delicious smell of the coffee. What Johanna had just said was true. Kick wasn't overjoyed that it was Johanna who said it.

BEN DROVE OVER to the fitness center after lunch. He'd called Lynn four times that morning and got her voice mail each time. That had been going on for days now. He'd spoken to her briefly the night before; he'd been at home and had gone out to the garage around eleven o'clock and called her on his cell. She'd begged off after a couple of minutes, saying she was tired and had to open the next morning.

His hesitation to put up the money for the gym had been based on his concern that she wouldn't commit to running the place. From what little she'd revealed of her past working history—as opposed to her sexual history, about which she was a little *too* forthcoming— Ben had come to the conclusion that she'd never been much for the working life. It appeared now that his fears had been unfounded. In fact, it had turned out that the opposite was true—she'd thrown herself into the running of the fitness center to the extent that she had no time for Ben. They hadn't had sex in almost two weeks. Ben had caught Meredith in the shower on Sunday morning and made it with her, standing up. That was not how it was supposed to work. He hadn't handed over fifty thousand dollars to his girlfriend in order to fuck his wife.

When he got to the gym Lynn was in her office, wearing white shorts and a snug tank top. She was standing up, leaning over her desk, clicking the mouse as she did something on the computer screen. It was as if she hadn't time to even sit down at the terminal.

He came up behind her, moved against her ass, and put his arms around her waist. "You look real nice like that," he told her.

"Hey, you," she said. "What are you doing here?"

"I'm here to see you."

She closed the program on the screen and wriggled out of his embrace. "I've got a Pilates class in five minutes. Why didn't you call?"

"I called," he said. "And called."

She picked up her cell phone from the desk and checked the display. "So you did." She smiled at him. "Sorry, babe."

Ben walked over to the little refrigerator. "Don't sorry babe me. I need a drink." He opened the door. "Hey, there used to be beer in here."

"I got rid of it," Lynn said.

"Why?"

"Mandy said it looked bad. This is a fitness club."

She was leaning against the desk now. Ben sat down in one of the leather chairs and looked at her long legs. She was wearing white runners with the tiny half socks that just showed above the shoes.

"Come here," he said.

"I got my Pilates class."

"What is that anyway?"

"It's an exercise program. It's based on … listen, I can't explain it in one minute."

"Okay." Ben shrugged. "Explain to me why we haven't gotten together for a month?"

"Chrissakes, it's been like a week." When he stood and stepped toward her she crossed her arms in front of her chest, the body language clear. Seeing the look on his face, she relented a bit. "Why don't you come to my place on the weekend?" she asked. "Can you get away?"

"Why don't we go to your place right now?"

"Because I have a class. Mandy says I should get my body fat down to twelve percent."

"I might have to buy a muzzle for Mandy."

"She knows her stuff," Lynn said. "Besides, I'm working."

"All you do is work."

"Well, that was the idea," she said. "Making this place work. I mean, we were gonna be filthy rich from your inheritance. But that didn't happen, did it? So now the plan is to make this place success-ful. I enjoy being here, Ben. I'm learning a lot about my body."

"I want to learn too."

"You got a one-track mind, you know that?"

"I'm your dog."

"Not today, Benjy."

"I told you not to call me that."

He walked out, knowing she would come after him, trying to smooth things over. By the time he got to his car, though, he realized that she wasn't going to do it this time. Driving away, he considered that he hadn't created a monster, he'd created a businesswoman. What he couldn't decide was whether or not that's what he wanted. After all, he'd been pretty happy with the old arrangement, although he hadn't known it at the time.

Driving along the thruway, he decided he would let it slide for the time being. Technically, he owned the gym. If there came time for a change, he could facilitate it quickly enough.

There were other, better, changes on the wind. Earlier in the day he'd had a conversation with Jack Dutton. He'd been continuing to send registered mail to Ethan, seeking counsel on one company matter or another. The girlfriend had shown up at the distillery again to reply to the missives and Dutton had refused to even meet with her. There'd been no response of any kind from Ethan. Dutton was keeping a record of the visits, and the instances of nonresponse.

Also, Ben had heard from Blaine Steward that Kick was back. She'd shown up at Great North, crying poverty, looking for money to finish whatever she and the hillbilly singer had started down in Nashville. Steward had, according to him anyway, shown her that there was no money available to help her, even if he wanted to. And he didn't, a fact that had to be pretty clear to Kick. His sister was a pain in the ass on many levels, but she was as smart as anyone Ben had ever known, a fact that he usually resented but was now hoping would work in his favor. Because it appeared that the prudent move at this point would be to abort the NIC project. If a compromise reared its head at this juncture, Kick would have to listen.

When Ben got back to his office he went online and checked out the real estate situation on Hilton Head Island. It was a little early to be looking at resort housing, but then Ben, a former boy scout, wanted to be prepared. Actually, he'd only been a cub scout, and even then had quit after a couple of months. The going had been a little too rough, with the rules and the outdoors stuff and the stupid salute.

EIGHTEEN

The seed arrived by special delivery late Thursday afternoon. Will sowed the pasture field behind the barn at Crooked Pear early the next morning. When he'd arrived with the seed drill, shortly after doing chores, he'd found Ethan waiting for him, as promised. He was standing by the corral, sleepy-eyed and his hair a wild tousle, but he'd been there. They talked for a bit afterward and then Will had come home.

By then the sun had burned the dew from the grass. Will hooked the mower to the John Deere and drove back to the ten-acre alfalfa field in front of the bush to cut it. After he'd made a couple of turns he saw Dalton coming down the lane with the baler. He went into the field opposite the lane from Will, the field Will had mown two days earlier and raked yesterday. Will watched as Dalton got down from the tractor and lifted armfuls of hay here and there to see if it was dry enough to bale. It was, Will already knew, because he'd gone through the same routine a half hour earlier.

When Will came around again Dalton was making his way across the field, kicking out bales behind him as he went. By the time Will made one more turn the baler was parked in the field, jacked at an uneven angle, and Dalton was driving toward the lane, the flat tire chained to the back of the tractor. Will veered off to meet him at the gate as he passed. Dalton stepped on the clutch and coasted almost to a stop.

"Thorn," he said and he kept on going.

It was after noon when Will finished mowing the field and headed back to the house. Dalton hadn't returned yet and Will wondered why, but then he met him coming down the lane. Will had to pull nearly into the ditch to let him pass. This time Dalton came to a complete stop.

"You got a visitor up at the house," he said.

"Who?" he asked. "Denise?" They were to sign the final papers that week and she was still pushing for his Mustang.

"I don't know who it is," Dalton said. "But it sure as hell ain't Denise."

When Will got back to the machine shed he pulled the John Deere up to the diesel pumps and filled the tank. He had the front field, an alfalfa-timothy mix, to cut at Crooked Pear that afternoon. When the tank was full he checked the oil and the hydraulic fluid and then walked around the barn and headed for the house.

He'd rescued an old pail bench from the barn a few years earlier and cleaned it up and painted it and placed it by the back door of the house. The rescue had been Denise's idea. Will had half expected her to ask for the bench in the settlement and he was glad she hadn't. It was a good spot to sit to remove boots, or to drink a cold beer after a warm day in the field.

And apparently it was also a good spot for Jonah Peck to be occupying, because that's what he was doing at this particular moment. He was wearing his dirty cowboy hat, and a buckskin coat, and he had his Hawkins rifle, wrapped in the doeskin, across his lap. It was a colorful image and Will, crossing the lawn, was pretty sure that the old man knew it. "Mr. Peck," he said, approaching.

"How are you, son?"

"Good," Will said. He tried not to smile. "Fancy meeting you here."

"Well, I'm stayin' over yonder," Jonah said and he pointed the barrel of the musket toward Crooked Pear. "I flew up for a few days to mix the record. I'm told Great North has got what we need to do it."

Will nodded. "I heard that Susie got cute with you guys."

"Cute isn't a word that comes to mind when describing that gal," Jonah said.

"I don't know much about mixing records," Will said. "Is a forty-two-caliber Hawkins standard equipment?"

"I was thinking about those turkeys you mentioned," Jonah said. "They still around?"

"They are. I saw a flock just yesterday back by the bush." Will turned and pointed.

Jonah got to his feet and looked suspiciously in that direction. "You said they were becoming a nuisance."

"Well, we have a season but the hunters don't take that many birds," Will said. "They're to the point right now that they're multiplying like crazy."

"Would a fella need a license for shooting them?"

"Not if he doesn't get caught," Will said. He took a step toward the house, then stopped. "You hungry? I was going to grab a sandwich before going back to work."

Jonah shook his head, still squinting toward the bush lot, as if he looked hard enough he might actually see the wild birds. "The woman over there fixed me something. What's her name?"

"Johanna."

"Yeah." He turned back to Will. "Good-looking woman."

"I won't keep you," Will said. "There's a lane just past the barn, follow it back. That other bush lot goes with Crooked Pear; I guess you can hunt there too, seeing how you're a guest of the family. You won't see a game warden but if you do, you're a trespasser. Okay?"

"Yup."

"I got a man back there baling hay, too. I'd appreciate it if you didn't shoot him."

"Is he a turkey?" Jonah asked.

"No."

"I'll let him be."

Will saw now that Jonah's canvas rucksack was beneath the bench. The old man picked it up and slung it over his shoulder. Then he nodded and started out.

"Hey," Will said, stopping him when he'd gone maybe twenty paces. "You're not gonna tell me you walked through customs carrying that rifle."

Jonah turned. "I did so."

"How the hell did you get away with that?"

"Easy as pie, son," Jonah said. "I'm a celebrity."

KICK GOT THE NAME of a local musician who was now producing music from an old high school friend who'd once played drums in the man's rock and roll band. An apologetic to the point of groveling Blaine Steward had agreed that Great North could afford to pay the man to help mix the recordings. Steward's contrition was such that Kick wasn't required to mention that the company was on the very cusp of unburdening itself of his own salary to help defray the costs. She wasn't required to, but she mentioned it anyway.

It took her the better part of the morning to set things up. It was hot and humid in the city and when she got back to Crooked Pear shortly after lunch she had a shower then made herself a cup of tea and carried it out to the south patio. Johanna had gone into town for a meeting and Jonah Peck, whom Kick had picked up at the airport the night before, was nowhere to be found. Kick sat in a chaise lounge, content for the moment in the afternoon sun with her solitude and her caffeine. She wondered if there would ever be a time when her contentment would not be measured in moments and, in the very act of wondering, knew that this moment was already gone.

Her minor despair at that realization was interrupted by the harsh sound of a diesel engine. She looked up to see Will Montgomery approaching down the road, driving a tractor with a hay mower behind. When he stopped and got off to open the gate to the front field, she set her cup aside and walked over. He didn't hear her approach over the tractor engine.

"Hello!" she called.

When he saw her, he propped the gate open and then went to shut the tractor off. He was wearing a faded gray shirt, the collar frayed. There was stubble on his cheek and he had a sorry-looking bandage on his right hand, dirty gauze wrapped with duct tape. Kick realized that she herself was still in the sweats and T-shirt she'd thrown on after her shower. She ran her hands self-consciously through her hair, although it was a little late for grooming at this point.

"Hello, Kick."

"How are you, Will Montgomery?"

"Pretty formal, aren't you?"

Kick shrugged and smiled. She realized she was being coy and the realization infuriated her. "You didn't come across a crusty cowboy singer in your travels?" she asked, looking to escape.

"Yeah. He was at my place when I came in for lunch."

"I thought maybe he'd gone to the meeting of the horticultural society with Johanna," Kick said. "Hey, I'm joking."

"I sent him back to the bush to look for turkeys," Will said. "He was like a little kid on Christmas morning. He's here to mix the record?"

"Yeah."

Will looked at the house. "Paige with him?"

Kick felt a sharp pang. If it wasn't Johanna, it was Paige. "No … she stayed in Tennessee. She, um … has a problem with the border. Drug convictions. Why?"

"Just wondered."

"I can get her phone number, if you want it."

"I could probably get it myself, if I wanted it," Will said. "What's wrong with you?"

"Oh, nothing. I'm just a little … wired. I guess being a music mogul isn't what it's cracked up to be. Especially a mogul with no money."

"So you're going to make your record," Will said. "That gets you clear on the will. Then what?"

"I've got a documentary to finish," Kick said. "I have to get back to Wyoming. There's a rancher who's about to be crucified or deified. Either way, I'd like to be there to record it."

"Where you gonna get the money for that?"

"I have no idea," Kick said. "Just like I have no idea how we're going to distribute this record, if we finish it. I'm taking it one financial emergency at a time these days. As Jonah says, either we'll all see the promised land or we won't."

"I don't know about that," Will said and he walked over to get back on the tractor. "But he's gonna surprise the hell out of me if he shoots a turkey with that old Daniel Boone muzzle-loader he carries."

"Don't count him out," Kick said. "I have a feeling he takes great delight in surprising people."

"You and him both," Will said.

She watched as he fired the tractor up and drove into the field. Putting the mower in gear, he looked back and gave her a wave, then began to cut the hay. Kick walked up the slope to the house. Her tea was cold now but she drank it anyway, sitting in the sun and wondering what he meant by that last remark.

THEY HAD WILD TURKEY for dinner that night. Johanna and Kick were picking weeds in Johanna's vegetable garden late in the afternoon when Kick looked up and saw Jonah approaching along the creek beyond the barn. He had the ancient rifle in his right hand and a dead turkey in his left. Kick stepped over a row of sprouting beans to give Johanna a nudge. When Johanna saw him, she smiled.

"Looks like he just stepped out of a history book," she said.

"He's posing," Kick said. She watched him for a moment. "But he did shoot a turkey."

They went back to their weeding. A few minutes later Jonah came through the twisted pear trees and across the expanse of lawn to where they worked. He nonchalantly tossed the dead bird to the ground, where it landed with a heavy thud, then he leaned on the barrel of the gun and nodded to the two women.

"Ladies."

Kick stood up from her row. She could see that the turkey hunter was himself puffed up like a peacock. She could also see that his pupils were rather large and that a familiar smell clung to him. It seemed that the great white hunter may have sparked a doobie on his walk back to the farm.

"Good lookin' garden you have there, ma'am," Jonah said then.

"Thank you," Johanna said. She stood up and tossed a handful of weeds onto the lawn. "My name is Johanna, did I mention that?"

"Yes, ma'am." Jonah shifted to indicate the turkey on the ground. "I don't know what you're planning for supper tonight but I'd be happy to add this bird to the pot."

"Sure," Johanna said.

"All right," Jonah said. "Now all we got to figure is who's gonna pluck this thing."

"We have a long-standing rule here at Crooked Pear," Johanna said. "Whoever shoots a wild turkey, plucks him. There's a garbage bin in the barn for the feathers."

Jonah looked from one woman to the other, then sighed and picked up the bird and started for the barn.

"Long-standing rule," Kick said when he was gone. "You're lucky he's as high as a kite or he wouldn't have fallen for that."

"Hey," Johanna said. "Do you want to pull feathers or do you want to go up to the house for a cocktail?"

"If you put it that way," Kick said and they started for the house.

SHE AND JONAH drove in to the studio the next day. It was quickly evident that Kick would be no more help there than she was during the actual recording. After the first day, which was interesting only because it was the first day, she let Jonah and the technician, whose name was Sam, work on their own. She'd been a little concerned about throwing the two men together. She'd rather expected Sam to show up looking like a castoff from a heavy metal band. Instead he looked like a baseball player, and wore a team jacket that suggested he was. Jonah circled him a couple of times in his own judgmental fashion. Then Sam began talking about George Jones and everything smoothed out from there.

It turned out that Great North had some decent equipment on hand. Sam brought along a very expensive laptop and through a combination of the two he was able to send audio files to Paige, who was sitting at her computer back in Tennessee. As such, she was able to contribute to the mix. It seemed an awkward arrangement to Kick but, according to Sam, it was entirely workable and that was all that mattered.

Jonah's working hours were typical. He'd sleep until noon at Crooked Pear—although on a couple of mornings he got up at dawn and went turkey hunting—and then Kick would drive him into Waterloo at around two. She'd hang around, or return to the farm, and then go back into the city to pick him up, usually after midnight. The odd hours left Kick with plenty of time to do other things, and she would have, had she anything to do.

She did, however, have a discussion with Ethan one morning while waiting for Jonah to wake up. She'd been expecting him to show up at mealtimes but neither he nor Janey ever did. Johanna reasoned that they arrived in the kitchen in the middle of the night, like mice, and made off with food.

Kick had been on the back deck, drinking tea and reading *The New York Times* on her laptop when she saw Ethan walk out of the barn carrying a rake and a hoe. When he disappeared behind the building, she followed. He was kneeling in the dirt of his garden patch when she approached. Just beyond the garden was the pasture field that Will Montgomery had recently plowed. It had been cultivated now, and planted in something. There were markers on steel posts here and there in the field, with labels she couldn't read from the distance.

"Hey, buddy," Kick said.

"You must leave now, take what you need, you think will last," he said.

"Ethan, I swear to God I'm going to slap the shit out of you."

He turned to her and in that moment she saw something in his eyes. "Hey, I was talking to the bugs," he said.

"I thought maybe I was the one talking to a bug," Kick told him.

He actually smiled at that. He stood and with the hoe deftly flipped a couple of weeds from between the rows of plants. The garden did indeed appear to be bona fide. It was maybe half the size of Johanna's large plot behind the house.

"All organic," Ethan said.

"We need to talk, Ethan."

He shrugged and then took a plastic yogurt tub from inside his jacket and walked over to the tilled field. Kneeling down, he scooped the tub full of soil. Just as he looked up, Janey walked around the corner of the barn.

"Hey," she said. "What's going on?"

"Good question," Kick said. "I don't know, and I have a feeling I'm not the only one. Johanna says you've been ignoring packages from the distillery, Ethan."

"I've been responding," Janey said.

"No offense, but your two cents isn't worth two cents. Didn't it occur to you guys that somebody's trying to set you up? You think McDougall needs Ethan's expertise to continue making whiskey? This is a power play."

"He's been busy," Janey said lamely.

"Hoeing this little patch of dirt? Let him talk for himself."

"I've been busy," Ethan said.

Kick looked at Janey a moment, then at Ethan.

"You want to grow tomatoes, grow tomatoes," she said after a minute. "But take care of business. Don't let these bastards walk all over you. You're not eleven years old, Ethan."

"I'm trying, Kick," he said.

"Just do it, Ethan. You've tried everybody else's way. Tell 'em all to go fuck themselves and just be Ethan Eastman. Remember, you're the only one qualified to do that."

She went back to the deck and her laptop and her tea. A few minutes later Janey came up from the barn and went into the house. She returned, carrying a file folder. She sat in the chair beside Kick, who was staring blankly at the screen.

"Son of a bitch," Kick said.

"What's wrong?"

"Stanley Dawe goes to trial in two weeks. They moved the date forward."

"Who's that?"

Kick turned the computer off. "A rancher in Wyoming. Took it upon himself to shoot up a drilling rig that was threatening ... well, all kinds of things."

"And you know him?"

"I'd like to think so. I do know this—I'm going to have to find a way to get to Wyoming by a week Monday."

"Listen," Janey said after a moment. "There's a couple of things I think you should know."

"Okay," Kick said.

"First, let me show you something," Janey said and she opened the folder. "I've been looking at these numbers from McDougall and they don't add up. Unless somebody's pouring whiskey into the

Grand River, this place should be making money. I'd need a more comprehensive breakdown on some of this stuff to say for sure. Equipment depreciation, for one, is a pretty vague thing to quantify. But it looks to me as if something's not right here."

"You think the place is losing money because it's being ripped off?" Kick asked.

"I don't think the place is losing money at all."

Kick looked at the pages Janey gave her. "I'm not the best person to be asking for financial advice. You understand all this?"

"Most of it. I'm sure some of the data is fudged."

"Who would do that? Ben?"

"Maybe. But it isn't just a recent thing. I do think that Ben and Jack Dutton are trying to suggest that Ethan isn't up to the challenge."

Kick looked toward the barn, where Ethan was still, presumably, toiling at his garden. "Why are you doing this?" she asked.

"What?"

"This. Why are you sticking around?"

Janey gathered the pages together. "This isn't about running a distillery. It's what Ethan's father wanted for him. If Jack Dutton cooperates, we're gonna make it work. If he doesn't, we're gonna make it work anyway. It's his father's wish. Did you think that part somehow escaped Ethan?"

Kick rubbed her eyelids with her fingers. "I think somehow it escaped me."

"And I'm doing it because I love him," Janey said. "You know what that's like."

"Well, shit," Kick said. "Thanks." She looked at the barn a moment longer, then turned to Janey. "All right—what else you got?"

THEY WORKED EVERY DAY for a week and finished the mix the following Wednesday evening at around eleven o'clock. The phone bills later showed that Jonah spent roughly fifty hours of the week arguing long distance with Paige. It seemed to Kick that Paige won most of the fights. Sam made a hundred CDs of the completed recording for demos and then he wished them luck and loaded his laptop in his van and said goodbye.

Kick and Jonah drove back to Crooked Pear in her car. Jonah sat slumped in the passenger seat as they drove out of the city. There was a half moon on the rise and no clouds and when they reached the river road Kick could see clearly the far bank of the stream. Jonah could have seen it too, except that he was staring straight ahead at the dashboard. The box of CDs was on the seat between them.

"How many of these things have you made?" Kick asked.

"I couldn't say for sure. Got to be ... forty. Maybe fifty."

"Doesn't anybody keep track?"

"Somebody probably does. Not me."

Kick touched the brake pedal as a jackrabbit ran out from the ditch, panicked in the headlights, dodged back and forth, then scooted back in the direction it had come.

"Well, you've heard it," Kick said. "How does it stand up? Is it good?"

Jonah pushed his long hair back from his face. "You gotta understand. You don't never make a record and say, That's not worth spit. They all seem good at the time. And it's a matter of individual taste too. Hell, I got records the critics say are classics that I don't much care for. And I made a few that never made a ripple that I still love. Same as mixing. Some of these guys nowadays will spend months and months on the mix. In the end, though ... well, in the end it's got to do more with emotion than knowing which knobs to turn."

"Stop beating around the bush, Mr. Peck."

"It's good."

Kick smiled. "That's what I wanted to hear. And, in my more sentimental moments, I might say that's good enough for me.

However, if there's one thing I've learned the hard way, it's that precious sentimental moments don't pay the rent. We have to figure out a way to get this thing out there. What would normally happen at this point? I mean, in your past experience?"

"At this point," Jonah said, "depending on what period of my life we're talking about, I would either get drunk, get stoned, go chasing a cheerleader, or maybe take a small role in a bad movie. Once, I even took a small role in a good movie."

"You're a lot of help," Kick said. She slowed down as they approached Crooked Pear and turned in the drive. The house was dark as they pulled up and parked. She shut the engine off and they sat there in the scant moonlight.

"I don't know a hell of a lot about music," Kick said after a while. "And the last time I listened to country music was when my marriage broke up. I had a Kristofferson CD and I listened to 'Help Me Make It Through the Night' about a hundred times. Might have been a bit obvious but I was looking for solace and old Kris was there for me. I've listened to these ten songs I don't know how many times these past couple of weeks, and I don't know if it's considered country or city or someplace in between." She looked at him; he was staring out the windshield, his eyes sharp. "But I can tell you, Mr. Peck, that I think it's absolutely beautiful. Paige told me that a record has to have heart. Well, this one's got a heart as big as a washtub."

He smiled at the phrase and turned to her. It seemed as if he would say something but in the end he just nodded.

"So," Kick said. "Tomorrow morning I'm going to go to Great North and I'm going to find a way to distribute it. Maybe I'll have to mortgage the company. Maybe I'll have to put Blaine Steward in a headlock and make him holler uncle. But I'll find a way to do it."

"You better be sure it's the smart thing to do. It's a new world out there. You heard Susie Braddock ... the business has passed me by. This thing could sink like a stone, Kick."

"You know, that's the first time you've called me Kick," she said. "And I'll have you know I don't set much store in Susie Braddock's opinion. You had a deal with my father. You held up your end, and now I'm going to hold up his."

THE REGISTERED LETTERS from Teddy Brock's office came the next morning.

Kick couldn't get in touch with Raney Kilbride until noon. He told them to come right over. Kick offered to drive but Janey and Ethan insisted on going in on their own, saying they had another stop to make first.

At two o'clock they met the judge in the library of his home. Alma Kilbride brought in date squares and tea then said that she would leave them alone. They sat silently while Raney read the letters from Brock's office. When he was done, he took his glasses off and looked at the three of them for a long moment.

"Oh, Ben," he said at last. "We should've drowned you in a sack when you were born, like they do kittens."

"Is it nonsense?" Kick asked.

"It is," Raney said. "But they'll get it before a judge. And if nothing else, they'll hold everything up. There's a timeline here and that's obviously going to work to their advantage. Ben wants to force the two of you into a compromise. What's this about McDougall asking for your input, Ethan? Is that true?"

"Yes."

"I've been responding on his behalf," Janey said.

Raney raised his eyebrows. "I can see where they're going there. They'll try to say Ethan's not fit to run the distillery and that as such the codicil is unrealizable. And if push comes to shove, they'll try to prove it. That's why they're offering this reduced role in ownership, thinking you won't want to subject yourself to a competency hearing, Ethan."

Ethan made no comment.

"As far as you're concerned, Kathleen—they're probably hoping to delay things until it's impossible for you to make the deadline."

"Who's this Brock?" Kick asked.

"I've never heard of him," Raney said. "There's lots of lawyers around." He picked up the papers again, sifted through them, frowning as he did.

"What do we do, Raney?" Kick asked.

"I'll go to court with you," he said. "I can certainly argue that Everett was competent. They'll claim that the challenges are unrealistic, proving that he wasn't. In the end, it will depend on how quickly a judge moves on it."

"I have to be in Wyoming next week," Kick said. "If I can pry enough cash from Great North to buy myself a plane ticket. I don't have time for courtroom shenanigans. Your esteemed presence won't tilt the board?"

"I'd be lucky if my esteemed presence got me a table at McDonald's. I'm looked upon as a colorful relic these days." Raney tossed the papers on the desk for the second time.

Kick got to her feet and walked to the window to look out at the street. "Can I at least fire Blaine Steward's fat ass?" she asked. "Come on, Raney … give me that satisfaction."

"You probably can," Raney said. "But if they were ever successful in this little coup attempt, he'd sue you for false dismissal and ask for punitive damages to boot."

"You're not much fun today," Kick said.

"Sorry," Raney said. "As far as you're concerned, Ethan, you're going to have to decide what you want. Your brother is basically offering you forty-nine percent of the distillery. You've shown no desire to meet the conditions of the will. Unless you've got a better idea, you might be wise to consider this, and hope they turn the place around."

"Um," Janey said, and then she got to her feet. "We might have a better idea."

WILL AND DALTON brought in four loads of hay late that afternoon and put three of them in the mow in the big barn before darkness stopped them. They ran the fourth wagon under the pole barn in case of rain and then they stood in the shed and drank a couple of beers each before Dalton said he had to be getting home.

Will walked to the house and put a frozen dinner in the microwave. He was standing by the counter waiting for his supper when the doorbell rang. At first he thought it was the microwave, then it rang again. He often forgot that he even had a doorbell; Denise had insisted on one although the neighbors never used it.

Before he got to the door, Kick and Jonah Peck walked in. They were a glum-looking pair and Will had to wonder if the recording had turned out badly. The microwave rang then. Will offered to nuke a couple more gourmet meals but they declined. He sat at the kitchen table and ate while Kick told him of Ben's latest maneuver.

"Maybe I ought to just knock Ben on his ass," Will said when he heard.

"Violence never solved anything," Kick told him.

"Yeah. You beat up any record producers lately?" Will asked.

"That's my point. Where did it get me?"

Kick was pacing. Jonah sat quietly at the far end of the table. He'd taken off his cowboy hat and laid it in front of him. There was a wild turkey feather stuck in the hat band.

"Is the record done?" Will asked.

Jonah reached into his coat pocket. "I brought you a copy. Appreciation for the hunting ground."

Will took the CD from him and walked over to put it in the player on a shelf. A few seconds later, Jonah's ragged tenor filled the room. Will listened for a moment and nodded.

"What do you do now?" he asked.

Kick stopped pacing and leaned against the counter. Will realized that the two of them hadn't really discussed the matter. It occurred to him that they had arrived at his place to do so.

"I can find a distributor," Jonah said. "I been around this business long enough to do that." He paused and looked a long moment at Kick. "Problem is, they're gonna want to take control. Great North will get paid, but you're only gonna get a itty-bitty slice of the pie. And that ain't fair."

"Fair or not, that's what you're going to do," Kick said. "Is the record good or not?"

Jonah shrugged and then finally nodded. Kick turned to Will. "There's more. The boys from the IRS are going to lock Jonah up at the end of the month."

"They won't put me in jail," Jonah said. "Hell, I'm a national treasure. I heard it said on TV."

"They *will* put you in jail and you damn well know it," Kick said. "They served you papers. You can't sit on this for a year, or two years, or however long it takes me to straighten out a situation that might not ever get straightened out. You made a good record, Jonah. You have to put it out. Find a distributor who'll advance you enough to keep the federal marshals at bay."

Jonah sat shaking his head and running his finger across the peeling finish of Will's kitchen table. The voice on the stereo sang—

I'd come back to you if you'd come back to me,
It's so nice to pretend that's the way it might be,
Instead I'll sit here and write another sad song,
Pretend I'm all right when I know I'm all wrong—

"I'd help out if I could," Will said when the song was done. "I'd mortgage this place but I just got done doing that to pay off my ex-wife."

Kick stopped pacing a moment. "We wouldn't let you do it anyway, Will. The music business is too risky."

"Look who's an expert all of a sudden," Jonah said. He put his hat on and got to his feet. "I do appreciate the thought. What I can't figure is how a girl who's so damn smart can be so damn dumb. He wouldn't mortgage the farm for me. He'd do it for you."

Kick looked at him, then she glanced at Will, who walked over to take his tray and cutlery from the table. He put them in the sink.

"Well ... it doesn't matter anyway," she said.

"It was always a long shot, with a limb in the way," Jonah said. "Don't give up yet. I had an auntie once, she always said if a man prayed hard enough he could make an elephant fall from the sky."

"Right," Kick said unhappily.

The track changed. Jonah was now singing "Big Man Coming Down the Road."

"I'm gonna head back to Tennessee tomorrow," he said. "And I'll make some calls. You can do the negotiating, Kick. It's your record."

"It's our record, Jonah."

Jonah walked over and extended his hand to Will. "I wasn't too sure about you, boy, back when I thought you was a lawyer. But you'll do. And this is some nice country. I suggest you take a look around and appreciate what you've got here. You do hear me, don't you?"

Will nodded and they shook hands. "Who's the big man in the song?" he asked.

"Well, that ain't for me to tell you," Jonah said. "I might say one thing today and something else next week. In the end, it ain't so much who I want him to be as it is who you want him to be."

"I have a theory," Kick said.

"I bet you do," Jonah said. "And a theory is all it is. I wouldn't—" His eyes fixed on something in the living room behind her. "What's that?"

Will followed Jonah's gaze to the gun cabinet on the far wall. "My guns," he said.

Jonah walked toward the cabinet. "That revolver. That a cap-and-ball Colt?" He leaned over to look through the glass at the old revolver in the holster where it hung beside Will's rifles and shotguns. "By God. Where'd you get that?"

Will followed him now and he took his keys from his pocket and opened the cabinet. He took the revolver out and handed it to Jonah. "It belongs to Kick. Her father left it to her."

"It belongs to Will," Kick said.

"No, I'm just looking after it," Will said.

Jonah took the Colt from the worn leather holster and turned it over in his hand. He examined the markings on the barrel and on the grips. He worked the ramrod and then put the gun on half-cock and spun the cylinder.

"Do you know what this is?" he asked.

"I know it's a black-powder Colt," Will told him.

Jonah saw the paper tucked into the holster and he pulled it out. "'Use this on them when they all start screwing up,'" he read. "Who wrote this?"

"My father," Kick said. "Those were his final instructions to me."

Jonah read it again and then began to chuckle, looking at Kick as he did. "I'll be goddamned," he said. He pushed his hat up on his forehead as he turned to Will. "Could I trouble you to use your phone? I need to call a friend about this."

"Right around the corner there," Will said.

Kick shrugged as Jonah went to phone, and then moved to sit at the table. Will looked at her a moment and then went into a cupboard for a bottle of whiskey. He mixed rye and water for them both. Shortly, they could hear Jonah talking excitedly on the phone in the other room, but they couldn't make out anything. After a few minutes he came back, still carrying the revolver. "He's gonna come over and have a look," he said. "Where'd your father get this?"

"I have no idea," Kick said. "He used to claim he won it in a poker game in New Orleans back in the fifties. That always sounded like a fish story to me."

"Nobody ever believes a fish story," Jonah said. "But everybody loves a fish fry."

They sat and finished their drinks. Jonah wouldn't have anything. He kept looking at the gun, peering down the barrel, trying to discern the hen scratching on the butt plates. After the first drink, Kick declined a second.

"Drowning my sorrows is too much of a country song," she said.

"Yeah, let's get going," Jonah said. "That woman Johanna promised me a game of checkers."

"I thought your friend was coming over," Will said.

"He'll be a while," Jonah said. "He's flying up from New Mexico."

Will hesitated. "He's coming here from New Mexico just to look at a gun?"

Kick reached over to take Jonah's hat off so she could see him better. "Come on, old man. Spill. What's going on?"

"Nope, I'm not gonna jinx it," Jonah said. "I been wrong so many times I'm surprised I never won a award for it. But I'll advise you both to watch your heads. Could be an elephant's about to fall from the sky."

NINETEEN

Ben met Teddy Brock in the parking lot of the liquor store on the outskirts of Guelph. It was Saturday morning. Teddy had never been to Crooked Pear and they had decided to drive to the meeting together. Ben was actually in the store when he saw Teddy drive in the lot and park beside his Vette. Ben paid for the champagne with his card and then walked out to meet him.

"Hello, Teddy." He opened the trunk and put the bag inside. "A couple bottles of Dom for afterward. I'm thinking Lynn and I might do some celebrating."

"You're a little on the optimistic side," Teddy said when they were on the road. "Your sister might have called this meeting to tell you she's going to fight you tooth and nail."

"I don't think so," Ben said. "I found out this morning that Jack Dutton is invited. And blubbering Blaine Steward too. She wouldn't have them there if she wasn't willing to make some sort of compromise. She's looking to cut a deal. If she was going to fight, she'd inform us through her own lawyer."

"Could be interesting, to see what she might propose."

"We stick to our guns, you got that?" Ben said. "They're coming to us on their knees. When they start whining, our position is tough titty. Fifty-one percent and everybody lives happily ever after."

Teddy nodded. "I'm sure that's how they'll look at it."

"I filed for divorce. Meredith got the papers Monday. I'm still at home but I guess I'm gonna have to take a room at the Hilton for the time being. A little early to move in with Lynn."

"Gee, couldn't you just kick Meredith and Ben Junior out of the house?"

"I thought about that," Ben said as they turned onto the county road. "After all, I bought the fucking place. The wolverine thought it wouldn't look good. You know, down the road, if we have to go to court."

"Yeah, you've got your image to think of," Teddy said.

"Fuck you, Teddy. You're not going to get to me today." They were approaching the river now. "Funny thing—Meredith didn't seem at all surprised when I told her. It was almost as if she expected it."

"Maybe she did."

"Doesn't matter," Ben said. "This is the day that all the dominoes fall at once. Look at me, Teddy. I'm Al fucking Pacino."

THE MEETING WAS SET for eleven. As it was a beautiful summer's day, and the assembly rather large, Kick decided that they would congregate on the south patio. Johanna brought out a pot of coffee and set it on a glass-topped table along the hedge. Kick had considered and vetoed the notion of snacks. It wasn't a social. She got Jonah Peck out of bed at ten o'clock and he came grumbling downstairs a half hour later. He'd been up late, talking in the kitchen with Johanna. Kick wasn't sure what that was all about.

Everyone was there on time. Jonah's friend from New Mexico, who'd insisted on staying in town as he had banking to attend to, arrived in a rental car. Kick asked him to remain in the house for the time being. Jack Dutton and Blaine Steward showed up, one after the other, each appearing a little put out at being summoned on a weekend. Will Montgomery rode his buckskin mare up the lane from the back of the farm, where he said he'd been checking out a crop. He tethered the horse on the lawn. When Ben rolled in, he was with his lawyer. Janey and Ethan were the last to come out on the patio.

Everyone found a spot to sit or stand and Kick stood in front of the French doors to address the group. She looked at Ben, who was leaning against a post that supported some lattice work. He wore a little half smile that would normally have infuriated Kick.

"I'm not going to bother with formal introductions," she said. "Everybody will figure out who everybody else is soon enough. Plus, it's Saturday and I'm sure everyone here has things to do. Jonah's got turkeys to hunt, and Will's in the middle of haying. And Ben, I'm sure you have a full-time job just trying to keep your head out of your ass."

Which removed the smug expression.

"Jack Dutton," Kick said then. "According to this takeover notice from Ben's lawyer, you have some complaints about Ethan with regard to the distillery. What are they?"

Dutton actually smiled at her in contempt. "I'll make it simple for you. He doesn't respond to anything. I mean, nothing. We've sent I don't know how many letters, asking for instruction, and received zip in return. Is this how he's gonna run the operation?"

"Maybe he's been busy with other distillery concerns," Kick said.

"Right," Dutton said, still smiling. "Maybe he has."

"Ethan," Kick said. "What've you been up to?"

"I've been … um … I've been researching some stuff on the internet," Ethan began.

"Oh, he's been *researching*," Dutton said mocking. "I had no idea. All I've been doing for the last thirty years is making rye whiskey. But the boy here has been researching. Guess I should apologize."

"Where do you buy your rye grain?" Ethan asked sharply.

Dutton hesitated. "What the hell is this?" he asked finally, looking at Ben. "Who cares where we buy our grain?"

"You don't use rye anymore," Ethan said. "You make rye whiskey out of ethanol. Most distilleries do. I've been doing research on organic grains. Rye grains, to be specific. Genuine rye gives you a more traditional taste, but more than that—going organic is a smart move from a marketing standpoint. Organic is very popular these days. And it's gonna stay that way."

"For Chrissakes, Kick," Ben said. "This is the best you could do? He read a fucking article on the internet."

"I read a bunch of articles, Ben," Ethan said.

"Oh well," Ben said. "You read a *bunch* of articles."

"That's right," Ethan said. "And last week Will and I planted five different organic ryes in the old pasture field behind the barn. Test plots."

"I don't believe it," Ben said after a moment. "You'd make anything up at this point."

"You'd better believe it," Will said. "I was just back there. We got grain showing already. Go take a look. If we get a good test, we could plant this whole farm in rye next year. Sorry to interrupt, Ben—you were about to call somebody a liar?"

Ben turned to glare at Jack Dutton.

"So he planted rye," Dutton said, recovering. "That doesn't excuse the fact that he never responded to company matters."

"You saying you've received no response from anyone?" Kick asked.

"Well, from the girl." Dutton indicated Janey with his chin. "She's nothing to do with this. I'm sorry but I can't take orders from a stray."

"The *girl* has a name," Kick told him. "It's Janey."

"Okay." Dutton shrugged and looked at Ben, lifting his eyebrows in amusement.

"And secondly," Kick said. "Since she's married to my brother Ethan, I'm pretty sure that she now owns half of the McDougall Distillery. We could get an opinion from Mr. Brock on that if you'd like. I assume you are Mr. Brock."

"Bullshit," Ben said. "They're not married."

"That big fella's a real skeptical sonofabitch," Jonah said.

"They sure as hell are married," Kick said. "Judge Raney Kilbride himself performed the ceremony and I witnessed it. You want a copy of the license, Ben?"

Jonah Peck began to chuckle. He was seated on a low stone wall, his hair tied back in a ponytail, his hand on his chin. Kick looked at him a moment before continuing.

"Back to you, Mr. Dutton," Kick said. "So you're telling me you've been ignoring correspondence from the owners? And *you're* the one making a complaint? That seems a tad peculiar. But maybe not as peculiar as your bookkeeping skills. My new sister-in-law is a smart woman. She's been over your accounts and she tells me that the plant should be making money. Matter of fact, she's pretty sure it *is* making money. It looks like someone's cooking the books to show otherwise. Why would a person do a thing like that, Mr. Dutton?"

"I don't know what you're talking about," Dutton said.

"No? Try this on. Maybe somebody wants the place to go under. Then that same somebody could buy the plant for—what—fifty cents on the dollar? Maybe less than that. Be a good move for somebody who knew how to make whiskey. Be a better move for somebody who also knew that the place has been running in the black all along."

Ben was now staring at Dutton.

"What's wrong, Ben?" Kick asked. "Mr. Dutton didn't provide you with all these little details when you were conspiring with him? Don't you hate it when you can't trust people, Ben?"

Ben refused to look at Kick, who turned back to Janey.

"Janey, I think Mr. Dutton will be leaving soon. Do you have anything you want to tell him?"

Janey was sitting, smiling, on a wrought-iron bench. "It's Saturday," she said. "We can talk next week. Is that all right, Mr. Dutton? Will you be able to find some time?"

Ben was watching Dutton with such malevolence that Kick
thought he might leap across the patio and strangle him. Dutton
finally looked at Janey and nodded.

"You can go now," Kick told him sharply, and he went. Kick
watched as he skulked across the lawn and disappeared around the
corner of the house. "Why do dogs tuck their tails between their legs
like that?" she asked. "Anybody know?"

"Just something dogs do," Johanna said. She smiled at Ben.

"I guess," Kick said. "You having fun, Ben? You want some coffee?"

"I'm real close to walking out of here," he replied. "Or have you
been researching stuff on the internet too? Or maybe you married
somebody? Whoever it is, he better have lots of money if he's gonna
pull your fat out of the fire over at Great North."

Everett's canvas bag was on the table beside the coffee pot. Kick
walked over to pick it up. She paused and then pulled the old
revolver from inside. "Remember this, Ben? The old gun that Everett
used to shoot the turtles with? Or at least shoot at them. I don't know
that he ever hit one."

"You gonna shoot me, Kick?" Ben asked. "If not, who gives a shit
about that relic?"

"Funny you should ask," Kick said. She turned and gestured
through the glass doors into the house. A moment later, Jonah's
friend walked out. He wore a tan suit and a brown open roader
Stetson. He nodded self-consciously to the gathering.

"This is Mr. Doby," Kick said. "A friend of Jonah's from Santa Fe.
Mr. Doby has agreed to buy my father's old revolver from me." She
looked directly at Ben and then continued. "He's going to give me
$325,000 for it. In U.S. dollars, I might add. I'm gonna just pause a
moment here so we can all appreciate the stunned silence that has
just arrived."

"What is this?" Ben asked. He was beginning to perspire.

"It's the Holy damn Grail," Jonah said. "That's what it is."

Mr. Doby took the gun from Kick. "This is a Walker Colt. Probably the most coveted handgun for the American collector. There were eleven hundred of these made, in 1847, by Samuel Colt and presented to Captain Samuel H. Walker, a former Texas Ranger. Roughly two hundred remain in existence. By the serial number, this gun's history is known to a certain extent. It belonged for several generations to the family of a man named Brown, one of Walker's original troop. But it disappeared about sixty years ago. It was last known to be in New Orleans."

Now Jonah, watching Ben, guffawed.

Kick looked at Steward. "Okay, Blaine. Truth is, I ought to take my money and leave Great North to stew in its own juices. But I won't. A couple hundred thousand goes to distributing Jonah Peck's new record. Aw shit, I was going to play the demo while I was doing this. Ethan, it's right inside the door. Would you mind?"

Ethan went in and turned the player on. Jonah's voice floated out from the house. Kick nodded to the beat for a moment.

"You like it, Ben?" she asked. "I'll give you a copy. No, I won't—I'll sell you a copy." She looked back to Steward. "The rest of the money goes into Great North's new documentary film division. Crooked Pear Films. I'm not sure why I'm telling you this. You'll be able to read about it in the paper while you're looking through the classifieds for a new job."

She turned back to Ben. His bottom lip was protruding now.

"Okay, that's that," Kick said. "I think this is going pretty well. We'll be done before lunch. Last thing I want to discuss, Ben—and I guess I should address this to your lawyer there. This audacious power play. I'd like to get this thing in front of a judge as quick as quick can. You see—Crooked Pear Films has a project shooting in Wyoming. What are your thoughts on that, Mr. Brock?"

Teddy Brock had been sitting in a patio chair. Now he stood up. "We won't be seeking to get this in front of a judge."

"I beg your pardon?"

"We won't be proceeding," Teddy said. He looked at Ben. "At least, I won't be proceeding." He nodded at Kick and then turned to go. "I'll be in the car, Ben. Whenever your sister finishes eviscerating you."

From inside the house came the voice of Jonah Peck:

I see his suitcase on the front porch,
I hear his footsteps in the hall,
I knew a man all my life
I never knew at all

Kick watched Ethan's face as the realization that he was hearing his own lyrics came to him, slowly, as comes wisdom or contentment, or even the elusive specter of happiness. And when he finally smiled, he smiled first toward Kick.

BEN AND TEDDY BROCK didn't say much on the drive back. Ben had a feeling they wouldn't say much to each other for a while, if ever. They wouldn't have talked at all, except Ben's cell phone rang as they were nearing the parking lot where Teddy had left his car. Ben listened, but said very little into the phone.

"Shit," he said when he hung up.

"What now?" Teddy asked. His tone suggested disinterest.

"I've lost the Toyota contract."

Teddy was laughing as Ben dropped him off. Ben squealed out of the lot and headed straight for Lynn's apartment. She would be home, he knew; he'd called earlier to tell her he was coming to celebrate. Strangely enough, she hadn't worked the previous day either. Maybe the appeal of working for a living was wearing off.

Ben ran the Vette up to eighty miles an hour and crossed from lane to lane, gauging as he did the extent of his hatred for his sister.

It was inexcusable what she'd done to him today, and in public to boot. Family obviously meant nothing to her. Ben had forgiven her any number of slights in the past, but this time was different.

He managed to calm himself by the time he reached Lynn's. When he let himself in she was standing out on the balcony, wearing tight jeans and a T-shirt. He was aroused as soon as he saw her; his anger and frustration seemed to inflame him. Then she turned toward him. It took him a moment to speak.

"What the hell?" he finally said.

"Hi, Ben."

"What the fuck is going on?"

"Come here, baby."

"No. Tell me what's going on."

"They were alien objects in my body, Ben," she said. "Mandy says it's a health disaster waiting to happen."

"Fuck! I knew she was behind this."

"I'm still the same person."

"I paid for them!"

She looked at him for a long moment and there was something dangerously close to pity in her look. "Are you saying my health means nothing to you?"

He sat down heavily on the couch and covered his eyes with his hands. "I don't believe this."

"There's more," Lynn said.

"Oh, God."

"Your wife called me today. Apparently your friend Teddy Brock has been talking to her. She knows about the fitness center. With the divorce, she's about to become an owner. That didn't occur to you? But get this, Benjy—she's enthusiastic about it. Asked me all kinds of questions. She's actually very nice."

By the time he got home he felt he was on the verge of a nervous breakdown. His breathing was ragged and irregular. He checked his pulse several times as he drove, thinking he might be suffering a heart attack.

It seemed no matter how hard he tried, he was destined to fail. And it simply was not fair. With Kick, everything always fell into place. There seemed no rhyme or reason in any of it.

He walked through the house and found no one there. He stepped out the back door and came upon the gardener Wilson, with Meredith by the pool. They appeared to be standing rather close to each other, and as soon as Ben appeared they stepped away. Wilson nodded to him and went to work skimming the pool. Meredith stared at him with an intensity he'd never seen before. He grew uneasy and went back inside. He made a vodka and tonic and went into the den, turned the TV on. He began to flip through the guide. *The Godfather* was on at four o'clock.

Ben turned the set off. Watching that particular movie was more than he could handle today. After what he'd been through, he didn't need to be mocked by his own fucking television. Maybe if things had gone the other way. But they hadn't.

In the end, it was Kick who was Al Pacino.

HER FLIGHT WAS SUNDAY AFTERNOON. After lunch she loaded her luggage and some equipment in the trunk of the Jetta and when she turned to go back to the house she saw the snapping turtle making his way across the lawn, angling a path from the riverbank to the creek. Kick closed the trunk and followed. He— and Kick had no doubt it was a he—wasn't as big as some she had seen, but he was big enough, and he appeared to be old as well. His beak was yellowed and brittle-looking and the folds of skin around his muscular neck looked as tough as saddle leather. He was missing a couple toes on one front foot, casualties of a past battle, no doubt. Seeing her, the turtle started to scramble for the stream, but then stopped and pulled his head and legs inside the shell.

"I might have figured you to show," she said, approaching him. She looked at him for a time and then put the toe of her Blundstone against his tail, and to her surprise the head and legs appeared and he began to move again. She decided to accompany him to the creek. Anyone watching would have thought she was walking a pet. When he got near the water he sped up and plunged in without hesitation, disappearing at once beneath the surface. Kick stood and watched the muddied, swirling water until it calmed and began to clear.

"All right," she said.

When she turned, Will was standing a few feet away. His truck was parked in the drive. She'd been less certain that he would show, but she didn't say so.

"Hi."

"Hey, Kick." He walked to the edge of the water and looked where the turtle had gone. It seemed he would say more but instead he knelt and gathered a handful of smooth stones, shook them in his fist like dice. He glanced toward the Jetta, with the trunk open, her luggage inside. "What time's your flight?"

"Four o'clock."

He plunked the stones one by one into the water. "How's the weather in Wyoming?"

"I'm thinking stormy." She watched the expanding ripples made by the stones.

"I'll bet," Will said. He indicated the broken Adirondack. "Your dad's chair is about to fall to pieces. I'll take it home and fix it while you're gone."

"You know, I don't remember ever calling him dad. I called him Everett. Mr. Eastman. Sometimes sonofabitch. But I never called him dad."

"He came through in the end though, didn't he?"

Kick laughed. "I guess he did. In his fashion. It's been quite an adventure, these past couple months. Maybe that's what he wanted to leave me—an adventure. Maybe he knew me after all."

"Or maybe he knew it would bring you back here." Will gestured to the house. "What about this place?"

"For the time being, it looks like it's going to be a harbor for tax fugitives."

"What?"

"Jonah's about this close to going to jail for his IRS problems. He can't go home. Not yet. Paige and I are forming a distribution company. Crooked Pear Records. She'll run it out of Nashville. If the record sells, Jonah can start paying off his debt. Till then, he's gonna hole up here."

"What's Johanna think about that?" Will asked.

"Tell you the truth, it was her idea. The two of them have been getting kind of cozy over the checkerboard. Although you might not like the picture."

Will hesitated. "Matter of fact, I do like it. Think about it. Johanna, checkers, fat turkeys—Jonah just might have found the promised land after all."

"That's what I was thinking," Kick said. "As for the place, I think I'm going to buy it, eventually. I need to be from somewhere. Crooked Pear's as good a place as any. It's the only place that feels remotely like home."

Will watched as a pine bough came drifting along the creek, its needles green against the muddy stream. It caught on a muddy plateau then freed itself and floated out to the river.

"It bothers me though," Kick said then.

"What does?"

"Everything seems too … perfect. Too synchronized. There were all these problems and now everything has just kind of dovetailed together."

"And there's something wrong with that?" Will asked. He was watching her brown eyes and thinking now of how she'd always been a kid to him, how it had taken all these years to separate the tomboy from the grown woman. Will's grandmother used to say that in order to really see something, first you had to look away. Until now, Will had never known what she meant.

"It's just that I don't trust it," Kick said. "I never have. It's not realistic to believe any of it will last. Something will fuck up somewhere along the line. Something always does."

"Maybe that's what life is about," Will said. "Endure the fuck-ups and enjoy whatever you can in between."

"Did you just tell me the secret of life, Will Montgomery?"

"I might have. Keep in mind I might not know what the hell I'm talking about."

"Okay," she said. "There's one more thing. Down in Tennessee, I kissed you. I kissed *you*. And now I'm standing here waiting for you to reciprocate. But I'm not going to wait forever. So, if you're going to do it, you'd better get to it."

And so he did.

Acknowledgments

Special thanks to legal eagle Amy Lee Ruff, music master Mitch Bowden, the insightful Lorraine Sommerfeld, and Turkey George Jurik. Thanks also to my editor at Penguin Canada, Helen Reeves; to permissions wizard Jennifer Notman for her deft stickhandling through the lyrics; and to my agent, Ann Rittenberg. And as always my undying gratitude to the permanently AWOL but always available Jen Barclay.

And, after writing about the joys to be found in real country music, I would be remiss if I did not thank Hank.

Copyright Acknowledgments